MW00586043

"I TRIED TO STAY AWAY FROM YOU,"

he whispered. "But fate conspired against me. You are here now, and I cannot let you go."

Slowly, tenderly, he bent her back across the bed. "You were made for this," he murmured as his hands moved over her. "Made for a man to cherish. And you are mine." He gazed fiercely down at her. "Accept me, Deirdre. I want you willing, for the thought of hurting you is a knife through me."

His entreaty left her dazed. The muscles in his arms and chest clenched with the force of his restraint. She was trapped and yet she was not. By waiting, by letting her decide, he made her free.

"Delacroix," she murmured on a thread of sound, "let there be no misunderstanding between us now. What I give, I will also take. You will be mine."

Beloved Enemy

MAURA SEGER

HarperPaperbacks
A Division of HarperCollinsPublishers

If you purchased this book without a cover, you should be aware that this book is stolen property. It was reported as "unsold and destroyed" to the publisher and neither the author nor the publisher has received any payment for this "stripped book."

This is a work of fiction. The characters, incidents, and dialogues are products of the author's imagination and are not to be construed as real. Any resemblance to actual events or persons, living or dead, is entirely coincidental.

HarperPaperbacks   *A Division of* HarperCollins*Publishers*
10 East 53rd Street, New York, N.Y. 10022

Copyright © 1992 by Maura Seger
All rights reserved. No part of this book may be used or reproduced in any manner whatsoever without written permission of the publisher, except in the case of brief quotations embodied in critical articles and reviews. For information address HarperCollins*Publishers*,
10 East 53rd Street, New York, N.Y. 10022.

Cover illustration by John Ennis

First printing: January 1992

Printed in the United States of America

HarperPaperbacks and colophon are trademarks of HarperCollins*Publishers*

10 9 8 7 6 5 4 3 2 1

PROLOGUE

ON THE THIRD DAY OF SEPTEMBER IN THE YEAR of our Lord 1601, a single-masted yawl entered the river Severn near Cardiff on the southwest coast of Britain. It proceeded several miles upriver to the fortress at Darkcroft, a holding of the powerful earl of Bradford. All day the weather had been clear and unusually warm for the season. But now as dusk approached, tendrils of mist rose from the water.

Three men awaited the yawl on the long stone pier. One was the earl himself, a tall, powerfully built man in his thirtieth year with chiseled features and an iron-hard gaze. The other two were men-at-arms who formed a token escort. They stood at a respectful distance, their faces carefully blank, as the earl watched the yawl's only passenger disembark.

She was a young woman of nineteen, medium of height and slenderly built. Her clothes were of excellent quality but worn and travel-stained. Her ebony hair was concealed by a veil that framed a face pale with exhaustion. The center of her wide skirt was flattened by a heavy chain fastened to each of her wrists. A similar chain secured her ankles, allowing her just enough room to move.

The chains clanged harshly in the stillness, causing river birds to start in alarm. The young woman shrugged off the hands of the sailors and straightened her shoulders. She stood without moving as the earl walked toward her. When he was directly in front of her, she raised her right hand, and despite the weight bearing it down, struck him full across the face.

The blow was powerful enough to knock his head back. It opened a gash along the square line of his jaw that immediately began to bleed. The men-at-arms leaped forward, as did several of the sailors, but a gesture from the earl froze them in place. He raised his own hand to the girl, a large hand, browned by the sun and strong in sinew; a warrior's hand. But its touch when it closed around her chin was gentle.

"Shall I presume, my lady," he asked softly, "that the battle is joined?"

Her reply was firm, though her emotions were not. "It was joined a long time ago, English. The time has come to finish it."

A flicker of admiration showed behind his storm-gray eyes. Looking down at the chains, he smiled faintly. "You don't perceive yourself as being at a certain disadvantage?"

The look she gave him would have shamed the greatest court lady. It combined generations of breeding with finely honed contempt. "No chains can hold my spirit, and it is that which will destroy you. You and all you stand for."

Coming from so young and vulnerable a woman, such a claim should have been absurd, but the earl knew better. The cold wind of certainty blew through his soul, reminding him of the long centuries during which her people had endured against a force that by any reasonable measure should have crushed them beyond memory. A force that in this time and place he was pledged to uphold.

On the stone pier by the river in the swirling mist they stood, a woman and a man, sworn enemies. But drawn to one another by passions greater than them both, passions that would not be denied.

PART
1

CHAPTER
1

IN THE BEGINNING THERE WERE THE STONES,
the sea, and the wind. Those three mighty elements of
God's great design made up all the world.

Or so Deirdre O'Neill sometimes imagined when she
walked along the Giant's Causeway at the northernmost
tip of her father's land. He was Hugh O'Neill, *the* O'Neill,
chieftain of Ulster and, some said, Ireland's savior.

Her memories of him were fond but fragmented,
for he came only rarely to the Abbey of St. Bernadine
where Deirdre had lived these seven years past. The
abbey was a small cluster of stone buildings set on a
hill within sight of the sea. The original foundations
had been laid down centuries before, when such places
were the only refuge from the Vikings raging out of the
north. Then Ireland was the haven of light and learning
in a darkening world. It still was in many ways, although it
was sometimes easy to forget that.

The wind picked up, blowing foam across the waters

and making the waves dance at the land's edge. It was the same wind that had worn the abbey stones smooth at the corners and stunted the trees to short scrub bushes. Even now, in the height of summer, it whipped Deirdre's cheeks to high color and sent her ebony hair dancing. Tomorrow her hair would smell of salt and she would have to wash it, this despite Mother Abbess's grumbling about waste and vanity. Being the daughter of the high chieftain did bring some advantages.

But the years of exile—as Deirdre thought of them—had been hard all the same, and the last few particularly so. Three years before, her family had risen in rebellion against the English crown. Since then, every day was lived on the knife's edge between glory and despair. It was a hard place to be, especially for a sixteen-year-old girl far from those she loved.

Staring out over the slate-gray water in the fragile fading light, Deirdre felt the yearning well up in her yet again. Tears threatened. She blinked them back determinedly, but she could not so easily suppress the need that seemed stronger within her with each passing hour. How she longed to go home!

Whatever ancient gods still inhabited the fiercesome shore, or perhaps the God the abbey itself served, may have heard her, for two days later her prayer was answered.

The man who stood before the abbess was so tall that he had to bend low to pass beneath the arched stone doorway that led to the refectory. His chest and shoulders were so broad that they blocked out most of the light. He wore chain mail and a great peaked helmet that even with the visor open made him appear as a deadly bird of prey. A long sword was strapped around his waist, a killing knife was in a scabbard tied around his right leg. A jagged scar ran across the left side of his face from brow to chin. That the eye in between was intact could have been taken as a sign of divine mercy.

Mother Justina did not see it that way. Her broad face was creased with displeasure as she confronted the man. "This is all well and fine for you, galloglach, but I should have had more notice."

Galloglach. The word reverberated through Deirdre where she stood well toward the back of the hall. She had been summoned so hastily that she'd barely had time to fasten her veil in place and smooth her plain wool gown. Now the first tremors of understanding quickened her heart.

Of all her father's warriors, none was so mighty or so trusted as those honored with the title of galloglach. The English corrupted their name into their own language, calling them "gallow glasses," for in them a man could read his fate. In battle they were the harbingers of death. But there was no battle here on the windswept tip of Ulster amid the cold gray stones of the abbey. So why . . .

"Ah, Deirdre, there you are," Mother Justina said, still looking mightily annoyed. "Don't dawdle, come here."

Swiftly, Deirdre did as she was told. Chieftain's daughter she might be, and privileged to an extent, but she knew better than to hesitate when Mother Justina spoke that way.

The man turned. He saw a girl of heart-stopping beauty, delicately poised on the edge of womanhood with a body made for pleasure and a face men would write songs about. The shock was considerable, but with it came a certain amusement. Lady Deirdre had changed in the year since her father had seen her. The O'Neill was in for a surprise. Gravely, the warrior inclined his head. "Lady, I come from your father. The tuath orders you to Dungannon."

Deirdre could not suppress the joyful smile that curved the soft fullness of her mouth. As though her father would think she needed to be ordered. Still, the wording was majestic. It left Mother Justina fuming but helpless. No one, not even she, could gainsay the chieftain.

Deirdre lowered her eyes, but not before the galloglach saw the glee shining in them and smiled. As humbly as she could manage, she said, "I shall gather my things."

"Hummph," Mother Justina said. She wasn't fooled for a moment, but there was nothing she could do. If the O'Neill wanted his willful, wayward spawn home, then home she would go.

A scant hour later, the warrior lifted Deirdre onto the short, shaggy pony brought along for her use. The animal might look unprepossessing but he could keep up a fast pace over rough ground long after more impressive animals faded. Still, he was rarely ridden by ladies of Deirdre's rank who used wagons or litters for long journeys. That neither of those was in evidence testified to the urgency of the summons. Confident he might be in his own land, but the O'Neill would not let his daughter linger out in the open where unknown danger might lurk. Similarly in the service of haste, there was no female chaperon. Mother Justina protested that, but the galloglach merely shrugged. A woman would have slowed them and his own life protected the lady's honor far more thoroughly than any woman could have done.

He swung up on his own war-horse, an animal of strength and speed usually used only in battle. To be riding him on a journey was a further indication of the precautions being taken. An escort of ten similarly mounted men-at-arms arranged themselves on either side.

On the verge of what she had yearned for so long, Deirdre was swept by a sudden wave of regret. The years at St. Bernadine had not been all bad; she had been kept safe and treated kindly. Mother Justina was gruff, but she was also fair, and she did her best to prepare her charges for the wider world.

Deirdre's throat was tight as she reached out and took the abbess's hand. "Thank you," she murmured. "I shall remember this place always. It, too, has been my home."

The plain, stern face softened. Gently, the abbess said, "God fare thee well, child. You will be in our prayers."

The horses turned, and the pony with them. The gate in the low stone wall stood open. Beyond led the winding road over the emerald hills and across the broad plain to Dungannon. To the future.

I will need their prayers, Deirdre thought as she looked back over her shoulder to where the abbess stood, a small black-garbed figure vanishing in the mist. God grant me strength to do whatever is required of me that I may bring honor to my family and grace to my name.

She straightened her shoulders and stared straight ahead. Behind her the wind blew softly and the sea sang, but Deirdre did not look back again.

✳ ✳ ✳

"Don't turn around," the small man whispered. "It's not much farther."

John Delacroix, earl of Bradford, stifled his annoyance and did as he was bade. It wasn't as though he had much choice. He could no more have found his way through the maze of tunnels beneath the Tower than he could flap his arms and fly out of the foul, dank place.

Whoever had laid out the tunnels in centuries past had undoubtedly had good reason; they provided an excellent escape route for a monarch who might find it prudent to leave London undetected. But in the long years during which they had lain unused and almost forgotten under the vast mound of the Tower, they had become filled with fetid water, the stone walls lined with slime, and the whole the sheltering place of rats that did not care much for intruders.

The earl kicked one of the bolder rodents out of his way just as the small man stopped. The guide lifted the smoking torch and exclaimed, "We've found it."

The man's obvious relief suggested he hadn't taken such success for granted despite all his assurances to the earl. They stood together before a low, iron-studded door draped in gossamer cobwebs.

"When was this used last?" Delacroix demanded as his guide struggled to open the door.

"I'm not sure. There are always rumors, but—" He broke off, wheezing from his futile exertions.

The earl looked pointedly at the rusted hinges. "You should have thought of this."

"Tell *her* that," the small man moaned, too worried of his own accord to summon the prudence he would normally have maintained. "There must be a way. We have to get it open."

Delacroix sighed. He pushed the guide out of the way and braced himself before the door. The muscles of his broad back and powerful arms clenched. An instant longer the door remained frozen shut. Then groaning metal bent to irresistible force and the portal swung open.

The guide smiled nervously. He had known that the earl was a man of enormous strength and will. Didn't the soldiers who had fought with him in the service of the Rus tsar call him "Strong Arm"? But still, that door must have been sealed a century or more, and he had opened it as easily as though it were the door to a lady's chamber.

Which, in a sense, it was.

Beyond the door, a narrow staircase wound up into the higher reaches of the White Tower, the oldest and most fabled part of the great fortress. It ended at what appeared at first glance to be a paneled wall. Only a closer look revealed the outline of a door set into it.

The earl knocked once. The door swung open. He stepped beyond into a small but luxuriously furnished chamber. A lady-in-waiting greeted him gravely.

"This way, my lord."

The guide remained where he was, inside the passage. The door closed again, leaving him to make his solitary way back out of the Tower. Not that he minded; he had fulfilled his task and been well rewarded for it. He did not envy the mighty who had to deal with far greater and more dangerous duties.

The small chamber was an anteroom that led in turn to a private "closet," the secluded inner sanctum of the apartment's resident. Long years before, Elizabeth of England had been its inmate, imprisoned there by her mad sister, Mary. Back then, of course, the passage had been unknown to her. Now she found it convenient—not to say amusing—to use it for her own purposes.

"My lord of Bradford," she murmured, extending a gnarled, beringed hand.

The earl went down on one knee. He bent his proud head respectfully. "Your Majesty."

Elizabeth smiled. In her youth, her smile had been her best feature. Now it appeared only a grim parody stamped on a face shadowed by death. At the age of sixty-five, she had outlived almost all her contemporaries. Slowly, with each passing day heaped one upon the other, her firm young woman's body had shrunk and withered until now she could barely recognize herself. There were times when she longed to lay down her burdens and rest forever. But she was not quite done, not yet.

"Rise, Bradford," she said. "You have had a long journey, and you must be curious about the reason for such . . . elaborations. Pour us both some wine, and I will enlighten you."

Bradford did as his queen instructed, filling two chased silver goblets with fine red Burgundy. Two things occurred to him as he did: he was alone in the queen's chamber without even a lady-in-waiting to attend her, a clear breach of royal protocol; and she was being unusually considerate of him, an even clearer indication that she wanted something he would not enjoy giving.

When the goblets were filled and he had handed one to her, she obligingly confirmed his suspicion.

"Sit down," she said, gesturing to the chair beside her. It was smaller and more modest than her own, but far from the humble footstool that was normally the only seating allowed in her presence, and then only by her highest nobles.

Ah, well, Delacroix thought, it's been amusing being an earl but there's always a piper to be paid.

"What I need is not so terrible," Elizabeth said suddenly. That ability to appear to have read the innermost thoughts of another had served her well over the years. There were even people who believed her to be possessed of supernatural powers inherited from her mother, the witch, Anne Boleyn. Delacroix, however, was not so gullible.

He stook a sip of his wine. "If you say so, Majesty, but in the final analysis, it doesn't matter. I will do whatever you require."

Elizabeth raised her eyebrows, or at least so much of them as her ladies could draw on the mask of white maquillage that covered her ruined skin beneath the fiery red wig she still affected.

"Are you so loyal, my lord?"

Delacroix looked at her directly. He answered simply, with the candor of a man who has seen too much of death to waste his life in lies. "You are the queen, I am your subject. Fate has raised me to a position of privilege within your kingdom. It is only right that I serve you faithfully."

"There are others not so clear in their thinking," Elizabeth said dryly. "But I'd had good reports of you, so I hoped for the best. Now you must be wondering at all this subterfuge."

He shrugged as though the matter was self-evident. "You have some reason for not wanting this meeting known."

"Clearly, but I also want to make sure that you are

not seen in London or at court. Word of your ascension to the earldom of Bradford has spread, but as yet only a handful know who you are or what you look like. That," she added, "is the advantage of being distantly related to a family that has shown a shocking penchant for ill luck."

Delacroix would not precisely have described what had happened to the Bradfords as bad luck, more as the scourge of God. The old earl had died fourteen months before. In quick succession his son succumbed to the sweating sickness, his grandson broke his neck falling from a horse, a great-nephew drank himself unconscious and drowned in his bath, and last but hardly least, the cousin who thought to reap the benefit of all that suffered a heart attack at his own good fortune and also died.

Which left one John Delacroix, distant relation of the Bradford clan, soldier of fortune, a complete stranger to the British court, and now England's newest earl. Had he not been out of the country when all the deaths occurred, suspicion might naturally have fallen on him. But he had been wandering the continent, enjoying a well-earned rest after several years in service to the Russian tsar. When word of his inheritance reached him, he was in Venice, savoring the pleasures of a particularly enthusiastic whore. He'd thought the man who brought him the news was a drunken fool and nearly kicked him down the stairs. There were still times when he wondered if he shouldn't have stuck with his first inclination.

Elizabeth tasted her wine and set it down absently. She tilted her head to one side as she looked at him, furthering the impression of a bright, curious bird.

"I understand that your lineage on your mother's side is equally impressive."

Delacroix frowned. He had no idea what she was talking about. His mother, God rest her memory, had been the daughter of an Irish merchant. Her family had cherished the usual stories about noble ancestors, but in their case, there might actually have been some truth to it. A gift for poetry ran in the line, enough to have won wealth and honor in Ireland, where such things were highly prized.

Again, Elizabeth seemed to read his mind. "One is naturally tempted to admire a people that put such store in poetry even if it is, shall we say, a shade impractical."

The earl did not disagree. He had built his life on soldiering, the poetry being only a thing for wine-lit nights and the eve of battles.

"I want you to go to Ireland," Elizabeth said. She paused a moment to savor the shock stamped on his rugged face. He was a handsome one, this rough-and-ready earl with his powerful body, golden hair, and a gaze that seemed to cut through steel. But there was a streak of sensibility to him that made her feel he could be trusted. Which was just as well, since she had no choice but to do so.

"Ireland?" Delacroix repeated slowly. His mind turned the word over as though he had never heard it before. Why in God's name would she want him to go to Ireland?

"To be a poet," Elizabeth said. She leaned back in her chair and pressed the tips of her fingers together. Peering over them, she seemed to see a great distance to a place where her wishes were made reality.

"They have need of such in Dungannon."

CHAPTER 2

LONG AGO, IN THE DAYS WHEN MEN SANG THEIR history rather than record it frozen on cold white paper, when Druids wandered the land casting their great spells and the barrier between this world and the next was very thin, Dungannon lived. It began as a simple log fortress north of the river Blackwater where people came mainly to trade and a few stayed on to raise their cattle and farm. Occasionally sortie parties ventured out to test their neighbors, but mainly the tribes lived in peace.

Even after the Norman came, Dungannon—and all Ulster with it—remained largely apart from the violence to the south. Centuries passed before the weight of the invader—who now called himself English—was truly felt. Then Ulster summoned the mightiest of her warriors and the wiliest of her leaders to fight for her freedom.

The O'Neills answered. They came singly, in twos,

by the dozens, and by the hundreds. They came out of the hills and the woods, from the copses and the glens. They came to fight and they stayed to win.

And they transformed Dungannon.

The simple log fortress became sheathed in stone rising proudly from the verdant plain. The design was Norman, for the O'Neills were never so proud that they couldn't learn from their enemy, and turn his wisdom against him. They crafted a vast keep of turreted towers and balustraded walls surrounded by a deep ditch crossed by a single drawbridge.

Before dawn on a day of low-hanging clouds and warm, heavy air, riders clattered across the drawbridge into the castle courtyard. Deirdre lifted her head and looked around her wearily. Home. The word was a benediction to her exhausted body and her troubled heart.

In the four days since the galloglach had come to St. Bernadine's, they had crossed almost the full length of Ulster without rest. Night and day they rode, picking up fresh mounts at prearranged points along the way. When Deirdre could no longer sit the saddle, the galloglach put her before him on his. That was hardly comfortable or dignified, but it did allow her desperately needed sleep. The men, if they slept at all, did so in the saddle with their horses still moving beneath them.

Now at last after all that effort, they had arrived. But to what? There was no one to greet them except the usual guards peering from the watchtowers. Deirdre had not expected any great ceremony, but she had thought that. . .

A man emerged suddenly from one of the small doors set above the courtyard. He stood looking down at the weary party for an instant before he bounded down the steps.

He was a very large man, as tall and broad as the galloglach. His hair was black as Deirdre's own, his eyes crystalline blue also as hers were, but deeply set in a face that showed the full extent of life's travails. Yet he smiled, joyfully and without restraint, as he embraced his beloved daughter.

"Blessed Mary and all the saints, you're here at last," Hugh O'Neill exclaimed. "I've been waiting, day after day, wondering when you'd come."

"We traveled without stop, tuath," the galloglach said respectfully. Inclining his head to Deirdre, he added, "A party of warriors alone could not have done better."

"Of course not"— the O'Neill laughed, engulfing his daughter in another bear hug—"for isn't my darling the seed of warriors? Let me look at you, lass. You're a sight for starving eyes."

Deirdre blinked back hasty tears and managed a smile for her father. He looked older and more worn than she remembered, but still much the same. And he was so glad to see her, so very glad. . . .

"Father, is anything wrong?" she asked softly. Instinctively, she lowered her voice, obeying the edict taught her since childhood that anything touching on the family was carefully guarded.

"Wrong? Now what could possibly be wrong? You're here—and without incident—so I'm the happiest of men and that's an end to it." To the galloglach, he said, "There's mead and meat in the hall for the men, and a sennight's rest for all of them. For yourself, you'll find my thanks in the stable, second stall to the right.

But watch yourself, those Moorish stallions can put a dent in a man's skull quick as they can look at you."

The warrior beamed, clearly delighted by his chieftain's generosity and not without cause, for the gift truly was a great and noble one. By the morrow, all would know how high he stood in the O'Neill's favor.

"You really were worried," Deirdre said softly as she walked alone with her father up the stone steps. "But why? We encountered no trouble of any kind."

"As well you shouldn't. Your escort and the pace they kept were precautions only. The English have been sensible of late. They've kept to the south of the border and not tried to trespass on us."

Deirdre was tempted to ask why, if that was the case, he had taken such care with her safety. But she was reluctant to press him further. It was not seemly in any case, and particularly not with a father who was little more than a distant though loving stranger.

Besides, at that point she was more interested in Dungannon itself. Her home looked much the same as when she left it seven years before. But after so long a time amid the austere surroundings of the abbey it might as well have been the fabled den of an eastern prince.

Stepping into the great hall, she gasped. In her mind, its dimensions had become somehow manageable but now she saw it for what it was, an immense space towering fully three stories high and running almost the full width of the keep. Despite the late hour, copper braziers set at intervals provided light. Fresh rushes covered the floor. The chieftain's table stood on a low dais with long rows of tables running down either side of the hall. It was a measure of the O'Neills' wealth that no retainers slept there. The soldiers had their own garrison hall and the servants had theirs. The family had private chambers, as did any noble guests who might come calling.

One such must be expected, Deirdre thought; otherwise, the great hall would not have been so gloriously alive in the hour before dawn. She said as much to her father, who furrowed his brow.

"Ah, lass, do you not know? Though I had no way to be certain of when you would arrive, I couldn't let you come home to a dark, still place." He laughed softly, a deep, rumbling sound that carried murmurs of her childhood when she would run to him and beg to be tossed high into the sky. He had called her the boldest of his children then, and there were times when she wondered if he didn't wish she were a boy. But now, seeing what he had done for her, she knew herself to be valued for exactly what she was.

"Thank you, Da," she whispered a moment before she hid her face against his broad chest and gave herself up to the tears that had waited so long to be shed.

Two days later, the tears were firmly gone, replaced by a steady smile, a light step, and a tendency to break into song. Deirdre was rediscovering Dungannon even as it was rediscovering her.

"Now will you look at that, my lady," the old gardener said with a smile. He gestured to the riot of tall orange and yellow lilies nodding their stately heads in the warm sun. "When they were nipped by a late frost a few weeks ago, I thought they might be done for. But they're Irish lilies, aren't they? The frost only made them all the better. Of course," he added on a more prosaic note, "the mulch I put down didn't hurt either."

Absently, he rubbed his left elbow, trying to ease in that one little place the ache that was always a part of him now.

"You work too hard, Liam," Deirdre said gently. "I've a liniment that would help your joints. I'll send some to you."

He looked both startled and pleased. "I thank you, my lady, but I must say, it's hard to realize that you're old enough now to know of such things."

Deirdre smiled. She resisted the impulse to point out that at her age—she would be seventeen in nine months—most women were already married and mothers. While she was living in the abbey with the good sisters, she hadn't thought much about that. But now, back in the world, it had crossed her mind.

Along with the possibility that it was for just such a purpose that her father had called her home.

Yet in the hours they had spent together—quite a few considering the extent of his responsibilities—he had mentioned no such thing. The O'Neill might be older and more burdened than she remembered, but she didn't believe he had become duplicitous.

She would have reason to reconsider that before the sun set. But first she luxuriated in the pleasures of being home, even if it was not quite as she remembered. In the old days, she had been free to come and go as she liked between the fortress and the nearby village with its surrounding hills and fields. There she had run and played with innocent abandon, learning the secrets of the forest and discovering her own deep love of the land of her forebears.

Now all that had changed. Her father had explained it to her plainly. "You will not go beyond the bailey wall without escort. And I don't mean some half-witted groom, but a troop of men-at-arms that only I can authorize. I know," he went on hastily, "you don't like the idea, but there's nothing to be done for it. Besides, there's plenty to keep you busy right here." Casting around for something to substantiate this claim, he said, "Needlework, for instance. It's been a long time since we had a lady of the manor who could supervise the needlework. . . ."

"I am a disaster with a needle," Deirdre said firmly. "Mother Justina should have told you that."

"Ah, yes, well, I do seem to remember her mentioning something to that effect in one of her letters. . . . "

"But I am learning to be a healer, which is far more important than any needlework. To do that, I must have access to the fields and the wood where many of the plants I need grow."

"We've perfectly good gardens right here," her father countered.

"Liam does a wonderful job, but there is much of worth that cannot be shut up within a garden walls."

"'Tis yourself you're thinking of, I suppose?" her father demanded, glowering down at her in the stance that never failed to intimidate even the largest and boldest of his subjects.

At least, not until now. "I was thinking of various tree fungi," his daughter shot back, "as well as mosses and lichens. They are important for controlling fevers and preventing the infection of wounds. If we are at war, surely those things are needed."

The O'Neill planted his hands on his hips and considered fuming but it wasn't likely to have any effect and she did have a point.

"I'll see what I can arrange," he said finally, "but in the meantime, you will obey me and stay within the walls." More gently, he added, "I mean this, mavorneen. You are too precious to me to be placed at any risk."

Which was hardly a sentiment with which a loving daughter could argue. Deirdre had to be content to stay where she was until her father decided otherwise. At least there was to be some diversion, as her old nurse breathlessly informed her the moment she set foot back in her chamber.

"There you are," Fionna exclaimed. She was a small, plump woman with a face red from her exertions and clear brown eyes bright with anticipation. "What were you thinking of, lass, wandering about like that? Your hair's dusty, you've mud on your nose, and . . ."

"And where's the harm in that?" Deirdre teased. She had been delighted to find Fionna still in residence, still very much the loving nurse and still thoroughly exasperating. "A little honest dirt never did anyone any harm."

"It would if the anyone weren't going to meet the O'Donnell this very night and, Mary save me, what will he think you looking like some hoyden a banshee wouldn't drag in?"

"The O'Donnell?" Deirdre repeated slowly. "I remember him, he's a fine old man." Soft-spoken and not terribly bold, as she recalled. Her father had never thought very highly of him. But their lands marched together, so it was just as well if they'd become friends, what with the trouble with the British and all.

"Not him," Fionna said, looking at her as though she'd been sipping fairy dew and gone daft. "Don't you know he stepped aside after the boy, his son, escaped the 'English.'" The word she actually used referred to the droppings of a diseased goat.

"The poor lad had been held four years in irons in Dublin," she went on, rising to the drama of the tale, "may the souls of his captors burn in hell for all eternity. He made his way back in the dead of winter with the snow so deep a man could drown in it. Then his father saw the worth of him and made him tuath of Donegal in his own right. Red Hugh, he's called to distinguish him from your father, and a fine, strapping man he is, as handsome as any lass could hope for. But not," Fionna added ominously, "one with mud on her nose."

So that was the way of it, was it? Brought back from the safety and serenity of St. Bernadine—she was angry enough to romanticize the place a bit—for the sole purpose of being paraded like some prize mare at the breeding pens? Ah, well, she couldn't claim to be surprised; it was the way of it. But the hurt was there nonetheless, a queer sort of aching hurt born of the wish that her father would see some other use for her than to simply give her to another man. Foolishness that, for why should her father be different in that respect from all the other fathers on God's earth?

"I'm tired," she said flatly, "and I've no appetite. You will take my regrets to my father"—the crafty old devil, "and I will stay here."

Fionna paled. She clutched her hands to her ample bosom and looked as though she was about to faint. "On my life, you will not! The shame of that is not to be borne. Have you been away so long you've forgotten what it means to be an O'Neill?"

Deirdre's teeth closed on her lower lip. The sharp,

stinging pain drove the froth of anger from her mind, allowing her to think more clearly. Fionna was right, of course. To refuse to appear before an honored guest would be the height of discourtesy, violating as it did every convention of hospitality by which the Irish lived. She would have to go, and she would have to make the best of it. But more than that she would not do. If Red Hugh expected her to be sweet and docile as befitted the occasion, he was in for a rude awakening.

Of the few clothes Deirdre had brought back with her from the abbey, none was really appropriate for her life at Dungannon. But her father, with his customary thoroughness, had thought of that. At the same time he dispatched the galloglach to being her home, he set a gaggle of seamstresses to working on a new wardrobe for her. There were beautiful soft wool gowns for day, wonderfully delicate muslin night rails for sleeping, frothy shawls, fitted jackets, full riding skirts, and even several court dresses that looked the next thing to royal if not already that.

"This one, I think," Fionna said, gesturing to a gown of burgundy velvet trimmed in fine bobbin lace and seed pearls. An underskirt of azure blue satin perfectly complemented the color of Deirdre's eyes. The bodice was modestly cut but sufficiently low to reveal the upper swell of her breasts. In it she would look like exactly what she was—a maiden of noble standing, great beauty, and immense worth who was also ripe for the plucking.

"I think not," Deirdre said primly. "After all, I have only just left the convent. It would not be appropriate for me to appear in such worldly garb."

That might have given someone other than Fionna

pause, but the old nurse had a low tolerance for any such ploy.

"You can always wear your school habit," she said succinctly, "awful gray thing that it is. But I'd be careful about that if I were you. The tuath might be getting the idea it was holy vows you wanted instead of a fine, upstanding husband to warm your bed and give you children. You could find yourself back in the abbey before you finished all the Hail Marys you'd have to say in penance for such deception."

"Perhaps I will wear the gown," Deirdre said hastily. Fionna did have a point. Loving though her father was, there was no sense seeing how far she could test his patience.

Which was how she came to be walking down the long stone staircase leading to the great hall, going rather slowly because the gown was very grand and she didn't want to trip over it. Paying close attention to her steps while trying to still the trembling in her stomach, it was a moment before she realized how quiet everything had suddenly become.

The great hall was silent. This despite the fact that it was no longer empty as it had been when she returned. Instead it was filled with people, two hundred of them at least. She saw in a glance that all the most important families of Ulster were represented, the men gloriously outfitted in velvet doublets and silken hose, the women equally impressive in gowns that almost but not quite rivaled her own. With them was the delegation from Donegal, headed by Red Hugh himself. But which one exactly was he?

Surely not that slender boy with the delicate features, farseeing eyes and heart-stopping smile who was walking toward her across the crowded hall with everyone making way for him? Even her father, the crafty old devil, who was standing off to the side beaming a smile that could have lit up the whole of Ireland.

"My lady," the young man said as he gently took her hand, "forgive my presumption, but I was delighted to learn of your return. You undoubtedly don't remember, but we've met before. It was. . ."

"You," Deirdre exclaimed, all her attempts at coldness vanishing like so much ice in the summer heat. "I don't believe it! You're the one with the bees and all that honey and the poor old MacSwiney running about like a stuck ram. . . ."

She laughed delightedly. How could she have possibly forgotten that long-ago summer when she was eight years old and her father had taken her north to the white stone castle at Fanat overlooking Loch Swilly? She'd met a boy there, six years older then herself, but unlike most boys that age willing to be kind to a girlchild eager to learn the world.

MacSwiney had been fostering him, but there'd been some secret about his identity, something unstated but important. Not that it had mattered. For a week, they'd roamed the fields and the wood, he sharing his knowledge with her while also taking seriously his role of protector and guide. It was he who had first made her see the possibilities in the simplest plant and understand the chance to make a difference in the lives of the people around her.

"*You* are the O'Donnell," she murmured, abruptly mindful of all the fine lords and ladies watching them, and of what they must be thinking, namely that this above all was going to be the easiest of Red Hugh's conquests for wasn't it already over and done by the look of it. Perhaps they hadn't bother to go home just to be called back for a wedding in a day or two.

Oh, no, Deirdre thought. A fine man he undoubtedly was—not to mention a tremendous relief—but no one was going to say that an O'Neill yielded easily to any man no matter what the circumstances.

"I am," Red Hugh said with disarming modesty. Solemnly, he added, "And you are every bit as beautiful as I imagined you would be." In fact, she was vastly more than that, so much so that his stomach was turning over itself. O'Neill might have given him a bit of warning, but that would undoubtedly have spoiled the joke. Telling himself to act like the chieftain he was and not an addleplated fool, he offered his arm. "Shall we?"

Together they walked the rest of the way into the hall where the O'Neill waited to greet them. The great bear of a man tried hard to conceal his delight, but it wasn't to be. He wasted no time calling for wine so that the company could drink a toast to his fine daughter, home from the convent for good, make no mistake about that, and the equally fine Red Hugh O'Donnell who was welcome under his roof any time at all, being practically a son to him.

After which it was only natural to call for the bard. He was a new fellow just come the day before by boat from—where was it again? Not that it mattered, for he had a fine voice, knew all the old songs, and was adept at crafting new ones.

The clear, liquid sound of the harp ran through the hall, summoning them all to listen. John Delacroix, earl of Bradford, looked up from tuning the instrument. His eyes met the gaze of a girl in burgundy velvet whose cheeks were flushed with excitement and whose ripe lips danced on a smile. For a moment, his breath stopped. She was the loveliest thing he had ever seen—beautiful, vibrant, pure. A woman to be won and to be treasured.

She was also smiling at Red Hugh O'Donnell, chieftain of Donegal, ally of the O'Neill, and rebel in his own right against the crown of England. O'Neill and O'Donnell, the two men who, if the earl succeeded in his mission, would shortly be laying their heads on the block on Tower Green.

The thought of which explains why the first song the bard called Sean Harpsinger sang was a decidedly gloomy one, all about circling ravens and the nearness of death. It sobered the company up for a bit, but he fell more into the way of things after that, so that the evening went merrily enough.

For all except the bard himself who went off to bed finally cursing the fate that had brought him to such a place and wondering if he hadn't been better off in the ice-swept tundra of the Rus.

CHAPTER 3

THE NEXT DAY IT RAINED, WHICH IS SAYING nothing at all since it rained most days in Ireland if only for a few hours. Deirdre woke to the soft, feathery sound of drops falling on the stone parapet beyond her chamber. She turned over in bed, her eyes still closed, and sighed contentedly.

She had been having the most delightful dream, all about herself and a wonderful man, strong, dashing, trustworthy, who. . .

Her eyes shot open. The man she was dreaming of was not Red Hugh—which would have been bad enough—but the bard, the new one, who had entertained the company so well the night before. What was he called? Something Harpsinger. His full name eluded her, but the sound of his voice did not. She could still hear it in memory, running through her like a silken caress that set her blood on fire.

Nor was she the only one so affected. Remembering

that, she frowned. Upon leaving the hall, she had heard several ladies whispering among themselves in terms that reddened her ears. How she would have liked to give Mother Justina just five minutes with any of them, but that wasn't to be. She was back in the world now, and the sooner she learned its ways, the better off she would be.

She had left the bed and was staring resolutely out the window when Fionna bustled in. "Awake already, mavorneen? You were late in hall last night."

This last part was said with a sidelong smile and a look that spoke volumes. Deirdre ignored both and began to brush her hair briskly. The rain had stopped and the sun was hot enough to dry the ground quickly, which gave her just the excuse she was looking for.

"Find an old dress for me, please, something from the abbey. I will be working in the gardens all day." She knew without having to think about it that her father would never authorize the necessary escort to let her go beyond the fortress while Red Hugh was still here. He would consider that discourteous to the guest who had come expressly—whatever else might be claimed—to see her. But no one, not her father or any-one else, could stop her from working out her frustra-tions in the good loamy soil of the castle gardens.

Fionna argued, as was only to be expected. She tried her utmost to wangle Deirdre into a silk and satin confection on the theory that she could spend the morning showing their guest the tapestries and other artworks that adorned Dungannon.

"He's been here before, hasn't he?" Deirdre point-ed out. "And he knows full well what my father intends for the two of us. He could probably inventory the place with his eyes closed."

Fionna's mouth tightened disapprovingly. "You didn't get that sharp tongue of yours from the good sisters, I'll wager. The O'Donnell is the finest man alive, saving your father himself, of course. If he marries you—and I mean that *if* lassie, for you're taking far too much for granted—if he does, it'll be because he thinks such a union will strengthen Ireland, not because of any dowry he's after getting."

Deirdre looked away, embarrassed by her hasty words. Fionna was right; she had no reason to think that Red Hugh saw her as so much wealth on the hoof. On the contrary, he was a gentle and sensitive man. She should be down on her knees in thanks for her good fortune instead of inventing ways to disparage the man who in all likelihood would shortly be her husband.

"I'm not fit company today, Fionna," she said softly. "The garden's the best place for me."

The nurse's face softened. "Mayhap you're right. You've been tumbled from one world to another with no chance to catch your breath. I'll tell your father that you're helping Liam, but mind you make yourself agreeable later."

Deirdre promised. Moments later, she slipped down the steps, a slender figure in a plain gray dress with a smile on her lips and lightness in her step.

From his seat in the shadows of a window deep set in the castle's thick stone wall, Delacroix watched her go. To the casual passerby, he was simply a bard tuning his harp in quiet reflection. In fact, he was doing that, but he was also carefully observing everything that went on around him.

The previous night, he had been struck by the extraordinary luxury of the O'Neill's court. Granted, the reception for Red Hugh O'Donnell had been something special. But even so, many a monarch would have been hard-pressed to mount such a display.

Two hundred guests had dined off plates of gold, working their way through dozens of courses ranging from minced lark's tongues and roasted swan to entire wheels of cheese, uncounted loaves of bread, and an array of pastries each more exotic than the last. The height of the meal had been the arrival of an entire roasted boar carried on the shoulders of footmen clad in doublets of silk and velvet. An endless variety of wines flowed like water from flagons of gold and silver. The entertainment included acrobats, minnesingers, and of course, himself. Although, strictly speaking, the bard was never thought of so lightly.

Touching a string of the harp, he listened to it resonate and wondered at his own reaction. Although he had known almost as long as he'd been alive that music and words lived in him in a way they didn't for other men, this was the first time he'd had his skill confirmed before an audience who truly knew of such things. He had to admit that their response was gratifying. Almost he wished he had no other purpose in being there.

He shook his head at the thought. A moment later, the harp was slung over his back and he was heading outside.

The day was already warm and heavy with the scents of summer. Birds circled against the azure sky, hunting and being hunted. A glance beyond the walls showed that the O'Neill had his men on the training fields, probably as much for Red Hugh's benefit as their own.

Delacroix counted a hundred or more archers and the same number of mounted men-at-arms. He knew that was only a fraction of the garrison that in its total stood at well over a thousand. And then there were the men who could be summoned within hours from the surrounding villages, not to mention the thousands more who would stream to the O'Neill's banner at the first call.

He frowned and rubbed the back of his neck thoughtfully. This part of his job was the easiest, but he didn't fool himself that there was nothing more to it. An estimate of the O'Neill's military strength was only the beginning. It didn't tell anyone how loyal his men would be when they encountered true difficulty, as they surely would if Elizabeth of England had her way.

That was a far subtler and more subjective matter that required much greater diligence. He waited until he saw the men taking a break from their training. They welcomed him among them with quiet respect, reminding him yet again that the Irish above all other people on earth honored the poet. He was offered a cup of mead to wet his throat and as encouragement for the exercising of his art.

He was willing enough to give them a song. But instead of selecting from among the hundreds he knew, he chose on impulse to compose one for the moment:

> *Hail, Tara, noblest of keeps,*
> *Perished gathering of a hundred hosts.*
> *Many were the bands whose home was,*
> *The green-shrouded keep of Tara.*
> *Heart of Erin secret and beating,*
> *Crumbled now even onto the clay.*
> *Tara, desolate in this day,*
> *All strength brought to nought.*
> *Hail, the men of Erin.*

Leaden silence hung over the circle. Delacroix knew full well the risk he had taken. Deliberately, he had sought to anger and provoke with talk of Ireland's vanished glory. He was not disappointed.

A young boy, one of those serving drink to the men, was driven to forget himself. "What bard sings such a thing?" he burst out. "It's an insult, it is. . ."

The blow that knocked him onto his back was finely gauged. It was sufficient to remind him of his manners without causing real harm.

The man who struck him was a large, burly archer with the farseeing gaze of his calling. "You dare much, Harpsinger," he said quietly.

Delacroix nodded. "Truth is never a little thing."

Around the circle, heads nodded. "Aye, truth it is. Tara is gone, but for the memory. 'Tis is the bard's place to remind us . . . keeper of memory . . ."

" 'Tis not Tara we seek to revive," a slender, red-haired young man said quietly. " 'Tis all of Ireland, one land strong and free."

"Free of the English," said another. "Plague in our house that they are."

"But not for long."

"Nay, they die as other men."

"As we have done."

"And will again," the burly archer said with quiet fierceness, "but this time they die with us."

Delacroix sat back, silent and attentive although he could not claim to like what he heard. This was worse than he'd thought. The calm strength and certainty of the men worried him more than the number of their arrows and swords ever could. Such men, so resolute in their purpose, did not break under even the harshest circumstances. They remained steadfastly loyal to the death.

Her Most August Majesty would not care for that. Even less would she care for the suggestion Delacroix was certain he had caught, the suggestion that the current state of affairs was not going to last much longer.

Not for long, one of the men had said, and the others had nodded with the matter-of-fact acceptance of soldiers who sense the approach of battle.

But where and when?

The men went back to their training, and Delacroix resumed his seemingly aimless wandering. Silently, he acknowledged Elizabeth's cleverness. Had she known or merely guessed that in Ireland poets were the freest of men, welcomed anywhere they chose to appear?

Even in the castle garden where he had earlier seen the O'Neill's daughter go. Not that he was hoping to encounter her, certainly not, he was merely getting the lay of the land, as it were. But as it happened, she was still there, kneeling beside a bed of herbs where she was busily working the earth.

Her hair was pulled back to hang loosely down her back. The dress she wore was of the plainest stuff. Concentrating on her task as she was, her expression was serene, but the vibrancy he had seen and been drawn to the night before was still very much in evidence. Physical beauty God had given her, that no one could question. The man in him responded to it, but the poet felt the beauty that was also within, beauty of the spirit, rarer and more enduring.

O'Neill's daughter. Only a fool would forget it. Or perhaps a poet.

The sound of the lute caught her unawares. She turned quickly, her light blue eyes large and wary.

Delacroix smiled. The song sprang to his mind without thought.

> *Fair is the daughter of Erin,*
> *Fairest of God's many gifts,*
> *Sweet balm to the emerald isle.*
> *Grace to the hearth,*
> *Comfort to the child,*
> *Heat in the blood of the man*
> *Who without her lives not.*
> *Fair daughter of Erin.*

Deirdre blushed. The song delighted her, most especially as she guessed he had made it for her. No one had ever done such a thing before. But that this man should do so, the very one who had invaded her dreams, filled her with trepidation.

Slowly, she stood up, dusting off her hands. She looked directly at him, taking in the broad sweep of his chest, the proud head crowned by thick golden hair, the intelligent, restless eyes that were the color of a storm-laden sky.

Restless? Now why would she think that? His gaze did not wander about, but remained steady on her. There was nothing tentative or uncertain about him; to the contrary. Yet she was left with the undeniable impression that his spirit was far from at peace.

He was simply dressed in rough-spun woolen trousers, a flaxen shirt, and a short cloak fastened at one shoulder by a brooch of bronze set with topaz and amethyst. It was the garb of an unpretentious man but one successful in his calling, a true bard in the old way.

Why then did she have a sudden, flashing image of

him in armor, helmeted and with a crimson-tinged sword in his hand? Ridiculous!

A cloud moved before the sun. Deirdre suppressed a shiver. Quietly, she said, "Thank you for the song, Harpsinger. You honor my father's hall."

The words were formal, but the tone was not. She was too young for that, and too uncertain in her feelings. Impulsively, she said, "Let me give you something in return."

Quickly, she bent and gathered a small bouquet of the herbs. She rose again and handed them to him, tied with a bit of the dried vine she carried for such a purpose.

"There is angelica here for warmth," she said, "and valerian to bring the ease of sleep, as well as rosemary to cushion the head in thought and hyssop to keep the lungs strong."

He took the small bundle from her. Their hands touched for the merest instant but long enough to make them both aware that the angelica was not needed. There was already heat enough between them.

"Thank you," Delacroix said gravely. He was playing a dangerous game, but he could not seem to stop. Ever since his first sight of her in the hall the night before, the girl had been in his mind. Up close, she was even lovelier than he remembered, with skin like sun-kissed silk and lips so firm and ripe that a man could—

Heaven help him, he was thinking like a randy boy instead of the seasoned trooper he surely was.

They stood a little while in silence, neither knowing what to say to the other. At length, Deirdre remembered her manners.

"If you are thirsty," she said, "there's water here." She gestured toward a small stone well set off to one side of the garden. It was one of many wells scattered around the castle grounds and beneath the fortress itself. In the everyday course of events, they were merely practical. But in times of siege they made the difference between life and death.

Deirdre drew up a bucketful, her slender arms pulling the rope smoothly and steadily. The motion stretched the fabric of her gown taut across her high, firm breasts. Delacroix looked away for an instant, staring into the sun to let the sharp, clear pain of that light remind him of who and why he was.

The water was sweet and cool. He drank it from the ladle she offered, then sat beside her on a garden bench. Bees hummed softly and a few bright-eyed birds darted about, but otherwise they were alone.

Softly, Deirdre said, "When I was a little girl, this was my favorite place. I played by the hour here. One day, I fell down on the gravel and cut my knees. My father was nearby and heard me crying. He left his men and came to comfort me."

She loves him, Delacroix realized. The thought was startling. Children, especially those of the nobility, rarely saw their parents as more than remote figures of authority. But this was different. Somewhere, somehow the O'Neill had won his daughter's deepest affection.

Which said more about the man than Delacroix cared to contemplate.

She turned suddenly, away from her memories, and looked at him directly. "Where do you come from?"

He smiled quickly. "From the same place all bards call home—here and there."

Deirdre laughed. Her easiness with him bewildered her. She knew little of men and was at a loss to understand her complex feelings for this one. He made her more vividly aware of herself than she had ever been before, yet she also felt completely safe and at peace. That odd sensation she'd had—of seeing him in a different, far more threatening guise—had not recurred. His songs had convinced her that he was truly what he claimed to be, a bard in the tradition of old. God did not grant such a gift to bad or narrow men.

"I suppose," she said, "that you've traveled the land a great deal?"

Delacroix hesitated. The simple thing was to tell the girl that he had and let it go at that. But he was oddly reluctant to lie to her any more than he had already done.

"I've been away for a long time," he said finally, choosing a compromise between truth and falsehood.

"Where?" she asked, eagerness shining from her. She was hungry for knowledge, and so excited by the thought of the vast world that he could not help but smile.

"In Russia mainly." He waited to see if she knew where that was.

"Is it as cold as they say?" she asked.

He laughed. "Colder. There are no words to describe it." Nor would he ever try. The priests said hell was a place of fire and heat, but men of the north knew better. They said hell was an endless cavern of cold and ice in which the doomed wandered forever. Delacroix suspected they were right, but such thoughts had no place in the midst of an Irish summer, seated next to a beautiful young girl.

Quietly, he began to tell her of his days among the Rus, of their great terem palaces of carved wood and inlaid marble, the sleds that carried them from place to place, the richness of their clothing and the fierce pride of their manner.

She listened, enthralled, which was as seductive to the poet in him as to the man. Time passed without their noticing. The sun slanted higher in the sky and a shadow fell across the garden.

Red Hugh stood watching them. Deirdre saw him first. She rose hastily, smoothing her skirt and trying not to look guilty.

"My lord," she said, "I did not realize the hour. . . ." A glance at the sky confirmed that it was later than she could have thought.

"It's my fault," Delacroix said quickly. He, too, rose, standing with easy grace as he surveyed the younger man. At first glance, the O'Donnell did not look much like a warrior, but he was not fooled by that. He knew full well that the most unprepossessing men could, when properly driven, reveal the least expected talents.

Besides, it was clear that Donegal's chieftain had the prime qualification for leadership—unshakable confidence. Another man coming upon them might have revealed uncertainty and anger. O'Donnell did neither. Clearly, he assessed the situation and found it innocent.

As well he might, for reality dictated that Deirdre was his and no other's. No bard, however great, could ever aspire to win a chieftain's daughter. And no such daughter would ever so disgrace her house as to think otherwise.

Standing straight and slim in the sun, Red Hugh held out his hand. His smile was gentle but commanding.

Yet Deirdre did not immediately respond. Instead, she turned to Delacroix.

"Thank you," she said gravely.

His reply was to lift the bouquet of herbs she had given him and touch it lightly to his lips. A moment longer they looked at each other before she turned away. Her hand in the O'Donnell's, Deirdre left the garden.

CHAPTER 4

"WALK WITH ME," RED HUGH SAID. THE HABIT of command was easy on him; he gave orders without thinking of them as such. Deirdre noticed that but did not mind it. At St. Bernadine's she had known girls who dreamed of being wooed in the courtly fashion with flowery speeches and beseeching looks. She had little tolerance for either. The world was the world; in Ireland, at least, women had some rights, but men still ruled. It was foolish to pretend otherwise. As for love, she believed it existed between parent and child, but between men and women—? On that score, she was unapologetically skeptical.

"It's been more than a while since I visited Dungannon," the young man at her side was saying. "Perhaps you could show me about?"

The tapestries, Deirdre thought, remembering Fionna's advice. She hid a smile. Red Hugh was mistaken if he imagined she would play the grand lady showing off the manor to him. The elegance and luxury of her home were important for what they said of her clan's power. But they were not what made her love each massive stone and blade of grass. It was the proud strength she cherished; that and the wildness.

"Come," she said, unconsciously matching his tone of command. "I'll show you my Dungannon." She glanced over her shoulder at him, her smile bright but with a touch of wistfulness. "I've also been away a long time. I'm still getting used to being back."

She did not add that her homecoming was tinged with the growing awareness that it might well be only temporary. If she was to leave Dungannon again—for a new life among his clan—she wanted to savor every moment while she could.

They went first to the stables. This was a long, low building set against the interior wall of the bailey. Like everything else at Dungannon, it was in excellent repair and meticulously clean. Deirdre's father might enjoy the excitement and intrigue of a life lived on the edge, but he despised disorder.

The stables housed more than a hundred mounts, mostly war-horses but with a dozen or so palfreys as well. The smaller and more docile ponies were kept apart. Together, Deirdre and Hugh walked beside the stalls, pausing here and there to pet an out-thrust muzzle and listen to a low whinny. Fierce in battle, the war-horses were unfailingly gentle elsewhere. That, too, was the O'Neill's doing, for he insisted that every horse be raised with gentleness so that none obeyed from fear but rather from love.

"When I was away," Hugh said quietly as he soothed a thick-maned gray, "horses were part of what

I missed the most. I lay awake at night thinking of long rides beside the cliffs near the sea. Sometimes I dreamed of them and then I felt truly free."

Deirdre's throat tightened. Without thinking, she reached out a hand to cover his. He looked so young and fresh, this tall boy with the bright red hair and the easy smile, yet he had endured suffering that would have destroyed most men. Safe in the sheltering care of her father, she had known nothing of it until it was over. Even then it had been left to sharp-tongued, but warmhearted, Fionna to make sure she understood.

"Four years," the maid had said the night before as she brushed Deirdre's hair before the fire still needed even on these summer evenings. "Four years he languished in a British cell chained to the wall like an animal. Barely a child he was, and the only friend he had in the world died before they could see Ireland again, but he never despaired. The courage of lions is in him. He escaped, walking miles through the snow, and coming finally half-dead to his father's hearth. Is it any wonder the old lord stepped aside for such a son?"

Deirdre had agreed it was not, but looking at him now, in the dust-dance light of the stables, she wondered at the core of iron within him. Had it always been there, even in that faraway day when they had roamed as children over the moors? Had he simply found it in himself when he needed it most? Or was it born in an English cell, birthed of hatred and the fearsome determination never to accept defeat?

She could not ask, and the man himself seemed disinclined to tell. Perhaps he did not know.

"I am sorry," she said softly. The words were simple . . . but the emotion was not. She was filled with regret for the cruelty of the world. For an instant, she remembered the convent, the wave-swept stones, the pure, unfettered isolation. The safety. And then she remembered how much it had nettled her and how she had dreamt of life beyond its walls. Life with all its heady, dangerous, demanding cost.

Hugh stared down into her eyes and knew what it was to plummet into deep, clear water, the kind a man will yield to even when he knows it will cost him his life. The daughter of O'Neill was beautiful; he had seen that in the first instant of meeting and been grateful for it. But she was also something more that he could not define, only wonder at. She was barely sixteen, fresh from the nuns, and as proper and obedient as befitted her position in life. But he felt beneath the cool, still water the pull of ancient, implacable tides that sang beneath the mother moon.

Her lips parted, he felt the soft exhalation of her breath. He was taller than her by half a foot. His head bent, a lock of red-gold hair falling over his brow. Deirdre's lashes drifted down, concealing her eyes. She waited, suspended, for the touch of his mouth.

On the parapet to which he had climbed after leaving the garden, Delacroix watched the pair until they were out of sight. They were well matched, those two. Both straight and slim with the same dancing eyes and ready smile. They would make beautiful children.

Mary and all the saints, why was he thinking that? The pain of it twisted in his gut even as his mind shrieked denial. And denial not for the only legitimate reason—if his mission succeeded, Red Hugh O'Donnell would not be alive to father any woman's children—but for the worst: the only seed he wanted in fair Deirdre's womb was his own.

God help him, somewhere between the Tower chamber and his present perch, he'd lost his reason, to be thinking any such thing.

He shook his golden head like a great beast throwing off lashes of water, only in his case it was thoughts he wanted to be shed of. She was only a woman. A girl, really, and the last of her sex he had any business noticing. He was the queen's man, let there be no doubt of that. Ruthless old harridan Elizabeth might be, but she had taken England from a piddling backwater buffeted by the whims of continental intrigues to a world power no one touched without peril. And she'd done it with far less of the customary brutality he'd seen so much of elsewhere.

Yes, he was for Elizabeth, which meant against O'Neill and O'Donnell. Against Ireland, if it came to that, for though it was the land of his mother, it was the back door to England, and as such had to be secured no matter what the cost. His mouth set wryly at the thought that if Deirdre knew for an instant how he felt, she wouldn't hesitate to drive a dagger through his heart. Nor would he expect her to do otherwise. They were enemies. If he forgot that, he was the world's worst fool.

And yet the loveliness of her made him ache. He shrugged, resigned to his own weakness. He'd find some pretty, accommodating woman around the castle. There were always such, and he never had any trouble persuading them, what with his looks and the liberality of his purse. A nice, uncomplicated woman who would ask no more than what he could give.

But the thought of any such involvement, however brief, left him oddly depressed. Women and the pleasures they offered were pitfalls even for the strongest man. War, now, that was a different matter. He understood war in a way he'd never understood women.

He went down from the parapet with his harp over his shoulder and wandered about in the aimless way that poets have when they are seeking inspiration. In fact, he was trying to get a rough count of the number of people at Dungannon, but it was hard, for there was much coming and going. The broad-beamed gates hewn of mighty oaks were thrown wide, and there seemed to be only a token guard on watch although closer inspection proved that wasn't the case. Several hard-faced young men were keeping a close eye on everyone who passed beneath the stone portico, but they did it without a great deal of display.

They nodded to him as he went by, proving that word of the new bard had spread. He'd been heard in hall the previous evening, and now already he was accepted. In England—and in Russia, which was the other place he knew well—a man could labor all his life and never earn such recognition. In Ireland it was given readily, even eagerly. The generosity of that caused him a twinge deep down inside. If only they were more sensible, these whole-hearted Irishmen with their enthusiasm for all that was beautiful. If only they could be trusted.

If only . . . If there were sadder words in either language, English or Gaelic, he didn't know them. Damned if he'd keep thinking of them.

Count, man, he admonished himself. How many

beneath the portico in five minutes, in ten? How many wagons, how many horses? How many armed, how many not? How many who look as though they could handle themselves in battle? And how many who will die like so much chaff before the wind if Elizabeth feels called upon to loose her full fury on beautiful, treacherous Eire?

Too many.

He gave up after a bit and decided to count something that stood still. Dungannon's armory was kept in a broad stone keep almost at the exact center of the castle complex. It was there the castle dwellers would retreat in the event of a breach in the wall by invading troops. An iron-studded door set at the top of a high flight of steps gave way to a cavernous chamber wrapped deep in shadows. A scattering of slit windows near the arched ceiling admitted grudging light.

Metal gleamed along the walls. Delacroix drew nearer, breathing in the familiar smell of steel wrapped in the faint chill that always, even on the warmest day, seemed to hover over the instruments of death. The razor tips of pikes arrayed in rows caught his eye. He drew nearer, remembering pikes in the Russian snows, crimson on white, and in the distance the howl of wolves.

The harp bumped against his back where he had slung it. He reached a hand around and for a moment caressed the warm, satiny wood. His fingers itched to touch the strings, but he pushed the thought aside. Song and the poetry that filled it had always been for pleasure alone. This was duty.

Along a farther wall hung broadswords, braced on double brackets to bear their great weight. No slender rapiers such as they favored in Elizabeth's court, but weapons of might and strength that a man could wield all day if he had the will, mowing down his enemies until there were no more. So too were the crossbows, aged but still lethal. And there, heaped in that deep corner, the iron seed for the cannons he had seen about, the cleavers of bodies and freer of souls to find their rest where they could.

The harsh planes of his face drew tauter; his eyes were grim, reflecting his thoughts. This O'Neill did not make his rebellion lightly; he had the weapons for war. As for the will, that his men at least seemed to have in abundance. He doubted they had come about it on their own.

How far exactly did the Irishman intend to go? A free Ulster under his own rule, or did he want more? All Ireland free with him as high king as there had not been in fifty generations of men? And if such should somehow come to pass, what then? How long before the lords of Scotland rose in fury, and Wales with them? England under such assault would be easy prey to the French and Spanish. They would dismember her, the worst fears of Elizabeth would be realized, and . . .

His thoughts were running away with him. He shoved them aside and went on determinedly with his inspection, going swiftly, for he did not want to be seen. When he was done, he went back again into the sunlight and stood for a moment letting the warmth sink into bones chilled by the memory of death.

He shut his eyes against the welcomed brightness and opened them again to find the O'Neill looking at him. Ulster's lord appeared surprised to come upon him, although not displeased.

"Bard," he said pleasantly but with the underlying note of wariness common to all powerful men. He glanced up toward the keep. "You have an interest in weaponry?"

"In history," England's newest earl said smoothly. "You have an impressive collection."

"Indeed," O'Neill said. "The fruit of centuries, although don't be misled, most of it is modern."

"I know little of such things." It surprised him how well he lied. He had never thought of it as a particular skill of his, but apparently he had been wrong. As soon as it was needed, the talent had emerged.

"Not in the usual schooling of a bard?" O'Neill said, still watchful of eye. "Well, then, if there is anything you would like to know, I will be glad to instruct you. Indeed, I would consider it an honor. When you compose the great sagas of our age, as I've no doubt you will, you will need to know all."

Give the man his due, he flattered as smoothly as any courtier, and why not? Like many of the Irish lords, he had spent considerable time beneath Elizabeth's various royal roofs. Indeed, in the silver and velvet doublet, with his cheeks freshly shaven and his hose neatly pressed, he looked as though he had just stepped from the queen's privy chamber.

Why the ceremony when he had spent the previous several days on the training fields with his men, bare-chested and sweating under the hot sun? It struck Delacroix then that something was afoot, not in the next week or next month, but something more immediate. Something that accounted for the air of suppressed excitement hanging about the big bear of a man before him.

"I would not take you from your tasks," Delacroix said cautiously. "These are busy times."

The O'Neill laughed. He slapped his bard on the back in a friendly gesture that would have disabled a lesser man but had little effect in this case.

"True enough, singer. The sun races across the sky and I wonder where each hour has gone, but surely that is a small price for the greatness of these days. I've noticed you on the training fields. Tell me, have you seen a greater host than mine own?"

Delacroix hesitated. He could easily have said that he had not, that the O'Neill's army was the greatest ever gathered. But he was realizing that there were some lies his newfound skill did not stretch to reach.

"It is mighty without doubt," he said slowly, "men of skill and fire, and notable for their loyalty to you."

The O'Neill stepped back slightly, looking at him from beneath his thick brows. "But . . ."

"In my youth, I journeyed far to the east and landed finally in the court of the Russian tsar. When his armies take the field, they darken it for miles around. The dust raised by their marching feet is enough to blot out the sun."

"Hmmm, I see. Very impressive. But Russia is far from here. Apart from that, what have you seen?"

Again a moment of hesitation before he said, "The English, I have seen them. They are not so numerous as the Rus, not at all, but they have a single great advantage."

"And what would that be, bard?" the O'Neill challenged with the look of a man prepared to indulge another who knows relatively little about the subject on which he speaks.

"Their discipline," Delacroix replied. He met the Irishman's eyes and did not flinch at their cold glitter. "The English soldier will not flee from battle, will not disobey orders, and will not suddenly switch his allegiance. He will fight to the end willy-nilly he dies in the process. How exactly they come by such obedience I do not know, but it is their greatest strength."

"Bah," O'Neill exclaimed, "they fight with armies of slaves. Their troops obey because they are like cattle, not capable of thinking for themselves. Why, a single Irishman of the lowest estate has more thoughts in his head in a single day than your average Englishman does in a year."

Delacroix smiled slightly. He had heard Britishers say the same thing, but in reverse. Each side liked to believe in the ignorance and stupidity of the other, and each was wrong. Still, this did not seem the time to try to convince the O'Neill of that.

"Be that as it may, you will need many more men to go against the force they can send. Will you have them?"

From another man, even a trusted lieutenant, the question would have been at best presumptuous. At worst it would have sown the seed of suspicion regarding loyalties. But a bard was cloaked in ancient authority that no one, not even Dungannon's lord, stood ready to question.

The O'Neill looked away, his gaze turned inward. Quietly, he said, "I know the British, singer. I dwelt among them too long not to understand them well. When I march to battle, it will be to win."

He fell silent for a moment, locked in the shadows of his thoughts before his mood suddenly changed. He clapped his arm around Delacroix's shoulders and laughed. "Enough of war. Tonight in hall let you turn your mind to happier pursuits. There'll be time enough later for the blood and glory. Time now for love and lingering looks, for the murmurs of a man and a maid, fresh born each time anew."

Delacroix restrained a sigh. Ireland's greatest warrior, fierce pride of her people and their hope for the future. And a poet too, as were they all, heaven help them. England had her poets, true enough, but they were kept apart. No singer soldiers for Elizabeth, no dreamers and sighers. Hackers and sawers only, slayers of renown.

Not unlike himself, John Delacroix, new-hatched earl of Bradford, late of the army of the tsar and Elizabeth's sworn man. What business had he wishing the world was different? Wishing there was time for a dark-haired girl with eternity in her eyes? If only . . .

Fie on that and all the rest. The O'Neill would have his songs, small gift that they were to a man shaking hands with death and not even knowing it. And he, singer of dreams, would put his mind to reality. There had to be a way to turn aside the rush to disaster, another path, another chance. Had to be. For if there was not, all this beauty and pride were like so much mist on the moor, burned off with the first harsh light of day.

The thought hurt him. He glanced away, and his eye fell on the stables. For an instant, he thought he caught a glimpse of ebony silk and the quicksilver ripple of laughter. But they vanished before he could be sure.

CHAPTER
5

TOWARD DUSK THE SPANISH CAME. THERE were three, gloriously garbed in black velvet and silken hose, riding silver-caparisoned Moorish horses of the kind the O'Neill so admired. With them came their retinue, fully fifty in number, on foot and on lesser mounts, along with two wagons, one of baggage and the other fitted out with a fringed roof to serve as a litter. That it had only recently been quitted by the Spaniards while still out of sight was obvious; each looked singularly ill at ease in the saddle.

Odd for a people who in their prime had used the horse to conquer everything in their path, Delacroix thought. He remembered fighting with men of Spain in service to the tsar and noting how fiercely they acquitted themselves. These three were apparently of a different sort. Their ivory skin, protected from the capricious Irish sun by broad-brimmed hats, the awkwardness of their perches on the spirited animals, and the relief they evinced as they dismounted all said strongly they were men of the court, not of the field.

Any thought that their arrival was unexpected was banished when Ulster's earl appeared to greet them. His booming voice could be heard from one end of the vast castle bailey to the other.

"At last, my lords, well come and met! Your journey gave you no trouble, I hope?"

The elder of the three, on whom faint wisps of graying hair showed from beneath his hat, stepped forward with some reluctance. He eyed the big Irishman cautiously.

"My lord," he said in English, for it was their only common language. Actually, to be fair, that is not quite true; they both spoke French, but neither would admit to it.

"I am Don Carlos de Alonza, duke of Medina Sidonia, by the grace of God and His Most Holy Majesty, King Phillip, emissary to the kingdom of Ulster." He gestured toward the two younger men. "I present my associates, Don Diego Flores de Valdez and Don Enrique Perez de Guzman."

Each of the men proffered a deep bow with the embellishment of their hats swept before them so that their plumes trailed in the bailey dust. The O'Neill appeared pleased. Ulster they called a kingdom, and him they acknowledged as a king. It was a good beginning.

"Be welcome," he continued munificently. "The gates of Dungannon are open to you, and the hospitality of my house is your own."

He walked beside the duke up the broad steps to the entrance as the other two followed. Behind them, their retainers began the business of dismantling the baggage wagon. Delacroix remained off to the side, watching. From the quantity of belongings the Spaniards had brought, they looked to be staying awhile in the *kingdom* of Ulster. A fine fit her exalted highness, Elizabeth of England, would be having were she to hear that.

The mystery of O'Neill's elaborate garb was solved, as was his unexpected good humor earlier in the day. The earl watched the baggage wagon a moment longer before turning away grimly. Sing of love in hall tonight, Ulster's *king* had said. Rather sing of treachery and foolishness so great as to pass all belief.

The Spanish, for pity's sake. Beaten ten years before when their great armada smashed against Britain's shores, their diseased king dead but a short time and an uncertain heir in his place, and now this. Clearly, they meant to challenge Elizabeth once more, but to do it this time through Ireland. So they had learned something after all. Too bad the same couldn't be said of their feckless host.

Delacroix went up the steps to the hall, knowing what he was likely to see and resigned to it. The Spaniards were being presented to Red Hugh O'Donnell. To the younger man's credit, it was impossible to say whether he'd been forewarned of their coming or not. No reaction showed on his slender, finely featured face.

Beside him, glorious in scarlet silk, Deirdre did not so easily deceive. The look that flickered behind her azure eyes said she was surprised and not entirely pleased. She gazed at the Spaniards coldly and withdrew her hand as quickly as propriety allowed.

Delacroix smiled to himself. He touched a hand beneath his jerkin and felt the soft, crushed flowers within. A moment later, he watched as Deirdre said something to her father. The O'Neill frowned but nodded. She inclined her head once more toward the Spaniards and moved gracefully from the hall.

He resisted the impulse to follow, strong though it was. Instead, he stayed until the formalities were concluded and the O'Neill withdrew to a private chamber accompanied by his guests and Red Hugh. The nature of their business was not difficult to imagine, only the exact terms. How much aid would the Spaniards provide, and when? On that rested much.

Briefly, he considered discovering what he might overhear from behind the closed door, but he decided against it when he noticed the two men-at-arms who had taken up position in front.

Meaning to leave the hall, he passed one of the curving stone staircases that led to the upper reaches of the castle. There he paused as Deirdre's voice floated down from the landing above.

"Don't be difficult, Fionna," she was saying. "I'll put this thing back on before supper, but in the meanwhile I'll wear something comfortable. You tossed me into it so fast I had barely time to draw a breath. If I don't get one soon, I'll faint."

She did sound a bit weak, he thought with a grin. Not to mention exasperated. The maid, however, was having none of it.

"Do you have any idea how hard it is to do up those stays, my girl? My fingers are aching already, and you want me to fuss with them again?"

"Just get this thing off me, for pity's sake. I truly

cannot breathe. Every rib I have is aching, and I've got this queer rushing noise in my ears."

"Pity's sake my own! There's not a girl in a million who wouldn't envy you such a fine gown, and you in a tear to be rid of it. What the devil's got into you, Deirdre O'Neill? Ever since you came back from showing young Hugh about—and I still cannot believe you did it in that awful old dress—you've been lost in a fog somewhere. The Spanish are here, and even I know what that means. Great things are afoot. Is it any wonder your father wants you to look your best?"

"My father . . ." She broke off on a thread of a whisper. Delacroix waited, straining against the silence. Beneath the jerkin, the flowers exuded their scent, prompted by the warmth of his body.

"My father has his plans, and the rest of us have but to follow them."

"And what's wrong with that, lass?" the maid asked, more gently.

"Nothing, I suppose. It's only that—"

"Deirdre, lass, did . . . did Red Hugh do something that frightened you?"

"Oh, no," she said quickly, "not at all. He's very kind and . . . sweet, I suppose."

"Then what has you like this?"

A moment's silence, before Deirdre murmured, "Fionna, he kissed me."

"Ah, well, then what's wrong with that, the way things are?"

"Nothing, except that I didn't feel anything."

Silence, followed more gently by, "You didn't feel . . . ?"

"Anything. Nothing at all. It was like the kiss of a

brother or a friend, even though I know he didn't mean it that way."

"Lass . . ."

"That's not right, is it, Fionna? I should feel something at least, shouldn't I?"

The maid hesitated as Delacroix leaned forward, hand pressed against the cold stone, listening unabashedly. Kissed her, had he, the red-haired rogue? And she'd felt nothing? She'd damn well feel something if he was the one doing the kissing. No woman could have eyes like that and be immune from passion. Young O'Donnell simply had no idea how to awaken it.

"He's a good man," Fionna said firmly, "and he'll make you a fine husband. It will all work out, you'll see."

Her conviction rang hollow, but either it reassured Deirdre or she was merely disinclined to continue the conversation, for Delacroix heard nothing more.

He sang in hall that night, a lonely Spanish ballad about the great warrior, El Cid, and the woman he had loved. The visitors liked it, but O'Neill looked disgruntled, perhaps because he could not understand it. Red Hugh sipped his wine and looked at Deirdre, who returned his gaze but only courteously.

Later, the bard walked the parapet, ghostly in the smoke of tar-soaked torches. The night was cool, and far below trees rustled. Ireland slept as her soul wandered through ancient dreams. Far to the south, against the navy sky, Orion followed the hunt. The moon was almost full.

From the window of her chamber, Deirdre gazed out at it. Fionna had gone to her own rest, and Deidre was alone. She breathed in the heavy scent of night and felt the weight of it deep within. Pining, Mother Abbess would have called it and mocked her for such indulgence. What, after all, was she pining for? The dream of a man who could never be?

Red Hugh was decent, honorable, even kind, which was a marvel considering what he had endured. She should be on her knees giving thanks to God for finding her such a husband. And yet . . .

She shut her eyes and heard for a moment the deep, caressing voice of the bard singing of deathless love. Sean Harpsinger, poet and wanderer, both honorable professions in the land of Ireland but hardly the seed of chieftains. Singers of songs were for the fireside, not the marriage bed. And yet . . .

She sighed and leaned forward to pull the shutters closed against the sudden chill. Above, leaning against the parapet, Delacroix caught a glimpse of slender, snow-white arms. He told himself it could have been any woman and went to find his own slumber, only to encounter in it dreams of raven-haired Deirdre embracing the bloodred moon.

"A tradition," the O'Neill said. "Nothing of any particular significance, only a small thing people hereabouts have enjoyed too long now to put a stop to."

"Blasphemy," Don Diego murmured. He was one of the younger Spaniards, inferior in rank to Don Carlos. Properly enough, he'd had little to say in public so far. But suddenly his long, finely drawn face was no longer bland. Behind the large, slightly protruding eyes, the fire of religious fanaticism sparked.

Red Hugh cast him a chilling look. "You misunderstand, it is merely a custom."

Don Diego did not reply, but neither did he appear convinced. He returned to his breakfast, sipping ale with fastidious care and declining the breast of quail proffered by a serving man.

"One must expect quaint customs wherever one goes," Don Carlos said. "Civilized men know what is real and true, but the peasantry is always the same. They wallow in ignorance and superstition. Naturally, we must all do whatever we can for the salvation of their souls, but one must not expect too much." He waved a hand, pale and languid. "After all, we are only men, not workers of miracles."

Deirdre waited, thinking her father would surely rebuke him, for the O'Neill loved his people well and would not care for the description of them as ignorant and superstitious. But, to her dismay, he merely changed the subject. What followed passed her by, for she made no attempt to listen to it. Instead, she fought the anger that had been building in the two days since the Spaniards had come.

Trust their dour guests to try to spoil something that for her had always been one of the high points of the year. Don Diego was the worst of them, but Don Enrique, the other young one, and Don Carlos, the eldest, were little different. All looked as though they would like nothing so much as to be elsewhere. They had cast a pall over what should otherwise have been a happy time.

Granted, the scent of war was in the air, but so far it hung but lightly on air perfumed by the earth's bounty. The first crops were being brought in from the fields, the fresh beans and marrows, and the hard little potatoes introduced only a short time before but already so popular. In the orchards, trees hung heavy with apples and pears ripening in the warm sun. In the fields, lambs cavorted. Calves, newly weaned, followed their mothers at forage. Ponies ran on their wandlike legs, tossing their heads to catch the breeze. Everywhere life in all its enthusiastic joy seemed intent on reveling in itself.

Who would not celebrate that? For uncounted generations, the people of Dungannon had come to the hill beyond the fortress to offer the first fruits of the harvest. It was an ancient ritual whose origins were lost in the mists of time, but it was also surely innocent. Proof of that lay in the fact that no priest had ever spoken against it. Or if one had, it wasn't recently. Granted, the priests absented themselves from the hilltop ceremony, but that didn't mean it was bad. Did it?

So, too, now that she thought of it, did the O'Neill absent himself along with all his major retainers. He had never expressly forbid her to attend, but he had certainly never encouraged it.

Still, she would go. It was seven years, the time she had been at St. Bernadine's, since she had attended the festival. As soon as she could, she slipped away from the hall and made her way to the bailey.

Her father had said she was not to leave the fortress without escort. Actually, what he had said was that she was not to ride out alone. But she wasn't riding, she was going on foot, slipping in among the cheerful, milling crowd that thronged the road leading north of the fortress to the tallest of the hills around Dungannon.

Padriac's Seat, it was called, named for the saint who had driven the snakes from Ireland. But then, so were at least a hundred other peaks in the land. The name meant little. Most people still referred to it in the old way. "Buan-ann" it was known as, "good mother" in the ancient language.

A winding track led up the hill, laid down so long ago that it had worn a deep trench in the earth. As Deirdre came around the last turn and emerged onto the flat plateau at the top, she heard the laughter and eager talk of the people who had gone ahead. The ascent of the hill itself was a solemn matter best done in silence, but once the top was reached such restraint slipped away.

The people had been gathering since before dawn, the old ones among them reading the wind to know what the weather would do through the remainder of the harvesttime. Already they were saying it would be fair, not too much rain or too little, so that the bounty gathered in would be ample. Unspoken was the knowledge that such was a mixed blessing. There would be no hunger if all the harvest could be brought in. But with the young men going to war . . .

Make haste, the wind said as it skirted over the top of Buan-ann. Take the long nights when the swollen moon illumines the fields and make haste. Hurry, for the time of reaping is coming, for crops and for men.

Deirdre gathered her skirts more closely around her and turned her face to the benediction of the sun. No one appeared to take any notice of her. Even Fionna, whom she glimpsed off to one side and who clearly saw her, gave no sign of recognition. That was as it always had been, at least in the lifetimes of all those present. Attendance at the festival was a private matter; it did not bear commenting on either before or after. The result was that each year the summer ritual appeared to happen spontaneously without anyone giving it prior thought or planning for it. No one spoke of going up to Buan-ann or of what would happen there. They simply went and did it.

Around her the people grew still, talk falling away into silence broken only by the excited murmurings of the youngest children. The oldest of them, a crone of gnarled bone and skin seamed to the texture of worn leather, stepped into the center of the circle and lifted her arms. The wind filled her plain black dress of humble homespun, giving it for a moment the contours of a holy robe billowing on the earth's breath.

She said nothing for nothing was needed. Perhaps in the past words had been spoken, but words could fall on the wrong ears. Better simply to act.

The old one turned in a circle, gazing at the assembled people. She turned once, twice, three times. Her arm stretched out, her hand pointed.

At Deirdre.

The young girl started. She had never thought to be singled out. Usually, the honor went to a girl of the village. Still, there was no refusing. The thought of doing so did not even occur to her.

In the back of the crowd, towering above those around him, Delacroix watched her. He had joined the throng going to the hill out of simple curiosity. No one had questioned his right to do so. On the contrary, he had received enough smiles and encouraging nods to know he was welcome. But at what? What was happening here on the high hill above the fortress on this bright summer morning?

And why was Deirdre summoned by the crone?

CHAPTER
6

ON HER KNEES, DEIRDRE DUG IN THE EARTH.
First, she used a short, blunt stick to loosen the hard-packed dirt immediately on top. Below was softer soil that she was able to scoop up with her hands. She dug until the opening before her was about the size of a woman's lap. When she was done, she waited.

From the crowd came half a dozen children walking with self-conscious pride. One held a stalk of early beans, another carried a basket of potatoes, a third brought fine, soft fleece, and so on. One by one, they handed their offerings to Deirdre. One by one, she placed them in the earth. That done, she scooped the soil back into the hole and patted it down gently.

Immediately, a cheer went up. The brief solemnity was banished and in its place came revelry again. Earthen jugs were uncorked and sipped from. Loaves of broad bread still warm from the oven were passed around. Cheese, meats, and fish were laid out.

Delacroix accepted a drink from a man standing near him and was surprised to discover it was whiskey, not ale. *Uisge betha*, the Irish called it, "water of life," and generally they saved it for special occasions. This was clearly one, even if he didn't understand it.

He lingered a while longer on the hilltop, but nothing else of consequence appeared to happen. The people now resembled nothing more than a happy group gathered on the spot to share a simple meal. No mystery to that except it was not a day the official calendar recognized as being set aside from work. Yet surely the O'Neill knew many of his people were not at their usual occupations. Did he also know his daughter's whereabouts?

Delacroix was wondering about that when he saw her bid farewell to those around her and set off down the hill. He followed and caught up with her quickly.

"Good morning," he said, softly so as not to startle her on the narrow track. She turned her head, and he saw the wariness quickly masked.

"Good morning," she replied. Nothing else, as though it was the most natural thing in the world for them both to be there in that time and place.

The wind blew strands of her ebony hair toward him. She had left it loose, falling in waves below her shoulders. He thought suddenly of the night and a crimson moon and Deirdre. But the thought was fleeting, and he let it fade.

"The going is steep here," he said as he offered his hand. "May I help you?"

She hesitated a moment, looking up at the golden-haired man above her. He was simply dressed as always, with the harp slung over his back. Her gaze focused on his mouth, hard yet full, unlike Red Hugh's. She looked away quickly, but not before accepting his assistance.

Her fingers were slim and warm in his. He fought down the sudden flash of desire that ripped through him. They reached the road going back toward the fortress before she spoke. "I suppose you have been to many such festivals."

Why did she suppose that? What was there he, a bard, was expected to know but did not?

"I have been away from Ireland too much," he began, falling back on an excuse he knew he was in danger of using too often.

Yet Deirdre appeared to accept it. "It is very ordinary what we do here," she said. "I understand at the Ring of Kerry and in some other places they do it more elaborately."

It. What it? What did the little ritual he had observed signify?

Rather than so expose his ignorance, he asked, "What is the hill called?"

"Buan-ann," she said.

Good mother in the very old tongue, not the Gaelic as it was presently spoken but an archaic form he had heard referred to . . . where? His mother had taught him the language of her people, and she died before his thirteenth year. Where had he heard the ancient words and grasped their meaning?

A fleeting memory, so shadowed as to be barely sensed, passed through his mind. The chant of voices, a singing stream, and himself very small, held safe and warm in arms . . .

The memory vanished, but the powerful longing it evoked did not. Something had happened on Buan-ann that carried shadows of a half-remembered dream. Yet to the several hundred people who shared it, the event had been as solidly real as the ground beneath his feet.

"You left before the others," he said.

She looked uncomfortable. "I have to get back."

Something in her tone told him more than she intended. He smiled slightly. "Before you are missed?"

She cast him a sharp look from beneath long, dusky lashes. "Why do you say that?"

"No reason in particular, only that your father keeps you close, understandably enough."

"It is not so understandable to me," Deirdre said before she could stop herself. The pent-up frustration of the last few days would no longer be denied. On a note of longing, she said, "When I knew I was coming home, I was overjoyed. I imagined myself free to roam as I had when I was child. But instead—"

"You are not a child anymore," he interrupted gently, "and your father is right to recognize that."

Deirdre bowed her head at what seemed to her to be a reprimand, however kindly meant. He was right, of course. She should be more obedient, more patient, more grateful. More of all the things a proper young woman of her class was supposed to be. Instead, she always felt at war with herself, caught between what she knew she ought to be and the wilder, freer side of her nature.

The true O'Neill side. Had she been a boy, her father would have had no quarrel with her. But instead he sought, as the bard said, to keep her close.

Sought but did not always succeed, as he was about to discover. Dust rose from around a bend in the road. Delacroix stopped. He heard what Deirdre did not, the clink of armor and the low voices of men.

The O'Neill was in the lead with Red Hugh beside

him. The Spaniards rode behind, and behind them came a brace of retainers fully ten ranks deep, mounted and armed. Behind them came a yapping army of dogs straining at their leads, keeping the handlers busy.

Ulster's *king* had decided on the spur of the moment to take his guests hunting. Partly, he was bored being stuck inside the castle walls playing host; and partly, he wanted to discomfit his guests in return for the discomfort they were inflicting on him. That these dour Spaniards were his allies troubled him greatly. Had there been a choice in the matter, he would have sent them packing. But choice was something he sadly lacked for a man of his presumed authority. Either he played loyal retainer to Elizabeth or he took every means available to fight against her. Rebellion was not for the fastidious.

Which was all very fine, but it also explained the strain to his temper before he ever rounded the bend in the road and came upon his only daughter, the cherished flower of his heart, standing dirt-stained and disheveled without an escort in sight save for the new bard. Who, now that he happened to think of it, seemed to keep turning up in unexpected places.

He scowled at the pair the instant he saw them, but the scowl deepened as his eye caught the swell of Buan-ann in the near distance and he realized where they had been. Granted, he looked the other way at what the common people did, but Deirdre at the summer festival! His daughter among such pagan ritual! And her poised but an instant between the convent and a good Christian marriage. Surely no man had ever been tried more sorely by the seeds of his loins.

Had the Spaniards not been present, he would

have dressed her down in a way she would never have forgotten. But pride demanded he not let the foreigners see how he had been disobeyed by his own whelp. Not that she mistook his restraint for anything but what it was. Her face was pale as she sketched him a curtsy.

"Father," she murmured.

Distantly, in the back of his mind, the O'Neill noted her fear and noted, too, the way the bard stepped beside her, interposing himself between her and the earl on his mighty roan. The bard . . . that bore more thinking about, but not yet.

"Daughter," the O'Neill said. "We missed you in the bailey, but no mind. Now that we have found you—" He gestured behind him to where the other horses pawed the ground in their impatience to move on. His expression was guardedly fierce, anger held in strict check but no less anger for that. "Mount."

If the Spaniards noted that none of the horses was riderless, they did not comment. One of the men-at-arms, seeing the red glare in their lord's eyes, made haste to remove himself from the saddle.

"You, too," O'Neill added, looking at Delacroix. On the spur of the moment, he decided to bring the bard along. It did not occur to him to wonder if Delacroix could ride well enough until he saw him approach another newly vacated mount. Concerned lest the man be biting off more than he could chew, the O'Neill almost rescinded his order. But the bard took the reins without hesitation and swung onto the stallion's back as though he had done the same every day of his life.

So, the O'Neill thought, a bard who is at home with war-horses. Who visits my armory. Who appears, now that I think on it, out of nowhere at a moment of crisis. Something or nothing? Time would tell, and he was content it should, being by nature a patient man.

That the O'Neill truly believed this about himself was eloquent testament to the powers of self-deception. In fact, he had never been much good at restraining his natural impulse, although he had learned a useful amount of guile at Elizabeth's court. With rebellion had come the urge to shuck off such foreign trappings. The Spaniards held him in unwitting check, but Deirdre—and the bard—offered a welcome outlet for his displeasure.

Riding next to Delacroix, her back straight and her head high, Deirdre looked directly ahead. She did her level best to keep her mind absolutely blank, although the effort was doomed to failure.

How could her father do this to her? True enough, she had violated his orders when she left the castle, but surely the punishment did not fit the crime. He knew how much she hated hunting, indeed how much she feared and loathed it. Not that she was any hypocrite about the matter; she knew animals had to be killed and eaten. It was the chase itself that horrified her, the sense of terror she seemed to share with the prey, and the desperate climactic moments when death could no longer be outrun. From earliest childhood, while all around her were chattering on and on about the joys of the pursuit, she had done her best to avoid it. Generally, she had succeeded. Until now.

Her knuckles gleamed white against the reins. She shifted slightly in the saddle and caught the bard looking at her. He saw too much, but then, poets always did. Flushing, she looked away.

Delacroix frowned. He didn't like what he saw in

her eyes. Why should Deirdre O'Neill be so afraid simply because her father had ordered her to join the hunt?
It defied explanation, yet afraid she clearly was, sitting
white-faced and so tense in the saddle that it was a
wonder the horse didn't catch her unease and buck
under her. Up ahead, Red Hugh cast a glance over his
shoulder, but he appeared to see nothing amiss. He
went back to chatting with the O'Neill.

They turned off the main road onto a branch that
ran through a tunnel of ancient oaks, their leaf-heavy
limbs spread out in a canopy above them. The horses
whinnied nervously. Like all of their breed, they disliked the shadowed places. Up ahead, a horn sounded.
Instantly, the hounds began to bay. The handlers
released them, stepping back quickly as the dogs shot
past the riders and tore into the woods.

The horses followed. Delacroix was about to urge
his mount forward, for truth be told he enjoyed the
hunt as well as any man. Only the realization that
Deirdre was holding back stopped him. Her face was
very pale. All the light and color he had seen in it on
the hilltop were gone. Even her mouth, normally full
and ripe for the tasting, looked bloodless.

All his life he had possessed the ability to separate
himself from whatever was going on around him and
observe them dispassionately. That did not desert him
now. Far in the back of his mind, he noted the irony of
his being so concerned with the welfare of the young
woman whose father and husband-to-be he was working to destroy. Ah, well, life was full of that sort of
thing. There might even be a poem in it if he thought
on it long enough. But in the meantime he had more
immediate concerns.

"Are you ill?" he asked softly as he drew up alongside her.

Deirdre shook her head. She kept her gaze steadfastly ahead.

He frowned. Not ill, then what? "Are you worried about your father? He is bound to be displeased, but surely he will forgive you."

"I disobeyed him by leaving the castle," Deirdre said in a low, strained voice. "And going to Buan-ann, he knows about it, of course, but I can't pretend he would want me there." She turned her head away, but not before he caught the glint of tears in the fathomless blue eyes. "I knew he would be angry, but not like this."

It was on the tip of his tongue to ask what was so terrible about being brought along on the hunt, but before he could do so, the horns rang out. The prey had been sighted. Dogs, horses, and men alike surged forward. Deirdre struggled to hold back, but her mount was too strong for her. It went with all the rest.

The silence of the wood was shattered by the sudden crash of hooves, the excited whinnying of the horses and the frantic yapping of the dogs. Birds, rousted from their perches, circled overhead, cawing shrilly. Again the horns sounded and again the pack turned, tearing through the underbrush.

Deirdre was a good rider, schooled to it from earliest childhood and more than at home on horseback. But her fear distracted her. She failed to notice the low-hanging branch coming at her at fiercesome speed until it was too late to avoid it. The branch caught her full in the chest, knocking the wind from her and throwing her from the saddle. She landed heavily, the breath knocked from her. Pain encompassed her and swirling darkness threatened to draw her down. She fought for consciousness, knowing full well the terrible danger she was in. Unseated in the midst of a rampaging horde of men and horses with the blood-scent hot in them, she was at real risk of being trampled. She had to move, and quickly, but when she tried to do so the pain and the darkness both grew stronger. She cried out and did exactly what she knew she must not. For the first time in her life, Deirdre O'Neill fainted.

Delacroix saw the slender form lying supine amid the crushed leaves. He was no stranger to fear, having counted on it to keep him alive in the heat of many a battle, but this was different. This was the sickle-swinger come for another, not himself, and one too vulnerable to resist. Already one of the Spaniards was bearing down on her, oblivious to what had occurred. Delacroix shouted a warning, but he was either not heard or ignored. He didn't waste time on another. Instead, he drove his spurs into the heaving sides of his mount and thundered straight ahead. His horse struck the Spaniard's flat-on, forcing it to shift direction. The animal, rightly disgruntled, took off at a gallop, oblivious to the frantic shouts of its rider.

Delacroix reined in and jumped from the saddle. He ran over to where Deirdre lay and knelt beside her. She was lying facedown and appeared not to be moving. The hand he reached out to her shook slightly.

"Mavourneen," he murmured, hardly noticing that he used the word. Singularly inappropriate it was, given who and what they were, but that didn't seem to matter. He turned her over with infinite care and was relieved to see that though she was unconscious, she was breathing deeply. Quickly, he gathered her into his arms and carried her a little distance away.

In a copse of oak trees, near a rock-strewn spring, he laid her down. The ground was covered with moss softer than any bed. Sunlight dappled through the canopy of leaves. He bent beside the water, scooping handfuls of it, and patted her cheeks gently.

She moaned, her eyelids fluttering. He stared at them, seeing the pale-blue tracing beneath skin delicate as the most finely spun silk. When her eyes were open—and all the spirit alive in her there to be seen—it was possible to lose sight of the fragility of her form. To him, a seasoned warrior, it seemed almost inconceivable that so vibrant a nature should be housed in so delicate a vessel. But then he remembered the deceptive strength of women even as Deirdre herself confirmed it. She stirred, her eyes opening, and stared directly at him.

"What happened?" she asked. Her voice was soft but clear. He murmured a silent prayer of thanks. Any slurring could have indicated that the fall had caused serious injury. As it was, she appeared to be recovering quickly.

"You were knocked from your horse. Lie still. The hunt's gone on, there's no point in trying to catch it."

Deirdre closed her eyes again for a moment in relief. She had followed her father's orders—and accepted his punishment—as best she could. Not even he could blame her for being unseated when such could happen to the most seasoned hunters.

It did not occur to her that he might blame her for being alone in the woods with Harpsinger. Of that she did not think at all. The cause for such omission was simple enough: she was too busy watching the bard even as he watched her.

He had beautiful eyes, large and almost golden with lashes that were absurdly long for a man. Nor were they the only beautiful thing about him. His mouth, for instance, but she had noticed that before and didn't need to dwell on it. Beautiful eyes, beautiful mouth, yet the face in which they were set was utterly masculine. It was a hard face, made of tough bone and sinew covered by skin burnished by the harhest weather. In the shadows of the oak trees, the planes of that face looked carved by a master hand concerned less with delicacy than with endurance. No sweet-faced boy this, no pale priest, no bleary scholar, yet a poet of such fire and directness as to make her understand how it was that poetry and prayer had begun as one and the same.

Still and all, it did not take powerful muscles to make a poem, nor long, tensile-strength limbs, nor a chest she could barely span within her arms were she to ever—which, blessed Mary, she would not—be mad enough to try. A warrior's body, she thought again, made for fire and the sword, not flowers in a garden and the song of the harp.

Her lips moved on a breath. "Who are you?" she whispered.

Delacroix started. Was she hurt more than he had thought? Surely she could recognize him?

He bent closer, blocking out the sun, enveloping her in the warmth and scent of him. "Deirdre, can't you see me?"

"I can," she murmured, and felt the quick relief in him. Still, the question remained: "I don't understand . . . I keep looking at you and seeing someone else. Someone different." She shook her head, winced at the pain, and stopped. Feeling foolish, she said, "You are a wonderful poet."

"Thank you," he replied, warming to the compliment, for truly what this slip of a girl thought mattered to him out of all proportion to what it should. All the same, he let it go swiftly, more concerned with other things.

"I am no one else," he said, and realized in the saying that lying had not come as easily to him as he had thought. This one stuck in his throat like a barb.

"Deirdre."

On his lips, her name was a caress. Warmth suffused her. The pain was forgotten, gone as though it had never been. She felt filled with light and air, lifted above herself toward some destination she could not so much as glimpse yet sought for all the same.

Until reality intruded, not subtly or politely but with a brute grunt and the pawing of ground. Delacroix heard it first and jerked around, tearing himself from the girl. Even as he did so, he cursed himself for having been so absorbed in her as to forget any possible danger. The hunt having moved on, he presumed the prey had, too. It was an elemental error, one that might now cost them their lives.

Facing him across the narrow space of not twenty feet was a full-grown male boar weighing several hundred pounds, armed with razor-sharp tusks and ready for battle. No trembling doe this, or even a powerful stag, but the most feared denizen of the woods aside from the wolf itself, and a match for it in combat.

Deirdre saw it at almost the same instant he did. She bit back a moan and froze in place, knowing that the worst thing she could do was draw attention to them. Delacroix noted her courage but was not surprised by it. He moved a hand slightly to touch her reassuringly, and said under his breath, "At the first chance, run for that tree over there and climb it. Can you manage that?"

She nodded even as her mind rejected the mere notion. What chance—first or otherwise? He was unarmed except for a kirk in the belt around his taut waist. Against the boar he had no chance at all. Their only hope was that the hunt would return quickly. Even now she thought she could hear it off in the distance, the sounds growing clearer with each passing moment.

The boar heard it, too, and did not wait. "Now!" Delacroix ordered as the animal lowered its great head, pawed the ground once, twice, a final time, and lunged. "Run, Deirdre!"

Merciful heaven, the man was mad, for he made no attempt to evade the beast but came out of his crouch to meet it headlong. In that instant, in the whirling darkness of the moment, Deirdre saw him again as he was, a great golden wolf, for surely in the world of dreams there was such a thing. Wolf to boar, clashing in all their power and wildness. She wasted no breath on a scream but got to her feet, ignoring the throbbing behind her temples, and began looking around frantically for a weapon. Never mind that nonsense about making for the nearest tree. She was the O'Neill's daughter, and while there was breath in her body, she would fight.

CHAPTER

7

THE KIRK CAME FROM ITS SCABBARD TO GLEAM silver-edged and deadly in the shadowed light. Against the boar it seemed scant weapon, but it was in the hand of a master, and one moreover with an incentive to fight that went beyond his own life. Behind him, he listened for the sound of Deirdre's escape. When it did not come, he dared a glance over his shoulder. What he saw angered him almost as much as the boar itself.

She stood, her midnight hair in glorious disarray around her shoulders, clutching between her two small hands a sturdy oak branch fully half her size. The look on her face was purest terror, but beneath it was iron-hard determination he could not fail to recognize.

"Sweet Lord, woman," he roared, "I told you to run."

"I won't leave you to fight alone," she cried. "You are a poet. The boar will kill you. Together we might have a chance."

Merciful father, give him strength. Deliver him from the desire to throttle the very creature he was trying to save. Preserve him from the desire, however understandable and undoubtedly shared by the deity himself, to beat a little common sense into what was surely one of the most infuriating females to ever bedevil hapless man.

"Deirdre," he said in a low and menacing tone, "you may wish the boar wins, for if he doesn't, when I am through with him I am going to teach you what your father has clearly failed to impart, namely that when you are told to do something, you damn well *do it!*"

This last part was uttered in a roar that shook the branches above them and gave even the boar pause, though not for long. Perhaps he didn't like the attention being diverted from himself, or the human squabble may have set him on edge. At any rate, he did what came most naturally, which is to say he charged.

The boar leaped, the kirk flashed; Deirdre had barely a moment to wonder at the queer proficiencies of poets before the battle was joined. For a time, it seemed evenly matched. The boar was an old campaigner that had gone against men before. He was strong, wily, and fearless. But this man with the wolf light in his eyes was different. He didn't flinch but met the beast without quarter. They surged against each other, two magnificent, primal beings. The boar raised its head, tusks gleaming, and ran straight at Delacroix. He stepped aside only enough to evade the full blow, but hurled himself at the raging animal and wrestled with him, fighting to get the head up that the knife might reach the soft throat beneath. The boar knew its danger and fought equally to keep its head down while maneuvering for a second chance to gore. It never came. Even as the sharp clamor of the hunters' horns shook the trees, Delacroix rammed the knife home. He did it cleanly, respecting the animal and not wanting to inflict needless suffering. As it was, the boar died almost instantly. It sagged against the man, who laid it heavily on the soft ground swiftly soaked by its life's blood.

Thus it was that when Hugh O'Neill, chieftain and father, came galloping into the clearing in the greatest fear of his life and cursing himself for the spawn of seven devils, this is what he saw: the boar lying dead, the bard standing above him with the bloodied knife in his hand, and his own daughter white-faced but unharmed standing amid the carnage with apparent calm.

The calm was false, of course; Deirdre was petrified, but beneath that, shining crystal clear, was the certainty that she had been right: Sean Harpsinger was no ordinary bard. He met danger coolly and killed with exactitude, suggesting it was not the first time he had done so. More to the point, he had killed for her, risking his life in the process. Something to think on in the quiet hours of night, which she would know once again thanks to him.

Something of the same thought flashed through the O'Neill's mind even as he was awash in relief more intense than any he had ever known. His daughter lived. She had not died through his own foolishness and cruelty. He was reprieved. As for the man to whom he owed it all, the time to consider what was known of him was fast approaching, but first there was the debt just incurred that must be recognized and honored in full. He slipped from his horse and strode toward him.

"Harpsinger," the O'Neill said, his voice carrying to all the rest of the company, who had come riding up behind him, "rather Boarslayer and preserver of the life of my daughter, only say what you would have of me and I will grant it, for truly I have never seen greater courage."

He looked again at the boar and thought of what that beast would have done to Deirdre. Coldness gripped his heart. More softly, he added, "Truly God is good that he sent you to do this."

Delacroix bit back the curse that sprang to his lips. If the O'Neill had a glimmering of the true reason for his presence, he would hardly be thanking anyone for it, much less the deity. As it was, he felt like a churl for accepting the chieftain's gratitude. And yet there was no way to avoid it. He could hardly claim to have done nothing considerable, for to say that would be to belittle the importance of Deirdre's life and by extension the honor of her father. Nor could he claim to have fought only to save himself since he would clearly have had a much better chance of escaping on his own without thought of her. To suggest that the boar was no great matter, being a sort of chicken with tusks of the kind he dispatched daily, was patently ridiculous. No, like it or not, he was stuck with the O'Neill's gratitude as well as his determination to repay the obligation implied by same.

Delacroix repressed a sigh. Only ask, the O'Neill said, and all those in the hunting party—retainers,

Spaniards, and a silently watchful Red Hugh—awaited his answer. Strictly speaking, he could claim any boon; indeed, the greater the reward, the greater the acknowledgment of O'Neill's own worth. However, certain limits were understood. He could not, for instance, ask for Deirdre, although the thought did cross his mind. That would have been beyond all bounds and made the greatest service into gross insult. Nor could he request an end to the rebellion, much as it was carrying them all down the road to madness. No, his obligation in such circumstances was to ask for something the O'Neill could reasonably grant yet which would reflect the honor and munificence suitable to the occasion.

Ah, well then, only one thing to do. "I have been a wanderer for too long," John Delacroix said, and it was true. "I ask leave to remain as bard at Dungannon."

The O'Neill stared at him for a long moment. He had prepared for a good deal else—gold, jewels, land, such were the things the bard could have claimed and would gladly have been granted. But he asked instead only for a place in hall—an honored place, to be sure, but one he was rightly entitled to by virtue of his own abilities.

"Nothing else?" he asked.

The Harpsinger shook his head. "That is all to me."

"Very well, then," the O'Neill said reluctantly, "it is yours. But should you change your mind, should there be anything more, you have only to speak." He held out a hand to Deirdre and said gently, "Daughter, you ride with me."

She went to him gratefully, glad for the love in his eyes, and was lifted onto the saddle.

"Bring the boar," the O'Neill ordered. "We feast tonight."

Don Carlos and the other Spaniards flinched at the thought; clearly, such fare was not their usual preference. There was nothing for it, though. The O'Neill was bent on revelry. After the long, tedious negotiations with his dour-faced allies, he was more than ready to kick over the traces. His daughter's deliverance merely gave him a welcome excuse.

So it was that the stone walls of Dungannon castle rang that night with song and laughter, with the drinking of many toasts and with much boasting about other feats, none so great as the Boarslayer's but worth the telling nonetheless. Sean sang for the company, but mainly he walked among them, sharing their pleasure and accepting as well as he could their gratitude. Before he had been welcome among them, but now it seemed as though he had become *of* them. The difference might appear slight, but was in fact great. He had a disturbing sense of loyalties slipping out of focus that was not helped by the quantity of mead he swallowed. Every time he set his mug down, someone was refilling it. He protested but no one listened, particularly not the pretty young serving girls who seemed intent on outdoing one another in their efforts to please him.

From her seat on the dais, Deirdre observed the goings-on and tried not to grumble at them. It was none of her affair who the Harpsinger turned his attention upon. But if that overblown wench with the tangled black hair and her bosoms popping out of too-tight bodice was a sample, he was sorely lacking in taste.

To be fair, the serving girl was actually a beauty, with hair more curled than tangled and breasts luxurious enough to deserve display. Certainly, Delacroix thought so as he studied them in their present position not more than a few inches from his nose. The lass was bending over rather more than she had to in order to refill his cup yet again. He grinned and looked up, meeting her eyes. They were brown, not blue. He felt a surge of disappointment and resolutely suppressed it.

"Are you're sure you've a mind to do that?" he asked. "There are times when it's wiser for a man to keep his head."

"And times to lose it," the girl said with a ready grin. All the same, she took his meaning. Ceasing her pouring, she plopped herself down on his lap and wiggled her body meaningfully. "You're not a man to be sitting up drinking all night, then?"

Delacroix shook his head. "Never saw the point of it myself."

"Indeed not, a terrible waste of time I always say. Of course, now this whole business here will drag on a while yet, and what with you being the guest of honor and all I can see that you can't be absenting yourself any time soon but—"

"I'm not the guest of honor," he protested. "I'm the bard, so I can't be any kind of guest."

The girl shrugged, unimpressed by his reasoning. The broad sweep of his chest and the pleasant weight she felt beneath her bottom were different matters altogether; they were most impressive. If only he didn't have this tendency to talk so much.

"You killed the boar and saved the Lady Deirdre, which is more honor than many a man could ever claim. But no mind." She hopped off his lap, tossed her ebony hair, and gave him a smile that could smelt steel. "I'm Megan, by the way. Do you lock your chamber door, Harpsinger?"

"Not tonight," he replied. Their eyes met in under-standing. She dawdled a moment longer, letting him feel the warmth of her gaze before reluctantly picking up the wine again and going about her duties.

Delacroix settled back in his seat. He told himself he was doing the right thing—nay, the only sensible thing. He was a man, thank the Lord, not a saint. He had a man's needs, and it had been a long time between women. Undoubtedly that was why he was having inappropriate thoughts about the O'Neill's daughter. They had nothing to do with her, really, not with her beauty or her spirit or the laughter he saw in her eyes or—

Her eyes weren't laughing at him now, they were spitting venom. Meeting her gaze, he drew back in sur-prise, not to say astonishment. What could possibly have happened to draw the lady's ire in such a way?

The warmth of the serving girl's bottom still linger-ing on his lap presented its own answer. Despite him-self, a smile quirked his mouth. Hot-tempered she was, and passionate as well. With that spirit and body, she would come on fire in bed. The man who awakened her to pleasure would have a memory to last a lifetime. But she had no business thinking of him in those terms, any more than he had thinking of her. The sooner he left her in no doubt about that, the better.

He waited until the feasting began to wind down before standing, still rock steady on his feet despite the mead. Megan saw him across the width of the hall. She stood, hands on her hips, and watched him saucily as he walked toward her. When he was standing directly in front of her, she put a hand out and traced a path down his chest to the wide leather belt at his waist. That earned them amused glances from those nearby. Even the O'Neill, normally not a man to take notice of such play, smiled benignly. Only Deirdre did not. She sat white-faced, her eyes averted, as the bard led a mightily pleased Megan from the hall.

Deirdre remembered very little more of the feast. She responded when Red Hugh or her father spoke to her, and what she said must have seemed reasonable to them, for they took nothing amiss. The sight of the food on her plate made her queasy, so she avoided looking at it, staring off into the middle distance instead. After a decent interval, she feigned a yawn and asked her father if she might retire. He granted her wish with a smile that faded as he saw her white, strained face.

"You should have spoken up before now, lass," he said with gruff tenderness. "You're exhausted, and why not after such a day? To bed with you."

She nodded gratefully, aware of his loving contrition, and bent to kiss him lightly on the cheek. To Red Hugh, she nodded cordially as she made her farewells. With Fionna behind her, she left the hall head high.

But once upstairs in her own chamber, that changed. Then the full depression of her thoughts slammed down on her. Harpsinger was . . . even now . . . he and Megan . . . A sob broke from her.

Fionna dropped the brush she had been using to smooth Deirdre's hair and looked at her anxiously. "Child, what's wrong?"

"Nothing," Deirdre managed to get out before her throat clenched and tears consumed her.

Fionna stood over her, making soft little soothing motions with her hands and tut-tutting. She was at a loss momentarily until her usual common sense reasserted itself.

"Ah, lass," she said softly, "'tis no wonder you're out of sorts, what with what you went through today. But never mind now, it's all over and done with. You're safe." She put her arms around the girl's slender shoulders and hugged her gently. "Put it out of your mind, mavourneen, there's a good girl. The boar's dead, you're alive, and that's all that matters."

But it wasn't, as Deirdre could have told her but did not. She did not feel in the least safe, not since she had discovered the perilous depths of her feelings for Sean Harpsinger. Anguish twisted in her at the thought of him with the girl Megan. It seared her skin and gripped her heart in a vise of jealousy. She wanted to scream out against it, to proclaim that he had no right to touch any other woman.

Dully, she shook her head. Surely the devil was inside her, telling her these things, for they were as far from everything she knew to be right and good as she could get. Red Hugh would be her husband; she would cleave to him as a good wife and give him children he would name with pride. All else was ashes.

"I'm all right now, Fionna," she said wearily. Her shoulders slumped with the tired droop of a defeated child. The maid looked at Deidre still with concern but said nothing more as she helped her gently to bed. Only as she was leaving the chamber did she turn back to look at the slender form beneath the covers. This was the baby she had held and cared for, the little girl on colt legs daring the world, the laughing imp of a thousand pranks. But also something new and different, a woman with a woman's secrets.

"Mary keep her," the maid murmured. For her part, she had done all that she could.

Alone in her chamber, Deirdre lay dry-eyed. She would not weep for him or herself. No matter how strong the urge, she would not give in to it. Tears were weak, useless things. She wanted no part of them. Or of the feelings coursing through her, the hot surge of passion and the searing burn of jealousy, the melting desire and the hollow pain of impossibilities. Sweet Lord, there were times when it hurt to be alive. Hurt so much she had to wonder how others had survived it, for surely she was not the first to long for what could never be; that much comfort, at least, was hers.

She squeezed her eyes shut. For more than an hour she courted it, until she finally had to admit it wasn't to be. She had passed beyond being tired into a state of strained wakefulness. Unable to bear the solitude of her bed any longer, she left it and after a moment's hesitation wrapped herself in a dark-blue cloak. It was warm against the night chill, but more importantly, it allowed her to blend into the darkness. Softly, her feet silent in calfskin slippers, she moved over to the door and stood listening for several moments. No sound came from the antechamber beyond. She cracked the door open and peered out gingerly. Fionna lay on her pallet, her back to the room. The gentle rise and fall of her chest showed that she at least had found her rest.

Deirdre slipped past her and opened the door to the passageway. She stared into total darkness. Working by habit, she found the candle kept in a small recess behind the door and struck tinder to it. Shielding the frail flame with her hand, she left the room.

In the great hall below, a pair of hounds raised

their heads as she passed and stared dolefully. One of the castle cats stalked the shadows, visible only by virtue of its white fur. Deirdre shivered. The day had been warm, but the old stone walls held the chill of winter. Toward the back of the hall a heavy oak door led to the castle garden.

Deirdre left the candle to burn within and ventured out into the darkness. A sliver of moon cast pale light over the neatly kept beds separated by gravel paths. She walked slowly, breathing in the delicate night scents kept hidden during the bold day. In the darkness, the air smelled of thyme and rosemary and of the precious, bell-shaped jasmine generations of O'Neill women had lovingly cultivated. Doves nesting in the eaves rustled softly at her passing. In her solitude, every sound, every scent, every movement sprang forward for notice. She wrapped the cloak more closely around her and settled on a small stone bench. In such a setting, she felt strongly the power and beauty of creation. She bent her head, the ebony hair cascading forward, and strove to empty her mind. If she could only stop feeling, yearning, imagining. If she could become what Mother Abbess had always told her she should be, a vessel for a higher will. Always she had rebelled against the idea, but now she sought it. To yield, to still the clamor of her tempestuous nature, to stop struggling and accept whatever came. How much better off she would be!

"Please," she murmured, "help me."

Only the wind answered, blowing softly over the garden. It lifted tendrils of her hair and ruffled the hem of her cloak. An owl called distantly, the sound seeming mournful beyond bearing.

A tear dropped onto her hand, and another. She stared at the glistening drops lying pale against her skin. Her mouth hardened. This would not do at all. She was an O'Neill, daughter of Eire's proudest house. Her duty might not come easily to her, indeed the path to it seemed strewn with sharp stones and treacherous traps, but she would walk it nonetheless.

"Help me," she whispered again, this time more firmly. A cloud blew across the moon. In the sudden darkness, the door to the garden creaked.

Deirdre straightened. She looked across the narrow distance to where she had entered the garden. The candle she had left inside flickered softly. "Who . . . ?" she murmured.

A shape moved in the open door. A man, formidable in height and breadth, standing dark against the night. Until the candlelight struck golden hair and the hard contours of a familiar face.

Harpsinger. Her heart hammered painfully. She sat motionless on the bench. He lifted the candle higher and took a step into the garden. Their eyes met.

Delacroix breathed in sharply. What demon was this sent to torment him with his innermost thoughts? Deirdre here? Not likely. She would be in her bed high within the tower, watched over by the old nurse. But then who was this creature with Deirdre's face, stark white against the midnight swathing of her cloak?

"Lady . . ." he said tentatively.

She stood, and the hood of her cloak fell, revealing the cascade of her hair gilded with strands of silver by the moon. Her head was high, her gaze unflinching. "Bard," she said.

Ah, good voice, the friend of deception. She sounded as unruffled as deep water beneath still air. But within, her thoughts were chaos. What was he doing here? Where was the willing Megan? Had they? Hadn't they? She had prayed and he was there before her, and now the consequence of that heedless plea filled her with trembling.

"You left the hall," she said quietly. The rest remained unspoken, but he knew it well enough. A deep sigh escaped him.

"I am a man, Deirdre."

"And how many times has that excuse been used?" she demanded, her temper flaring. To the hindmost with dignity and discretion. I am a man, he said, and that was supposed to settle everything. Not with her, it didn't.

"And what of Megan?" she demanded. "What if you get her with bairn? What happens to her then? Do you think of that, any of you *men*, when you're rutting in your pleasure?"

Delacroix's mouth dropped open. He couldn't help it, he'd simply never been so taken by surprise. Demon, he'd thought, and he'd been right. She had the face and form—so far as he could see the latter—of Deirdre, she even had the voice, but that was no sheltered virgin daughter of a great clan speaking of rutting and false-get bairns.

"What do you know of it?" he demanded, coming closer. Whatever this was in the quiet castle garden, it drew him powerfully. He wanted to know it for the truth of what it was. Distantly, he remembered the ancient tales of spirits in the shape of beautiful women luring men to their doom. But it was not death he sensed in the pale, beautiful face, the haughty stare and the flashing eyes. Life was there in all its untrammeled glory, the life of fire and passion such as he had sought with Megan and found only dimly.

It had been a mistake to go with the girl, however willing she had been. He'd known that almost at once, but having committed himself he felt compelled to continue. In the end, it had been a matter of going through the motions. He had found the release he sought, but hard on it came the gnawing emptiness that would not be ignored. It drove him out, into the garden, to this strange, moonlit meeting with Deirdre-yet-not-Deirdre.

"I know," she said on a thread of sound, "what is too great to be treated lightly."

"You are too young," he protested, "too sheltered to know of such things."

"What I am doesn't seem to matter." She laughed, hearing the recklessness in her voice and not caring. Nothing mattered except the night, the stillness, and the man. "Perhaps it has to do with not dying. Mayhap the boar was meant to kill me and when he did not I became something new."

He took another step toward her. "You are tired, and your mind is prey to imaginings. You are the same as you always were, daughter of O'Neill."

"Who are you reminding, Bard?"

"Myself," he said, becoming angry now. This child-woman was playing with weapons she did not understand. Harshly, he added, "*You* should need no reminder, but I wonder if that is the case. Go to bed, Deirdre."

"I tried to." She sounded so plaintive that he could not help but smile. But his good humor faded quickly as he considered the effect she was having on him.

Poor Megan, it was just as well she would never know.

He came nearer, close enough to see the faint flush of color darkening her cheeks. "What is it that you want from me, daughter of O'Neill?" Deliberately, he called her by the same name, driving home the point of all that lay between them. "A memory? Something to recall when you are safely married to Red Hugh and have his child in your belly? Something for the days when you are bored with being safe?"

"Safe?" she echoed. "There is no such thing. We are at war, bard, in case it has escaped your notice. My father makes rebellion against the English crown. Do you know what happens to people who follow that path? Do you know how they die?"

He frowned. This was the first he knew that she worried about what her father was doing. The fear was sensible enough, but he hadn't realized she perceived it.

"I thought you would have more confidence in your father," he said.

"I love him," she said quietly, "and whatever he orders, I will do. But even I know the seriousness of his course. Everyone who has gone against Elizabeth has died. It is that simple."

Delacroix tried to think of an example that might soothe her. He could not, for she was right. Everyone who had challenged England's monarch had found not glory but the chill of the grave.

"Deirdre," he said softly, "your father is an intelligent man. He may come to some compromise."

She blinked, staring at him as though he had spoken in a foreign tongue. Finally, she said, "You *have* been too long away from Ireland, bard, if you truly believe compromise is within our characters. Nay, my father knows only one way, to fight until he either wins or dies. Nothing else is possible. But," she added swiftly, "that is neither here nor there. You are right, I must go to bed."

She made to pass him, but on impulse he reached out suddenly and took her arm through the enveloping cloak. The realization of how much this small girl knew struck him hard. She was not the innocent he had believed; rather, she dueled with the looming reality of death as stalwartly as any warrior.

And for that she deserved—what? Comfort, respect, honor? He would give her all that and more, yet he could give her nothing.

"I would . . ." he began, but she stopped him with a finger to his lips.

Gently, without recrimination, she said, "I smell Megan's scent on you, bard. That, more than anything, is the only reminder I need."

"Of what, Deirdre?" he demanded, resenting the embarrassment she made him feel. He had done nothing wrong, after all, except in the eyes of a girl, wise beyond her years, who knew how much of himself he denied.

Her mouth curved in a smile that made him ache to crush it beneath his own. "Why, that you are a man, Harpsinger," she said, and so saying slipped away, leaving him alone in the empty garden beneath the slivered moon.

CHAPTER
8

ON THE FOLLOWING DAY, HUGH O'NEILL,
father, chieftain, rebel, and would-be king, announced
that he would host a tourney to honor his foreign
guests. In fact, his desire to do so had nothing whatsoever to do with the Spaniards of whom he was heartily
tired. Rather it was a bid to entertain himself, to mis-
lead another, and, last but not least, to take the better
measure of his bard, Sean Harpsinger, poet of many—
possibly too many—parts.

The announcement was met with glee. His warriors rejoiced because it meant a break from the routine
of training and a chance to show off their prowess. The
common people delighted because of the opportunity
for trade. As was the custom, a market would be set up
around the tournament. All matter of business would
be done there, from scriveners to clothiers, surgeons to
whores. But the main business was still the tourney
and the chance to let a little blood in the name of sport.

Word spread quickly throughout Ulster. Before the week was out a steady stream of travelers poured into Dungannon. The weather held warm and fair. Tents were pitched in the open fields around the town, barefoot children ran among the stalls that sprouted everywhere, and the nights bloomed with a hundred campfires around which people gathered to sing, drink, and praise Ulster's chief.

Red Hugh extended his visit, causing speculation that on the one hand, his marriage to Deirdre was imminent and, on the other, that the courtship that had begun so well was not proceeding as smoothly. In fact, the O'Neill's fair daughter was not uppermost in his mind. Delightful though she might be, he had other things to concern himself with, chief among them the O'Neill himself. Ulster's chieftain was proving an unexpected source of concern. To the serious young man, veteran of four years in a British prison, he seemed too casual about the rebellion they made, cavalier almost. This business about a tourney in the midst of preparations for war set Red Hugh's nerves on ends. He tried to talk about it with his host, only to have his efforts skillfully deflected.

"Sir Henry Bagenal is reported growing restless in Armagh," Red Hugh said. It was the morning before the tourney was due to begin. He had managed to run O'Neill to ground near the horse pens and was determined that this time he would not be brushed off. "While we make sport here, my agents report he is boasting that he will annihilate us before the summer is done."

"Bagenal is a fool," the O'Neill replied without taking his gaze from the prancing stallion before him. He had scant respect for England's high marshal in Ireland, thinking the man no more than a lickspittle servant of that vicious old hoyden, Elizabeth. Sweet Lord, would the woman never die? She had been there all his life, voracious in her hunger for power, never satisfied, never ceasing, always prattling on about the greatness of England and the need to protect it. To do that, she would sacrifice anything; for that he grudgingly credited her. Had she been Irish, he might even have followed her. But she was the enemy from across the water, the clever, relentless, merciless foe whom in this high summer of his life he must finally bring to the battle too-long postponed.

"We will meet him on our terms," he said, "at the time and place of our choosing."

"And when will that be?" Red Hugh demanded. They stood alone, their retainers a discreet distance away. He pitched his voice low so that no one would overhear them, but his words were vehement. "How long do we wait, my lord? The men are ready, the Spaniards are with us. Now is the time to strike, not"— he waved a hand in the direction of the gaily colored tents—"not to disport ourselves."

O'Neill cast him an amused glance from beneath his massive brows. He liked this young man well enough to want him for his ally and his son-in-law, but he had to admit Red Hugh lacked any lightness in his nature. Undoubtedly that was the result of his sojourn in one of England's grimmer prisons, but understanding the cause didn't always make it easier to deal with.

Patiently, he asked, "Have your agents in Armagh reported what Sir Henry thinks of our tourney?"

Red Hugh's narrow face flamed. "He says it's typical of the Irish to talk much and do little. He says we are drunkards and imbeciles, he speculates that we are not actually human, and he sends messages to Elizabeth pleading for permission to attack."

"Permission she withholds," O'Neill said. He was a good deal less troubled by the high marshal's slurs than his young friend, but then, he'd had more years to get used to them.

"For how long?" Red Hugh demanded. "She feels the same way he does. They all do. They hate us, and they won't rest until Ireland lies devoured."

"Easy," O'Neill said gently. He laid a hand on the younger man's arm. "No less an authority than the noble Pericles tells us to wait for the wisest of all counselors, which is Time."

"Ireland is not Athens," Red Hugh countered, "and time slips quickly by. We must act."

O'Neill sighed. He took his hand away and turned to look at the horses again. Softly but with steel in his tone, he said, "We will, but cleverly this time, not with the impulsiveness that is the curse of our race. Let Bagenal be drawn out, let him rant and strut until the fury of his hate engulfs his better reason. Then let him act *without* Elizabeth's foreknowledge or support." He moved his great head slightly, eyeing the younger man. "Do you understand me, lad? Bagenal is the best friend we have right now. If we can only push him far enough, he will do exactly as we wish."

"Leave Armagh?" Red Hugh murmured, turning the thought over in his mind. "Without the queen's authority?"

The O'Neill barred his teeth in the semblance of a smile. "The lady does not like to be crossed. If Sir

Henry can be convinced to play the fool, it will be him she devours, not Ireland."

"If he loses."

"Ah, yes, there is that. Victory knows no substitutes."

Red Hugh sighed, deflated but not discouraged. On the contrary, now that the O'Neill had seen fit to confide at least the broad outlines of his plan, he could see it had much to recommend it. However, it also came laden with risk. If Bagenal responded as expected, if he marched his men to battle without his monarch's approval, if the Irish met him in fury and defeated him, then might the English be thrown into such confusion as to be swept before Eire's victorious sons and Ireland would be free again.

If.

"And so the tourney?" he said.

The O'Neill grinned. "An amusement, nothing more, indulged in by a man not serious about rebellion and begging for the stern hand of English chastisement."

Red Hugh nodded slowly. "So be it," he said. Head high, eyes alight, he murmured into the wind, "Then let the games begin."

Deirdre stepped carefully around a pile of horse manure and stopped for a moment to get her bearings. It was the hour before dawn. The first faint rim of gray light had given way to blazoned colors signaling the birth of a glorious day. The carpenters were hammering together the last rows of benches, hawkers offered hot breads and cold cider to the crowds already streaming onto the fields, and the men who would compete were out in force, stretching their muscles in the morning air, eyeing their opponents and boasting of the victory that would be theirs.

All very exciting and almost enough to shake her from the leaden mood that had dogged her these past few days. The meeting in the garden with the bard seemed a half-remembered dream, but one from which she was hard-pressed to wake. She kept recalling exactly how he had looked, what he said, how he moved. All of it was firmly etched on her memory. The compulsion she felt to relive it all made her acutely self-conscious. She had gone out of her way to avoid Sean Harpsinger since that night, and had glimpsed him only in passing. Until now, that was.

She raised a hand, shading her eyes, and stared into the rising sun. Before that glittering light, silhouetted against it, was the too-familiar figure, tall, broad-shouldered, lean-hipped, head tilted proudly. He even had his harp slung over his back, which, as she recalled, he had not in the garden. Then he had been only a man, not poet or singer. Sweet heaven, let her remember who and what he really was. Let her not disgrace herself this time.

"Bard," she said as she walked past him quickly, inclining her head to precisely the right degree of recognition and nothing more.

"My lady," he murmured. She heard surprise and something that sounded suspiciously like pleasure, as though he, too, had found the recent days barren. Fool! She must not think like that.

She went on quickly and found her father standing with the Spaniards near the dais. He smiled when he saw her, and held out a hand. Since the incident with the boar, he had gone out of his way to be gentler and more patient with her. She appreciated that deeply, but it filled her with a sense of melancholy whenever she thought how quickly all she cherished could be lost. Not from the war, for truth was, she thought little of that. It was her marriage she contemplated. Nothing had been said directly, but each day she sensed it growing nearer. A part of her wanted the matter settled, but another and for the moment stronger self wished time could simply stop, that she might forever be the O'Neill's dark-haired daughter standing in the sun of his smile and his love.

"Deirdre," he said, "you are up early. Is anything amiss?"

She shook her head quickly and returned his smile. "I was too excited to sleep."

He accepted that readily, knowing the feeling well enough. Of course, his excitement had a different source from that of his innocent young daughter. He was thinking of Bagenal, that fly-blown braggart, sitting down there in Armagh slurring the Irish and going on about his own great courage. Let him show it, then, only let him. The O'Neill's smile deepened. Beside him the Spaniards shifted nervously. Already they had come to know some part of what that smile meant. They could not feel the whole of it, not yet, but they sensed the ground shifting under Ulster as a fierce beast, long slumbering, began to wake. It was their task to ride the beast, to bring it to heel if they could. Amid the cool, shadowed halls of Madrid, that had not seemed so daunting. In the brilliant light of an Irish summer, it had entirely a different character.

"My lords," Deirdre murmured courteously, "if you do not mind, I would borrow my lord father for a few minutes. We have had little time together since I came home, and I have need to speak with him."

They nodded gravely, not really hearing her but glad of any excuse to absent themselves. The O'Neill chuckled as they hurried off, their black velvet doublets puffed out behind them like so many anxious crows.

"Sweet Mary," he said, "but they're a dour bunch, hard enough to take at any time but doubly so first thing in the morning. I swear they turn my stomach, and it empty of nought but ale. Come with me and we'll break fast while we have this serious conversation you're after wanting." He cast her a teasing look as though to say he knew exactly what was on her mind. But when they sat at one of the trestle tables set up near the field, he sipping fine mead to go with his bread and cheese, his mood turned graver.

"I'm sorry I haven't had more time for you, lass, but these are busy days."

"I know," she said quietly. A cup of the mead sat near her right hand, but she had not touched it. Her hand was steady as she pushed it a little distance away. "You mean to make war soon."

His face went blank, the whole ruddy visage with its brilliant eyes and expressive brows becoming immobile. He did not withdraw, but he might as well have. She all but heard the clank of iron shutters coming down between them.

"Why do you say that?"

"It stands to reason."

"Does it? I have not said I will, I have not called up the levies into the field, I have not threatened or blustered. So why then do you imagine I am set on conflict?"

Her head tilted to one side in a gesture he remembered from her childhood. Softly, she said, "Red Hugh is here, with all that implies. The Spaniards have come. The levies are not called, true enough, but the heart of them, your personal army, is training so rigorously that when the battle does come they will think it a Sunday romp. And then there are these games."

He crossed his burly arms and stared at her forbiddingly. "You overstep yourself. You are only a woman, and you cannot understand such things."

"Perhaps, but I stand by what I said. War comes, and swiftly. The high marshal—"

"Bagenal? What do you know of him?"

Deirdre repressed a sigh. She did not like wasting time any better than her father, but he seemed determined to take the long way around. "I spent the last few years in a convent, rightly enough, but it was not on the other side of the earth. Everyone knows about Sir Henry. He's the worst kind of fool, a man who imagines himself wiser and braver than everyone else when in fact he's the opposite. He fairly begs you to take him. Indeed, the only surprise is that you have waited this long."

"I see. . . ." The earl hesitated, torn between chagrin at her perceptiveness and pride in the same. Pride won. "All right," he said quietly, "suppose I do have plans. How does that concern you?"

Her cheeks warmed. "Am I not also an O'Neill?" she demanded. "Does being female disqualify me from caring about what happens? Perhaps you would prefer me to weep and faint at talk of war, but I cannot. There are serious matters that require attention."

She had the satisfaction of seeing his composure crack before he growled, "What are you talking of, girl? War is no business for women."

"Tell that to the mother who sends her sons to fight or the wife who loses her husband," Deirdre shot back. She had promised herself she would keep a firm hold on her tongue, but the provocation was too great. He insisted on treating her like a child, and a not very smart one at that. It was time he learned otherwise.

"When I came back from the abbey, I mentioned to you that the store of medical supplies I found here was inadequate. The more I consider it, the worse it seems. There will be wounded to deal with shortly. They have a right to the best care we can provide. As it is, they will have virtually nothing."

"I have surgeons aplenty," the O'Neill retorted. "Do you think me daft? Some of the best barbers in this country are in Dungannon right now preparing to march with us. Why, I challenge anyone to provide better—"

"Surgeons? Say, rather, butchers. They have no more idea of how to save a man's life than you do. All they know is to cut. Those of their patients fortunate enough to live are maimed for life, but the great majority die, in agony I might add, and for no good reason." Her hands clenched into fists as she stared at him with fire in her eyes. "You have to do better than that. *We* have to. It is one thing for a man to lose his life in a great cause. It is quite another for him to die through carelessness and stupidity."

"What do you know of it?" the O'Neill demanded. That his daughter would dare to question him was bad enough, but that she would suggest—nay, say outright—that he was failing to do right by his men was intolerable. No one insulted him like that and escaped unscathed. "You overstep yourself," he said coldly. "I begin to think I do Red Hugh no great favor giving you to him. He will have his hands full making a proper wife out of a fledgling harridan."

Deirdre breathed in sharply. The attack stung, but she had expected it. Her father was a great man in many ways, but his vision could be overly narrow. Women to him had always been ornaments, childbearers, or pawns in political intrigues. So she might also have been had she remained at Dungannon, but the years in the abbey had made her something different. She had a mind of her own and she wasn't afraid to use it, especially not in a cause that cried out to be championed.

"Say what you will, but it changes nothing. Your men deserve better medical care than they will receive. You cannot in all conscience take them into battle knowing that some of them will die unnecessarily."

For a moment, she thought she had gone too far. The O'Neill's face was red, almost purple. His stony black eyes glittered dangerously. She held her breath, waiting for the explosion that seemed certain to come, only to be taken aback when he suddenly subsided.

"Ah, lass," he said softly, "you've too much of myself in you."

"And why would that be a bad thing?" she demanded. Seizing the advantage, she pressed on. "I am indeed your daughter, and for that reason I will dare what I must. Let me see to better care for the men. I can do it quietly," she assured him quickly, "since no one wants to be reminded that it will be needed. But believe me, when the time comes it will make a difference."

"What does this seeing to involve?" her father inquired dryly. He knew he was beaten, but he wasn't sure how it had happened. The boar was involved somewhere, and not wanting to hurt her again, but this was different. He could have stood firm, perhaps should have. What had stopped him was the sneaking knowledge that she was right. He had seen too many men die of the fevers that could spread after even minor wounds, and knew the surgeons were powerless to help them. They hacked off limbs and applied leeches with great dispatch, but the men died anyway. If there was some hope of saving them, he had to take it, even when it came from so improper a source as his cherished daughter.

"I need more herbs," she said quickly, "many more, and I must gather them quickly before the summer fades. There are ointments and tinctures to be made, bandages to prepare, all manner of things. . . ."

He raised a hand, stopping her from reciting each and every one of them. "All right, do what you must, but be discreet about it. If word gets out that I've turned to such a chit for help, there could be panic in the ranks." He smiled to take the sting out of his words, but she knew there was truth to them.

Gravely, she nodded. "I will be careful. Does this mean I can leave the castle without escort?"

"No, there must be someone with you. I will think on who's best to be trusted."

When she would have protested, he downed his mead quickly and stood up. "Be satisfied with that, lass, for it's the best you will get."

Deirdre subsided, however unwillingly. She had won for the most part, and whoever her father chose, at least she would have more freedom then she did now. The trick would be to put it to the best possible use, for truly summer was fading. In the old days, the days of Buan-ann, people had understood that after the nurturing mother of the bountiful fields there came the crone, the devourer who swept over the land with a bloody scythe. All any of them could do was prepare for the dark time fast approaching.

A trumpet sounded in the near distance, interrupting her grim thoughts. "Come," her father said, holding out his hand. He gave her fingers a reassuring squeeze. "We have this day, let us enjoy it."

She lifted her head, letting the wind catch her hair, and the smile she gave him was brilliant.

Standing off to the side where he had been watching them unobtrusively, Delacroix saw it and wondered at its cause. They had seemed at odds a moment before, but now they were at ease again. Truly it was difficult to understand these O'Neills, father and daughter both, but for different reasons. He was a canny warrior who kept his intentions close to his chest, while she was—what? Moonlight and dreams, the stuff of poetry. Nothing at all to do with the real world, with his mission and his duty. He must remember that at all costs. Fiercely, he repeated the words to himself: *he must.*

The trumpet blared again, and he welcomed the surge of excitement it brought within him. Grinning, he thought he was like an old war-horse who couldn't resist the call to action. His blood stirred and he lifted his head, looking out over the fields where the contestants were beginning to assemble. They were as fine a body of men as he had seen anywhere. That did not bode well for Elizabeth, but at least it promised much for the tourney. He made his way through the milling crowds, thinking to find himself a good spot from which to watch. He was passing near the dais when the O'Neill saw him and raised his hand in summons.

"A fair day," he said when the bard stood before him.

"Indeed," Delacroix agreed. He was aware of Deirdre sitting beside her father, radiant in a gown of tawny silk embroidered with tiny crimson flowers, but he took care not to do more than glance at her. Red Hugh was there as well, although shortly he would excuse himself to enter the competition. The Spaniards were seated together beneath an awning, protecting their pale skins from the capricious Irish sun.

"Will you compose a ballad in honor of these games?" the O'Neill inquired pleasantly.

"If you wish, my lord."

Ulster's chieftain grinned, his black eyes alight. "I would have no high-sounding tale of what we do here this day. Rather I seek the truth of it—the grunts and groans, as it were, the mud and sweat. Can you give me that?"

Surprised, for such was not the custom, Delacroix said, "I can try."

The O'Neill sat back in his high, carved chair and regarded Harpsinger. "Do not take offense, but I am concerned that you may fail, for gifted though you are, only a man who has experienced it for himself can know the thrill of such contests. If only . . . " He paused as though weighing the other man in the balance. "But no, I cannot ask that. It would not be proper."

"Ask what, my lord?" Delacroix inquired with a smile. The notion of O'Neill tripping over propriety was amusing, since the Irishman was far more inclined to ignore it altogether.

"You could join the games, if you would. Mind you, it is only a suggestion. I understand full well that you are not trained in such things. However, it's all meant to be clean fun, with honor to the winners and losers alike."

This last part was patently false, and both men knew it. So did Red Hugh, who shot a sharp glance at his host and said nothing. Only Deirdre spoke.

"Tourneys must have changed a great deal while I was away," she said with pretended lightness. "I remember them as the nearest thing to actual battles."

"My daughter exaggerates," the O'Neill rejoined. "She has the tender heart of a female and does not understand such things." His eyes met Delacroix's with unmistakable directness. "But we do, do we not, bard? Will you enter?"

Delacroix hesitated. O'Neill's "request" was clearly more in the nature of a command, but what lay behind it? Did he hope to see his bard injured, and if so, why? He had, after all, saved his daughter's life scant days before. Or had O'Neill concluded from that incident that Harpsinger could handle himself well enough and would be in no real danger, might in fact—as it was in truth—enjoy himself? Whatever the case, Delacroix had only one answer for him.

He bent his golden head and said, "Of course, my lord. I would not miss so noble an opportunity."

When he straightened, his gaze fell on Deirdre. Her

face was pale, all the light and joy suddenly gone from it. To his credit, he felt mildly guilty about being pleased by that, but he felt it all the same. On an impulse, he removed his harp from around his back and handed it to her.

"Will you care for this, my lady?"

She took it slowly, with both hands. The smooth, golden wood was warm beneath her touch. Her lips, full and enticing for all their sudden lack of color, moved stiffly. "Be careful," she said.

He nodded once and bowed again to the O'Neill. His step unabashedly eager, he returned to the field.

CHAPTER 9

*THE HARD THUD OF BODIES COLLIDING PUNC-*tured the breathless silence of the crowd. A roar went up. In the fury of the moment, new wagers were laid, the early ones having gone mostly against the bard, respected though he was, but now second thoughts were setting in and it occurred to more than a few of the watchers that they might have judged wrongly.

The same thought was passing through the mind of one Eamon Dougherty, loyal Ulsterman, happy rebel, and, up to the present moment, championship wrestler. Despite—or because of—the ringing in his ears and the lack of air reaching his lungs, he was getting the definite impression that things weren't going too well. This was a novelty for him and caused him to examine the situation with uncharacteristic care.

Eamon was one of those big, bumbling men, essentially good-natured, who go through life shy of women, boyish at heart, and without a malicious bone in their bodies. He took to wrestling at the urging of his friends, discovered he was good at it, and stuck with it for the simple human reason that he liked to win. It was pleasant to be the acclaim of the crowd, to have the men thump him on the back afterward and tell him what a good fellow he was, and for the women to glance at him with interest he knew no other way to stir. At least it had been all of that until his path crossed that of the bard and what should have been a routine match turned into something far different.

He grunted and arched his back, trying to throw the other man off, only to find that he could not. The fellow had a hold on him that he wasn't sure how he had gotten, something between his neck and his shoulder blades that didn't so much hurt as seem to freeze him in place.

Merciful heaven, this from a harpsinger. It passed believing. Eamon took a firm grip on himself, remembering that, big as the other man was, he was a full three inches taller and had a good fifty pounds to boot. Of course, too much of that weight was courtesy of the good lager and meat he so enjoyed, whereas the bard was stripped down to muscle and sinew. Curious that, now that he thought of it, for weren't bards supposed to spend most of their time sitting around, thinking up songs? How the fellow had managed to hone himself the way he had was a mystery that didn't bear solving, at least not right then.

He twisted hard to the right and at the same time rammed his shoulder down. It was his favorite maneuver, one that never failed him. Opponents lost their balance and fell hard. Other opponents, that was. This one merely shifted slightly and kept his grip. Worse yet, in the next moment he turned the tables and flipped Dougherty onto his back, where he lay, stunned and disbelieving, for the regulation count of the referee to declare him beaten.

The crowd roared its approval, for never mind where the bets were laid, everyone liked to see a job well done. It roared again when the bard held out his hand to help Eamon up. The Ulsterman took it willingly enough, though he still looked stunned. Together they left the field.

From her perch on the dais, Deirdre watched them go. Her hands unclenched slowly, her heartbeat returned to normal. She took a deep, restoring breath and congratulated herself on how well she had managed to conceal her feelings.

For a horrible moment, she had thought he was surely going to die or at the very least be seriously maimed. The other man was so large, and from the way the crowd called out to him she knew he must be a champion. The notion that a bard should wrestle against such a one as that had almost—but not quite—blocked out the far larger and more ominous sensations she experienced when Harpsinger appeared on the field.

Of course, men wrestled half-naked. They always had, they always would. She knew that. It had never before struck her as remarkable. Indeed, it still didn't. It was only the sight of the bard shorn of his shirt, wearing only snug-fitting chausses, that cast all thought of propriety clean out of her mind. Golden hair gleaming in the sun, he stood broad-shouldered, iron-hard muscles moving beneath taut, burnished skin. When he moved, he had the grace of a great hunting animal. He tossed his head slightly, and a woman sitting near

Deirdre murmured deep in her throat. Deirdre shot her as nasty a glance as she could muster, half-stunned as she was, and did her utmost to avert her eyes without success.

Why exactly did God make certain men to be so beautiful? What element of the divine plan was thus accomplished? Was it merely an indulgence—did God indulge? Or was it a snare for unwary females likely to betray themselves when confronted by so much splendor?

Only an instinct for self-preservation remained, and that was barely enough to enable her to sit through the match without disgracing herself. When it was over, and the Harpsinger victorious, she had needed every ounce of her self-control not to leap from her seat and join in the cheers that greeted him. As it was, her cheeks were becomingly flushed and her azure eyes glowed with a fire they had rarely if ever possessed.

None of which escaped the notice of the slender young man at her side. Red Hugh had sat frowning through the match from the moment he became aware of Deirdre's excessive interest. At first he told himself he was wrong, she couldn't possibly be drawn to the bard. Then he insisted he shouldn't care, it made no difference. She was young and impressionable, but she was of good blood and when she was his wife she would behave herself.

None of which changed the fact that the way she looked at Sean Harpsinger made his own blood run high and brought him close to forgetting that his rank placed him above such paltry considerations. He waited, thinking the other fellow would surely win, only to discover the most peculiar thing, namely that the poet wrestled better than any man he had ever seen. His long, sinewy body was perfectly fashioned for the sport; he had bulk but also grace, and somewhere in his life—where exactly?—he had learned moves that would not have disgraced the masters of ancient Greece.

Red Hugh was still thinking on that when Delacroix returned to the field. He had donned a simple woodland green tunic over a fresh pair of chausses, and his thick golden hair shone damply from the wash he'd had. He looked, the younger man thought, quite noble. A lord's by-blow perhaps, raised in the old ways by a doting mother? Whatever the explanation, there was more here than met the eye.

"My lady," Delacroix said quietly as he stood before Deirdre, "thank you for keeping my harp." He held out his hands to relieve her of it as Deirdre rose. To Red Hugh's eyes she looked a shade unsteady. Silently, she offered the instrument. Simply, she said, "I am glad you won."

"So am I," he replied with a flash smile that made him look suddenly boyish. "It's been a long time since I enjoyed such a contest."

"Not too long, I would say," the O'Neill interrupted. He had observed the whole without comment, missing nothing, including Red Hugh's reaction. About time that boy stirred to notice what was happening under his own nose. Deirdre was his daughter and he loved her, but she was like all women, fundamentally weak in the head. If not, why would she prattle on about the wounded-to-come—what sensible person wanted to think of such a thing?—and why would she look at the bard with her heart in her eyes when she was bound for a good Christian marriage and the sooner the better?

"You are well-skilled," he continued smoothly. "Who taught you?"

"My late father," Delacroix said cautiously, "and friends of his. He was a soldier for hire who wandered far from Eire and took me with him."

"Didn't your mother object to that?" Deirdre asked, her tender heart troubled.

Gently, he said, "She died young and, as I was without other family, it was best for me to remain with my father. At any rate, it was also greatly to my benefit. I saw much of the world and learned things I would otherwise have missed."

"How does a soldier's son become a bard?" the O'Neill asked, interested now despite himself. He had only the dimmest notion of how bards were made, something about the ancient ways and half-remembered gods reasonable men did not think on. Where had a soldier of fortune's son acquired the training?

"I had some skill," Delacroix admitted. He had no experience talking about himself and was uncomfortable doing so. When he saw that did not satisfy them, he went on reluctantly. "My father saw that, and arranged for me to study. I spent several years on Inishmore."

"Ah," the O'Neill said as though he had it now. "Inishmore, a barren place but holy for all that." Odd sort of place, too, for a soldier to send his son unless he'd thought to save him from the sort of life he himself had known. "Yet for all that, you learned to fight."

"Indeed, you did," Red Hugh said, suddenly expansive. His expression was passingly pleasant, even eager. Only the hard light of steel in his eyes warned of its falseness. "First the boar and now this. Truly you have been denying yourself, bard." He looked Delacroix up and down as though seeing him for the first time. "What's this, dressed for song, not the field? Surely you don't mean to retire already. Not with the melee about to begin."

"I have had my sport." And had fair warning in the bargain for every nerve ending prickled as he studied Red Hugh. Something had changed in the serious, aloof young man, something dangerous come alive and kicking. He sighed, thinking of the complications women wrought even when they were the next thing to children and knew nothing.

"In your late father's memory, then?" Red Hugh suggested. "Surely you would do him honor?"

"Actually," Delacroix said, "my father had much to say on that subject, and little of it was good. He was of a practical turn of mind."

Red Hugh nodded sagely, but the gleam in his eye held nothing of wisdom. "I suppose he would be," he drawled, "being a hireling."

Delacroix told himself not to be a fool. His father had been what he had been; the demands of his life had taken nothing away from the man himself. But heaven help his son, for he was an earl now and must concern himself with such niceties as honor like it or not.

"However," he added, "my sire did like a good brawl, there's no denying that. The melee, you said?"

"I did," Red Hugh confirmed, "and may it be my pleasure to lend you a sword, presuming you have none of your own?"

"Bards travel light, but I will take the loan and thank you for it." He gestured toward the field. "Shall we?"

"Wait!" Deirdre exclaimed. She stood, straight and slim, all softness gone from her face. This was really too absurd. Granted, men didn't have the brains lambs were born with, but there were times they surpassed themselves in stupidity.

"You can't be serious," she demanded of Delacroix. "It was one thing to win at wrestling, but men can be killed in the melee or scarred for life. And as for you," she went on, turning her fury on Red Hugh who eyed her nervously, thinking here was something he hadn't anticipated in his bride-to-be. "I don't know what game you are playing, but it is a false one. Would you take the life of a bard to satisfy your own spleen?"

Nicely put, but not wisely. The question hit its target squarely and dug in for good measure. Red Hugh flushed. "What are you prattling about, woman? Spleen has nothing to do with it. Go back to your needlework and leave men's business to men."

The O'Neill chuckled. This was turning out to be more entertaining than he'd hoped. Not that there weren't serious implications to what was happening between his daughter and Red Hugh, but they could be worked out in time. For the moment, it was the sport that mattered.

"Yes, daughter," he said, grinning hugely, "go back to your needlework and leave these two to what they do best."

Deirdre opened her mouth to speak, but no sound came out. She was furiously, coldly angry. Needlework indeed. The only needle she was interested in was a long, sharp one she could dig into all their addled skulls, anything to let a little light in where it was so desperately needed.

"I give up," she said. "Do whatever you like. Hack and saw, blast and break, go to it with a will. You're all the same, every last one of you." Just for good measure she added under her breath, "I should have stayed in the abbey."

"What was that, lass?" the O'Neill inquired. "Something about the good sisters and your desire to join them?"

Red Hugh snorted loudly. "Put that out of your mind. You would make the world's worst nun, but I'll be damned if you'll be as poor a wife. You'll learn what's proper and you'll do it. But first—" He bowed stiffly to the O'Neill and left the dais without looking to see if Delacroix followed. He didn't ask himself why he was so confident that the other man would, not wishing to consider the question of how much they had in common. First a sword for him and some mail, too, just to make it fair. And then to the melee where, damn whatever training the upstart had received, he would discover he was no match for his betters. The lesson would be harsh but well deserved, and in the end he would be thankful for it, for truly a man was ill-served to forget his station in life.

Which was all well and good, except that Sean Harpsinger could not be reminded of his true place in life, because he had none. How could he when he was nought but a figment of the imagination of the great red-haired spider dwelling in Londontown, spinning her endless web and drawing the unsuspecting to death within it? Sean Harpsinger was a lie, but John Delacroix, warrior earl, was all too real.

Blare trumpets beneath the burning sun. Come men in armor and peaked helmets, wielding deft

swords. Bring pride, honor, fear, anger, all to this field
nestled between emerald hills. Feint and parry, thrust
and meet, metal clashing, horses whinnying, and the
crowd in its deep-throated roar, scenting blood and
excited by its lure. Deirdre was right, the melee was as
close to battle as any could come outside of war. The
rules said care was to be taken to avoid injury to an
opponent. In fact, anything was acceptable short of outright murder, and that, too, had been known to occur.

Red Hugh was in the thick of it, shield up, sword
slashing. Mounted and in full regalia, his slight figure
seemed to grow larger. He shouted his challenge, wading ever deeper into the center of the milling, surging
mob. Men fell before him, not out of courtesy, but
because they felt the force of his blows and wisely withdrew. All those days and nights buried in an English
prison had to come out somehow. His eyes were reddened, his face corded with tension. He drove his
mount forward, slashing, always slashing, and imagined as he did so that the enemy was fat Sir Henry
Bagenal, going on about the stupidity of the Irish even
as his guts spilled out onto the good earth of Eire.

No English here, more's the pity, and no real sport
since few seemed willing to engage him. But wait, there
was the bard, on foot since he had declined a horse,
and holding his own against three others. Red Hugh's
brows shot upward beneath the visor of his helmet. He
knew at least one of the three and respected him as an
able fighter. Yet the man was yielding, as were the others, falling back before this . . . this poet.

Delacroix fought with controlled intensity, gauging
each blow perfectly so that it whistled by the man, hit-
ting his shield square and knocking the air from him

even as it sang its intended message: I am playing, this is sport, but were it not, or were I to forget, you would lie food for the carrion crows.

He thought of it as exercise and found nothing remarkable in that. His opponents saw it differently. They sensed the fury honed to ice, the discipline and training, and beneath it all, the lethal power of a warrior inured to battle and to death. A man who has stood in the dank shadow too often to fear it. A man without limits who would fight and fight all day, wading through gore, then sit down by the fire come evening and calmly strum the harp.

All of which was true enough so far as it went. He had learned to fight well, because for a long time that was all life offered him. But he had never learned to like it. Other men he knew were different, they wallowed in carnage, loving the power over life that the sword gave them. Berserkers, they were called, the old Viking word still being more than adequate to describe the killing madness that swept over them. Such men were formidable in battle, but eventually the madness betrayed them. A false step, a lost moment, and it was their blood that poured onto the insatiable ground.

Not Delacroix. He found his refuge in poetry and kept his reason. Meanwhile, his body went its own way, seeking action. For him, the melee was the perfect compromise. A healthy outing without the direr consequences.

At least until he glanced up and saw Red Hugh bearing down on him. A curse slipped from his lips. What was the boy playing at?

No, correct that, this was no boy, but a man filled with hurt that without release would devour him alive.

Red Hugh did not draw rein until he was almost upon Delacroix. Other men would have run, but the bard stood his ground. In the midst of the chaos, a circle of silence grew around them. The O'Donnell dismounted and released his mount, which reared its front hooves before wheeling and racing away. The two men eyed each other.

"Still more surprises, bard," Red Hugh said.

Delacroix shrugged, but without taking his gaze from him. "A day's sport, nothing more." He hefted the broadsword he wielded. "Thank you for the loan, by the way. She handles well."

"Does she? Suppose we see?" Red Hugh raised his own weapon and brought it down, slashing inches in front of Delacroix's face.

The bard stood perfectly still, refusing to respond. Quietly, he said, "My lord, think on what you do."

The thin, sensitive face grew crimson. "Merely sport, bard, that's what you called it. A day's amusement, not unlike killing a boar or wooing a girl. Fight, damn you! You know how well enough, I've seen that. Turn coward now and I'll cut you down."

As though to illustrate the threat, he raised his sword again and struck the shield Delacroix raised barely in time.

"Fight!" Red Hugh exclaimed again.

Delacroix suppressed a sigh. He blamed himself, for surely he should have known. Plump Venetian whores and obliging tavern wenches were enjoyable enough, but ladies were nothing but trouble. It must have been the moonlight, or perhaps the strange Irish air with the way it held the memory of day long after it should have faded. Whatever the cause, he had erred with Deirdre and now he was going to pay.

His choices were limited. He could let Red Hugh best him, although it seemed unlikely he'd be satisfied with less than a blooding. Delacroix had been wounded only three times, far less than most men in his line of work, and none had been life-threatening. But they'd been bad enough for all that, and he'd be damned if he'd put up with the inconvenience, the threat of fever, and the sheer galling of it.

He could apologize and hope the lad would be satisfied with that, but every instinct he had told him that wouldn't work. Once he admitted any fault, Red Hugh would be driven all the more to gore him.

Which left meeting him blow for blow until one of them became too exhausted to fight. Long experience and the simple differences in their physiques told Delacroix who that would be. The only problem there was that the tactic called for patience, which at the moment he had in short supply.

He breathed deeply, as he always did at such moments, and felt the clear, sweet air flow within him. A well of stillness opened at the core of his being, the place he had found as a child, the place where he went to make his poems and, strangely, the place he went to fight.

He raised his sword. Red Hugh crouched, ready, his face hard and narrow. The battle light was in his eyes. He was telling himself he had the training, the skill, the breeding to take this upstart poet. He would not kill him, for he was a guest in the O'Neill's house and he had saved Deirdre's life. Only a little wounding to assuage pride and make the point on who was lord and who was hireling. Only that, and then the lesson done, he would—

A cry split the sky. It came up out of the ground, shook the air, and tore the clouds asunder. Birds rose from the trees fully fifty yards away, screaming in their terror. People in the stands choked on their own shouts and grew suddenly still. Horses froze, eyes maddened, withers heaving. Men in the midst of combat dropped their guard and turned to stare.

Again, Delacroix raised his face to the heavens and let loose his battle cry. Again, the heavens responded while the earth trembled. Barely had the sound begun to die than he was on Red Hugh, slashing and driving, forcing the man to keep his shield high and try desperately to parry while he was driven back, step by painful step.

Men fled before them. Brave men who would never run in battle picked up their heels and ran when confronted by the spectacle of death, armored and weaponed, come among them. For surely that was what the bard must truly be, death in disguise mocking them all this time, reciting his great poems, stirring their blood and all the while thinking of the harvest that would be his.

Children screamed and hid their faces in the skirts of mothers who clutched them close and murmured prayers. On the dais, Deirdre leaped to her feet only to be dragged back by the harsh hand of her father. Her face was pale, her eyes dark and haunted. She wanted to weep, to scream, to run between them and demand they stop, to beat both their stupid heads together until they promised they would never do such a thing again.

"Do not forget yourself," the O'Neill ordered grimly. His eyes were fixed on the battle. Never had he seen such fierce strength and ability, such deadly grace and unrelenting force. For a moment he pitied Red Hugh, but then he remembered that the lad had gotten himself into this mess and his anger surged. Bloody fool! What of the rebellion, their great plans, the need for their earldoms to present a united front against Elizabeth? O'Donnell dead would do him no good at all.

He rose, pushing Deirdre back into her seat and bellowed for his guards. "Stop them!"

The men obeyed, give them credit for that. A half dozen leaped onto the field without hesitation and raced toward the offending pair. But before they could intervene Red Hugh raised his sword arm in a desperate parry, threw his full weight behind the blow, and, without regard for whatever shreds of honor were left, sought to ram his sword up beneath Delacroix's shield.

In battle against a sworn enemy, the ploy was perfectly respectable. In the melee, it was not. What he was trying was murder, and everyone who saw him knew it. There was a collective in-drawing of breath followed hard by its release. For surely heaven flung its answer back as, poised for the kill, Red Hugh suddenly lost his footing and went down. He landed winded at Delacroix's feet. The bard raised his own sword high.

Time stopped, or at least slowed to a crawl. Every man, woman, and child there watched the scene being etched in memory to be retold round the fire on nights long removed.

"And then the O'Donnell fell," they would say in the hushed tones of high drama.

"And the bard raised his sword. Oh, but it gleamed in that summer light like the eye of death itself. Only an instant it took before—"

Before what? The bard paused, sword frozen, looking down at the other man. Red Hugh O'Donnell, sworn enemy of England, coconspirator in treachery. Kill him and the rebellion is cut in half. Do it now, quickly and cleanly. The provocation was clear; he acted in self-defense. No one could fault him, least of all Elizabeth, who would be mightily pleased, perhaps even enough to be talked into treating Ireland more gently. And Deirdre . . . Deirdre would be husbandless and perhaps, only perhaps, fair for the taking.

Hireling, Red Hugh had called his father, and been right enough, but the hireling had spawned a son burdened by conscience. In the quiet place he could hide from everything except himself. He could not, would not, kill out of lust for another man's woman. Had it not been for that, had it truly been only a question of treason, he might have done it. But desiring Deirdre as he did, he could not.

Damn women, always complicating what should be a simple matter. Sighing, he lowered the sword and held out a hand to Red Hugh. It was the same hand he had given to Eamon Dougherty, erstwhile champion, and the same gesture. The crowd, recognizing it, cheered mightily. Truly, here was a poet of the old ways. A man who treated all with the same noble dignity. A man of courage and strength—sweet Lord, could he fight! A man worthy of his own epic to be sung over the hills and in the meadows. A man for the ages.

Red Hugh took his hand. His own shook slightly as he was pulled to his feet. He stood looking into the eyes he would have shut forever, until shame overcame him.

"I thank you," he murmured under his breath.

Delacroix nodded curtly. He turned away and walked off the field. The guard formed a path for him to get by. People screamed his name and tried to clutch at him, but he ignored them all. Only one he saw, Deirdre standing fair and silent. Her head covering had slipped off, and her ebony hair blew in the gentle breeze. Tawny silk clung to her high, firm breasts and the slender curve of her waist. She looked like a magnificent idol, all ivory and gold in an ancient temple. Only the light in her eyes was thoroughly human and unmistakable. He smiled grimly. The lady was fit to be tied and would cheerfully have finished off what Red Hugh began. Not that she would get the chance. He had learned his lesson. Until his mission was done, he was clear of women. A monk would have nothing on him.

For several hours, he actually managed to believe this. Only after he had bathed, eaten, and retired to bed did it occur to him that he might be overly optimistic. The thought arose from the discovery that when he closed his eyes, he saw the vision of Deirdre. He imagined he could smell her perfume and hear the soft timbre of her voice. His body, single-minded creature that it was, found this notion pleasing and responded at once.

He cursed into the darkness and briefly considered ending his solitude. Megan had made it clear she was more than willing and there were others enough for any man. But the thought had no appeal for him. Rolling over on his side, he resigned himself to an unrestful night.

CHAPTER

10

DEIRDRE WITHDREW THE SMALL KNIFE SHE carried from her pocket and began to carefully scrape a clump of fungus loose from the rotting tree bark where it nestled. When she had a sufficiently large piece, she dropped it in the basket hanging from her arm and moved on. Next to catch her eye were lichen clinging to a dull-gray rock. Bending closer, she confirmed they were of a sort useful for easing swellings. Removing them was harder than with the fungus, but she managed finally and added them to the basket.

She paused for a moment, rubbing the back of her neck where it was sore from constant bending and craning. She had been in the woods since early morning, and it was now midafternoon. So far the effort had proved even more worthwhile than she had hoped. In the heavily laden basket were bell-shaped foxglove to ease the heart, blackberry root for the bloody flux that so frequently plagued armies on the move, hyssop to ease breathing, St. John's wort for bleeding, and far more. Dungannon's fields and hills held a bounty of life, but it had to be gathered carefully. The wrong plants, or the right ones in the wrong proportions, could mean death.

The strain of her efforts was beginning to take its toll. Although she was loath to miss anything, she knew she had done far better than expected. It was time to return to the castle to sort through her finds.

"I think that's enough," she said, and smiled when she saw the look of relief that flashed across the face of the galloglach. Poor man that he was, he had followed her patiently up hill and down, fording streams, crawling under rocks, moving fallen tree trunks all at her behest. Perhaps he'd get another Moorish stallion for his trouble, but she doubted it. The O'Neill was not in a giving mood.

Rather he was coldly, implacably angry—at Red Hugh for his childishness at the tourney, at the hapless Spanish for merely being themselves, and at Sir Henry Bagenal for staying snugly in Armagh when any decent man would have sortied out to risk life and limb in accordance with the O'Neill's plan.

But he had kept his promise to his daughter, and for that she was grateful. Not merely did it allow her to go out seeking what she needed, it kept her away from Dungannon for the day. And it gave her time to think.

Who was Sean Harpsinger? She was no closer to the answer now than she had when she'd asked it of him after the boar attack. From the beginning, she'd sensed the difference in him. Hadn't she seen him, harp in hand, yet with the phantom sword crimson-tipped wielding around him? What he'd told grudgingly of his father and his own life explained some of what he was, but not all. Hirelings did not fight like that, at least not usually. Lords were supposed to but rarely did. Which left—what?

"Cuchullain come again," Fionna had called him the night before, clutching her breast and rolling her eyes to heaven. Nor was she the only one calling up the hallowed name of Ireland's greatest hero as the only possible comparison to the bard's noble feat. It was an exaggeration, of course, for Cuchullain had enjoyed a lifetime of derring-to and death-defying to pave his way into the epics, whereas the bard had only a single boar and Red Hugh to secure his place. Yet for all that, it wasn't totally outrageous.

She straightened on her mount and drew in her wayward thoughts. Sternly, she reminded herself that she had more immediate concerns. First to her workroom to prepare what she had gathered, then to the castle garden for more of the tame plants she needed, then to the weaving sheds to make sure the bandages she had ordered were ready. When that was done, she had to begin sorting each medicinal, the dry ones into cloth packets, the others into stoneware vials. Each then needed to be packed in something she could carry readily. Not the usual wooden box, she thought, but a large pouch to sling over the shoulder. If her father knew what she was plotting, his already strained temper would have burst all bonds, but the O'Neill was busy enough with matters of his own and did no more than note her return.

Deirdre was too busy herself the remainder of the afternoon to take much notice of anything. Some of the herbs needed more time to dry, but she was reluctant to give it. A sense of urgency was growing in her that increased steadily as night fell. Sending a message to her father, she begged leave not to come to hall for the evening meal. Fionna took it clucking, anticipating trouble, but came back with surprise.

"He said it's all right," she informed her young charge. "Now, why would he suddenly be so accommodating? Especially when he looks as though he'd like nothing better right now than to bite the head off a bear?"

"Off Sir Henry's more like it," Deirdre murmured absently. She was at a key point in the preparation of a tincture and didn't really pay attention to what she was saying.

Fionna hurrumphed under her breath. "There you go again, interfering with men's business." She peered at the light-brown liquid dripping from the sack of cheesecloth Deirdre had immersed in water. "What is that, anyway?"

"A tincture to ease fever."

"My mother had one of those, but you had to bury a fish under the moon and say three Hail Marys backward or it wouldn't work."

"That's ridiculous," Deirdre said as she squeezed the last few drops into the vial. "Either a remedy is effective or it isn't. The rest is only superstition."

Fionna looked unconvinced. Churchgoing woman that she was, she wasn't above burying a bone near a thorn tree to gain good fortune.

"Where did you learn such things? I'll warrant the holy sisters didn't teach you."

"They certainly did. Mother Justina is a learned healer, and so are several other of the nuns. Much of the abbey's income comes from the cures they make."

Fionna clucked her tongue. "That's what comes of being up there near the top of the world instead of down here in a respectable place. Did your father know of such goings-on when he sent you there?"

"I have no idea," Deirdre said, "but it didn't do me any harm. Besides, why would you think it ill? Mother Justina told me that some of the remedies they use date from the time when places like Buan-ann were the only churches. You go there right enough, but you don't think the old ways should be continued?"

"I didn't say that," Fionna muttered, flushing. "But sensible folk don't talk of Buan-ann or other such matters. You've been too sheltered, or you'd know."

"I do know," Deirdre said softly. It was warm in the chamber, but she suppressed a shiver. They still burnt witches in England, Mother Justina had told her, and in Scotland as well, not to mention the atrocities done on the continent in the name of holiness. Any woman who dared to stand apart from the crowd was liable to an accusation of witchcraft. A powerful family might be able to protect her, but there was no guarantee of that.

"Never mind," she murmured. "I'm almost finished here."

"Good," Fionna said briskly, "then you can go console that lad of yours who's skulking around as though the world had ended."

"What lad?" Deirdre asked, still preoccupied with her work.

"Red Hugh, of course. Have you no sense at all, lass? Everyone knows he made a mistake yesterday and you've done nought to comfort him. That isn't wise, given as how he's to be your husband."

"That remains to be seen," Deirdre replied. Her eyes narrowed and her mouth set in a thoroughly no-nonsense line. "It was more than a mistake he made, it was an act of dishonor."

"And don't you think he knows that? Think, lass. What do you suppose provoked him to act as he did?"

Deirdre paused for a moment. She placed a stopper in the last vial before she said, "I have been thinking on it, and be sure my thoughts aren't happy ones. I know I had a part in what happened."

"Then you aren't totally daft," Fionna said gruffly. When she saw the look on the young girl's face, her own softened. "There now, lass, no one really blames you. He shouldn't have done what he did no matter what the circumstances. But it wouldn't hurt you to let him know you aren't angry at him."

"But I am," Deirdre said. "I'm angry at all of them." She waved a hand over the worktable crowded now with packets and vials. "Look at what I'm doing here, Fionna. If I'm lucky, all my efforts will save a few lives, but a great many more will be lost. And for what?"

The older woman was shocked. "Why, for a free Ireland, of course. Don't tell me you don't think that's worth dying for."

"I'm not sure," Deirdre said slowly. "If I really believed war would bring a better life, then maybe I'd be more enthusiastic. But what are the chances of that truly? Aside from Red Hugh, who are my father's allies? Spaniards, that's who, not other Irishmen. We're still a badly divided people."

"That will change," the older woman insisted.

"When himself is victorious, other clan chieftains will rally to him."

"Will they?" Deirdre asked skeptically. "Or will they see him as a rival to their own power and seek to destroy him? That's what has always happened in the past. We haven't done ourselves any good being our own worst enemy."

"I don't know what to say to you, lass. You must have faith, you must believe Ireland will be free, otherwise there's no chance for it at all."

"I want to believe," Deirdre said softly, "but I think of the men who will die, of how their families will suffer, and I wonder if things couldn't have been handled differently. If father could have built a stronger alliance to the other chieftains before rebelling, if he could make it clear that he doesn't necessarily want to be high king himself, merely one among equals, then perhaps—"

Fionna raised a hand, cutting her off. "Child, you canna go on like this. We're women both of us, and our minds aren't suited to wrangling with such problems. You'll only give yourself the migraine if you try. Now, it's a fine thing that you worry about others and want to help them, but don't be fretting yourself over things you canna affect."

"I suppose," Deirdre murmured, though her tone made it clear she was far from convinced. To her way of thinking, her mind seemed as sharp as any man's, indeed sharper than some. Red Hugh's, for instance, who, for all that he could be kind and gentle, had that rock-hard stubbornness that afflicted males and made them act so rashly.

"Go find the lad," Fionna counseled gently. "Comfort him in his shame, for later you will be glad of it. He will remember what you do now and be the better husband as a result."

"Is that all I'm supposed to be concerned about?" Deirdre asked.

"Yes, lass, it is, and if you've any sense, you'll accept that. If you can't do it because it's the womanly thing, then do it as an act of Christian charity. But whatever your reason, don't let him go another hour without seeing your face."

Still, Deirdre hesitated. She knew her old nurse was being practical and that her advice was good, but it galled her all the same. She was still mulling it over, trying to decide whether or not to do the sensible thing, when the decision was taken from her.

Shouts broke out in the courtyard. Deirdre ran to the window and opened the shutters, leaning over to look out.

"Not so far!" Fionna said in alarm. She ran to hold on to her and ended up draped over the sill herself, craning her neck.

Armed men were crowding out of the hall to greet the messenger who had just ridden in. By the light of the torches, Deirdre could see his face streaked with dust and utterly weary. Questions were shouted at him, but he ignored them as he lowered himself stiffly from the saddle. He moved toward the hall, the crowd following, and disappeared from sight.

"Now what could that be about?" Deirdre wondered as she came back inside. "I didn't recognize him. Did you?"

Halfway to the door, Fionna shook her head. "Not I. Come on."

Deirdre followed, unable to deny her curiosity. By

the time they reached the hall, the messenger had vanished from sight, sequestered with the O'Neill and Red Hugh in a private chamber. Speculation about who he was and what word he brought ran rampant through the hall. "From Armagh," someone said. "Ridden all night and day," said another. "Mayhap the witch in London wants to surrender," one man suggested, laughing, and others took it up, bragging that the English had already seen the light and realized the folly of coming against Eire's proud sons.

Deirdre's blood chilled. She stood a little apart, unable to share in the giddy confidence. In the distance, a drum began to beat. Another followed, and then the pipes, high and haunting, filled the air with a robust marching tune. The crowd took it up, singing lustily, all about blood and greatness, battle and honor. For Deirdre, the words were ash. She could think only of the savagery about to be unleashed and whether or not it could possibly have any purpose. Watching the others, knowing they did not share her doubts, she felt completely alone until she saw one other, standing as still and apart as herself.

Sean Harpsinger had not joined in the singing. He remained, his face grim and watchful, trying to determine what was happening. When he saw Deirdre he hesitated a moment before making his way toward her. As he reached her side, he said quietly, "It appears something is afoot."

She nodded, her expression as somber as his own. All day he had been at the back of her mind despite her best efforts to banish him. Try though she did, the memory of him on the field kept returning. He had come so close to dying, the maddening, infuriating man! And he had behaved so well, damn him for it, for it made it all the harder for her to remember the differences between them. Why couldn't he have been the lord, her father's ally, her chosen husband! Oh, sweet heaven, she must not think like that. It was disloyal to Red Hugh, who for all his failings was a decent man and deserved better of her. And it was a betrayal of her father, who had more than enough to concern him without a weak-willed daughter to add to his troubles.

Bitterness washed over her. She grimaced, unable to hide her dismay. "Fools, the lot of them. Do they seriously believe the English would just surrender or that my father would want them to? It's war he seeks and war he's got, God help us all." Her voice broke. She turned away from him, embarrassed by her weakness, only to be stopped by his hand on her arm.

His grip was gentle but implacable. He moved slightly so that she was between him and the stone wall, sheltered from the view of the crowd. Grimly, he said, "What do you know, Deirdre? Tell me."

She raised her head, meeting his eyes, and was struck by the coldness in their steely depths. Her throat closed. She had to swallow hard before she could speak. "You'll all know soon enough. Let me go."

She might as well have saved her breath, for all he did was tighten his grip fractionally and repeat his demand. "Tell me, what has your father wrought?"

Fear stirred in her. This was the man who had saved her life, the man she desired despite her best efforts not to, and yet there was something in him— something secret and dark—that made her afraid. When still she did not answer, he moved closer. She felt the hard length of his body pressing her against the wall. Her eyes widened at the heat that flooded her. His scent engulfed her—leather, smoke, and the essence of manliness. Her senses swam, but still she would not yield to him.

"You forget yourself, bard. Release me." His grip hardened yet further. In response, she tried to twist away, only to find the effort bruising. "You are mad," she said from between clenched teeth. "If anyone sees you, if I scream . . ."

She stopped, aware suddenly of the taut, hard face looming above her own. His features were stripped of all gentleness, honed to the battle hardness she had seen before. This was no sweet-voiced bard, but a warrior, implacable and relentless.

Harshly, he said, "If your father has provoked war, he will rue this day and every Irish man and woman with him. He cannot possibly win. His only hope lay in compromise."

"What do you know of it?" Deirdre demanded. She refused to quake before him, never mind that her insides were turning over. "My father is a great leader. He knows what is best for his people."

"Then why were you cursing him yourself only a moment ago?" Delacroix demanded. The feel of the girl against him was blurring his reason. He was close to forgetting that they were in a crowded hall where they might, as she had said, be noticed at any moment.

"I wasn't . . ." she gasped, "I only . . . oh, sweet heaven . . ." Hot tears stung her eyes. She bit her lower lip hard, trying to stop them, but succeeded only in wounding herself.

"Don't," Delacroix said roughly. He touched a hard finger to her mouth, tracing its line with unexpected delicacy. "Don't," he repeated more gently. "Deirdre . . ."

Whatever he had meant to say, the words were not spoken, for just then a cry went up as the O'Neill emerged from his private chamber. All eyes turned to him. He stood, head back, feet firmly apart, his face alight with ruthless pleasure.

"To arms!" Hugh O'Neill shouted. "The filthy blackguard Bagenal marches from Armagh intent on battle. Blessed Mary and all the saints, we will give it to him."

The roar was deafening. Deirdre shut her eyes against it, but she could not close her ears. Despair filled her. Engulfed in it, she barely noticed that Delacroix had released her. When she looked again, he was gone from the hall.

CHAPTER
11

DELACROIX PAUSED BY THE CISTERN WALL. HE stood, hugging the shadows, black against the black of night. The moon was gone, riding to its rest. Nothing stirred in the bailey yard. A lone guard walked the rampart above the castle gate. It was closed, naturally enough, and could not be opened without great clamor. But the smaller postern gate could be managed. Beyond, the village slumbered. He had already marked the location of the stables from which he meant to appropriate a likely mount. With luck, he would be heading south well before dawn and could intercept Bagenal by evening.

Stealthily, he came away from the wall and crossed the distance to the gate. Nothing stirred in the darkness. Dungannon might as well have been under a spell, so deeply did the castle and all its occupants slumber in the aftermath of their great excitement, aided in no small measure by the quantities of mead and ale poured forth after the O'Neill's announcement. Heads would be heavy come morning, but he would not be there to see it.

The postern gate stood in a recess even more deeply shadowed than its surroundings. Delacroix reached it with relief and put out a hand to find the iron hasp. He lifted it slowly, making no sound, and eased the gate open. One step, another, and he was out, shutting the gate carefully behind him. A gentle slope led down from the castle to the road. He followed it quickly and was almost there when, without warning, the night exploded.

"Take him!" a voice cried.

Men came at him from all sides. He cursed and struck out, felling the first few, but they kept coming, holding nothing back. Still he fought, knowing it was for his life. So great was his power that he might have broken free had not one of the men raised a heavy club and brought it crashing down against his head. Pain tore through him. He fell before it and was swallowed by darkness greater than any night.

The darkness gave way to a thin crack of light. Delacroix opened his eyes gingerly. The pain was still there, throbbing but bearable. "Who?" he murmured, surprised when his voice cracked. How long had he lain like this?

"Come," a hard voice said. He was dragged upright and hauled down a long corridor before being shoved into a small chamber.

He straightened slowly, his mind shrieking caution, and glanced around him. The chamber was windowless;

either that or thick hangings were drawn over the openings. The flagstone floor was covered by a rich Araby rug. A carved oak table stood at one end with a large, high-backed chair behind it. The chair was occupied.

Hugh O'Neill barred his teeth in a smile. "The night grows long, bard, and I have tired of waiting for you. Sit down and nurse your head while we talk." He gestured to a chair opposite him, which Delacroix took gratefully enough even though he knew his trouble had only begun. Worse yet, he had only himself to blame. He had been incautious; first that business with the boar, then the wrestling, and worst of all, the melee. Had he stood on the ramparts and shouted, "I am John Delacroix, earl of Bradford, sworn man of Her Most August Majesty, Elizabeth," he could hardly have raised more interest in himself.

Which was all well and good in hindsight, but did nothing to help the throbbing in his head or the glint of murder in the O'Neill's eyes.

"You had me watched," he said unnecessarily.

"I have a little voice that talks to me from time to time," the O'Neill said, "and when it does, I listen." He leaned back in his chair and regarded his guest benignly, much as the cat does the mouse. The thought rankled Delacroix. Granted, his present circumstances were hardly good, but he wasn't finished yet. Was he?

"I could have been wrong," the O'Neill went on. "You might have simply been what you said, a mercenary's son who learned his father's trade but also followed his heart to become a bard. And yet, I admit I did wonder almost from the beginning. Your turning up here when you did was a shade too convenient."

"Your little voice misleads you," Delacroix said. "I

am what I have said and nothing more."

"Indeed? No common man fights as you do. If I thought I could trust you, I would offer you a position in my own army. Indeed, I might have if you hadn't seen fit to absent yourself from under my roof scant hours after word came that we will shortly be under attack. Either you are a coward, which I do not believe, or you had some other motive for leaving when you did."

"A willing wench in the village was my motive, nothing more."

"Indeed? What is her name?"

Delacroix shrugged. "We didn't get that far. She has red hair, blue eyes, or perhaps they're green, and a body . . ." He smiled, leaving the details unspoken.

The O'Neill frowned. "You didn't know her name but you did know where to find her?"

"At the tavern, she said."

"Hmmm, mayhap, but my little voice is unconvinced. I owe you a debt, bard, for there is no denying that you saved my daughter's life. For that reason alone, I will not hand you over to those in my service who would wring the truth from you, whatever the cost. But you will remain here in confinement until I return."

"You mention your debt to me in one breath and order my imprisonment with the next? A queer sense of honor that."

"Do not irk me, bard, for my temper is not good at the moment. In truth, I like you, you've too much spirit for me not to. But"—he leaned forward, his great arms spread out across the table—"I'll crush you like so much chaff before the wind if I find out you spy for Bagenal."

"Bagenal is a fool," Delacroix said with feeling.

"On that we agree." The O'Neill rose and signaled the guards. "Confinement is never pleasant, but yours will be decent enough. When I return, we will talk again. Mayhap you will convince me to trust you after all."

"Mayhap you will not return," Delacroix suggested unkindly.

The O'Neill laughed and returned his attention to the maps littering his desk, signaling thereby that the audience was over. Delacroix was escorted away by a pair of watchful guards, who saw him to a small cell deep within the castle bowels. There they left him, behind a steel door, to contemplate the folly of his own behavior and consider how it might yet be remedied.

Six hours later, the O'Neill rode out. With him went his army and Red Hugh O'Donnell's, several thousand strong thanks to the reinforcements summoned during the night. The entire castle, minus a certain prisoner, turned out to see them off. Deirdre stood in the bailey yard, watching her father as he mounted the big, black destrier he customarily rode to battle. The horse pawed the ground in its eagerness, its breath snorting mist into the morning air.

She was determined to remain calm. It would avail her nothing to reveal what she felt, that confusion of fear and anger that had kept her awake through the night. And now added to it was the bewildering sense of betrayal.

"The medicines," she said, standing close beside her father and looking up at him. Unknown to her, her anxiety was stamped clear on her face. He frowned as he looked down at her.

"What about them?"

"You said they could be gathered, you seemed to understand the importance, but now—"

"Now you wait," the O'Neill said with unintended harshness. He was impatient to be gone and did not like the reminder that this raven-haired daughter believed he was in error.

"The wounded will be sent back to Dungannon," he said more gently. "You may care for them here."

"By then it will be too late for some."

His eyes darkened again, the heavy brows drawing close together. "That is as it must be. Surely you could not have believed I would allow you anywhere near the field?"

In truth, she hadn't thought it out at all, merely presumed that she would be where she could do the most good. How foolish of her. She was expected to wait behind the castle walls, a good and dutiful daughter, until the dead and dying were brought to her to succor as best she could.

"If I were a man," she began, her small fists clenched in frustration.

The O'Neill stared at her for a moment before abruptly throwing back his shaggy head. His laugh drew startled glances. "Now that I truly cannot imagine. Accept what you are and be thankful for it." He gestured toward Red Hugh, seated some little distance away on his own war-horse. "Make your farewells, daughter."

Deirdre heard the warning in his voice and knew better than to ignore it. Reluctantly, she went over to the younger man. Part of her hesitation came because she was uncertain of how he would respond, but the moment he saw her, his features brightened.

"Deirdre," he murmured with such palpable yearning that she could not help but be touched by it.

"My lord, I wish you godspeed and a safe return."

He nodded gravely. "Thank you, my lady. I assure you, we will trample the English most vigorously."

She suppressed a sigh, thinking what a boy he sounded despite all he had endured. All she had known was the abbey and Dungannon, yet she had an instinct for the truth of battle that told her it had no glory. Nonetheless, she said, "You will be in my prayers until we meet again."

The words were no more than she would offer anyone, yet he appeared touched by them. He reached down for a her hand and raised it to his lips. "My lady," he said again, almost reverently. "Deirdre . . ."

The rest was lost as the trumpets blared assembly. The O'Neill's destrier pranced to the head of the force. The banners were unfurled. A mighty cheer went up. Deirdre's throat tightened. She fought back tears as, slowly and then with growing speed, the army of Ulster began its march. Two dozen noble retainers led on horseback followed by rank on rank of archers and then the pikemen, their sharp-pointed weapons gleaming in the sun. The baggage train followed with its assembly of cooks, servants, and hangers-on, all looking as cheerful as though they were heading not to war but to a fair. To glory or to death, the old motto said, and there seemed little doubt which they thought to find.

Deirdre remained where she was, unmoving, until the last supply wagon rolled out of sight. The dust was settling in the bailey yard before she finally turned away. Inside, the great hall rang with silence. In the aftermath of so much hustle and bustle, the world was strangely still. She looked around, seeing in her mind's eye the space crowded with laughing men and women, smoke rising from the immense fireplaces at either end, servants laboring under heavy trays, and near the high table, in a place of honor, the bard singing of—

The bard. Abruptly, she stopped. Where was he? She had not seen him since the previous evening in hall. The memory of that encounter sent a tremor through her. Had he gone with the army, she would surely have seen him. At the very least, he should have been there to witness its departure. Instead, there was no sign of him.

Dread flowed through her. He had been so concerned about Bagenal and, even more, about what her father was planning. And now he was gone. To where?

She glanced around, confirming that she was unobserved. In the aftermath of the army's departure, those left behind had scattered to their separate duties. For the moment, the hall was empty. Cautiously, she made her way through it and up the short flight of stone steps that led to chambers set aside for guests.

The Spaniards had the largest and grandest of those close to the hall, but farther down and around a corner was the room allotted to the bard. She stood before it, hesitant, and looked again to make sure no one else was in sight. Were she seen now, there was absolutely no excuse she could give that would be tolerated. Her danger was real, but so was the desperate need to know.

Hardly breathing, she tried the door. It was unlocked. Softly, she called, "Is anyone within?" Silence answered her, but in the next instant she heard the unmistakable sound of rustling. There was a step and then another as someone came across the room toward her. She drew back quickly from the door, wondering if she should flee at the same time she debated what in heaven's name she could say to him to explain her presence. She needn't have bothered, for the door, thrown open, did not reveal the harpsinger. It was Megan who stood there, black hair tumbling around her shoulders and her eyes red-rimmed with tears.

"You," she gasped when she saw Deirdre. "What do you want here?"

The challenge was improper coming from a serving girl to a lady. Had she been older, more experienced, or simply more set on her dignity, Deirdre could have chastised her for it. As it was, she barely noticed the slight.

"What is the matter?" she asked, stepping into the room and shutting the door behind her. A glance around the sleeping chamber showed that everything appeared to be in order, too much so. The wall pegs were empty of clothes, and, most tellingly, no harp was anywhere in evidence. Sean Harpsinger might never have been, for all the trace of himself he'd left.

Megan stared at her defiantly. " 'Tis all your fault," she murmured, "hoity-toity miss that you are. When Seamus told me, I said he was in his cups and a liar to boot, but now I see it's true."

Deirdre's face flamed. Did everyone in Dungannon know of her feelings for the bard? "If he's gone, I'm not the reason. "

"Fool," the girl snarled, "he isn't *gone*. He's below in the dungeons where your noble father sent him."

Deirdre breathed in sharply. Her mind reeled.

Please God, let this be some terrible dream she would wake from in a moment. "How would you know such a thing? It's a lie, it is."

"Oh, no, it's true enough and curse you for it." Megan turned away, hiding her face in her apron. Her shoulders convulsed.

Deirdre's anger faded. In its place was compassion and genuine concern. She reached out a hand and touched the other girl gently. "Whatever's happened, there'll be an answer to it. Only tell me what you know."

Megan sniffed. "What's the use? There's nothing anyone can do."

"That remains to be seen. Who is Seamus and why does he say Sean is in the dungeons?"

Perhaps Megan wasn't used to such gentleness, or perhaps something simply snapped inside her. At any rate, it had the effect of a dam bursting. "My brother, he is," she said, speaking very fast, "half brother, really, and a sorry excuse for one, let me tell you. He works in the kitchens and sees more than he should. He was bringing ale to the guard last night when he heard them saying something was afoot. Being the little badger that he is, he hung around to see what would happen. He found a corner for himself out of sight and fell asleep. Hours later, in the dead of night, he hears noises and wakes to see them dragging in a man who looks unconscious. They threw him into one of the cells, but about an hour later they came back and took him out again."

She swallowed and dabbed at her eyes. "Took him to the O'Neill, they did, and this time Seamus saw him clear. Why that's the bard, he says to himself, and shocked he was for we all thought so well of him. He

153

couldn't hear what passed between them, but after a few minutes the guards brought Sean back to the cell and left him there."

Her voice rose, becoming shrill. "Now the O'Neill's ridden out and Sean's left below to rot. Merciful saints, 'tis an evil world we live in."

"Easy," Deirdre said, shushing her. "I can't imagine why my father would do such a thing, but I'll get to the bottom of it, you can be sure."

"You will?" Megan asked, eyeing her doubtfully.

"Depend on it. I'll not let any man pay such a price through my own foolishness."

" 'Tis good of you, milady, but still the dungeons and all? What chance would you have?"

"I don't know," Deirdre admitted, "but I'll find a way. You go on about your duties, let no one know that we've talked. All right?"

Megan nodded hesitantly and did as she was told, but not without a backward glance that said she was glad of Deirdre's intervention but gladder still not to be in her shoes. Deirdre wouldn't have minded not being there herself. Confronted with the problem she had already promised to solve, she set about trying to decide what to do.

First thing was to confirm that Sean was where he was said to be. For that alone, she needed all her courage. Dungannon's dungeons were hardly the worst of their sort, but Deirdre had always steadfastly avoided the part of the castle where they were located. Reminding herself that she was an O'Neill and as such could never give in to fear, she went back to the great hall. Near the passage leading to the kitchens, she found flint and tinder, and slipped both into her pocket. Cautiously, she returned to the bailey, still deserted in the aftermath of the army's departure.

The day mocked her with its sunshine cheer. She walked quickly across the yard to the wing of the castle that housed the garrison hall. The dungeons were beneath it. Ordinarily, several hundred men would have been living in the hall, but almost all had gone. Only a routine guard remained, and he was not in evidence. Praying that her luck would hold, she slipped inside.

The dungeons were below ground. Deirdre shivered as she left the warmth of day. Dank air rose up, filled with musty odors she did not want to identify. She found a torch and lit it, but took scant comfort from its presence. As quickly as she dared, she moved down the worn stone steps and along the passageway. This part of the castle dated from the first round tower built on the site more than three hundred years before. Originally, the space had been used to store food and weapons. Now it served a far different purpose.

A dozen or so heavy wooden doors lined the passage on either side. Each had a small iron grill set high up within it. Trembling, she went to the first, stood on tiptoe, and peered in. Nothing. The next was the same, and the next. She had just begun to think that perhaps Seamus had been wrong after all when a sudden sound froze her in place. She heard the lilting sound of a harp, soft, almost imperceptible.

Deirdre ran toward it. She stopped before an iron-studded door. A thin ray of light shone through its grille.

"Sean . . . ?" she called softly. The harp fell silent. "Sean?"

In the midst of a suitably melancholy tune about

vanquished dreams and evil fairies, Delacroix paused. He was surprised to discover he had so little stamina. Already he was hallucinating. He could have sworn he'd heard Deirdre's voice.

"Sean?"

There it was again, more urgent this time. Reluctantly, he laid the harp aside and moved toward the door. "Who—?"

"It's me, Deirdre. What are you doing in there?"

"Sweet Lord." He moved closer to the door, gripping the bars of the grille. It really was her, standing there pale and defiant, gripping an ill-lit torch that was quickly smoking up the entire passageway.

"What in the name of heaven are you doing here, woman?"

Her temper flared. Trust him not to be the least bit grateful. "Looking for you, of course. Megan told me you were down here, and I had to find out for sure."

He tried to wrap his mind around the image of Megan and Deirdre consulting as to his whereabouts, found that he could not, and gave up. "Well, now you have," he snarled. "Get away with you."

"No."

His pewter eyes widened. Hellfire, what was this about? What was she thinking to come to such a place and then refuse to leave? "Don't you know what would happen if you were found here?" he demanded.

"I know you could hardly be in any worse position," she said.

Delacroix frowned. Had he imagined the small choke in her voice? The thought that she was truly worried about him did queer things to his stomach. It seemed to somersault. "Now, Deirdre, lass—"

"Let me finish. I know this is all my fault, what I did was foolish, but for my father to go off as he has done . . ." She paused, thinking for a terrible moment that perhaps Harpsinger had not known of his abandonment. "Did you realize? Down here, you might not have—"

"I know the O'Neill rode out this morning," he assured her quickly. "But what was that about it being your fault?"

"Don't try to spare my feelings. I don't deserve it."

Was that what he was trying to do? He hadn't realized.

"He should never have done this, never," she went on vehemently. "And he wouldn't have if he'd been thinking right. Obviously, he wasn't, so it is up to me to remedy the injustice. Of course, you cannot be left here."

"Of course," Delacroix said slowly. It was beginning to come together now. Deirdre thought he was in the dungeon because of what had passed between them. Really the idea wasn't that farfetched, it just happened to be wrong. Further, she thought he'd been abandoned to his fate, dropped, as it were, into an "oubliette" to be forgotten to death. In fact, he wasn't being treated all that badly, taking everything into account. His head no longer throbbed, he'd been brought food and drink, and he'd even been allowed to keep his harp. Hardly evidence of the O'Neill's desire to find him dead when he returned.

His conscience reared its unrelenting head, telling him to straighten out the misunderstanding at once. It was unforgivable for him to let her go on believing as she did, and placing herself at risk as a result. A few small words and she would realize that she had nothing to be sorry about.

And she would go taking with her any chance he had to get out before the O'Neill's return.

Poised on the particularly sharp horns of a dilemma, Delacroix said, "Deirdre, what is it you mean to do?"

"Find the keys and let you out, of course. It may take me a while to do it, but—"

"The keys are hanging on a board at the far end of the corridor." That much he had been able to ascertain, along with the fact that the guards made few appearances except when his meals were brought. Apparently, it didn't occur to anyone that he might escape.

"Wonderful," Deirdre exclaimed. "As soon as it is dark, I'll return. Once you're out of the castle, you can head for the coast. There are always boats going to Scotland and Wales. With my father so distracted, he'll never know you're gone." But she would know it, and the knowing filled her with anguish. Still, there was nothing to be done. "I'll be back—"

"Wait!" Delacroix thought quickly. What she said made sense enough; he should wait for dark, even though he had no intention of making for the coast. He still had to find Bagenal, but the longer he waited, the more likely it became that he would be too late. "Let me out now," he ordered. "I'll take my chances in the daylight."

"You're mad! Darkness will give you cover. Without that, you cannot hope to escape."

In fact, he could, but he was not about to tell her how, at least not yet. His conscience roared a protest, but he refused to heed it, telling himself what he was doing was for her ultimate good as well as everyone else's. Peace had to be the first objective, and to attain that he had to reach Bagenal.

"Now, Deirdre," he said urgently. "Almost all the garrison is gone. Find me an old cloak to wear and no one will notice me. By tonight, who knows? Your father could return suddenly, or Red Hugh." He hated himself for misleading her so callously, but at least it worked. Through the grille, he saw her face pale.

"I hadn't thought of that," she said. "If you're willing to take the chance—"

"I am."

She met his eyes, hers dark pools of worry. Abruptly, she nodded. "Of course, I didn't realize . . . I'll be right back."

True to her word, Deirdre returned within scant minutes. She had an oversized cloak filched from her father's own chamber and, in her other hand, the dungeon key. Quickly, she opened the door. It creaked slightly on its hinges. Delacroix stepped out, his pouch over his shoulder. He smiled reassuringly as he took the cloak.

"You are a brave one, lass," he said softly.

She flushed at the praise. "Come, we must go."

Swiftly, she led the way above. They came out onto the bailey where a few servants were in evidence once again, attending to their duties. Delacroix pulled the hood of the cloak more securely over his face. "The stables," he said.

Deirdre nodded. Together, they crossed the open space, garnering a few curious glances along the way but nothing more. Inside the stables, almost all the horse stalls were empty. Only a few palfreys remained. Delacroix selected the best of them. He saddled the gelding quickly and then surprised Deirdre by going down the rows, releasing the remaining horses.

"Open the doors," he told her.

"Why?"

"To keep any of the guards from following. They'll be able to round them up in a few hours, but this way I'll have a decent head start."

She nodded, seeing the sense of that, and went to do as he said. The horses milled about for a few moments, but scents of wind and sun soon made them take the chance for freedom. As they bolted for the bailey yard, Delacroix swung into the saddle. Deirdre looked up at him, thinking how golden he looked. The hood of the cloak had fallen back, exposing the glistening mane of hair and the hard perfection of his features. She wanted to remember him exactly as he was, storing the memory in her heart for the long, cold years ahead.

A pretty notion, but one that didn't match the sudden look of implacable determination that flashed across his face. She had a moment to wonder what he could possibly be thinking when he spurred the palfrey forward, riding directly at her. The clatter of pounding hooves resounded off the stable walls. Closer and closer the powerful horse came. A scream rose in her throat. This could not be happening, it could *not*. And yet it was. She pressed back against the stable wall, trying vainly to escape. In the final instant before the horse would have trampled her, Delacroix reached down a steely arm and scooped her up. She was slammed onto the saddle in front of him, held in a rock-hard grip as the horse surged toward the castle gate.

"What are you doing?" Deirdre screamed. "Are you mad? If you take me, they will hunt you down. You will never escape."

"Be silent," Delacroix ordered. He was feeling badly enough about the whole business without her adding to it. The look on her face as he spurred the horse forward had been terrible to see. The thought of her in such fear hurt him more than he would have believed possible. Still, he told himself he was doing the only thing he could.

"Good hostages don't annoy their captors," he told her gruffly, and was rewarded by an indignant gasp.

"You *are* mad. The guards—"

But the guards, what was left of them, were racing about in disarray, trying to recapture the rampaging horses. Delacroix rode directly past them, taking time only to shout a warning to a startled fellow on the ramparts.

"Come after us and she dies."

Deirdre had a glimpse of the man, gray with horror, before they were through the gate and racing down the road her father had lately marched along in glory. There was no evidence of that now, only the fierce gallop of the horse and the harsh grip of the man holding her. The man she had thought to save who suddenly, inexplicably, had become her enemy.

CHAPTER
12

FOR SEVERAL MOMENTS, DEIRDRE WAS TOO paralyzed by shock to do much of anything. She could not believe what was happening to her, that she had been so wrong, that the bard would dare, that her life would take such a dark and astonishing turn. But belief really didn't matter. Whether she could comprehend it or not, what was happening was nonetheless real. There was no place to hide from the truth.

It was that more than anything else that broke the grip of shock. She began to struggle wildly.

"Stop that!" Delacroix ordered, tightening his hold on her. "Behave yourself."

Her answer was to lash out with her feet, kicking him in the shins while also managing to land a solid blow to his nose. He grunted in surprise. She was stronger than she looked, not to mention faster. It was all he could do to hold on to the fighting bundle of femininity and maintain control of the horse.

But Deirdre wasn't done. She hit out in all directions until Delacroix finally lost patience. He let the horse have its head while he turned all his attention to her. His grip became implacable, momentarily robbing her of breath. Whereas before he had sought merely to contain her, now he deliberately drove home the message that she was helpless against him. Deirdre was loath to accept it. She continued to struggle until her strength was exhausted. Only then did she slump against him in weary defeat.

Delacroix took no pleasure in that. Like any warrior, he applauded courage even in an enemy. He also greatly disliked hurting women. She would have bruises by the next day. That they came largely from her own struggles made him feel no better.

He reined in the horse slightly to stop its mad rush and looked down at the pale face lying in the curve of his arm. Her eyes were closed; he could see the blue tracing of veins beneath the delicate skin. Both her hands were caught in one of his. They felt small and fragile for all their strength.

His mouth tightened. By all rights, she should have been safe at home instead of caught up in the madness of men intent on war. Had she been his daughter, or better yet, his intended wife, he would have moved heaven and earth to keep her safe. Yet that team of blunderheads, O'Neill and O'Donnell, had gone marching off down the road to war with never a thought for what they left behind. Fools!

A notion, tempting in its starkness, spread through him. He was an earl, sweet heaven, enjoying enormous wealth and power, and a loyal servant of Elizabeth's to boot. England was effectively at war with Ulster. Was not Deirdre therefore a prize of war, possession of the man strong enough to claim her? Would not his queen gladly honor such a fitting reward for his efforts, especially given that it would cost Elizabeth herself nothing?

It was something to mull over as the horse's swiftly pounding hooves carried them over the miles. Following the narrow tracks away from the main roads, they changed direction often. Toward dark, Delacroix drew rein in a small glen surrounded by high, concealing trees. A brook ran nearby, gurgling over stones whose moss drapings gentled the sound. All was fragrant earth and night stillness.

He dismounted holding Deirdre, and laid her down gently before turning his attention to his mount. She woke a short time later, confused, and sat up quickly. She was wrapped in a soft cloak that smelled of wood smoke. Some little distance away she could make out the shape of the horse, grazing placidly. Another shape loomed by a small fire set in scooped-out ground to hide most of its light.

Harpsinger. She shrugged off the enveloping cloak and struggled to her feet. She was disoriented, still tired and plagued by thirst, but she heeded none of that. Without thought or hesitation, she ran.

Delacroix cursed under his breath. He should have expected this, but she had been sleeping so peacefully, and looking so innocent in the bargain, that he had told himself she wouldn't do anything foolish. Instead, here she was flinging herself into the woods without thought of what that would mean to her own safety. Apparently, she found the solid darkness and the threat of predators, human and animal, both preferable to his company. A sobering thought, but one he undeniably deserved for being so witless where she was concerned.

Grimly, he shot to his feet and went after her. Deirdre heard him coming and swallowed a scream of purest terror. Her lungs burned and her heart pounded wildly. A moment more she ran, another, and then he was on her, bringing her down with a swift, remorseless surge. She fell heavily, and would have been hurt had he not shifted his weight enough to take the brunt of the fall himself. He landed on his back with her above him, but turned swiftly, holding her flat beneath.

"Are you witless?" he demanded. His breath came harshly as the full impact of what could have happened to her sank in. Rage rose in him at the thought that she would dare to put herself at such risk. "Do you have any idea what could have happened to you out there? This bedeviled land of yours is falling toward war. Violence scents the air. You could have ended praying for death."

Deirdre gaped at him. She couldn't help it; what he said made absolutely no sense. He was angry at her for trying to get away because she might have been killed as a result? Was this the same man who had threatened to take her life if her father's guards dared follow them?

"I, witless?" she shot back. "You said you would kill me. What choice do I have but to try to get away?"

Delacroix stared at her. In the faint light, he could just make out the pale oval of her face, the unnaturally big eyes luminous with unshed tears and the full, moist lips trembling slightly.

"Damnation," he muttered, "don't tell me you believed that?"

Deirdre hadn't thought it possible to be more befuddled, but she managed it. Had she been sipping fairy dew? Had she wandered unknowing behind a waterfall and slipped into the nether world? Or had she simply lost her senses? "Of course I believed it. What was I supposed to think?"

He had the grace to look abashed. "I only said that for the guards." Regret was clear in his eyes. His tone was soft, almost caressing. "Deirdre, you must know I would never hurt you." Indeed, the mere thought of his being the source of fear to her disgusted him. He wanted only to cherish and protect her.

All right, not only that. Holding her as he was, he was becoming aroused. The sweet softness of her body pressed to his, the rapid beat of her heart discernible beneath the thin tunic she wore, the knowledge that they were at last truly alone, all combined to make him desire her even more than usual. Only the fear he felt in her stopped him. He could not, would not, indulge his own needs when she was in the grip of such terror.

Abruptly, he got to his feet and pulled her upright. Keeping a firm hold, he led her back to the fire. "You will behave yourself. I have enough to think on without worrying about keeping you safe. I'll tie you if I must, but I would rather have your word you will not try anything so stupid again. Do I have it?"

Deirdre hesitated. He really was the most insulting man, not to mention infuriating. Lying to her, kidnapping her, berating her for trying to escape, which was clearly her right as well as duty, and then turning around and saying he would accept her parole not to try it again.

Without relinquishing his hold on her, he tossed

another piece of wood on the fire, sending up a shower of sparks. As they settled back down, Deirdre said stiffly, "I cannot give my word until I know who I am giving it to."

"You know who I am."

"I know you entered my father's house under false pretenses. To think otherwise, I would indeed have to be witless. You are not what you claimed, and until I know who you are, I can promise you nothing."

Delacroix hesitated. She was right, of course. No man would give his word to one he did not know, and a woman could not rightly be expected to do otherwise. And yet if he told her, she would hate him without restraint.

So be it, then, there was no alternative.

"My name is John Delacroix. I am the earl of Bradford and various other things. Her Majesty, the queen, sent me to Ulster to learn what I could of your father's intentions."

The ground seemed to move under Deirdre. She feared she might actually faint. Her cheeks flushed as she glared at him. "You are lying. I have heard you in hall. You are a true bard and you have the Gaelic. How can you be this thing you say, this . . . this *earl?*" She uttered the last with such curdling disdain as to make Delacroix think that all the nobility of England, living and dead, must surely rise up to protest her contempt.

But as for him, he could not do it. She had every right to despise him. He accepted that and yet, lackwit that he was, the fact that she still called him a true bard was as a tiny ray of light in the gathering darkness of his soul.

With great dignity, always handy in moments of

such crisis, he said, "I am exactly as I have told you. My mother was Irish; hence the language. As for being a bard, I never thought to be any such thing until Elizabeth bade me here."

"You don't just wake up one day and say now I will be a bard. You have studied . . . worked . . ."

"It was a gift from my childhood," he said softly, "long ago. Since I became a man, I have been a warrior. The rest . . . was a half-forgotten dream."

Deirdre refused to believe him. She had heard him, she knew he had the gift. How could he deny it, how could he claim to be this . . . this thing he said he was? If a true bard could be an English spy, chaos had the world by the throat and nothing could be trusted anymore.

"You remembered well enough when you came to Dungannon," she said. "You were welcomed there, honored. Damn you! How could you do so foul a thing?"

Still holding her, he said grimly, "I am earl of Bradford, Elizabeth's man. My loyalty is to her. Your father must be stopped. Now, do I have your word or not?"

When still she hesitated, he said more gently, "There is no dishonor in this, Deirdre. Parole has always been honorable, even between adversaries. Give it and we will get through this business with as little fuss as possible."

"What business? What exactly are you about?"

"I must find Bagenal and convince him to withdraw. There is still time for negotiation. Your father can see reason, and so can Elizabeth. There does not have to be war."

Her eyes, drowning pools that they were, drew him in yet further. A look of sorrow flitted through them, so intense that for a moment he was pierced to the quick.

"You are a dreamer," she murmured, "and you do not even know it."

Stung, he shook his head. "We are finished discussing what I am. Your word or no?"

She lifted her chin and met his eyes. "If you speak truth, if all you want is to find Bagenal and convince him to withdraw, then you have my word. I will not try to escape unless I discover you have lied. If you go to join Bagenal, to betray our defenses, I swear before almighty God I will kill you myself!"

Coming from so delicate and vulnerable a woman, that could have been funny. But Delacroix saw no humor in it. He did not question that she meant exactly what she said. Further, he didn't dismiss the possibility, however unlikely, that she might actually manage it.

With a low mutter, he put her from him. Deliberately, he ignored her as he went over to the brook to drink. She watched him warily as he returned and opened the pouch he'd brought. His harp was inside, along with a few extra clothes, a loaf of bread, and a chunk of cheese.

He broke off a piece of the bread and offered it to her. She drew back from his outstretched hand and shook her head. He shrugged and proceeded to eat.

Silence reigned for long moments before Deirdre spoke. "How long have you been an earl?"

"Since Candlemas last. Why?"

"I wonder how it is my father did not know you. He spent a great deal of time, too much, at the English

169

court, and other of our people have done the same. If he didn't recognize you, Red Hugh certainly should have."

Delacroix sighed. At least she was talking, which was preferable to the cold silence that was one of womankind's most tried-and-true weapons—along with tears, which saints knew would have been even worse. All the same, he could be pardoned for wishing she had picked some other topic.

Reluctantly, he replied. "I was a distant relative of the family, lately come to the earldom through a string of deaths hard upon each other. No one knew me because I had never been to court. That was part of why Elizabeth chose me for this mission."

"I see," Deirdre said slowly, although indeed she did not, at least not yet. "Lately come," he had said, and "since Candlemas last," so he had been earl not yet a year. And he had never been at court. Truly, Elizabeth must have rubbed her gnarled hands with glee when she learned of him.

"You spent your life fighting other people's wars until being summoned home to England?"

"Something like that," he admitted, hardly liking the description though it was apt enough. "I had left the service of the tsar and was traveling when word of the deaths reached me."

"Convenient for you that you weren't in England when they happened."

"Indeed," he said, taking no offense. Suspicion was the way of the world. Indeed, if her people had remembered that a bit more, his would have been a different story.

"So you haven't actually lived in England?"

"Only a few months when I was a boy."

Deirdre smiled. Never mind the outrageousness of the situation. There was something about a good debate that stirred the blood, especially when she knew she was going to win it.

"No wonder you support Elizabeth. You don't know any better. If you'd lived under her rule, suffered her oppression, you'd have other ideas, you would."

Delacroix was not impressed. He took another bite of the bread, swallowed it, and said, "Oppression? I knew a captain in the tsar's personal guard who slaughtered two hundred men, women, and children because a wheel of his carriage had come off on a road that went through their village. It put him in a bad humor, and he unleashed his troops on them. That's oppression."

"Elizabeth has burned Catholics," Deirdre countered.

"After the pope named her heretic and excommunicated her. She executed people she believed were trying to overthrow her. Any sovereign can be expected to do the same."

"She denies Ireland its freedom. We have no need of English rulers, and they have no rights over us."

"Perhaps not, but Ireland is the back door to England. So long as Irish chieftains connive with her enemies, Elizabeth can be expected to use any measures in her reach to stop them."

"Forgive me," Deirdre said sarcastically, "but I don't see Ireland in quite those terms. For me, it is a good deal more than anyone's 'back door.'"

"It doesn't matter what it is to you," Delacroix said. "What matters is who is stronger, and that is England.

English power keeps the peace, and will continue to do so given half a chance. Your father has to see that. An alliance with Elizabeth is as much in his interest as anyone else's."

Deirdre shifted slightly on the ground, seeking a more comfortable position. Her stomach rumbled, but she ignored it. "You keep speaking of alliance, but you must know it is impossible. Elizabeth wants far too much power for her to accept an independent ruler in Ireland."

"That remains to be seen. Given the right incentive, people will surprise even themselves. But enough, it grows late and we must rest. Come here."

She froze, staring at him. The night closed in, reminding her of their solitude. It was madness to be alone in the night far from home and without even her maid to keep watch on her.

"No," she said.

Delacroix stood up. He put the remainder of the bread and cheese back in the pouch and laid it carefully aside. He poked the fire a bit with a long piece of green wood. Only when that was done did he walk toward her.

Deirdre stiffened, but she had given her word not to flee again. Besides, there was no point; he had already proven how easily he could control her when he chose.

Standing over her, dark and tall against the night, Delacroix put his hands on his hips and considered what to do. She was frightened, that much was obvious, and not without cause. Difficult though it was to remember sometimes, she was a gently reared maiden. Add healer and hellcat and you more or less had her.

He smiled inwardly. Simple, straightforward women had always been his natural preference. Lately, though, he had come to think them boring. Deirdre was anything but.

He bent down slowly so as not to startle her unduly. Softly, in the same tone he would use to a frightened mare, he said, "It will grow cold in the night, and animals may come prowling. I would have you near to me to keep you warm and protect you should the need occur."

"How noble," she murmured, almost choking on the words. The thought of lying in his arms . . .

Hail Mary, full of grace, the Lord is with you. Blessed art thou—

Prayer didn't work. Her mind kept wandering in contrary directions, all of them sufficient to make her blush.

"Your word," she said. "I would have it."

"What word?"

Her flush deepened. "That you would not . . . that is . . . you would respect . . ."

"You fear for your virtue."

"Have I no cause?"

Ah, honesty, betrayer of the fondest deceptions. How infinitely satisfying to affect shock, even offense that she would think him capable of any such thing. How pleasing to clutch his sterling moral character to his breast and gaze hurt-eyed at the source of such unmerited offense.

How false. His loins were already hard, although, praise her innocence, he didn't believe she had noticed. The long night ahead promised to be among the least comfortable he had ever experienced, but he would get through it. And he would keep her safe no matter what she thought.

But he was damned if he was going to plead with her in the bargain. "I will not harm you," he said stiffly. "You will have to be satisfied with that. Now do as I tell you."

He expected her to obey then as any reasonable man would, for surely she understood his temper had its limits? But Deirdre had another thought.

"What, exactly, do you mean by harm?" she persisted.

Delacroix stared at her. He had heard of certain men in Elizabeth's court who argued thusly. They were called lawyers, and there was some discussion about whether they might benefit from burning.

"You astound me," he said, meaning it. "I guarantee your safety—indeed, I pledge to protect you—and still you argue with me?"

"I am not arguing. I am simply trying to define terms. When one is giving parole, that is very important. There are men who might think . . . or claim . . ."

To his surprise, Delacroix discovered that he was suddenly enjoying himself. She looked so adorable when she blushed, and her attempts to describe what certain men might think, presumably about deflowering maidens, were the far side of ridiculous. Still, it wouldn't do to laugh.

"Deirdre," he said gently, "not harm means exactly what it sounds like. It holds no falsehood within it. I will do nothing improper, immoral, illegal, or illicit. Does that convince you?"

"I suppose it will have to."

"Good," he said with heartfelt relief. "Then perhaps we can get some rest."

Perhaps he could, but she could not possibly be expected to sleep wrapped in his arms, snug against the hard length of him, with the cloak spread over them both and the soft Irish night gathered around them. There was no chance of that at all. She would be awake to dawn and beyond. But that was to the good, for it would give her time to think over the failings of her nature that led her to feel a rush of gladness at merely being near to him. She would pray and repent of her sins, she would beseech God to make her a better person, worthy of her position in life. She would remember all the good and wise words Mother Justina had said to her all those years in the abbey hard by the stones and the sea. Even now, she could almost hear the waves pounding against the beach, carrying her with them far from thought and worry. She would think on that, consider its meaning, and . . .

She slept.

CHAPTER
13

A WARM, SEEKING MOUTH DREW DEIRDRE FROM her dreams. She smiled and moved closer, wanting more of the delightful sensations being unleashed within her. She murmured and raised a hand, brushing the hard strength above her. At the contact, remembrance flooded through her. Jerked to full wakefulness, she stiffened and had to force herself not to cry out.

John Delacroix, earl of Bradford and her captor, was still deeply asleep. He lay on his side with her drawn close against him. His face, darkened by the night's growth of beard, was nestled into the curve of her shoulder. He moved slightly, and his mouth brushed her throat again. A shudder went through her. She told herself it was fear and revulsion, but it was anything but. Desperately, she closed her eyes, fighting the treacherous pleasure. A moan rose within her.

Delacroix's arm tightened. Even asleep as he was, the warm, willing woman in his embrace filled him with desire. His hand moved, cupping her breast, the thumb caressing the rigid nipple through the thin linen of her gown. He pressed his hard length on her. A muscled thigh slid between slender limbs. She moaned again, her hands clutching his hair, and called his name.

"Harpsinger . . ."

The sound penetrated sleep, and more. It reached beyond the languid heat of passion to bring him suddenly, acutely awake. Who called him that? Only one person he could think of, and she surely the last he should be lying on, pressed between her legs and scant moments from delving deep within her inviting warmth.

For a long, tense moment, they stared into each other's eyes. Deirdre's heart pounded. The heat, the scent, the touch of him all engulfed her. Desperately, she struggled not against him but against herself, fighting the temptation to forget duty, family, honor, and be only the woman she became in his arms.

Deirdre might have won that struggle or she might not have. As it happened, Delacroix decided the matter for them both. He pushed her away abruptly and got to his feet. With his back to her, he ran a hand through the thick, golden mane of his hair and struggled to gather his thoughts.

The glen was flooded with the gray light that precedes dawn. Songbirds twittered in the branches above. The horse stirred nearby, tossing his head and beginning to graze. Tendrils of mist moved among the trees. The air was sweetly scented, soft with moisture, and refreshingly cool. He drew it into his lungs, hoping it would ease the raging heat that threatened to consume him.

So much for honor. Where she was concerned, he apparently had none. The simple release of sleep was enough to free his baser nature and make a mockery of his pledges to her. Grimly, he turned back to her intent on apologizing, only to be stopped when he saw the look on her face.

She appeared . . . ashamed. Yes, that was the word, although for a moment he was at a loss as to understand why. Only gradually did it occur to him that he had not been alone in his passion. She had been there with him. Moreover, she knew it.

"Deirdre," he said softly as he took a step toward her.

She raised a hand, holding him off. "Please, don't say anything. I know I behaved very badly. I am so sorry. I don't seem to be myself around you. That is, I am but I can't control . . . What I mean . . ." Her blush deepened. She gave up and got to her feet, hoping that a merciful God might allow her to simply disappear or, failing that, turn her into something useful—a tree, a bush, a bird—as had been done to wayward maidens in sensible times gone by.

No more, though; she was stuck exactly where she was. Delacroix had the most peculiar look on his face. She dared a peek at it and wondered what would make a man appear so oddly tender at such a moment.

"Never mind," he said gruffly. "See to your needs. We are leaving."

Deirdre needed no urging to obey. She hurried off, glad of the few minutes of privacy to gather the shreds of her composure.

Left alone in the glen, Delacroix began saddling the horse, but his mind was on other things. Specifically, he was trying to remember how many men he had killed over the course of his life. He had always held to the belief that a man coming at him with a weapon and murder in his eye rightly deserved death, but apparently he had been wrong. Certainly, God must be punishing him for something. If it wasn't the killing, what was it? What had he done to condemn himself to this fever of unrequited and most inappropriate desire? No answer immediately presented itself.

Deirdre returned, still not looking at him, and suffered to be lifted onto the saddle. She held her head high, but the flush remained on her cheeks. When he slid up behind her, she stiffened.

"Easy," he murmured, reaching carefully around her to secure the reins. "We have a long way to go."

She nodded but said nothing. They rode in silence through the morning. At midday, they stopped to finally break their fast. Deirdre accepted the bread and cheese but ate only a small amount. Delacroix lacked appetite as well. All his senses were keenly alert. He was aware of Deirdre in every possible way, but there was more as well. Every tread of the horse, every movement in the underbrush reminded him that danger could erupt at any moment. He had no weapon except his knife, unless his harp could be counted. That was a whimsical notion that made him smile, but the good humor was fleeting. Soon enough they had to leave the trails they had been following and venture out onto the main road. It ran along the river Blackwater that flowed south of Dungannon. They crossed the river at a place called Yellow Ford and had continued only a little way before they saw the first evidence of Bagenal's troops. Several hundred strong, they were making camp for the evening.

Among the tents already pitched and those being raised, good English archers and pike men settled at their fires to heat a pot of water, chew a bit of beef, and crack a keg of ale. Some of the men were sharpening weapons on whirling whetstones set in motion by foot pumps. Young boys stood behind the stones throwing water on them to keep the grinding fine. Some of the archers were restringing their longbows and oiling the steel rasps that aimed the arrow true. But for the most part there was only quiet talk absent any sign of revelry. Bagenal's army looked fit enough, but somber.

A few of the men glanced up as Delacroix guided the horse through the camp, but no one made any effort to stop them. Presumably had they been a horde of attacking Irish, the response would have been different. Still, Delacroix was not impressed by their security. It bespoke overconfidence, which in his experience never led anywhere good.

Deirdre's hands were tightly clenched as she fought against the fear rising in her. In the heart of the enemy's camp, she had never been more vulnerable. If her identity became known, she would be lucky to find death. Worse, Bagenal might decide to use her as a weapon against her father. It all depended on what Delacroix chose to do. He had promised his protection, but could she trust him?

They continued without restraint until they reached the scarlet tent set in the center of the encampment. There a guard finally challenged them. He was a young man, dressed in breastplate and helmet with a pike held upright before him. Although he tried his best to look the grizzled veteran, he failed utterly.

"Hold," he demanded. "State your name and business."

Delacroix looked down at him coldly, his eyes narrowed to steely glints. "Go tell your master, Sir Henry, that the Earl of Bradford is here."

The guard's mouth dropped open. He stared at the big, hard man on the horse with the beautiful woman in his arms. Nothing in the man's garb supported any such claim, but there was an aura of power and danger that communicated itself clearly.

Still, the guard wasn't totally a fool. "I can't go tell him that," he protested. "He'd have me head if you're lying."

Delacroix smiled. Bagenal might be an idiot when it came to setting up a camp in unsecure territory, but at least this plain English soldier had his wits about him. From a pocket sewn into his shirt, he removed the ring Elizabeth had given him. "Show Sir Henry this," he said.

They waited perhaps two minutes before the guard was back again. He handed the ring back with great deference. "Your pardon, milord. Sir Henry bids you welcome."

Delacroix repressed the urge to voice his doubt of that. He swung from the saddle and lifted Deirdre down. "Chin up, lass," he said softly. "Think what a story you'll have to tell round the fire when this is all said and done."

She managed a wan smile, which vanished when they stepped into the tent. Three men were seated among ornate furnishings better suited to a Moorish palace than an army in the field. Sir Henry clearly liked his comforts. Two of the men were relatively young. They wore velvet doublets slashed to show their brightly hued silk linings and short breeches to the knee, with tight hose held by satin garters below. Great froths of lace rose at their throats and wrists. Their hair was styled in elaborate pompadours, their beards and mustaches waxed. Jewels gleamed at their fingers and along the hilts of the ceremonial daggers displayed at their sides.

The third man was older, thick around the waist with thinning brown hair, and even more elaborately turned out. He sat in a thronelike chair. Delacroix wondered how they managed to haul that along with an army on the march. His expression was cautious, but the plump cheeks were flushed and the small mouth drawn taut. Clearly, Delacroix's arrival did not please him.

"My lord," he said as he stood ponderously, coming not quite erect in reluctant acknowledgment of the other man's far greater rank. His small, black eyes flitted from the big golden man to the woman at his side and back again. "We are hardly fit to receive you. You sent no word of your coming."

"Had you remained in Armagh," Delacroix said "you would have received word. Instead, you go off half-cocked and put me to the trouble of tracking you across the face of Ulster."

Deirdre's eyes widened. He sounded every inch the aristocrat, this mercenary's son come to the nobility through the most unlikely circumstances. Bagenal certainly thought so, for though his angry flush deepened, he made no attempt to defend himself. The ring was proof enough that this devil earl came from Elizabeth herself, but his knowledge that Bagenal had left Armagh without royal authorization made his importance unmistakable. He had the confidence of the queen even to the extent of knowing what she had ordered and what she had not.

"We will discuss all this," Delacroix went on in the same way, "but first—" He turned to Deirdre and deliberately gentled his manner. "The lady requires rest." His glance fell on the two younger men who gazed at her with undisguised lechery. His voice hardened again. "She is under my protection and will receive every courtesy. I trust that is clear?"

"Perfectly, my lord," Bagenal said hastily. He glared at his young aides. "Farthington, vacate your tent. He'll quarter with you, Blansworth. Send a servant for the lady, also wine." On an afterthought, he added, "Food as well. I trust you will dine with me, my lord? You won't be disappointed, my table's among the best. Can't leave civilization completely behind, can we? Although I don't mind telling you, its damnably hard to maintain any sort of standards in this country. The people are the worse sort of villains—lazy, stupid, dirty. But if you've been here any length of time, you know that. Now, then—" He broke off his nervous chatter as a servant entered, bowing low.

"Show the lady to Sir Charles Farthington's tent and give him what help is needed clearing out of it." He turned to Deirdre but avoided actually looking at her, which was just as well. If looks could kill, Sir Henry would have been on his way to his maker. "I trust you will be comfortable, madame. Whatever you require, we will endeavor to provide it."

She took a step toward the door but was stopped by Delacroix. He lifted her hand in his own and, holding her eyes, kissed it gently. "I will be with you shortly."

The touch of his lips burned. For an instant, she was back in the glen, held beneath him. She was tempted to yank her hand away, but forced herself to smile instead. Nothing could protect her better in this camp of armed men than the clear understanding that she belonged to the haughty earl of Bradford. Never mind what that did to her pride and dignity, she would simply have to live with it if she wanted to live at all.

"My lord," she murmured. Her lips smiled, but her eyes were as defiant as he had ever seen them. Ruefully, he released her hand and watched as she followed the servant into the cool evening air.

"Lovely thing that," Sir Henry murmured when she was gone. "Wherever did you find her?"

"In Ulster," Delacroix said. He took the chair the high marshal had been using, leaving the other man to find himself a smaller and less comfortable seat. "I have been there at Her Majesty's behest." Sir Henry's small eyes widened. Clearly, it had not occurred to him that Elizabeth had an agent in the rebellious province.

"You understand," Delacroix went on, "that Her Majesty has laid her plans very carefully? Interference with them is neither welcome nor wise."

"With all respect," Sir Henry said, his voice trembling, "it is easy for those at court to decide what needs to be done. Here in the field we often see things differently."

"*We*, sirrah? Don't you mean yourself? *You* made the decision to leave Armargh and sally across the border. *You* took it upon yourself to challenge the O'Neill directly and give him the excuse he wants to turn talk of rebellion into true revolt. God's blood, man, how do you imagine this will be received at court? Her Majesty will be enraged. All her careful strategy, all the months of planning, wiped away by one idiot marshal who couldn't follow orders."

This last part was a gamble. First, he had no idea if

Elizabeth was planning anything at all, much less that she had a careful strategy. All she had done was send him to Ulster, not take him into her confidence. Secondly, he had to hope Sir Henry truly was acting without authorization. If he was wrong . . .

He wasn't, not if Sir Henry's reaction was anything to judge by. Sir Henry paled and reached for the wine the servant had brought, pouring a generous measure but slopping even more on the table. He took a long swallow and wiped his mouth with his hand. "No one told me Her Majesty had any grand design. Pacify Ireland, she said when she sent me here. How am I supposed to do that when that spawn of hell, Hugh O'Neill, is running loose in Ulster?" Gaining strength in his outrage, he went on. "Do you have any idea the problems he creates? Every hopped-up bog dweller fancies himself a king. He declares rebellion, trains an army, and then what does he do? He holds a tourney, that's what. He thinks to me a fool, to flaunt himself before me. Well, let me tell you, before I'm through he'll regret the day he slighted Sir Henry Bagenal!"

"No, Sir Henry," Delacroix said, rising from his chair. A shudder ran through the smaller man at so much power uncoiled in cold rage. "Any regret will be your own. You will return to Armagh and leave the O'Neill to Her Majesty. *If* the day comes when she orders you into battle, then you will fight. But by God you will not take it upon yourself to lead England into war because of your injured pride."

"You have no right!" Sir Henry sputtered. "Earl you may be, but I am high marshal. I hold the queen's authority, I speak in her name. Yes, it is my decision to fight, but I stand by it. O'Neill must be crushed. We will rid Ireland of his loathsome presence once and for all. The queen will applaud my efforts. She will recognize the good I have done and reward it. I will not fail!"

"Fool! You will shatter any chance of peace with Ireland for a hundred years. There will not be another moment like this, with a strong Irish leader on the rise who can unite the country as England's ally. Think, man. All Elizabeth wants is for Ireland to be secure. Friends are always far more trustworthy than a foe nurturing its hatred and plotting vengeance."

For a moment, doubt flitted across Sir Henry's porcine features. But it vanished quickly, washed away in the desperate confidence that had the man in its deadly grip. "Friends? Ally? Ireland can never be that. Your sojourn in Ulster has dulled your wits if you believe otherwise. We fight for the glory of Britannia, and by God, we will win! Stay and observe our victory or go, it makes no difference to me. But we hold to our course."

Delacroix turned on his heel and walked from the tent. It was either that or throttle the man. Nothing drained his patience faster than stupidity, and that Sir Henry had in astounding abundance. So much so that he didn't even have the sense to bow before the greater authority of the queen's agent. The lust to avenge an imagined insult wiped out even the simplest survival instinct.

How much time was left? He and Deirdre had managed to reach Bagenal in little more than a day. They were traveling by fast horse, whereas the O'Neill was hampered by the need to move an entire army. He would be a day off, but not more. Scant time to make any difference now. From all he had seen, the armies were well matched. The battle would be close. A decisive outcome was unlikely. All that would happen would be a quantity of men being slaughtered for no good reason, just as he had seen so many times over the course of his life.

In the grimmest of moods, Delacroix stalked into the tent lately vacated by the hapless Farthington. It was smaller than Sir Henry's but no less plushly outfitted. Were they going to war or a court ball, these half-wit lords playing at being warriors? They seemed to think it was all some glorious escapade designed to load them down with glory, when in fact war was—

He broke off in midthought and stared at the vision before him. Clearly, Deirdre had expected him to be gone some time yet. Otherwise, she would not have ordered bathwater and begun to disrobe. The pale ivory length of her back was exposed, as well as the soft curve of her breasts. She clutched the gown to her and stared at him in shock.

"I thought . . ." she murmured.

Delacroix grimaced at the remorseless surge of passion that tore through him. He had given her his word, he could not violate it, but sweet lord, surely the rack would be better than this? Harshly, he said, "Garb yourself."

He turned away as she did so. When he turned back, his face was grim. The tent seemed to shrink. There was no room to move, no safe distance to separate them. Deirdre's face was white. Her ebony hair, unbound, hung to her waist in thick, wavy tendrils. She stared at him warily.

"It did not go well?"

"Bagenal is an idiot. He has some half-wit vision of glory he cannot relinquish."

Deirdre shrugged. She was not at all surprised.
"He is English."

"What's that supposed to mean?" Delacroix
snarled. He was in no mood to bandy words when all
he really wanted to do was lie her beneath him and
sheathe his aching manhood to its hilt. She would feel
so good around him, so tight and hot. The release
would be rebirth, but afterward? Honor, cold mistress
that she was, reared her unforgiving head.

Deirdre ignored the trembling in her limbs and
refused to be cowed by him as any sensible woman
would have been—sense being highly overrated in her
estimate. "It means that the English always do this sort
of thing. They like to say we're the ones who are emo-
tional and undisciplined, but how many times have
they gone raging out to kill Irish simply because their
tempers got the better of them? Too many times. My
father knows it, and that's how he lured Bagenal to . . ."

She broke off, horrified by what she had just
revealed. The look on Delacroix's face was terrible to
see. He crossed the small distance between them and
took hard hold of her.

"Tell me," he demanded. "I should have forced it
from you yesterday, but I let it go by, thinking Bagenal
would listen to reason. Now it is clear he won't. What
is your father planning, Deirdre? What has he done?"

"Nothing," she insisted, shaking her head frantically. The cloud of ebony silk floated around them both,
brushing his hands and filling the air with the scent of
lilacs. Desire roared through him. He shut his eyes
against it. When he opened them again a moment later,
his gaze was as cold as the icy tundras of the Rus where
he had learned so well the lessons of war.

"The tournament was no whim," he said, almost to himself. "It was a lure to draw Bagenal out of Armagh. But why? I saw your father's army; it matches ours but no more. Why would he choose to provoke battle now?"

At her silence, his grip hardened further. "You will tell me, Deirdre. What has led your father to do this?"

"Ask Bagenal," she snapped. "He will tell you that we Irish are irrational. Clearly, my father is mad."

"Don't be a fool, and don't think me one. Your father may be many things, but there is nothing wrong with his wits. Why does he do this?"

"Perhaps you are the one who is mad, English, if you think I tell you anything. Even if I knew the answer, I would die before I revealed it."

"You don't know," Delacroix said, confirming what he saw in her face. "But you do suspect. You have had a day and more to wonder at it, and you've come to some conclusion. I can see that."

"You see nothing, English! You understand nothing. All you know how to do is lie."

He ignored her outburst and continued to study her face with care. Softly, he said, "The O'Neill declares rebellion, trains his army, allies with Red Hugh, courts the Spaniards, and then . . . he throws a tourney. He lures Bagenal out, intending to meet him in equal combat. Or does he? I saw the army march . . . I saw . . ." He broke off, his gaze suddenly shuttered. As though from a great distance, his voice came. "I saw *an* army march. It was there for anyone to see. Even a blind man would have known what was passing. God's blood, I *am* a fool!"

A harsh laugh broke from him. He thrust her away so hard that she lost her balance and fell. Staring up at him, she saw the understanding etched starkly on his face. "You Irish truly do love a good performance, and you know how to give one yourself. Your father has other forces, doesn't he? Secreted away from Dungannon but ready to join him at a moment's notice. He doesn't mean to rout Bagenal. He intends to destroy him and end English rule in Ireland once and for all."

"And why not?" Deirdre demanded, fury in her eyes. You Irish, he said, making clear how great was the chasm between them. Never mind the poetry and the Gaelic, he was all English, this proud earl. And as such he was lost to her forever.

"Stay here," he ordered. "Do not attempt to leave this tent, or I swear before God you will be severely punished."

"Where are you going?" she demanded, all but choking on the words.

He turned and looked back at her, still lying tumbled onto the soft Araby rug. His expression was inscrutable. "To Bagenal. It is still not too late to make him see reason."

The tent flap swung shut behind him. Deirdre remained where she was, all the strength gone out of her. It would return, she had no doubt of that, and when it did, she would act. But for the moment, there was only terrible, wrenching grief.

He went to Bagenal to tell him of her father's forces, exactly as he had promised he would not when he demanded her parole. The pledge between them was broken.

Shakily, Deirdre got to her feet. In the midst of the enemy camp, threatened with the direst consequences if she took a step outside the tent, she began to plot her escape.

CHAPTER
14

SIR CHARLES FARTHINGTON DID NOT REGARD war casually. He required nothing less than three trunks of clothing, each item seemingly more glorious than the last. Deirdre made no attempt to go through them all. She helped herself to hose and a doublet, and dressed quickly. As she did, she kept watch over her shoulder, fearing Delacroix might suddenly reappear. When he did not, she breathed a small sigh of relief. It faded quickly before the enormity of the task still confronting her.

Grief still throbbed deep within her, but she refused to yield to it. Only duty mattered now, and for that she needed all the courage she could muster.

From the tent's entrance, she surveyed what she could see of the camp. Little stirred. In the gathering twilight, the English soldiers continued about their small, domestic tasks, seeing to their comforts as best they could. No one so much as glanced in her direction when she slipped from the tent and moved as quickly as she dared toward the nearest horse pen. With her hair tucked beneath a rakish cap festooned with a purple plume, she looked like a slender boy outfitted for a day at court, not a desperate woman fleeing an enemy camp on the verge of war.

Her heart hammered painfully. Despite the balmy weather, she was cold with fear. A step, another, she was at the edge of the pen, close to the simple rope barrier that enclosed it. Horses milled around, a few whinnying nervously as they caught her scent. Farthington favored a pungent perfume that permeated his clothing. Deirdre wrinkled her nose at it. Her eye caught a medium-sized gray mare standing a little distance from the other horses. Gathering her courage, she slipped under the rope and approached the horse. In her hand, she held the bridle and reins she had found in the tent.

The horse whinnied and danced sideways. "Easy, girl," Deirdre murmured. She reached out a hand, gently stroking the mare's silken nose. "We're going for a nice ride, just the two of us. You'll love it. Over the hills we'll go, like the wind. I'll be light on your back, I promise, and you'll miss all that man-fool battle nonsense that's coming. You're much too sweet for that anyway. Here now, almost done . . ."

She had no saddle, having decided that any effort to obtain one would risk drawing attention to herself. But in her childhood, she had often ridden bareback and had no hesitation about doing so now. With the help of a convenient rock, she clambered onto the mare's back. It wasn't graceful, and she did have to wonder if she mightn't have picked a smaller mount. But the feel of the mare's strength beneath her was reassuring. She patted her side as she murmured, "Good girl. Now we ride. Like the wind, sweetling, like the wind."

A young archer only lately come from his home in the green hills of Wessex, and wishing with all his heart that he was back there, looked up in time to see the dandy riding out on his fine gray mare. Trust the nobs, he thought, to go prancing about as though they hadn't a worry in the world. Any sensible man, among which he counted himself, drank his beer, said his prayers, and tried his best not to think of the morrow. Certainly, he did not bestir himself to wonder why the nob was riding without a saddle. If he broke his neck, he could explain it to the devil.

The archer turned away to refill his mug. When he looked again, the gray horse was gone, vanished into the fading light.

An hour later, Delacroix returned to the tent. He came weary in heart and soul. Bagenal refused to be moved. He dismissed out of hand the notion that O'Neill had deliberately lured him into a trap. The Irish weren't capable of such sophisticated planning, he asserted. They were a primitive, simple people much given to grandiose notions but no good at all turning them into action. And besides, even if Ulster's force was larger than originally thought, it made no difference. He would defeat them anyway, and the victory would be all the more glorious.

Delacroix shook his head in disgust. It did not escape him that the same monarch who sent him to Ulster had also chosen Sir Henry as her high marshal. He still nurtured the hope that Elizabeth and the O'Neill could be brought to see reason, but any chance of that was fading fast.

War had always struck him as a wasteful business, no matter how good he got at it. Now he was more certain of that than ever. When this was over, he was going back to England, settle on his land, and devote himself to whatever it was earls did. Hunting maybe, although he found that boring. Perhaps he'd learn about farming or study Greek. Or he could raise horses, he liked them. A few dogs would be nice as well. Anything but war.

While he was at it, he ought to think about acquiring a wife. A man of his position was generally expected to have one, if only for the necessity of getting heirs. After all the trouble he was going to, he'd be damned if some third or fourth cousin would claim the earldom after him. He'd have a son of his own to do that, perhaps more than one, for the world held plenty more opportunities for those strong enough to seize them.

A wife. He almost flinched at the thought, having so little experience with such creatures. But women he did know, and one in particular had lately come to occupy his attentions far too much. He smiled wryly, thinking of the progress he was making. Wasn't it only a day since he'd been thinking of her as a prize of war, a favored possession to be kept and enjoyed? Now here he was making the leap to matrimony. Mayhap Sir Henry's stupidity was contagious, but the notion didn't seem all that terrible.

Until, that is, he entered the tent. Quiet reigned, the deep, unnatural quiet of emptiness where there is supposed to be activity. She should be eating, sleeping, bathing, sulking, ranting, throwing things, anything. She should be right there where he had told her to be, and dammit, she was not!

What kind of fool woman would go wandering around an enemy camp? Obviously, she had been overly indulged as a child. Her father must not have the faintest notion of discipline. He was left with no choice; he would have to be harsh at first, but afterward she would understand he acted in her best interest, she would be contrite and repentant exactly as a woman ought to be. Then he could be gentle, then he could let her see—

It had to be the air, the light, the water, something about this fairy-addled Eire that so distorted his reason. But he would fight it. He would not indulge in this maddening mixture of desire and tenderness that shook the very underpinnings of his nature. He was a warrior, and it was past time he acted it.

Delacroix stormed out of the tent. No expression that but simple truth. He came with the fury of the bursting heavens, startling the men lounging nearby so badly that several of them stumbled to their feet reaching for their weapons. They subsided when they realized it wasn't a horde of crazed Irish invading but just that fellow who had come riding in a few hours before, whoever he might be.

Half an hour later it dawned on Delacroix that the reason Deirdre was nowhere to be found might be that she was no longer in the camp. He came to this conclusion after peering into every corner, upsetting anything that got in his way, and generally making a nuisance of himself. A grizzled veteran was nearest to him at the moment Delacroix realized the truth. The man blanched at the string of curses that erupted even as he marveled at their creativity.

Delacroix strode to the horse pens. He picked out

the biggest, strongest, meanest-looking destrier he could find. Grabbing a hapless groom by the scruff of his neck, he sent him racing for tack.

The horse's owner happened by as it was being saddled. Sir Percy Blansworth had been the third man in Bagenal's tent when Delacroix and Deirdre arrived. As foppish as Farthington, he cherished a robust sense of his own importance and considered every privilege of his rank to be no more than his God-given due. The horse was a gift from his younger brother, given in the hope that dear Percy would end up trampled under his hooves, thereby clearing the way to the family barony. So far the horse hadn't obliged, but only because his owner gave him a wide berth. He'd brought the four-legged devil along on campaign for show, but had absolutely no intention of ever riding him.

Which was not to say he approved of anyone else doing so, especially not without his permission.

"I say there," he shouted when he saw Delacroix, "what do you think you're doing?"

The big golden man on the horse made no attempt to answer him. Indeed, he seemed unaware of his existence. Blansworth would have protested, but he was too busy diving out of the way. He and the hapless groom lay facedown, breathing dust, as the destrier charged by.

Well beyond the camp, riding for all her life was worth, Deirdre suddenly flinched. She felt as though the cold hand of doom had swept over her. Trembling, she caught her breath and told herself not to be a fool. Danger there certainly was, but so far she was doing extremely well. Nothing had happened to change that, nothing at all.

The horse moved on, more slowly as the going became rougher. Deirdre murmured to her reassuringly. Ahead lay a section of the trail overhung by trees where the darkness was even greater than on either side. The mare whinnied nervously.

"Easy," Deirdre said, "it's all r—"

She broke off. In the distance, muted but still unmistakable, came the sound of something crashing through the underbrush.

An animal of some kind, but what? Something large, moving fast, dangerous. The thoughts tore through her mind in less than a heartbeat. Reacting instantly, she gripped the reins and turned the mare toward the cover of trees beyond the trail.

"Quiet, girl," she whispered tensely, "not a sound."

The mare seemed to understand, for she stood trembling but silent. Deirdre bent low across her back, hiding herself as much as she could and listening intently.

Not a wolf, too big for that and too loud. Please God, not another boar, that would really be too unfair. A bear? There hadn't been one sighted in Ireland in living memory and beyond. A unicorn bound on faery business? No, they were silent as the softest breeze. Perhaps the devil horses that drew the banshee's coach on its screaming death search? Certainly it sounded as though it could be that, but the truth was worse still. Deirdre edged up to it, skirting round the edges, until at last her mind could no longer deny what confronted it.

A horse and rider coming from the same direction she had, from Bagenal's camp where there were only villain English. What were the chances that one of them had taken it upon himself to go for an evening gallop?

About the same as she had of convincing herself that she was not in the worst possible trouble.

Delacroix, traitor bard and Elizabeth's man. Please God, it could not be he. He should still be with Bagenal, making their new strategy to deal with the greater Irish force. He should be planning, scheming, drinking, eating, cursing, anything but what she most desperately feared he was doing— namely, hunting her.

Terror twisted her stomach and raised burning bile in her throat. Of all the dangers she had thought to face, this was the worst. He would be—what? Enraged didn't even begin to describe it, but then, so was she. That he should be who he was filled her with fury. Ten thousand curses on the man! Let the devils take him. He would not have her!

"Fly, sweetling," she cried to the mare, and dug her heels into her sides. The horse whinnied fearfully and bounded forward. Branches crashed around them, tearing the cap from Deirdre's hair, catching at the ebony strands and scratching at her skin. She felt none of it. Nothing mattered except the rush of wind, the pounding of the horse, and the frantic need to escape.

A moment passed, another; time slowed and stretched, all the ordinary rhythms cast askew. She would escape, she would, another moment, another. Holy Mary, let the darkness hide her, let the night be her shelter, let—

A scream tore from her. Hard, unrelenting hands ripped her from the mare's back. She was flung across a saddle, the breath driven from her. The world swam, direction turned upside down. Dizziness overcame her. She fought it frantically, fighting for air. The pressure around her middle eased, if only fractionally.

"Cease," Delacroix said. His tone was deadly. It went through her with the force of an ice-tipped dagger. She obeyed, not from any lack of courage but because of the obvious futility of any further effort. Better to save her strength for what was coming, whatever that might be.

He rode on a short distance to catch the mare. Drawing rein, he steered both horses toward a small clearing. He dismounted quickly and with equal speed pulled Deirdre from the destrier's back. So rapidly that she hardly grasped what was happening, he twined a length of rope around her wrists, securing her hands.

"What are you doing?" she demanded. "You can't—?"

"Be silent!" Looming above her, his face taut with rage, he said, "Your parole is broken. You will be punished for that and punished again if you try anything further. Do you understand me?"

"Oh, yes, I understand full well!" Typical man. Tell her to be quiet—which she had absolutely no intention of doing—and then ask her a question to boot. Illogical, unreasonable, infuriating man! Also terrifying the way he was looking, his mouth drawn into a hard, narrow line and his eyes like steel. But she wasn't going to dwell on that, not she. Head up, her own eyes flashing, she met him head-on.

"I broke *my* parole? What about you racing off to tell Bagenal about my father's armies when you said— nay, you swore!—that you would not? You broke parole, English, and when you did you released me from mine. I will do anything I must to be free of you, and when I am, I will run a knife through your black heart. I will—"

To the hindmost with restraint, Delacroix thought, which was stretching it a bit since very little of his brain was involved, and those only the most primal parts. She had driven him mad with hunger, with rage, and with fear. Never in his life had he experienced such a chaos of emotions as he had since wandering all innocent and unknowing into the life of Deirdre O'Neill. Madness the woman was, and madness she provoked. So what would any sane man do but—

Kiss her, hard and long, restraint forgotten. His mouth was hard, hot, demanding. He gave her no quarter but took all, claiming the taste and feel of her, the intoxicating femaleness, all so longed for and at last possessed.

His body surged. Heedless of his strength, he bent her to him. His hands ran over her, learning the tapered smoothness of her back, the narrow indentation of her waist, and the soft curve of her hips. Without thought, he clasped her buttocks and pressed her hard against him. His arousal was plain even to one as sheltered as Deirdre had always been.

The kiss and all that accompanied it tore her from the cloud of protective ignorance to which she had hitherto clung. Not a shadow of doubt remained as to what he felt or what he intended. She cried out and wrenched her head away. Struggling, she managed only to bruise herself, for he was prepared this time for her resistance and easily overcame it. Her hands bound, her hair falling in dark masses over her shoulders, she was held relentlessly against an angry and fully aroused male.

Still, all was not yet lost. He had failed in his distraction to take all possibilities into consideration.

Deirdre still had her feet, and she wasn't afraid to use them. "Now, girls," Mother Justina had said one day while they were sitting in the tiny garden beside the abbey, "'tis a difficult world we live in, and there may come a time when it would behoove you to know a bit about men."

"So that we may please our husbands?" one young lady inquired innocently.

Mother Justinia's face gave little away. "Not exactly. 'Tis not husbands of whom we speak." At which point, she proceeded to explain exactly the type of male she had in mind and exactly what could best be done to inconvenience him.

Deirdre hadn't been sure it would work, but amazingly enough the moment she lifted her knee and rammed it up between Delacroix's legs, his grip on her loosened. Unfortunately, it didn't yield entirely. Try though she did, she couldn't get away.

"You bitch," Delacroix snarled through clenched teeth.

Deirdre's eyes widened in shock. Kidnapping, mayhem, and horrible threats were all one thing, but bad language was quite another.

"How dare you speak to me like that?" she demanded, and for good measure tried to deliver another blow.

She didn't succeed, because Delacroix swerved to one side. At the same time, he threw her from him. She landed heavily on the ground and had but a bare moment to try to gather herself before he was upon her.

"A word of advice," he said, grasping her bound hands and stretching them above her head, "when you try to unman a male make sure you really do it, because if you don't, the results are likely to be unpleasant."

"Unman? Oh . . ." She flushed scarlet. Mother Justina really should have explained things a bit better, but then, come to think of it, what had she done exactly that was wrong? Hadn't he been trying . . . hadn't he meant . . . ?

"You deserved it. Now let me go."

Delacroix stared down at her. She was stretched out beneath him so that he could feel every inch of her body through the absurd doublet and hose that, incidentally, left very little to the imagination. Her hair was in glorious disarray, her mouth swollen from his kiss, and her hands held bound above her.

And she was telling him to let her go.

His answer was a low, feral growl. She had a single moment to realize that something had snapped inside him before he reached out with one hand and tore the doublet open. Beneath she had only a thin chemise that was little more than a semitransparent veil. Through it, her nipples could be clearly seen, rose-tipped and hard. Delacroix lowered his head. His mouth moved over hers, down along the sensitive line of her throat to the hollow between her collarbones. His kisses were hot, heavy, unrelenting. Deirdre tried to evade them, but she could not move. She could only lie helpless under him as he did exactly as he wished.

His big, hard hand, the palm callused, cupped her breast, the thumb rubbing over her nipples. She bit down hard on her lip to stifle a cry. He lifted his head, his eyes molten, and watched her for a moment before his gaze drifted down to the perfection he had revealed. Again, there was a low sound in his throat before he lowered his head and claimed her nipple. The touch of his mouth through the thin fabric sent shards of pleasure through Deirdre. She fought them desperately, knowing that she must, even as they redoubled in intensity. His teeth grazed her lightly before impatience seized him. Fabric rent as the chemise gave way. Cool night air touched her skin before he claimed her yet again.

Urgently, he suckled her as his rock-hard thigh drove between hers. The tugging of his mouth at her nipple triggered deep, rhythmic shudders within her. Her body, heedless that it was, remembered the man she had yearned for but her mind rebelled. She could not, would not let him use her in such a way.

And yet, what choice did she have? He was a battle-hardened warrior capable of defeating the strongest and most determined man. What chance did a mere girl have against him? A sob choked her. That it should be like this after all the dreaming, the wishing, the song and the poetry. That he should take her on the hard ground, heedless of her struggles, and in hatred, was more than she could bear. A remorseless pit of despair opened beneath her. Abruptly, she went limp.

Delacroix didn't notice at first. He was caught in the coils of passion that held him as relentlessly as he held her. The beauty of this woman, the silken smoothness of her skin, the perfection of every line and curve, the heat within, beckoning him, were all more than he could resist. To take her once would never be enough. He needed a lifetime, an eternity, to make her his. But first—

Only gradually did the realization that something was wrong pierce his awareness. Through the red haze of his passion, he stared down at her. She lay with her head turned to one side, her face pale and still. Her eyes were closed. A single tear trailed down her cheek to fall away onto the ground beneath.

A curse broke from him. Yes, he had wanted to frighten and even hurt her, so maddening was her insistence on escape. But not this, not this blank and hopeless woman who seemed scarcely half alive.

"Deirdre," he murmured, horrified by what he had wrought. This was wrong; she should be sweetly eager, as filled with desire as he himself. Instead, he had taken what should have been a moment to be cherished and filled it with the worst dread.

"Deirdre," he said again, entreating her. Already, his weight was easing as he started to rise, to draw her to him, to offer whatever aid and comfort he could. He would apologize and reassure her. She had done wrong, that hadn't changed, but so had he. They would work things out, come to some understanding, and—

Scalding pain shot through his skull. He jerked his head back, fighting it, and tried to get to his feet, but the pain was too great. A maw of darkness opened beneath him. He teetered on the edge, fighting it. Her face floated before him, white, shocked, her lips moving as though she called his name. But Delacroix heard nothing. He fell as though from a great distance, his last thought piercing regret that he had failed to protect her.

Deirdre stared, dumbstruck. Ahead, behind, on all sides men were coming out of the trees. They surrounded her and the unconscious Delacroix. Frantically, she grasped the edges of the doublet closed over her breasts.

A bewhiskered face loomed close to hers. Panic swept her. She looked around frantically for any means of escape, only to realize that there were none. So be it. Defiantly, she lifted her head.

"Do not touch me." The words were uttered calmly, yet also with the unmistakable ring of authority. There was also something else about them that struck the band's leader. He was a big, burly man, built much along the lines of an ill-tempered bear with a gap-toothed leer and small but shrewd eyes.

"You have the Gaelic?" he demanded.

"Of course I do. I am Deirdre O'Neill, daughter of Hugh O'Neill. Harm a hair on my head and—"

"By God, it is!" one of the other men declared. "I saw her not two days ago at the tourney. No one could forget that face or that hair or—"

"Shut your mouth, Doyle," the leader snapped. "Praise the Lord we've found you. Your father's mad with worry. He's turning this countryside up from one end to the other in search of you." Abruptly, he demanded, "Who's this, then? Filthy English, I warrant. Here, lads, roll him to one side. We'll cut his throat and let the good Irish earth drink his blood."

"No!" Deirdre exclaimed. She scrambled to her feet and stood over the unconscious man. Heaven knew, she should hate him, but try though she did, she couldn't manage it. At the last there, as he held her, she could have sworn she had felt something—regret, tenderness, something—starkly at odds with his harsh treatment of her. And she could not forget the poetry, the song he had made for her, the look in his eyes when he saved her from the boar.

"No," she said again. "Leave him. He doesn't matter anymore."

Lie it was and lie they knew it, for they were not

blind to what had been happening before they came along. But she was the O'Neill's daughter, and they were reluctant to go against her. Besides, perhaps they hadn't really seen what they thought they had.

The leader brought the gray mare forward but gave the destrier wide berth. One look at it was enough to decide that it should be left to the Englishman. He used his knife to cut Deirdre's bonds, then lifted her onto the mare and handed her a cloak to put around herself. "As you will, my lady. We ride for your father."

"Where is he?" she asked numbly. A cold, jagged stone seemed lodged in her heart. She looked at Delacroix, lying unconscious on the ground. His face was turned slightly toward her, the golden hair falling over his forehead. The hard planes and angles of his features appeared uncharacteristically relaxed. He might have been asleep. Regret surged through her. So much longing, so much . . . if only . . .

"Yellowford, my lady, hard by the river. He will meet the English there tomorrow with all his armies."

The breath rushed from her. "All his armies, then he was right. The battle . . . ?"

"Is fast coming, praise be to God. We shall fall upon our enemies in fury and drive them from this land."

The other men echoed the sentiment but Deirdre remained silent, for really what was there to say? Desire, love, hope, all died when war came. It blew the carefully ordered structure of life away and left only chaos in its place. So be it. She would pray, for that was what women were supposed to do, and she would heal, for that she could.

But one other thing she would also do in the sanctuary of her most private self: She would remember.

A final glance at the man lying still on the ground, a final thought for the men who would soon be stiller yet, and then she dug her heels into the mare and urged it forward. Ahead lay the war-riven future. Behind was only memory.

PART

2

CHAPTER 15

JOHN DELACROIX, EARL OF BRADFORD, DIS-
mounted in the stable courtyard. He glanced up at the
mid-September sky, clear but for a handful of clouds
skittering east toward England. There was no rain in
sight to mar the beginning of the harvest. His fields
were ripe, his people eager; everything he had seen in
his ride that morning had been to his satisfaction.

A groom leaped forward to take the reins and lead
His Lordship's mount away. The boy moved quickly,
not eager to linger in the earl's presence. A good man
he was, and fair by all standards, but undeniably
somber and with an air of restrained threat that gave
pause to anyone foolish enough to even think of crossing him. Not that any of them would. They counted
themselves lucky to have so great a lord and blessed
the day he came.

That day was now almost two years past, a fact
much in Delacroix's mind as he left the stables and

walked along the gravel path that connected to the main house. Darkcroft it was called, and the name suited it. In some distant time, his Norman forebears had built a tower there to show their might over the surrounding peasantry. Much later, the tower was expanded into a pleasant stucco and cross-beam manor house with two stories, several high chimneys of red brick, and surrounding gardens. It was all very comfortable and civilized, the envy of its neighbors and the admiration of the nobility.

Delacroix tolerated it. He thought little of the vast hall furnished with fine tapestries and Araby rugs, the immense quantities of plate and silver stored in cupboards against the day he might deign to receive guests, the silk and velvet hangings, the fine cushions, the carved chests and armoires, the old revered swords and battle pennants. All were of scant interest to him. Occasionally, he walked in his gardens and more often he sat in his library, reading from the enormous and hitherto untouched collection there. Daily he rode out among his fields and was often gone until dark, for his holding stretched miles in either direction and emcompassed fully half a dozen villages.

There were other holdings as well, one in East Anglia, another in Dorset, and a fine town residence in London itself. But it was Darkcroft he preferred, close to the banks of the river Severn on the western edge of Wales. There was an untamed enthusiasm about the place that appealed to him, that and the ever-present rumble of rebellion in the populace that reminded him of Ireland.

The less said of that, the better. He had almost died in Ireland, and indeed, a part of himself had perished there. There were still nights when he woke cold with sweat, awash in the memory of Yellowford.

Motes of sunlight danced in the stillness of the great hall as he stepped within. As usual, the vast space was empty. He maintained a sufficient garrison, but housed in its own quarters removed from the main house. He trained his men, permitted no slackness, and saw to it that his orders were unquestioningly obeyed. All this he did, but no pleasure did he find in any of it.

Tonight he would sup alone as he always did, this to the consternation of his steward, who alone among Darkcroft's servants dared to address his master on terms approaching, though not quite reaching, familiarity.

The steward was waiting now as Delacroix entered the library. He was a tall, slender man with pale-brown hair and farseeing eyes. His ostensible reason for being there was to tidy up the books, which were too precious to be left to an ordinary servant. But in fact he had seen his master coming from the stables and hurried to waylay him. Such tactics were necessary because the earl was inclined to ignore household matters. The land and people he cared for, but the house itself could have gone to rack and ruin for all he cared. That Ewan Vaughn would not allow.

"My lord," he said, ignoring the frown his master bestowed on him, "if you would, a moment."

Delacroix sighed. Ewan was indefatigable and inescapable. He might as well listen now and get it over with rather than be plagued.

"Make it quick," he said as he lowered himself into a high-backed chair. A decanter of port stood nearby, but Delacroix rarely touched it. He ate plainly, showed little interest in finery, and paid no mind at all to the local women. This last occasioned no little disappointment and more than some concern, for not only did his lordship show no interest in the fair sex, he showed no inclination to marry and get himself an heir. So long as that remained the case, nothing would be quite settled or secure.

Ewan dared a cautious glance at the big, silent man. At thirty-two, John Delacroix was as formidable a specimen of raw power as could be found. Broad of chest and long of limb, he was dressed entirely in black. His face was darkly tanned, evidence of his preference for being outside, and the thick, unruly mane of his golden hair hung almost to his shoulders. No member of the garrison could claim his lord worked him harder than he worked himself. Yet there was an aura of sadness and reflection about him that could not be denied. More than once, Ewan wondered what accounted for it. In two years, he had come no closer to the answer, but he did have a few theories.

The steward cleared his throat and said, "Margaret is with child."

Delacroix raised an eyebrow. "Who is Margaret?"

Ewan sighed. It really was remarkable how ignorant His Lordship was about his staff. A Barbary ape could have served his supper and it was doubtful he would notice. "One of the kitchen maids, sir. She joined us six months ago."

"The father?"

"One of the garrison." Ewan sniffed as though to make it clear that was the one aspect of Darkcroft that did not involve him. "A certain Kerwin Osborn, so she says."

"A good man," Delacroix said. "Handy with a

bow."

"Margaret's a good lass, sir, and she's frightened now. The babe needs a father."

Delacroix glanced at the port but decided against it. No solution there. "I'll have a word with the garrison captain. If Osborn acknowledges responsibility, he will marry her."

"And if he does not?"

"I'll settle a sum so that she can care for the child and herself."

Ewan permitted himself a small smile of relief. "Very good of you, sir."

Delacroix glanced up, catching his eye. The corners of his mouth quirked. "Did I handle that right, Ewan?"

The steward cleared his throat. "Perfectly, sir."

"Just curious. It's somewhat outside my experience."

"Of course, sir." Ewan hesitated a moment before he added, "Ordinarily, I would not have troubled you. But given the absence of a lady . . ."

"Noted, you did as you should. Is there anything else?"

"Only this, sir." He handed over the heavy parchment packet the messenger had brought while Delacroix was out. It was from London and bore the unmistakable royal seal. Such missives invariably raised excitement in the house, but not as much as they once had, it now being accepted that the elderly queen communicated readily with her most reclusive earl.

Delacroix accepted the letter, but he did not open it until Ewan had bowed himself out. Alone, he read it quickly and without expression before refolding the single page and putting it aside. Elizabeth invited him to court, but she did not go so far as to demand his presence. He smiled at that. Mayhap she was softening in her old age, or perhaps she had merely learned the futility of trying to confine him within what passed for civilization.

He had gone to court after recovering from the wounds he suffered in Ireland, and he had achieved great success there as such things were measured. The ladies adored him despite—or because of—the lack of attention he paid them, and the gentlemen found their fear and envy eased when they realized he was singularly lacking in ambition. As well he might be, since he was already one of England's wealthiest and most powerful nobles *and* dear to the heart of the queen.

Elizabeth left no doubt about that. She called him her "most noble Delacroix" and sought to cultivate him as she had other hard young men. He eluded her, but she blamed him not. Rather, she seemed to understand the sorrows that drove him. As much as she could, she left him to Wales's wild comfort.

On this day, she wrote to say that matters did not go well in Ireland. Since his great victory at the battle of Yellowford, Hugh O'Neill had truly become high king in Ulster. He ruled there unopposed and through much of the rest of Ireland, where the English were hard-pressed to keep more than a toehold. Bagenal was long gone in disgrace; others tried to hold the line in Dublin, but the outlook was not good.

Delacroix tried to bestir himself to care. He knew she was right to be alarmed. Nothing had changed; Ireland was still the key to England, and the Spaniards were still intent on trouble. Something had to be done, but he saw no reason to involve himself. He had paid dearly for his time in Ireland; not even Elizabeth could ask more of him.

So he told himself and so he wanted to believe, but doubt remained. Ancient though Elizabeth was, she had lost none of her wiles. Her continued efforts to woo him suggested she had some further purpose in mind. He refused to contemplate what it might be.

A rigorous afternoon of swordplay with the captain of his garrison improved his mood. So, too, the brisk run he took over the hills and along the river that covered a circuit of five miles. He had discovered running when he was recovering from his wounds, having heard of men who did it in the east and swore by its effect. That his people thought the sight of their earl running over hill and dale strange did not trouble him.

By the time he returned, long shadows stretched across the courtyard. In the garrison hall he could hear his men laughing and joking among themselves. Their easy camaraderie reminded him of a time when he had shared the same kind of life. That all seemed very long ago, almost as though in a different world. The man who ruled Darkcroft was not the man who had sallied out to Ireland at the behest of his queen. He was older, wiser, somberer, and in some way he did not care to explore, more dangerous. It was as though having lost so many of his illusions, he had nothing else to risk.

His private chamber was on the upper floor. It was a large room dominated by a four-poster bed of heavy, carved wood softened slightly by luxuriously embroidered hangings. Leaded glass windows stood open to admit the scents of the gardens directly below. Behind a screen near the fireplace was an oversized tub. As per his standing instructions, it was filled with steaming water.

Delacroix stripped off his clothes and lowered himself gratefully into the bath. He winced slightly as the hot water touched the long, puckered scar along his left thigh, but he was used to the discomfort and at any rate it passed after a few moments. The wound was a souvenir of Yellowford. It had almost cost him his leg, if not his life. Even when the infection finally eased, there was considerable doubt that he would ever walk again. Faced with the prospect of living the remainder of his days as an invalid, he chose instead to ignore the doctors and drive himself relentlessly. Despite pain that would have felled most other men, he learned to walk again, and then to ride and run. In doing so, he regained a part of who he was, but not the whole. There were other wounds from Yellowford, much more deeply hidden, that no amount of determination could heal.

He leaned his head back against the rim of the tub and closed his eyes. Muted sounds reached him, birds singing in the trees, servants moving quietly around the house. The servants were always quiet around him; he swore they tiptoed. He never entertained, and only a few travelers had overnighted at Darkcroft before passing quickly on. It was a somber house, perhaps too much so, but it suited him. Once he had thought to make it different, to fill it with life and the sounds of children. But that no longer interested him.

In the back of his mind, he knew he could not go on forever as he was. Something would happen to intervene, to send him back into war, perhaps, and to death. He accepted that and made no attempt to evade it. Until then, he merely waited, tending his people, reading his books, training his men.

He rose from the tub some time later. Water matted the golden hair on his chest, at his groin and down his long, steely legs. He toweled himself briskly and dressed again in the snug black breeches he favored and a white lawn shirt loosely tied at the throat. He needed a shave, but he saw no particular reason to bother with one. He would have a light supper, go over the account books, and perhaps finish the translation of Euripedes he had been reading of late. He slept little and lightly, preferring that to the nightmares that came when he allowed himself to slip too deeply into unconsciousness.

Supper over, he settled in the library with the heavy velvet curtains closed against the night and the soft glow of the fire softening the hard edges of the room. The account books were before him, and he had begun their perusal when a flurry of hooves shattered the silence. He rose from behind the desk and strode over to the window. He could make out the shape of a horse and rider. Ewan was hurrying to greet them.

Most likely a traveler caught out after dark and seeking shelter. He would be given a bed and a meal. In the act of turning away from the window, Delacroix paused. The rider had handed something to Ewan, who hurried back toward the house clutching it.

A moment later, the steward was at the library door.

"My lord," he said, a bit breathlessly, "there is a further message from the queen."

Delacroix took it, frowning. Usually several weeks passed between missives from London. What could be so urgent as to require a letter hard on the heels of another?

Reluctantly, he broke the seal and read. Ewan, his own curiosity caught, watched unabashedly. Delacroix's eyes narrowed. A thin white line appeared near his mouth. He crumpled the letter in his fist with such ferocity that Ewan jumped back a pace.

"My lord . . . ?"

Delacroix said nothing. He didn't need to; every inch of him radiated furious, cold rage. Ewan gulped and backed up farther. "Sir . . ."

"A pox on them," Delacroix said between clenched teeth, "queen, whore, every damnable one of them. Truly when God made woman he cursed mankind."

There being no acceptable response to this, Ewan held his tongue. He would have liked nothing better than to withdraw, but he was too afraid to move.

The earl dropped the crumpled letter on the desk. His voice heavy with strain, he said, "Her Majesty has decided to lodge a royal prisoner with us. See to it that appropriate quarters are prepared."

Ewan blinked. The last thing he wanted was to unleash any of that barely controlled rage in his direction, but His Lordship really wasn't thinking. What kind of quarters? Darkcroft had no dungeon, although he supposed something of the sort could be improvised. Was that what he meant, and if not, then what?

"Uh, sir, your pardon, but isn't this actually a subject for the garrison captain? A prisoner will need guarding, after all, lest escape be attempted. . . ."

The earl laughed, a harsh sound that held no mirth.

"This prisoner is a woman, and you are quite right, escape is a problem. Pick a room as far from mine as you can find; tell the smithy to place iron bars across the windows and another on the door."

Glad to have a concrete task he could use to absent himself, Ewan nodded. "As you say, my lord, it will be done at once." He headed for the door.

"Wait."

"Sir?"

Reluctantly, as though the words were dragged from him, Delacroix said, "The prisoner apparently was captured several days ago. That being the case, there will probably be things she needs—clothes, for instance."

Ewan frowned. Iron bars in one breath, concern over a lack of clothing in the next. Something wasn't quite right here. "What sort of clothes, my lord?"

"How would I know what sort?"

Fine for His Lordship to say, but let his instructions not be carried out and Ewan had no doubt where the blame would fall. "Is she old or young?" he inquired, determined to be helpful. "Tall or short, plump or slim? Is she noble or not? All that affects what sort of clothes should be provided to her."

Delacroix grumbled, but he did relent. "She is of noble birth and gently reared, young, tallish for a woman, slender but not too much so. Her hair is black, her eyes are blue, she likes bright colors." Abruptly, he waved a hand dismissing the subject and Ewan with it. "See to it."

The steward needed no further encouragement. He fairly flew from the room, agog with surprise and eager to share it. Not only did His Lordship know the lady, but he also knew a great deal about her. Young, noble, quite presentable from the sound of it. Ewan chuckled as he hurried down the corridor. Bright colors, indeed.

A man did not notice that about a woman unless he had some feeling for her. They had been praying for a lady at Darkcroft, and now it seemed she was come. That it was in so peculiar a manner only made it all the more exciting. Ah, sweet intrigue! There would be extra mead in the servants' hall tonight, for truly they would talk enough to dry their throats many times over.

Alone in his chamber, Delacroix's thoughts were grimmer. He wouldn't put it past the wily old creature in London to at least suspect what she was doing sending Deirdre to him. She would relish the complication and enjoy jarring him from his self-exposed solitude.

He walked back to the desk and picked up the crumpled letter. Gingerly, he unfolded it and scanned the queen's words. No, he had not been mistaken. "The daughter of the traitorous O'Neill," she wrote, "Deirdre O'Neill, now our prisoner and shortly to be lodged with you at our pleasure."

Deirdre O'Neill, daughter. Not Deirdre O'Connell, wife. Yet how could that be? O'Neill had been determined on the marriage, and Red Hugh was surely willing enough. What had happened in all this time to prevent it?

He would know soon enough. Deirdre, at Darkcroft, with him. He shook his head, rejecting the thoughts that unleashed. She came as a prisoner placed in his custody, and undoubtedly her wrath was great. So, too, must be her fear, although she would do her utmost to disguise that.

He would do his duty as he always had. She would be kept at the queen's pleasure, properly cared for as her station required, but nothing more. This was Wales, not Ireland, and he was no longer subject to the fairy madness of might-have-been.

The breeze stirred beyond the window. A night bird called mockingly. Around Delacroix, the shufflings and murmurings of the great house settled down. In time, Darkcroft slept, but its master did not. He remained awake, gazing into the night and thinking of what the morrow would bring.

CHAPTER 16

DEIRDRE WINCED AS SHE TRIED TO SIT UP. Every inch of her body felt bruised and stiff. She was lying on a filthy straw mattress thrown into a corner of the yawl's hold. The skittering of rats had kept her awake most of the night. There were dark shadows beneath her eyes, her mouth was parched, and her hair hung in tangles down her back.

Slowly, she righted herself and looked around. It was early morning; soft, gray light filtered through the half-dozen portholes in the hold. Each was far too small to offer any hope of escape. Even if they had been larger, she would have drowned the moment she reached the water. Heavy chains weighted down her arms and legs. They had been put in place almost a week before, shortly after her capture. The chafing around her wrists and ankles was becoming steadily worse. Ignoring it, she got to her feet and peered out one of the portholes.

Since leaving Ireland the previous day, they had

been surrounded by the gray, choppy sea, but now, off in the distance, she could see land. Her eyes narrowed, taking in every detail. The rolling hills and rock cliffs revealed little. They might still be near Ireland or they might not. It was impossible to tell.

The uncertainty plagued her, but there was nothing she could do about it. Rather than waste her strength trying, she straightened herself as best she could and sat down again to wait. For all the drawbacks of captivity, she was at last learning patience. Mother Justina would be proud.

She could hear the crew moving about on deck, but no one approached her. When her thirst grew too much, she drank a little from the jug of water left with her when they embarked. There was also bread, but poor, mealy stuff her stomach rebelled against. She occupied herself trying to remember the name of every herb, where it grew, and how best it might be used. Someday, God willing, she was going to write a herbiary.

Time passed with aching slowness. The afternoon was waning when at last the hatch opened and a burly guard lowered himself into the hold. He approached her with caution that would have seemed excessive but for the black eye she had given him the day before. Gruffly, he said, "Up you go."

Deirdre shook off his hand and climbed the ladder to the deck herself. The effort strained her strength, for the chains were heavy and her limbs aching, but her face revealed none of that. The guard nudged her forward toward the yawl's prow. Beyond it she could see the mouth of a river and realized they were heading into it.

The yawl's captain was a young Englishman named Sidney Rutledge. He came of middling good family, which had managed to secure his appointment to the force garrisoning Dublin. Possessed of a normal share of ambition, he took himself and his duties seriously, but he had clearly never thought to be placed in charge of such a prisoner. His relief at approaching land was palpable.

Deirdre stood, head back, the breeze catching her unbound hair, and eyed him disdainfully. "Where are we?"

Rutledge would have liked not to answer, but fear of appearing ridiculous stopped him. She was only a woman, after all. It was some weakness of his moral fiber that caused him to see something else every time he looked at her. He was irresistibly put in mind of the ancient furies, those creatures of beauty and power who wreaked such havoc on hapless men. Too much reading was clearly bad for the brain; he would have to give it up. Yet seeing her standing there with her glorious ebony hair streaming back and the light of battle in her azure eyes, he couldn't help but wonder if cursed Ulysses wouldn't have recognized her and impetuous Achilles as well. There was something old and terrible in her that defied chains. Wales was welcome to her, and the earl of Bradford as well. The sooner she was off his vessel, the happier he would be.

"That is the river Severn," he said reluctantly. "We approach Cardiff."

She knew Cardiff; her father had received traders from there in better times. The news cheered her slightly. It was not so far from Eire, and anywhere was better than England proper. "Is that our destination?"

Again he hesitated, but he could think of no good reason not to answer her. Indeed, there was some satisfaction in it. Let her know the nature of her captivity that she might rightly fear it.

"No, we are going to a place called Darkcroft farther up the river. It is a holding of the earl of Bradford. There you will be held secure so that—"

He broke off, startled by the sudden draining of color from her face. Her lips moved stiffly. "B-Bradford?"

"Why, yes, the earl of Bradford. He is to be your warden." Emboldened by her reaction, he added, "You would be well advised to give him no trouble. He has a most fearsome reputation."

Deirdre hardly heard him. She reeled from the sudden and completely unexpected mention of the man she had known as Sean Harpsinger. For two years, he had lain buried deep within her memory, emerging only in dreams and during those stray times of the day when her self-control slipped. Now suddenly he was back in her life in the worst possible way she could imagine.

Sweet Lord, how could she face him? Those moments in the clearing when she had lain beneath him were etched into her soul. So, too, was her last sight of him lying unconscious on what so shortly afterward became a killing ground. How many times had she almost yielded to overwhelming temptation and sought news of him? Was he alive, was he well, had he married, did he dangle a babe on his knee, on and on until she feared she would be driven mad by the thought of him. And now, at the lowest moment of her life, she was about to come face-to-face with him again.

Mary and all the saints, give her courage. Protect her from the terror raging within her. Shelter her, too, from the treacherously sweet yearning he aroused. Don't, above all, let her do anything to shame herself.

He was her enemy. She had to cling to that, had to make it her shield and her sword. She owed that to her father, her clan, and her heritage.

The river slipped past; too quickly Cardiff was behind them. Tendrils of mist rose from the water, softening the shoreline and giving a dreamlike quality to the surroundings. Ahead lay verdant hills and sheltered valleys dotted by peaceful farms until at last, around a curve in the river, a high tower rose. It was built of darkly weathered stone and looked very old. A manor house stood nearby, and beyond that she could make out the shape of other buildings, stables and the like. But it was the dock at the edge of the water that drew her eye. Three men stood there: two guards and another who was tall, powerfully made, and dressed all in black.

The icy hand of fear numbed Deirdre. She stood unmoving, hardly blinking, as the yawl eased toward the dock. A gangplank slipped into place. Two sailors came up on either side of her and took her arms. Before she scarcely knew what was happening, she was lifted from the boat.

The chains around her wrists and ankles clanged harshly in the still air. River birds rose in alarm. She shrugged off the sailors' hands and straightened her shoulders.

John Delacroix, earl of Bradford, walked toward her. A golden wolf she had thought him, and that had never seemed so right. Against the fading sun, he appeared invincible, wrapped in an aura of power and will that could never be defeated. His face with its strong, masculine features appeared older, stronger, and even more unrelenting. His hair was thick and almost to his shoulders. His clothing was black, luxuriously made but with no adherence to feeble fashion. He looked, she thought unwillingly, like a splendid barbarian utterly in command of his domain.

And of her, if the gleam in his silvered eyes was anything to go by. She was his prisoner, given to him by none less than England's monarch. By all reason, she was helpless before him.

Anger surged in her. Fear be damned, she was the seed of Ireland, and it was past time these English devils knew it.

He stopped in front of her. Heart in her throat, Deirdre raised her right hand and, despite the weight bearing it down, struck him full across the face.

The blow caught him completely off guard; otherwise, it could not possibly have been so successful. It knocked his head back and opened a gash along the square line of his jaw that immediately began to bleed.

The men-at-arms leaped forward, as did the sailors who were standing nearest, but a gesture from the earl froze them in place. He raised his own hand, large, browned by the sun and strong in sinew; a warrior's hand. But its touch when it closed around her chin was gentle.

"Shall I presume, my lady," he asked softly, "that the battle is joined?"

The sound of his voice reverberated through Deirdre. Hard on it came sweet, seductive heat, threatening to shatter reason. Desperate to fight it, she jerked her head away. "It was joined a long time ago, English. The time has come to finish it."

A flicker of admiration showed behind his eyes. He glanced down at her chains. "You don't perceive yourself to be at a certain disadvantage?"

Again, the sweet surge of pleasure brought by the mere sound of his voice. Again, the desperate determination to deny it. She lifted her head and glared at him. "No chains can hold my spirit, and it is that which will destroy you." For good measure, she added, "You and all you stand for."

He sighed, and for a moment she thought she felt the sadness in him. But it vanished before she could be certain. He raised a hand and signaled to the men-at-arms.

"Show the lady to her quarters. I will be along shortly."

A moment more their eyes held before she turned away and walked slowly up the path toward the dark stone tower.

Behind her on the pier, Delacroix turned to Sidney Rutledge. His face was grim as he addressed the young officer. Curtly, he said, "I would speak with you, sir."

Rutledge swallowed hard. He was stunned by the woman's action in striking the earl and equally shocked by His Lordship's response. Rather than punish her swiftly and mercilessly, as anyone would expect, he had treated her with what could only be described as indulgence. There was no sign, however, that such clemency extended to anyone else. "Of course, my lord," he murmured.

Delacroix gestured for him to follow. They moved a short distance away to where another path gave access to the manor house itself. Rutledge, who fancied himself a student of architecture, observed it admiringly. The elegance of its construction, the pride with which it stood against the surrounding countryside, the subtle but unmistakable aura of luxury all confirmed the might and power of England, exactly as it should. Beside it, the dark and somber tower appeared as a vestige of another time, yet it seemed to suit its master all the better for that.

The earl did not speak again until they were seated in the great hall. A servant—a rather nervous one, Rutledge thought—brought mead before departing hastily. He glanced around as discreetly as he could, taking note of the luxurious furnishings, the tapestries and Araby rugs, the fine carved furniture, the leaded windows, and the weapons boldly displayed. Truly, the earl was as he had heard him to be—rich, mighty, and dangerous.

He took a quick sip of the warm honeyed wine, hoping it would calm his nerves. That they would need it was not long in question.

"How was she taken?" Delacroix demanded, his face taut. He sat in one of the high-backed chairs, his long legs stretched out before him. A goblet of chased gold rested in one burnished hand, but the wine within it was untouched.

Rutledge paled. He tried to tell himself that the black rage he sensed in the earl was merely a misunderstanding of some sort. There was no reason for Darkcroft's master to be angry at anyone other than the prisoner and she he treated with astonishing forbearance. Instead, the dark, boiling rage seemed directed at hapless Rutledge who could only seek to deflect it as best he could.

"A landing party was sent in near Dungannon to gather information," he said quickly. "They happened upon her gathering plants in the hills. Her guard was overpowered and she was seized."

To his inexpressible relief, the earl smiled. But whatever the source of his amusement, it did not last. Tautly, he asked, "Why is she chained?"

"Not by my design, my lord, I assure you. I was ordered to do it."

"Why?"

The stark command spurred the young officer to speedily recite everything he knew. "When she was captured a week ago, she injured two of her guards in an attempted escape. At that point, it was decided to secure her hands with rope, thinking that would be enough. But it turned out she had a knife hidden somewhere about her person. She used it to cut herself free, fled again and was recaptured, but injured several more guards in the process. She was then chained and shipped south to Dublin. Once there, the chains were removed, but she tried yet again to flee, so they were put back on. When she was handed over to me for transport here, I was ordered to keep her secure and to take no chances. I don't mind telling you that I count myself fortunate to have managed that."

"I see," Delacroix said. How many was that, one, two, three attempted escapes? Despite himself, he smiled. There was a certain relief in knowing that Deirdre was little changed. Abruptly, he put his goblet down and stood. "You are welcome to spend the night, but for now you must excuse me."

"Of course, my lord," Rutledge replied, hastily getting to his feet. "A few hours' rest and we will be on our way." Much as he would have liked to linger, Darkcroft and its master overwhelmed him. He would not breathe easily until he was gone.

Delacroix nodded but said nothing more. He left his guest in the great hall, clutching his mead and thanking his stars that the eerily beautiful Irishwoman was no longer his responsibility. Surely the earl was far better suited to deal with her.

The earl himself would have found that confidence amusing had he known of it, for he had no such certainty. Indeed, doubt assailed him as he strode from the house. The anger he had felt when he saw Deirdre, weary, disheveled, and chained, still threatened to engulf him. He had gone so far as to permit her to strike him in front of his men, something he would ordinarily not have tolerated under any circumstances. The blow still smarted. He touched a finger to it thoughtfully as he strode toward the tower. When Ewan had told him what quarters were prepared he had been surprised at first, but upon reflection he realized the steward chose wisely. The tower did meet the two qualifications he had set: it was as far removed from his own chamber as possible, and it could be readily secured. Beyond that, he would see for himself.

Despite its age, the tower was in excellent repair. Its walls were six feet thick and made of dressed stone that provided no handholds to would-be attackers. The only entrance was twenty feet above the ground at the top of a wooden staircase that could be readily doused with oil and burned if needed. The door was heavy oak crossed by iron bars. Immediately beyond it was the original hall, a wide, high-ceilinged space that took up the entire first level. Slit-windows admitted light but little warmth. Even on a pleasant September day, the air within was chill.

Curving stone steps led to the upper level where the family's private rooms had been. A pleasant solar for the manor's ladies took up most of it. The windows were larger there and the remaining furnishings more gracious. Opposite the solar was a small chamber that until the previous day had been made private by an old and increasingly fragile door. That was gone now. In its place was a new door of freshly hewn wood made even sturdier by the iron bar across it. As though all that were not enough, a guard stood before the door. He leaped to attention when he saw the earl.

"Open it," Delacroix ordered.

The man obeyed instantly. He lifted the bar, then used a large iron key to release the chain-and-lock combination that further secured the door. That done, he stepped aside swiftly.

Delacroix stepped into the room. For a moment, it appeared empty. A surge of fear went through him. She couldn't possibly have escaped yet again, could she? There was a flutter of movement. One side of the heavy bed hangings stirred. Deirdre stepped from the shadows. His relief was so intense that he felt momentarily weak.

Gruffly, he said, "Come."

Her eyes widened. Instinctively, she took a step back. He looked so formidable standing there all in black with his face grimly set. Her gaze fastened on the gash along his jaw. She trembled inwardly as she contemplated her own daring.

Still, it wouldn't do to let him know that. She straightened her shoulders and raised her chin in what was becoming an all-too-familiar exercise. "Come where?"

He stared at her disbelievingly. Did she imagine she had some say in the matter? Ah, well, let it never be said he wasn't a tolerant man. "With me."

This further explanation did not strike Deirdre as adequate, far from it. "Why?"

Delacroix shook his head in exasperation. Perhaps she had been dropped on her head as an infant. "Because I say so."

Typical male logic. *I say, you obey*. It seemed to Deirdre that women had been hearing that for an awfully long time. Sheer, unreasoning stubbornness— always useful in such circumstances—took control of her.

"No."

Darkcroft's master crossed the room with steady, implacable strides. He came to a halt directly in front of her. Deirdre drew an unsteady breath. The space between them was very small. She was vividly aware of the broad wall of his chest directly in front of her eyes. Slowly, she raised her head. Her voice shook slightly, but her words were clear enough. "I am a prisoner. I am under no obligation to cooperate with you. Indeed, it is my duty to resist."

Delacroix shut his eyes for a moment. He was not as a rule much given to praying, having concluded long ago that God apparently had better things to do than pay attention to humanity, but now he made an exception. He would most dearly like an added measure of patience. What he already had was being exhausted at an alarming rate.

Slowly, speaking as though to a backward child, he said, "You cannot resist. You will do exactly as you are told or you will be compelled to do it. If I have to carry you, I will. If you struggle, I will stop you. In the end, you will do as I say. Is that clear?"

Deirdre swallowed with great difficulty. Under her breath, she muttered, "Yes."

"What was that?"

"*Yes!* It is clear. You are the same arrogant, insufferable man you always were. Nothing has changed. Fine, we understand each other."

In high color, she strode past him. The guard started, but stopped when he saw the bemused look on his master's face. Delacroix followed her down the curving stone steps and out through the great hall. All the while, he was mindful of the possibility that she would suddenly bolt. But apparently even Deirdre had more sense than that. She stopped when they reached the outside.

"Where are we going?"

Delacroix hid a smile. Even the indomitable "Princess" O'Neill, as he was coming to think of her, couldn't decide everything.

"To the smithy."

She shot him a startled look in which hope flickered. "Why?"

"To have your chains removed."

Her breath caught. With as much dignity as she could muster, she nodded. The chains were more than mere restraint, they were a symbol of degradation. She loathed and feared them, but she would not allow herself to show how profoundly the news that they were to be removed affected her.

Nonetheless, Delacroix saw what was in her eyes. Inwardly, he cursed the countrymen who had done this, but outwardly, he managed to look stern. "Do not imagine this means you can escape. You will be most closely held, and any attempt to get away will be punished. Understood?"

Once again, Deirdre inclined her head. The gesture served to hide the sudden darkening of her cheeks. Much as she tried, she couldn't help but think what had happened the last time she fled from him.

Better to think of nothing at all, which she tried most sincerely to do as they walked across the courtyard toward the blacksmith's shed. The smithy was a big, bearlike man, typical of his kind, with massive arms and a patient, deliberate air. The sudden appearance of a young woman in chains accompanied by no less than the earl himself drew no reaction whatsoever. Such might be an everyday occurrence at Darkcroft, for all the surprise he showed.

"My lord," he said, his voice deep and smoke-roughened, "how may I serve you?"

"You may remove these chains," Delacroix said.

The smithy frowned. He bent down and peered closely at Deirdre's wrists. Without warning, he lifted her skirt and similarly studied her ankles. "Won't be easy. The locks are welded shut."

"They did that in Dublin," she explained, her voice very low.

Delacroix took a deep breath. Rage would avail him nothing, and neither would dread. What must be, must be.

"Quality work this," the smithy went on. "Solid, well made." He looked at Deirdre curiously. "How long have you been carrying them around, miss, if you don't mind my asking?"

"Four days."

He shook his head. "Can't have been pleasant. Well, then, let's give it a try." Somberly, he looked from Deirdre to his master. "You need to know, miss, and you, too, my lord, that this won't be easy. It'll take hot pincers to cut through iron like this. The lady may be injured."

"I don't care," Deirdre said quickly. "I just want them off."

The smithy shrugged and turned away to pump his fire. Deirdre clasped her hands together, trying vainly to stop their trembling. Even so close to the flame, she felt freezing cold. Exhaustion, fear, and now the near-certainty of pain all combined to sap her will. Her knees buckled, and for a terrible moment she thought she would fall.

A rock-hard arm wrapped around her, holding her upright. "Easy," Delacroix murmured. "It will be over soon."

She nodded, her throat thick. He was so strong, so certain and unflinching in his will, while she felt so much the opposite.

"I am ready, my lord," the smithy said.

Deirdre shut her eyes tight. She had to go through this, but she didn't have to watch it. Delacroix guided her to the large anvil set up near the fire. "Kneel," he said softly.

She obeyed and felt the hard ground beneath her. Her arms rested on the anvil. Unable to resist, she peered from beneath her lashes only to immediately regret it. The pincers the smithy held were large and glowing red hot at the tip.

"I cannot," she murmured brokenly.

Delacroix knelt behind her. He took her hands in his and stretched them out across the anvil. "Do it," he ordered.

The smithy hesitated barely an instant before he obeyed. Deirdre gasped and squeezed her eyes tight shut. The smithy grunted. Slowly, going little by little, the pincers bit into the iron and sliced it through.

"Done," the smithy murmured as one end of the chain fell away. "Now for the next."

Deirdre took a deep breath and held it. She was pressed close against Delacroix, held immovable by his strength. His own breathing was harsh in her ear. Again the pincers, again the fear as iron bent before fire.

The smithy straightened. He put the pincers back into the flame to heat again and wiped his brow. "Not too bad. You all right, miss?"

Deirdre nodded. Speech was beyond her. Her arms were free, but her legs remained shackled. Modesty notwithstanding, she raised her skirts, exposing slender legs, tapered ankles, and delicate, if grimy, feet. When captured, she had been wearing boots, but they were taken from her when the chains were put on. Delacroix moved behind her again, and she accepted his steadying strength. Twice more she submitted to the red-hot pincers before the last of the hated chains fell away.

The smithy beamed, rightly proud of himself. He had done a difficult job well, leaving the lady unscathed. Which was not to say she had no injury.

The skin around her wrists and ankles was red and chafed, the joints beneath beginning to swell. A pulse beat in Delacroix's lean cheek as he gazed at the evidence of her suffering. Without a word, he lifted her into his arms.

"Put me down!" Deirdre exclaimed. This was absurd; they were out in the open where anyone could see them. She was supposed to be his prisoner, yet here he was carrying her across the courtyard and up to the steps of the tower, her skirts billowing around his powerful legs and her hands beating ineffectually against his chest.

He did not pause until they reached the tower chamber. Only then did he set her down again. He stood, hands on his hips, showing no sign of exertion, and studied her calmly. "You will rest now."

Deirdre opened her mouth to tell him she would do no such thing, but weariness overcame her. It was all she could do to remain on her feet until he left the room. When the iron bar clanked across the door, she walked tiredly to the bed. It was big, soft, and irresistible. Still fully dressed, she stretched out and pulled a cover over her. Her eyes fluttered shut, her breathing slowed. Scant moments passed before unconsciousness claimed her.

CHAPTER 17

AN HOUR OR SO LATER, THE DOOR TO THE tower chamber opened again. Darkcroft's master stood for a few moments, letting his eyes adjust to the darkness. Only then did he approach the slender figure stretched out on the bed.

He looked down at her, his expression carefully shuttered. She showed no sign of waking, but he was taking no chances. His feelings needed hiding from himself; they most certainly could not be revealed to her.

Slowly, his gaze swept over her. She was lying on her side. Her hair, matted and tangled, flowed over the pillows. Most of her was hidden by the blanket, but he could see the streak of dirt across one cheek and the chafing around her wrists. Had she not been so obviously exhausted, he would have insisted that she be cared for immediately. But sleep was her first and greatest need. Anything else would have to wait.

An old-fashioned copper brazier fetched from the manor storerooms emitted some heat, but the room still felt chill. He had expected that and come prepared. Careful not to disturb her, he unfolded the fur coverlet he held and laid it over her. Deirdre sighed softly and snuggled farther into the bed.

He watched her a few moments longer before turning away. The door closed behind him softly. He eased the bar back into place. The guard stood rigorously blank-faced and at attention. "If she wakes," Delacroix said, "if anything is needed, send word to me."

He did not wait for the man to reply. His orders would be obeyed as they always were. Only Deirdre dared to challenge him and would undoubtedly continue to do so. The peaceful sameness of his days at Darkcroft was no more. He let it go with undeniable relief.

Ewan had supper waiting for him when he returned to the manor house. There was no sign of Rutledge, who, sensible fellow that he was, had absented himself. The steward waited, watching critically as a servant offered roasted quail, peas flavored with butter and mint, freshly baked bread, and a small round of tart yellow cheese. It was a simple meal as the earl preferred, lacking soup, pastry, and sweet, and particularly without the elaborate collations the cook so longed to prepare.

Ewan poured the fine ruby wine himself, then stood back, waiting. Some evening his master was going to taste the wine and comment on its excellence. He would notice the exquisite damask cloth, the perfection of the table setting, the attention given to each and every detail. Some evening, perhaps, but not this one.

Ewan bowed his head and started to withdraw, but the earl stopped him. "The tower chamber appears acceptable," he said.

The steward resisted the impulse to inform His Lordship that he and six other members of the household staff had worked virtually without halt since the previous day to clean and otherwise prepare the prisoner's accommodation. The chamber had lacked even the most basic furnishing, let alone anything approaching comfort. Dogged labor had changed that; the bed found in the ever-useful storerooms, carried to the chamber piece by piece and assembled there, the fine French rug unrolled and beaten clean of decades' worth of dust, the carved Moorish chest freshly scented with shaved cedar, the chairs and table, the inlaid garderobe, all were better suited to an honored guest than a prisoner of the crown. Still, Ewan had no doubt the effort was justified. Weary, frightened, dirty, the woman was nonetheless a vision to be reckoned with.

"Will there be anything else, my lord?" he asked.

Delacroix shook his head. He took a sip of the wine. The steward was backing himself out when he stopped. From the shadows beyond the candlelight, the earl spoke softly. "This is quite good, Ewan, as always."

Ah, well, that would be how it would be, coming without any warning and hardly time for a man to savor it. The woman was behind this change in the earl, Ewan was sure. He went off smiling inwardly, but careful to conceal it. In the privacy of his own room he reviewed the instructions he had given until he was certain all was as it should be.

✳ ✳ ✳

The first of these instructions was carried out early the following morning. Deirdre woke from a sleep deeper than any she had ever known to confront the sight of two young maids straining under the weight of a heavy tub. They staggered into the room with wary smiles and bobbed their heads in unison.

"Good morning, my lady."

Deirdre blinked once, twice. Something had happened to her vision during the night: she was seeing double. Two carrot-headed, broad-faced, plump and smiling maids, with identical blue eyes, stood before her, dressed in identical brown skirts, white blouses, and tan aprons.

"Who . . . ?"

"I am Libbie, my lady," the first one said. "This is my sister, Lizzie. 'Tis honored we are to serve you."

"Serve . . . ?"

"Put up the screen, Lizzie, and give that wee fire a poke. How's Her Ladyship supposed to bathe with it so chill in here?" Clucking her tongue, Libbie bustled over to the bed. Her eyes widened slightly as she took in the fur coverlet, which she most certainly had not placed there when preparing the room and which, if she remembered rightly, she had last seen in His Lordship's chamber.

While she mulled that over, she went on, "Fell asleep in your clothes, did you? Oh, well, no loss for them if you don't mind my saying so. Good quality, but I doubt they'd come clean now. Here, let me help you up. We'll get you out of these and you'll have a nice hot soak. Breakfast is on its way." Her gaze fell on Deirdre's chafed and swollen wrists. "Oh, my lady, that must be hurting something dreadful!"

Her wrists did ache, as did her ankles, but Deirdre was more concerned by the sense of unreality that threatened to overcome her. The luxurious room, the willing maids, the obvious concern for her comfort and well-being were all starkly different from anything she could have expected. Only the solid oak door blocking the entrance to the chamber and the iron bars on the windows confirmed that she was indeed a prisoner.

There was no time to consider that, however, for the maid kept up a running chatter. "Lizzie, fetch that salve Ewan keeps for burns and suchlike. And be quick about it. Beautiful hair you have, my lady. Lizzie will be dressing it for you; she's quite good at that. The soap's lilac, by the way. I hope that's all right."

Deirdre murmured her assurance that it was. The words were indistinct, for Lizzie was pulling the worn gown off over her head. She tossed it on the floor and made short work of the chemise below. Hastily, before she could get cold, Deirdre was hustled into the tub. The maid draped a linen sheet over it to keep in the heat, then set herself to washing the heavy mass of ebony hair.

Deirdre closed her eyes and let herself relax. The warm, soft water, the soothing touch of the maid, the sense of comfort and security were more than she could resist. Later there would be time to fight again—far too much time, probably—but for the moment she would let her bruised and battered body regain its strength.

By the time she stepped from the bath to be wrapped in a warm wool robe, Lizzie was back, weighed down by a heavy tray. She set it on the table near the window and took a small jar from her apron pocket.

"The salve's our granny's own, my lady," she said shyly. "No better you'll find. You'll be fit again before you know it."

Deirdre took the small jar and opened it. She smelled chamomile, mallow, and thyme, all beneficial to the treatment of wounds. But there was also something else she couldn't identify.

"How does your granny make this?" she asked.

Lizzie flushed and looked confused. It was left to Libbie to answer. "We don't rightly know, my lady. She says we're good girls but without the brains to learn such ways. Mayhap she's told Ewan, he's our brother and steward here, but I don't really think so. It be woman's lore, she says, and not fit for men to know."

Deirdre pondered that as she spread a little of the salve on one of her wrists. She felt a slight tingling, followed by immediate relief. Having applied the salve everywhere it was needed, she recapped the jar and put it carefully away.

"Thank your granny for me, will you?"

"Oh, yes, my lady," Libbie assured her, "and most pleased she'll be. We'll just fetch your clothes now while you have your breakfast."

The girls hurried from the room, leaving Deirdre to contemplate the meal set out before her. Should she be expecting guests? Surely there was enough food to feed at least three or four other people, everything from porridge and honeycake to rashers of ham, stewed lentils, chicken pie in glazed pastry, fine white bread, and a pot of crushed strawberries. After subsisting on water and stale husks for a week, Deirdre was understandably hungry, but even she doubted she could do justice to the meal. Moreoever, she wasn't sure she should try. She was a prisoner, held by a relentless enemy. That the enemy happened to be a man for whom she had decidedly mixed feelings really shouldn't matter.

Resolutely, she moved away from the table. Uncertainly, she moved back. Aromas assailed her. Her stomach growled. A small piece of the bread wouldn't matter, would it?

Half an hour later, having eaten the better part of the porridge, three pieces of bread, and a rasher of ham, she accepted that she wasn't made for martyrdom. Maybe it was just as well. There were still things she wanted to do in this life before seeking the next. Chief among them was the need to hold her own against one John Delacroix, misplaced bard and misbegotten earl.

The door opened again. She jumped, thinking for a moment that it might be he. But it was only Libbie and Lizzie. Each had her arms full of garments.

"Ewan says to tell you there will be more, but in the meantime he hopes these will suit."

Suit what? Deirdre wondered. A royal wedding? An emperor's ball? For where else would she wear such garb? There was a bodice of azure silk cut low and with a cartwheel ruff around the throat. Attached to it was a bell-shaped skirt of matching velvet slashed to show the underskirt of rich green taffeta. Leg-of-mutton sleeves ended in froths of lace. There were also silk hose with embroidered garters, a chemise of finest batiste, and delicately made slippers secured by golden ribbons.

Dazedly, she shook her head. "There must be a mistake."

"Oh, no, my lady," Libbie insisted. She thought it was Libbie; she was the talkative one. "Ewan doesn't make mistakes. He was most precise."

Deirdre reminded herself to meet the formidable Ewan at the first possible opportunity. In the meantime, there didn't seem to be much she could do about it. Her own clothes really were filthy, and she was loath to put them on again after finally getting clean.

"Isn't there anything else?" she asked, half hopefully. "Something simpler, plainer?"

Libbie shook her head firmly. "His lordship said you were to be dressed properly, my lady."

"I didn't realize he was such a connoisseur of women's fashion," Deirdre muttered.

Libbie looked shocked. Chidingly, she said, "If you don't mind my saying, my lady, it's best to just do as His Lordship wishes. I don't know anyone who's ever disobeyed him, but I wouldn't care to be the first."

"You wouldn't be," Deirdre said. Libbie's mouth tightened as Lizzie looked anxious. Before their combined pressure, she relented. "Oh, all right, do your worst, but I don't like this one bit."

Which was stretching things, to say the least. She wouldn't have been human, much less female, not to be thrilled by the gown. Yet once she had donned it, her doubts returned full force. The neckline really was quite low, exposing to an alarming extent the generous swell of her breasts. The cut of the bodice emphasized her narrow waist and the swell of her hips. Even the ruff around her throat drew attention to its slenderness and made her appear even more vulnerable.

"I don't think—" she began.

"Your hair, my lady," Libbie interrupted. "Lizzie,

get the brushes. If you'll just sit here, my lady." Briskly, she directed Deirdre into the chair.

Lizzie went to work with a will. She might not talk much, but when it came to hair, there was no holding her back. She brushed until tears came to Deirdre's eyes from the prickling of her scalp. Only when every tangle was gone did Lizzie relent. She put the brushes aside and with fingers flying constructed two narrow braids on either side of Deirdre's face and more toward the back. These she laced with ribbons, securing the ends with tiny pearl clasps.

"Very nice," her sister said when she was done.

Deirdre said nothing. She was too busy looking at herself in a large, gilt-framed mirror that stood in one corner of the room. The woman who gazed back at her was a stranger—beautiful, sensual, with luminous eyes, a full, ripe mouth, and a body made for a man's delight.

"Oh, my," she said.

"Help me with the tub, Lizzie," Libbie said. She smiled reassuringly. "If there's anything you require, my lady, you've only to tell the guard. We'll be back at midday with your dinner." With the tub between them, the maids headed toward the door.

"Wait," Deirdre said.

They stopped obediently, looking at her. She hesitated, embarrassed but determined nonetheless. All her life there had been only one thing she could not bear, and now it threatened to descend on her. "I would like something to do."

The girls glanced at each other in bewilderment. This was a problem neither of them had ever confronted. They began work when they rose in the morning and ended it when they went to bed. Ladies were different, of course. They must do something—mustn't they?—but what that might be remained a mystery.

"We could ask Ewan, my lady," Libbie suggested, ever helpful.

"Then he can ask His Lordship," Lizzie chimed in.

"Oh, no," Deidre said quickly. The last thing she wanted was to draw their master's attention in any way. "Never mind. I'm fine just as I am."

Libbie looked unconvinced. "If you say so, my lady . . ."

"I do, most definitely. Please don't trouble your brother."

And above all, she thought, don't trouble His Lordship. She would gladly accept idleness if it meant avoiding his notice. Wouldn't she?

By afternoon, she was no longer so sure. She was overjoyed to see Libbie when the girl brought her the midday meal, but then only picked at it. The maid tut-tutted when she saw how poorly "my lady" had managed. This would not go down well in the servants' hall where they were waiting with bated breath for every scrap of news about the prisoner.

Speculation was rampant despite Ewan's best efforts to contain it. She was His Lordship's lost love, so the thinking went, daughter of a king, torn from the earl in battle and the reason for his lonely exile at Darkcroft ever since. Oddly enough, unlike most gossip, this was remarkably accurate. However, it failed to explain the scene on the dock, which was hashed over again and again. She had struck him and lived! No one would have believed that possible. Not only that, but he responded by draping her in furs, dressing her in silk and velvet, and keeping her high in a tower, guarded constantly. Truly no troupe of traveling players, no minstrel or jester had ever presented so diverting a tale. What a pleasure, indeed what a privilege, to witness its unfolding. Truly, life was good!

But not, Libbie declared, if the lady failed to eat, if she pined and saddened. Then, put bluntly, there would be hell to pay.

Ewan agreed. He saw no reason to dither but laid the problem squarely where it belonged, before His Lordship.

"What do you mean she isn't eating?" Delacroix demanded. He had just returned from a morning's hard ride, hoping to escape the thoughts that tempted and tormented him. For a time he'd succeeded, but no longer. Barely had he drawn rein when Ewan was at his side.

The big black stallion he favored was led away, prancing and snorting, as Delacroix confronted the problem. He stood, a proud, compelling figure dressed all in black, and stared toward the tower.

Damnable woman. If she thought he would allow her to play with him like this, she was very much mistaken.

"I will see to it," he said, so grimly that Ewan was taken aback. By the time he recovered, it was too late, the earl was gone. He shook his head in dismay. Perhaps he should have phrased it differently, made it clear she had eaten a good enough breakfast. Instead, he seemed to have given His Lordship the impression she was refusing food.

Not good, that. Not good at all. Still, it wasn't as though there was anything he could do about it now. The lady would have to manage for herself.

CHAPTER 18

DEIRDRE WAS LOOKING OUT THE BARRED WIN-
dow, trying hard not to feel wistful for the bright-
sunned day, when the door flew open. She turned
quickly, her hand at her throat. Delacroix stood there,
big and formidable, the guard quaking behind him and
the door itself swaying on its hinges.

"You ought to be more careful," she said. Never
mind the sudden thudding of her heart, Hugh O'Neill's
daughter was no ninny to be frightened by a display of
bad temper. "You might have broken it, and then
where would you be? One prisoner, no prison. Can't
have that, can we? That nasty old thing in London
wouldn't like it."

The guard was a brave man, seasoned in battle, but he
closed his eyes to block out what he was sure must be
coming. A moment later when he heard nothing, he edged
them open. The earl was still standing there, still staring at
the woman. He looked transfixed—and who could blame

him?—for surely she was a vision, haughty and magnificent, a dream to stir the loins and addle the wits.

Which described the earl's condition precisely. With what breath he could muster, Delacroix uttered two words. They were directed at the guard. "Get out."

Rarely had any order been more swiftly obeyed. The man fairly dove for the door, slamming it shut behind him.

A faint and not at all encouraging smile touched the earl's mouth. Deirdre couldn't stop herself from taking a quick step backward. The smile deepened. His gaze moved over her with unrelenting thoroughness. Deliberately, he stalked her across the room.

A burnished hand reached out to lightly touch the lacy ruff around her throat. Again, his gaze raked her. "Pretty."

"I didn't want to wear this," she said hastily. "There wasn't anything else."

His silvered eyes gleamed with amusement. "I must think of a suitable reward for Ewan. He has outdone himself."

Deirdre flushed deeply. The way he was looking at her, the caressing rumble of his voice, the nearness of his big, powerful body all left her dazed. She felt exposed, vulnerable, and more helpless than ever before. Desperately, she retreated another step, only to feel the cold stone wall against her back. "Surely you have better things to do than being here."

She was wearing some sort of perfume, lilac, he thought, that was making it difficult for him to concentrate. Not that he would have had much luck even without it. She looked so damnably feminine arrayed in the beribboned gown with the soft swell of her breasts clearly visible above the low-cut bodice. Her hair was different, softer, more elaborate. Her eyes glowed and her mouth was so full and tempting that he was hard-pressed not to crush it beneath his own.

"I would," he said gruffly, "if you hadn't taken it upon yourself to be a nuisance. Why have you refused to eat?"

Deirdre's eyes widened. "Refused? I did no such thing."

Delacroix looked at her narrowly. "Ewan said you hardly touched your dinner."

"Did he also tell you I stuffed myself at breakfast? I haven't refused to do anything even to the extent of wearing this ridiculous gown. You have nothing to reproach me about, and no reason to be here. Now, please go." She turned on her heel, presenting him with her stiff and resentful back.

Clearly, Delacroix thought, a chat with his steward was in order. But not quite yet. Reassured that Deirdre was actually behaving herself, he allowed his good humor to return.

"Go? What kind of host would I be to so grievously neglect a guest?"

Deirdre shot him a look over her shoulder that would have reduced a lesser man to smoldering ash but sadly did not faze the earl at all. "I am not a guest, and you are most certainly not a host. Surely even a prisoner has some right to privacy?"

"Perhaps. I'll have to think about it. But, for the moment, it pleases me to spend a little time with you. Come and sit down."

"I will not."

Softly, with lethal precision, he said, "I can compel you."

A shiver ran through her. The thought of him touching her was terrifying, and not simply because she feared him. He also made her fear herself.

"This is very childish," she said. With as much reluctance as she dared, she took the chair he indicated. He sat opposite her. A single swift glance was enough to tell her he looked insufferably pleased with himself, sitting at his ease with his long legs stretched out, his hands folded across his broad chest, and a satisfied smile playing about his hard mouth.

Pointedly, she looked away. He could make her stay in the same room with him, he could make her sit, but he couldn't make her pay any attention to him.

"You are astonishingly beautiful," he said.

She sniffed and stared at the opposite wall, but the words had their desired effect; like it or not, she could not ignore him.

"Of course," he went on pleasantly, "I've always thought that about you. It's no wonder Red Hugh was so anxious to make you his wife. Which reminds me, how is it you aren't wed yet?"

"That is a personal matter which I have no intention of discussing with you."

Delacroix nodded sagely. "I see. Backed out, did he?"

Despite herself, Deirdre gasped. "How dare you? Have you no decency at all?"

Delacroix leaned forward slightly. "If I had no decency," he said, "you would be over there on that bed right now with your skirts up to your waist and your legs spread." Ignoring her shocked recoil, he

went on remorselessly. "No one—I repeat, no one—
would stop me. You surely could not, and nobody
else would be so foolish as to try. The only thing
standing between you and that is the fact that I do
indeed have some decency. However, I can be provoked into forgetting it. You would be wise to keep
that in mind."

"You bastard—"

He raised a hand in warning. "Careful."

"You . . . you . . ." Heaven help her, he had her
neatly trapped, unable to fight him even with words,
yet blocked from retreat into silence.

"Now, then," he went on when he was certain she
had gotten the point, "I was asking how you happened
not to be wed."

Grudging him every word, she said, "My father
decided it was not advisable."

Delacroix frowned. She could be lying, but somehow he didn't think that was the case. But why would
the O'Neill change his mind about so obvious and beneficial a union?

"Red Hugh is still your father's ally, still part of
this insane rebellion. Why should he no longer be
acceptable as a husband?"

"It wasn't him. It was . . ." She broke off, her cheeks
scarlet. If God were truly merciful, the floor would
open and swallow her whole.

It didn't. She was left exactly where she was to
manage as best she could.

"Not him," Delacroix said slowly. "You mean . . . ?"
Understanding dawned, and with it came a spurt of
anger. "Are you telling me your father somehow decided you were no longer worthy to be Red Hugh's wife?"

"He decided it would be better if we didn't marry," Deirdre said tightly.

"Why?"

"Because he did."

"That's not a reason. It was an important alliance. Why would he change his mind about the marriage?"

"Because he feared for my safety, damn you! He believed me dishonored, and he thought when Red Hugh discovered that there would be unpleasant consequences."

Delacroix's eyes narrowed. What was she talking about? "Dishonored? You mean not virgin? But why?"

"Because, you dolt, of what his men saw in the clearing when they rescued me from you."

His mouth dropped open. He stood up even as she did the same. They glared at each other. "Surely," he said, "you know that nothing happened between us? At least nothing . . . irreparable."

"Of course I know it."

He shook his head, more bewildered by the moment. "But then why didn't you tell your father?"

"I did."

"Didn't he believe you?"

"He wasn't . . . sure. Enough doubt remained in him to make him feel it best to cancel the marriage."

"But there are ways to prove such a thing . . . midwives . . . examinations . . ."

"No. I gave my father my sworn word, and it was not good enough for him. The matter is closed."

Delacroix stared at her for a long moment. He felt astonishment, anger, and beneath it all, tenderness for this beautiful, proud woman who would defy the world out of a sense of honor. Yet he remained just a tiny bit suspicious. If she had truly wanted to marry Red Hugh, would honor have stood in her way?

"I see," he said slowly. "I am sorry for my part in this confusion. However, I must say your intended doesn't seem to be much of a man."

"Why do you say that?"

"Because if he were, he would have claimed you and found out the truth for himself."

"*He* happens to be a gentleman. *He* would never dream of doing such a loathsome thing."

Delacroix laughed. "Then he's a fool." More gently, he added, "Deirdre, truly, I regret what you've suffered."

"I don't understand you," she blurted. "How can you say that when just a few moments ago you suggested you would make my dishonor real were I to provoke you too far? Which is the truth?"

Her candor startled him, but he did not try to evade it. Instead, he said bluntly, "The truth is that I am a man and a warrior, and that I desire you. But the truth is also that I have no wish to harm you. Obey me and you will have nothing to fear."

"Obey you," she repeated. Her eyes met his unflinchingly. In hers was a depth of pain and confusion that struck him to the quick. "What if I cannot? We are enemies. How can there be anything but hatred between us?"

He came toward her again, but slowly and far less threateningly than before. Steeling himself, he asked, "Do you hate me, Deirdre?"

She breathed in sharply, hating him truly for the question. But that was a weak and shallow hatred, a thing of no account, gone in a moment. What he was asking was far more profound.

The air in the room was very still. He thought he

could hear her heart beating, although he wasn't sure. She thought of poetry and passion, of the boar and the mad ride through the woods the day he escaped, of his berating her for putting herself in danger by fleeing him, and of the tender strength of his caress as he held her. Her enemy, heaven help her, for she could find no hatred of him in her heart. "No," she murmured finally, "I do not."

Elation roared through him. He fought it down, struggling for some semblance of control lest he frighten her again. Quietly, he said, "I'm glad to hear it. We'll talk again, but in the meantime I think you should rest."

He walked over to the door but did not open it at once. Instead, he stood looking at her silently for a moment before he said, "I cursed Elizabeth for sending you here, but now I think perhaps I should thank her. At least here you will be safe."

For a long while after he was gone, she did not move but remained staring at the door unseeingly. What a strange man he was, terrifying one moment, comforting the next. *Obey me*, he said. Everything seemed to hinge on that. She shook her head ruefully. Trust him to pick the one thing she'd never been any good at.

Very well, she would try. But he had to realize there were limits. This feeling between them, this frightening passion, controlled them both. He might not be willing to admit that, but she had no choice but to do so. Where he was concerned, she might truly be her own worst enemy.

When Libbie came a few hours later with her supper, she found Deirdre sitting near the window, staring out at the gathering night. She hadn't bothered to light the brazier, leaving the room deep in shadows. The maid clucked her tongue as she hurried to set matters right.

"Come now, my lady, this won't do. You've a fine supper here, and the seamstresses have finished more of your clothing. Isn't this the loveliest night rail you've ever seen?"

Deirdre glanced at the confection of silk and lace the maid held out. It looked like something made for a bride to wear on her wedding night. She sighed. Delacroix she had to avoid, but Ewan she must see as soon as possible.

"It's late now, but would you ask your brother to call on me tomorrow?"

The maid looked startled. "Certainly, my lady, I'll tell him you want to see him, but he'll have to ask His Lordship."

"Why? Surely a man with the responsibility of steward can come and go as he pleases?"

"Not here, my lady. Only Lizzie and me are allowed to wait on you. Why, not even the guard can come in."

"I see," Deirdre said slowly. "I had a visit from the earl this afternoon. Do the rules not apply to him?"

Libbie giggled, a most incongruous sound to come from so sensible a creature. It was inspired by the fact that she had heard about His Lordship's visit; indeed the details of it, scanty though they were, had kept the servants' hall abuzz all afternoon. Crashed in the door, had he? Stayed awhile but only talking? Ah, well, it was early days yet. "Hardly, my lady. After all, he makes the rules."

Oh, yes, he most certainly did, and he made them to his convenience. He could do anything he wanted, and so could—indeed, must—everybody else.

"I would still like to see your brother," Deirdre said firmly.

Libbie bobbed her head. "As you say, my lady. Now, about your supper . . ."

She wanted to say she wasn't hungry. She wanted to send it away untouched. Two things stopped her: the certain knowledge that such an action would inspire another visit from her captor, and the undeniable fact that the food really did smell delicious.

"The cook here must be very talented," she murmured.

"Oh, indeed, he is, my lady, and I don't mind telling you he's ever so pleased to have someone who appreciates good food. His Lordship's taste is as plain as you please, although he did compliment Ewan on the wine last night."

"Did he? Was that unusual?"

"Oh, yes, my lady. Ewan could hardly get over it. His Lordship's never said a word about anything to do with the house. Now, the rest of the manor's a different matter. He knows the number of lambs born each spring to the very last one, the condition of every field, even who's ailing in each and every of the villages. Marvelous, it is. But the house, that he's never paid any mind to. Shame, really, for it's a lovely place."

Deirdre gave her an encouraging smile, blessing the fates who had placed so talkative and well-informed a maid in her service. "Tell me, do the people here like His Lordship?" Swiftly, she added, "Be frank, for as you must know, there's no reason not to be. The earl and I are not exactly on friendly terms. I will not carry tales to him."

Libbie's eyes widened. From her point of view, a man who provided such luxurious surroundings and tender care ought to be regarded in the most friendly way possible. But the nobility was different, everyone knew that, and Her Ladyship was Irish after all. Good people, the Irish, but fairy-addled. Everyone also knew that.

"We bless the day he came, my lady," she said, "and that's the truth. The old lord, all he did was sit around drinking and complaining. Awful, he was. After that there was a bunch of them all at once, I couldn't keep them straight. They kept dying something terrible one after another."

"I heard about that," Deirdre murmured. "And then the present earl came."

"Oh, yes, my lady, he did, and terrible it was." Libbie rolled her eyes.

"Why? I thought you said you blessed the day?"

"Oh, and we do, but he was hurt so badly there were fears he wouldn't live. Then for a long time the doctors he had up from London said he couldn't hope to walk again. He got so angry at them he sent them fleeing in the dead of night. Oh, and then, we were all close to weeping, for he forced himself despite the most terrible pain to show they were wrong. I've never seen a man with such courage, although it near broke our hearts. He walked finally, and rode and even ran, but there's still nights when Ewan says the pain takes him something horrible."

Deirdre's face was white. What was this, Delacroix injured and badly so? In pain for a long period of time, struggling to walk again? He had taken a blow to his head when last she saw him, but his coloring had been good and his breathing regular; she'd had every reason to believe he would recover without difficulty. What had gone so terribly wrong?

"How," she murmured, her voice thick, "how was he hurt?"

"At that battle, my lady, you must know of it, at

Yellowford." Libbie's voice dropped, becoming confidential. "They say he was trying to stop the fighting and got caught between the two armies. Awful it must have been. They didn't find him for two days, and then he was almost gone with fever. I'll tell you, my lady, if he weren't so fiercesome strong and with the will of ten ordinary men, he wouldn't be alive today.

"Oh, my lady, what troubles you?"

"Nothing," Deirdre said shakily. It was an obvious lie. She was ashen, her hands trembled, and her eyes were dark with pain. Quickly, she sat down, fearing her legs would not hold her. Images too horrible to be endured darted through her mind. She felt as though her entire body was being wrenched apart.

Libbie ran over to the door and banged on it. Instantly, it was opened by the stern-faced guard. "Her Ladyship's ill," the maid blurted. "You must tell the earl. She went all over queer without any warning."

"Wait!" Deirdre called as strongly as she could manage. "It's all right, there's nothing wrong."

The man looked at her uncertainly. A little of her color had returned, but she still appeared shocked and weak. If she was ill and he failed to report it, it would mean his head. On the other hand, he didn't relish disturbing the earl unless he was sure he had reason.

"I'm fine," Deirdre said. With effort, she got to her feet. "I'm sorry you were both troubled. I must still be weary from the journey here. A good night's rest and I'll be fine." She managed a smile that was far more confident than she felt.

The guard remained uncertain. "Are you sure, my lady? Maybe it would be better if I just told His Lordship. He can decide what's best for you."

"He's already doing more than enough of that," Deirdre said firmly. "There is absolutely no reason to disturb him. It was a momentary weakness, completely gone now."

Libbie nodded slowly. The maid was remembering just what they'd been talking about when Her Ladyship was taken over so queerlike. My, but didn't she seem not to like the idea of the earl being hurt? Not on friendly terms, were they? Her Ladyship might have some other word for it, but Libbie knew better. She smiled broadly.

"There, now, it looks as though everything's right again," she said to the guard. "Sorry for troubling you. I'll just finish up here and be on my way."

He lingered a moment later, assuring himself the crisis was past, before securing the door once again. When they were once more alone, Libbie said, "Come now, my lady, let me help you out of that gown. You'll feel better when you're more comfortable."

Deirdre lacked the strength to refuse. In the aftermath of what she had learned, she felt bruised and exhausted. Mutely, she allowed herself to be disrobed, the luxurious night rail slipped over her head, and her hair brushed smooth.

Libbie placed the gown away in a garderobe, checked the brazier to make sure it was burning well, and patted the fur throw on the bed just for the pleasure of touching it.

"You will eat a good supper, won't you, my lady?" she asked.

"I'll do my best," Deirdre promised.

"I'll be back in a bit to collect the tray. Is there anything else you'd like?"

Only to be taken out of herself, freed of all responsibility, and able at last to follow her heart, none of which was remotely possible. "No, thank you."

Libbie bobbed a curtsy and was gone a moment later. Deirdre glanced at the food reluctantly. Her appetite was gone, but she would have to make some effort. Despite the brazier, the thin night rail made her feel chill. She took the fur throw from the bed and wrapped it around herself. With her legs folded under her, she managed the soup and bread but left the rest untouched. She would owe the cook her apologies.

Wearily, she returned to the bed and got under the covers. The scent of crisp, clean linen enveloped her. When Libbie returned for the tray, the room was silent except for the deep, even breathing coming from the bed. Libbie glanced at the figure lying there and thought without rancor that she had never seen anything so beautiful. It was no wonder that the earl was behaving as he was, and he such a splendid figure of a man. They were a good match for each other. All that remained was for them to discover it. She went off briskly, anticipating the tale she had to tell in the servants' hall, all about how Her Ladyship had paled, indeed come close to fainting when she learned of His Lordship's suffering. She would spin it out, making the others wait for the best parts, perhaps with appropriate gestures and long sighs. Oh, but it would be wonderful, and the best part of all being that there was more to come. Not on friendly terms, indeed. Speed sweet day to reveal what next would happen between this pair of fated lovers!

CHAPTER
19

AS IT HAPPENED, DAY DID SEEM TO COME quickly. Deirdre woke feeling as though she had laid her head on the pillow scant moments before, only to discover bright sunlight streaming into the room. She barely had time to blink the sleep from her eyes before Libbie and Lizzie arrived with her bath. An hour later, bathed, dressed, brushed, and beribboned—and having disposed of an adequate portion of breakfast—she faced the task of getting through the remainder of the day.

There was absolutely nothing to do. Obviously, this was Delacroix's plan. Stuff her full of food, smother her in silk and lace, and let her mind turn to mush. At the end of the process, she would be his ideal woman, sweet, compliant and grateful for the smallest morsel of attention.

If she hadn't known what he had suffered, she could have armored herself in outrage. As it was, all she could manage was growing dread that he might succeed. But only if she let him. There had to be some way to occupy herself. She could . . . or she might . . . or . . .

Nothing. The room, gracious as it was, provided absolutely no release. Had she been better at mathematics, she might have amused herself counting the number of stones in the walls and devising complicated equations involving them. Had she been more diligent, she could entertain herself with prose and poetry from memory. Had she been holier, she could find solace in prayer. But she was as she was, and there was no sense regretting it.

She could, of course, simply request something to occupy her time. But that would mean asking Delacroix, and that she could not bring herself to do.

Perhaps if the steward came to see her, she might ask him. Yes, that was the best solution. Surely, the earl would allow him to come. This idea of keeping her isolated except for himself and the maids was ridiculous. He couldn't possibly mean to keep it up.

In fact, he could. When the door to her chamber opened a short time later, it was not the steward who entered.

"Good morning," Delacroix said. He was dressed, as usual, in black, and as usual, he looked devastatingly handsome. His thick golden hair was still damp, falling in thick waves below the collar of his doublet. His eyes, set in the deeply tanned face, were piercing. She resisted the impulse to shrink before them and instead matched him stare for stare.

"Good morning. Don't you believe in knocking?"

His mouth quirked. "If I did, would you bid me enter?"

"No, of course not."

"There you have your answer. Now tell me, how are you? Did you sleep well? Have you eaten?"

"I am fine, I slept perfectly." It was untrue; she had experienced nightmares she thankfully could not remember. "And if I eat much more, I will not be able to wear these absurd gowns your steward keeps providing."

This morning's gown was scarlet silk, the perfect foil for her ebony hair, as low cut as the previous day's and if possible even more frivolously feminine.

"I asked to see Ewan," she went on, "but I was told he had to have your permission first. Is that really necessary?"

"Absolutely. With your penchant for escaping, I wouldn't send any poor male into your coils unless he was well prepared to deal with you."

Deirdre's azure gaze narrowed to shards of ice. "I do not have *coils*. I merely wish to inform your steward that the clothing he is providing is not appropriate. I require something plainer and more restrained."

"I see," Delacroix said. His teeth flashed. "Then it isn't Ewan you want, it's me. He merely follows my instructions."

Deirdre hesitated. She had presumed the steward was responsible, being unable to imagine Delacroix concerning himself with such foolishness. "Yours? I didn't realize you were so knowledgeable about fashion."

"I'm not totally ignorant," he informed her. "You look much better than the ladies at court. What's that thing they're wearing nowadays to puff out their skirts, what's it called?"

"Farthingales," Deirdre said.

"That's it. Awful things. They can't sit in them,

they knock over anything they get near, and they look like beached whales. I can't understand why women would do that to themselves."

"Perhaps to put some distance between themselves and the men," she suggested tartly. "Did that ever occur to you?"

"Not really. From what I saw, that's the last thing they have in mind."

Deirdre fumed inwardly. It was plain enough what he meant, but that obnoxious smile made it crystal clear. Arrogant as sin, he was, and didn't care who knew it. So what if the court ladies made a fuss over him? It meant nothing at all, as far as she was concerned.

Maybe so, but it did mean something to the little green imp who stirred deep within her. The good Deirdre hammered it back into its box where it stayed, however reluctantly, kicking and hissing.

"You were at court then," she said. "How exciting. What was it like dancing attendance on that evil old thing?"

"Elizabeth isn't evil," he corrected matter-of-factly. "She's merely determined. She has a vision of how she wants Britain to be, and she does anything she has to in order to protect it."

"How nice for you English. The rest of us see it somewhat differently."

"I suppose you would, but remember, this rebellion was your father's idea. He seems to have jumped into it without any thought of where it would lead."

"He did no such thing," Deirdre protested. "He wants Ireland to be strong and free, in control of her own destiny."

"And I'd like roses to blossom in winter, but that

has about as much likelihood of happening. A free Ireland would be an immediate target for Spain and France. They'd be fighting each other to carve you up because, like it or not, Ireland is the key to all of Britain. Your only hope for survival lies in a strong alliance with England, and the only way you will get that is to come out of this fairy-addled dream of reviving some romantic past and accept reality."

"The reality is that England has raped and plundered Ireland for almost five hundred years," she shot back furiously. "How do you expect us to accept that? We can never forget what you have done."

Delacroix closed his eyes for a moment, fighting the almost irresistible urge to take her by the shoulders and shake some sense into her. "You can't live in the past. You have to build for the future; otherwise, nothing ever changes, there can never be any progress. Don't you understand that?"

"Yes," Deirdre said softly. "I understand it perfectly, but I am a woman. Women have to think of the future, because we're the ones who have the children. It's you men who never seem to care."

"I care," he said with such intensity that she could not help but believe him. "I have seen far too many men die and been responsible for far too many deaths myself."

She shook her head in bewilderment. "If you truly feel that way, why do you still say you are a warrior? Why don't you renounce it?"

His eyes met hers. Quietly, he said, "Because I have responsibilities to safeguard those placed in my care. Sometimes the only way to do that is to fight."

Abruptly, he shook his head. "How did we go

from talking of your gowns to talk of war? Surely there are better occupations for so pleasant a day."

"Are there?" she murmured, trying not to sound too hopeful.

"Come for a walk with me," he said.

Deirdre steeled herself. It was on the tip of her tongue to agree. To be free of the confines of the room was almost too tempting. But more tempting still was the urge to be with Delacroix himself. Softly, her voice trembling slightly, she said, "I cannot." He started to speak, but she went on quickly. "This is not disobedience, it is a matter of honor. There is something very strong between us. I cannot deny it any more than I can yield to it. For that reason, it is better if we are not together."

Delacroix looked at her for a long moment. He was very much of two minds. Her admission that she was vulnerable to the feelings between them gave him a certain satisfaction. He would have been less than human if he'd been content to suffer along. On the other hand, she clearly meant what she said. She would rather stay confined in the tower chamber than accept his company.

So be it. She set her terms; now he would set his. Without a single qualm, he said, "I won't place the responsibility for keeping you secure on anyone else. If you refuse to be accompanied by me, you must remain here."

Deirdre's breath caught. He had been so accommodating thus far, indeed so much more so than she could have hoped, that this suddenly uncompromising position caught her unawares. He presented her with a stark choice—risk being with him or stay confined within her prison. The sense of being trapped rose up, almost choking her. She had to fight against it with all the will she possessed.

"Then I will stay," she said, very low.

Delacroix looked at her for a long moment before he nodded. "As you wish." He turned to go.

Deirdre held out a hand to stop him. "Wait." She hesitated. "I . . . I have nothing to do."

He frowned. "Do?"

She strained for patience. "To occupy my time. Otherwise, the hours pass very slowly."

"I hadn't thought of that."

What did he imagine? That she was content to while away the day doing nothing? Tightly, she said, "I am used to being busy."

He nodded, remembering how she had worked in the garden at Dungannon, her hands coaxing beauty from the fertile earth. "I suppose you are. Let's see . . . you could do needlework."

"No, I couldn't."

"Why not? That's what ladies do, isn't it?"

"Perhaps so, but I'm not any good at needlework."

"That doesn't matter," he assured her. "You can just amuse yourself."

Deirdre gritted her teeth. In another minute, he'd be patting her on the head and telling her to be a good little girl. "The only use I have for a needle is to stitch up wounds," she said firmly. "I would greatly appreciate it if you could suggest something else."

Delacroix hid a grin. It wasn't kind to provoke her, but he couldn't resist. She looked so adorable standing there with her cheeks flushed and her eyes alight with anger. He'd always preferred sweet-tempered women, mainly because they gave the least trouble, but Deirdre made him reconsider. "All right," he said, relenting slightly, "I have a good library. It is at your service. You may read whatever you wish."

Deirdre almost sighed with relief. Books offered at least some form of escape, however temporary. "Thank you," she said softly.

He nodded. "I will send Ewan with a selection. You may speak with him then about your wardrobe." His eyes wandered over her, lingering on the ripe swell of her breasts visible above the low-cut gown. He smiled faintly. "Who knows, you may even be able to convince him that you should be plainly dressed. However, I doubt it."

"We will see." She hesitated again, trying to decide if he was disposed to grant her another favor. "One other thing, if you wouldn't mind. Libbie mentioned that her grandmother is a healer. Is that right?"

Delacroix nodded. "Granny Dru, she's called, and she's better than any charlatan physician. Why?"

"Since I can't go to her, would it be possible for her to come here? I would like to talk with her, find out what she knows about herbs and such."

"I don't see why not. I'll tell Ewan you'd like to see her."

Deirdre did her best to contain her excitement. The books were welcome, but the chance to meet with the woman who made the salve she'd used was an unhoped-for benefit. Much as she hated the idea of staying confined in her room, perhaps it wouldn't be so bad after all.

She almost said as much to Delacroix. Only one thing stopped her, the sudden gleam in his eyes as he took in the full extent of her satisfaction. From his perspective, that simply wasn't right. Here he was aching for her, accepting that her modesty and sense of honor drove her to remain apart from him, and all the while she was looking like the cat who swallowed the canary.

Not right at all. And not to be borne.

"You shall have whatever you wish," he said, "so long as I choose to grant it. But I, too, have wants. . . ."

A steely arm reached out, enveloping her and drawing her hard against the long length of his body. Deirdre had but a moment to gasp before his hand covered the back of her head, fingers twisting in the thick, fragrant hair. Frantically, she tried to escape, only to discover that she could not. He held her gently, but with implacable firmness.

She watched, eyes wide with apprehension, as his golden head bent. In the instant before his mouth touched hers, he murmured, "Hold still."

She most certainly would not. She would resist him to the last ounce of her strength. She would . . .

She was melting. Sweet, hot desire pulsed through her. The muscles of her abdomen clenched. Her nipples were suddenly achingly sensitive. The tension centered in the delicate tissues of her womanhood, where she felt a swelling tenderness.

"No," she managed in the instant before his mouth took hers, his tongue plunging deeply, allowing her no retreat. Shocked, she gasped. It was an elemental mistake born of innocence, for it allowed him to consolidate his victory. Boldly, he claimed her even more thoroughly, stroking and caressing until she thought she would be driven mad by the sensations he unleashed. She fought to keep from responding, but his hands, wandering over her, made her defeat even more inevitable. He palmed her buttocks, squeezing lightly, and brought her firmly against the unmistakable evidence of his desire.

Deirdre's senses whirled. Another, more primitive self seemed to be taking control of her. Desperately, she struggled against it. Delacroix raised his head. His eyes had gone dangerously dark. Passion drew his features taut. He had meant only to kiss her once, in small compensation for his tolerance, but it wasn't working out that way. She was a fever in his blood, a wind howling in his soul, a devouring need that blocked out all else.

And so pliant in his arms, despite the resistance he could feel pouring from her. His mouth grazed the slender line of her throat down to the hollow between her collarbones. He savored the sweetly female taste of her, only to find it made him ravenous for more.

His hand slipped into her bodice, straining the fragile silk, and fastened on her firm, uptilted breast. Dimly, he heard her gasp again, but the sound made little impression. He was lost in the swirling fury of his own desire. He grasped her nipple between his thumb and index finger, bringing it to even greater hardness. A low sound came from his throat. He pushed the gown aside, baring both breasts.

Slowly, with deliberate thoroughness, he drew a nipple between his teeth, sucking and stroking with his tongue. Deirdre cried out. Her fingers tangled in the thick mane of his hair, trying frantically to pull him away. His arm tightened around her commandingly. Savoring her with unbridled deliberation, he kissed and caressed each breast in turn, as the tender pink flesh tightened and puckered. Her skin gleamed, moist and flushed. Her eyes grew heavy-lidded and luminous. Bared to the waist, her hair tumbling around her shoulders, her mouth full and ripe, she was the incarnation of sensuality.

Sheer will had carried Delacroix into battle again and again, through the snows of Russia, into worlds and dangers other men quailed before. Now it, just barely, enabled him to step away from Deirdre. He stood, his body taut, his eyes smoldering, and fought for control.

He could take her now while her body so clearly overruled her mind; she wouldn't even fight him. But afterward?

Afterward, he would have to live with the knowledge that there could be a fine line between seduction and rape, and that he had crossed it. Her innocence made her especially vulnerable to a skilled and commanding lover, but it was also her best shield. He simply could not bring himself to take it from her in such a way.

Had he been able at that moment to drive a sword through his conscience, ridding himself of the merciless thing, he would have done so.

"Perhaps you are right," he said thickly, "it would be best for us to avoid one another."

Deirdre did not even try to answer him. She was trembling from head to toe, drowning in the sensations he unleashed. Only belatedly did she realize how exposed she was. A moan tore from her as she crossed her hands over her naked breasts.

"Get out," she said brokenly.

A moment longer he lingered, drinking in the sight of her until the torment became too great. Only then did he go, the door thudding behind him, the iron bar slipping back into place.

CHAPTER 20

"NO, NO," GRANNY DRU SAID, "IT HAS TO BE stirred more slowly and not so close to the flame. Here, now, let me show you."

Deirdre stepped back from the table where they were working. She watched carefully as the tiny, gnarled old woman moved the stone bowl farther from the candle and gently stirred its contents with a fragrant twig of hawthorn.

"Slowly," she repeated, "always slowly. The good things can't be rushed. If you want it to set right, you've got to remember that."

Deirdre took the twig and with great care continued to stir the pale-yellow mixture simmering gently in the bowl. Granny Dru watched her for a few moments before nodding in satisfaction.

"That's it. You're a fast learner. But then, you weren't exactly a beginner, were you? Truth is, you've taught me a thing or two these past few days."

Deirdre smiled but kept her attention on what she was doing. "I'm flattered. You're a good teacher, and you're more knowledgeable than any healer I've ever met."

"Known a few, have you?"

"Not really, but some of the nuns at a convent in Ireland where I lived for several years were skilled in healing. Afterward, I had to learn on my own, mainly by trial and error. Mostly error, I'm afraid."

"That's how it's been for all of us," Granny Dru said. "So much of the old ways have been lost, and there's so few who seek to recover them." She cast a speculative look at the younger woman. Deirdre was swathed from neck to ankle in a white apron she had improvised out of a sheet. It was intended to protect the magnificent blue silk gown she wore, yet another of Ewan's additions to her wardrobe.

Ewan, it seemed, was deaf, at least so far as her entreaties were concerned. He smiled, he nodded, he even commiserated when she expressed her dismay over how she was being dressed. Then he ignored her and went on exactly the same. Daily, he brought her new books when he escorted Granny Dru to see her. Each time she beseeched him anew, and each time he assured her he was doing his best. Slowly but inescapably, it was dawning on Deirdre that Ewan's principal concern was pleasing his master, and that he clearly intended to do by rigging her out in the most blatantly feminine garments he could have devised. It was an exercise in futility, so far as Deirdre was concerned, for Delacroix had not come near her since their last tumultuous encounter.

At the thought of the earl, her hand stilled. For

three days, she had managed to keep him from her mind at least while she had work to do. The rest of the time, she didn't even try. He was a constant presence, haunting the daylight hours and filling her fitful sleep with dreams she did her best not to remember.

"Something wrong?" Granny Dru asked.

Deirdre shook her head hastily. "Not at all."

The old woman smiled to herself. When the mixture had cooked sufficiently and Deirdre was pouring it into a stone bottle, Granny Dru said, "'Tis a shame you won't come gathering. I've rarely seen such a fine year for the wild things."

"I'd like to," Deirdre said softly, "but I can't."

"Because His Lordship won't trust you to another."

Deirdre looked up quickly. "You know about that?"

Granny Dru chuckled. "Gentry always think they've got secrets from the ordinary folk, and they almost never do."

"What makes you think I'm gentry?"

"The same thing that makes me think the sky is blue, the evidence of my own eyes." She shook her head chidingly. "It's as plain as the nose on your face, and would be even if I didn't know you were Deirdre O'Neill, daughter of Hugh O'Neill, taken during an English raid and brought here for safekeeping."

Deirdre stared at her openmouthed. "Libbie never addresses me by name, and neither does Ewan. I presumed they didn't know."

"Of course they do. We had it all from a sailor on the yawl that brought you. What I don't know is where the harp comes into it."

"Harp?" Deirdre repeated. She set the stone bottle

down before she could drop it and stared at the old woman. "What harp?"

"The harp I saw in the smoke," Granny Dru said calmly. "It's something you might try yourself sometime, for truly I think you have the gift. Night before last when the moon was full I went a wee bit out of the village to a spot I know where the old ones used to come. There I made a fire of oak and white birch. It has to be those woods, for they were sacred to the Mother and still are. When they had got to smoking good, I looked into the flame and there I saw a harp."

"It's superstition," Deirdre said vehemently. She would not listen to this.

"Nay, child," Granny Dru went on relentlessly. "It's a gift, and not to be scorned. The earl's a good man. Hard as nails and brutal when he needs to be, but he'd keep you safe and cherish you for all time. Why reject that?"

"You don't understand," Deirdre blurted. All the pent-up confusion and anguish she had been feeling for days threatened to burst forth. Her voice was thick with emotion as she said, "He is English, I am Irish. There can never be anything between us."

"Indeed? 'Tis a strange thing, you know, but nature never seems to care about such like. A man sees a woman, a woman sees a man, the fire leaps between them, and the rest takes care of itself."

"Not always. There are other concerns—duty, honor . . ."

Granny Dru scoffed. "Child, your only duty is to fulfill the purpose for which you were born into the world. You're more likely to discover that by listening to your own heart than anything else. As for honor, it's a cold word and one that's been twisted even more than most. What dishonor is there in cleaving to a good man who cares for you?"

"This good man, as you call him, serves my country's most ruthless enemy."

"Elizabeth," Granny Dru murmured. Her sharp brown eyes grew thoughtful. "Now, there's a tale. You know her mother, the Boleyn, was a dappler."

"A dappler? What does that mean?"

"She tried to find the old ways and use them to her purpose. Smart enough she was to know what to look for, and with just enough of the gift to succeed for a while. But she was betrayed by ambition and fell into the darkness."

"Does Elizabeth have any of her ability?" Deirdre asked nervously. Never mind her claim that it was all superstition. She, too, had felt the pull of something ancient and remorseless swirling under the swollen moon, felt it even on the most sunlit day when the breeze blew just so and all of nature shone forth. If Elizabeth could make that power her own, Ireland was truly doomed.

But Granny Dru shook her head. "Not her; she turned her back on it while she was still a child. Feared the darkness that took her mother, and rightly so."

"Thank God for that."

"Maybe, but don't underestimate her for it. She's survived against odds that would have had any man in his grave long ago. There's times I think something protects her—her or England, it's hard to say. If it's not the darkness—and it isn't—then you have to wonder."

"Great evils have been done in her name in Ireland," Deirdre insisted.

"Here, too. Don't ask the Welsh to sing England's praise. But nothing's ever simple. People are weak, they make mistakes. What counts is how it ends. Myself, I wouldn't oppose her, and not out of fear. I've a suspicion that when all is said and done, we'll be more glad than sorry that she was here."

Deirdre shook her head wearily. She didn't want to dispute the old woman for whom she had great respect and growing affection. But she had been raised from earliest childhood to see Elizabeth of England as a vile enemy. It was too much to expect her to do otherwise, no matter how much easier that might make her situation.

Granny Dru began to gather up her pots and bowls, her vials and boxes. She packed them away in the worn leather bundle she carried. "Shall I come again tomorrow, lass?"

"If you would. I greatly appreciate the chance to learn from you."

The old woman smiled. "Aye, old Granny knows the way. I'll teach you all I can so long as your heart's open to it." She laid a gnarled hand on Deirdre's arm and looked at her deeply. "I can only see the harp, I can't see who sits in the shadows behind it. But I wager you know."

"Perhaps . . ."

"I thought so. Listen with your heart, child. 'Tis the power speaking to you."

Long after she was gone, Deirdre sat by the tower window, her mind turning over what the old one had said. It was all well and good for Granny Dru to speak of higher duty, ancient power, and such like. Her words wove reverence over the earthy sweat and strain of simple lust.

How she ached for him! The torment of unfulfilled desire left her feeling bruised and battered. For three days—and nights—she had fought to deny the creature he had awakened within her, that wanton, sensual woman who had stood bare-breasted and let him do as he would with her.

She hadn't succeeded. If anything, the struggle made her need all the greater. The remainder of the afternoon passed with painful slowness. By the time night came, she had a throbbing headache. Libbie brought her one of Granny Dru's teas, which she drank gratefully, but not even that helped. She lay down in the bed certain she would be unable to sleep, but her body surprised her. Before long, a curious peace settled over her, stripping away fear and frustration. Far off in the distance, she half thought she heard a muted sound, the call of a flute, perhaps, or merely the wind. Her eyes grew heavier. She drifted in the shadowed place between sleep and wakefulness, listening to the flute. A flame leaped. From deep within it, the strum of a harp sang out. Flute and harp, playing, joining, voices raised together. No, wait, it wasn't a flute, but something older, ancient even when the harp was young. Pan pipes, teasing, rejoicing in their celebration of life unbridled.

Her eyes flickered open. She stared into flame.

"My lady," Ewan said.

Deirdre started. She must have been asleep after all, or perhaps she still was. What could the steward be doing in the tower chamber?

The flame was a torch he carried. Behind him the door stood open. A guard was there, looking anxious.

She sat up slowly. "What is it? What's happened?"

"'Tis the earl, my lady. He's in great pain. When he finds out I've come to you, he'll have my head, but I've no choice. He's got to have help."

"Granny Dru . . . ?"

"I sent to the village for her an hour ago. She's not to be found. It's as though she disappeared."

A suspicion began to dawn in Deirdre. She wouldn't put it past the healer to do exactly that. Likely as not, she was off among the sacred wood, communing with her old ones and laughing over the folly of poor mortals.

"I'll come," she murmured. "Just give me a moment."

He withdrew, leaving her in darkness except for the flickering brazier. She dressed as quickly as she could, cursing the tiny buttons and elaborate fastenings. Ewan was waiting directly outside the door when she was done.

"I have no medicines," she warned him. "Without them, I can do little."

"The man I sent to Granny Dru had the sense to bring back her calling bag."

Deirdre nodded. That would have to do. What mattered now was to get to Delacroix and assess the situation for herself.

Her teeth clenched the moment she entered his chamber. She fought the urge to cry out. He lay in the center of a huge, four-poster bed, the covers twisted and sweat-stained, his face contorted in agony. His hair was matted, his skin gray. Only his eyes remained as fiercely alive as ever.

They darkened with terrible anger when he saw her. Hoarsely, he said, "Get out."

Deirdre ignored him. She was far too busy trying to determine exactly what was wrong. "Pull the covers back," she instructed Ewan.

He leaped to obey, but thought better of it as Delacroix let loose a savage curse.

"Don't pay any attention to him," Deirdre said. "He's out of his head. Just do as I say."

Reluctantly, with the utmost caution, Ewan complied. Deirdre swallowed a gasp. Two things she observed immediately. The first was that the old wound to Delacroix's leg was far worse than she had imagined. The second— or perhaps it really was the first, it being hard to say—was that he slept naked.

And why not? So did many another man. She'd never been caused any discomfort by it before, and she didn't see why she should now. He was just like any other man, after all, only more so. Definitely more so.

Laughing and those damn pipes again. Her head whirled. Granny Dru's tea flowed hot through her veins. "Get me a basin of warm water," she instructed. Her voice seemed to come from a great distance. "Also towels and the calling bag."

Delacroix made to move. She laid her hand firm on his chest and said sternly, "Don't. You've obviously already been a great fool, but that stops now. Lie still and do as you're told."

He muttered something under his breath.

"What?" she asked.

"I said," he rasped between gritted teeth, "you'll do the lying and I'll do the telling. But for now get the hell out of here."

She smiled coolly even as relief crashed through her. He wasn't as far gone as she'd feared, but then, he was a man of immense strength and will. Even so the wound had almost undone him. She winced as she touched the livid red scar that ran down his left thigh almost as far as the knee.

"What did this to you?" she asked tautly.

"A pike wielded by one of your lovely Irish lads, the ones you're always saying want freedom and dignity. All he wanted was my blood, and the fact that I wasn't armed made no difference."

Deirdre paled. "Not armed?"

"My sword was sheathed. I was trying to reach Bagenal to convince him to withdraw rather than stay and be massacred the way he was, the stupid fool. Anyway, it's done. I'll pay the price for forgetting I'm still half a cripple, but I don't have to let you stand by and watch it. I'm warning you, Deirdre, get out now or I won't be to blame for anything I do!"

This was too much. Here she was doing her utmost to help him, and how did he thank her? Typical male, thickheaded and bossy. She was absolutely fed up with it. "You great galoot! Barely able to lift your head, and you're threatening me? You mind your manners, or I'll forget I'm a lady."

He stared at her dumbfounded until, through all the pain, a gleam of rueful humor appeared in his silvered eyes. Softly, he said, "I think I'd like to see that."

She flushed, memory rising to taunt her. She hadn't been a lady three days before when she stood half-naked in his arms, yearning for his possession.

"Oh, be quiet. I've work to do. Where's Ewan?"

As though in response, the steward hurried through the door, sloshing a basin of water as he came.

"Careful with that," Deirdre snapped. "Set it down

there. Here, now, you keep an eye on him while I see what Granny Dru's bag contains."

A bit of everything, it seemed—salves, tinctures, infusions, poultices, needles, clamps, bandages and a few things Deirdre couldn't identify all carefully organized and, thankfully, labeled. She found what she needed and set quickly to work.

"The muscles are tightly knotted," she said. "That's what causes the pain. How did you do this to yourself?"

"Running," Delacroix muttered. He clenched his teeth as her long, slender fingers dug into his thigh, seeking the source of the trouble.

"Running? Were you chasing something?"

He shook his head. "Just running."

Her eyes met Ewan's. Perplexed, she asked, "Why would anyone just run?"

"He does it for the exercise," the steward murmured.

Deirdre had never heard of such a thing. Men rode out to hunt, wreaked mayhem in the training yard, or sat around sharpening their weapons and boasting of their exploits. Otherwise, they were underfoot, drinking, belching, and generally causing trouble.

Not that it mattered. He'd done what he'd done and she had to deal with the consequences. But he was also a man of pride, and he would not appreciate being seen by a servant in his weakness.

"You may go now," she said gently. "If I have need of you, I will call."

Ewan nodded, grateful for release. Later, he would have to face His Lordship, but he preferred not to think of that.

When he was gone, Deirdre soaked a towel in the water and placed it carefully over the wound. As she did, her fingers grazed the soft nest of golden curls at his groin. She flinched, her cheeks fiery.

Delacroix stared down the length of his body and, despite everything, laughed. Here he was in some of the worst pain of his life, and did his manhood care? Of course not. Even as he watched—and Deirdre tried futilely not to—it hardened and thickened, preparing itself for dalliance.

"I'm sorry," he murmured, although truth be told, there was nothing at all contrite in his tone. On the contrary, Deirdre thought he sounded smug.

Deliberately, she said, "Oh, don't be. That happens all the time."

He scowled. "What the hell are you talking about?"

"I wouldn't be much of a healer if I didn't know how a man's body works."

That sounded about right, straight and to the point, even a bit bored. Exactly as she wished she felt, rather than this queer melting sensation that had hold of her. The sight of his magnificent body, the touch of his hair-roughened skin, the heat radiating from him, all threatened to overcome her. He was a patient, saints preserve her, in need of her care, and yet all she could think of was how he would feel deep within her.

"You're blushing," Delacroix murmured. The pain was easing. In its place came another ache that in its own way was just as insistent.

"I'm not."

"You are. Aaahh, that feels good. What are you doing?"

"Loosening the muscles, also stretching the tendons. Some of them are shorter now than they should be because of the wound, also less resilient. It's really remarkable that you recovered so completely."

Remarkable and almost inconceivable. She had some idea of what such a recovery must have cost him.

"I didn't know you'd been in the battle until Libbie told me," she said.

"Who's Libbie?"

She shot him a surprised glance. "One of the maids who waits on me. Ewan's sister."

"I didn't realize Ewan had a sister."

"He has two, twins, Libbie and Lizzie."

"Indeed, imagine that."

"Granny Dru is their grandmother. Did you truly not know this?"

"I'm afraid not."

"Libbie did say that, too. She claims you know the exact count of every lamb born in each of your villages but couldn't recall what you were served for dinner last night if your life depended on it.

His brow furrowed. "It sounds as though she has a great deal to say."

Despite herself, Deirdre smiled. "Oh, indeed, she's been a fount of information. Among other things, she informs me you make all the rules here and that it would be wise to follow them."

"Sensible girl, Libbie. I must compliment Ewan on her."

"Why? He's hardly responsible for her good sense. It's just like you men to be taking credit for something you had nothing at all to do with."

"Don't be silly. All I meant was . . ." He broke off, staring heavenward. "What's the use? You're the prickliest woman I've ever met. I can't see why I . . ."

"Why you what?" Deirdre demanded. In for a penny, in for a pound.

A moment later, she had reason to reconsider that. His burnished hand closed around her wrist. Weak as he was, his grip was still compelling. Holding her firmly, he said, "You know perfectly well what. Indeed, you have the evidence before you. Or perhaps you need a more detailed explanation."

"No," Deirdre said hastily. She managed to pull away, but only because he let her. "You go to sleep, that's the best thing for you. I will put a poultice on the leg to further draw out the pain. By tomorrow you should feel much improved, but you will have to go easy for several days."

"Do your worst," he murmured. He closed his eyes, only to open them again a moment later. "Ewan took you from the tower."

"He had to. He couldn't find Granny Dru."

"It's the middle of the night, isn't it? Where would she be but in her cottage?"

Deirdre shrugged. Not for the world would she tell him. "There are certain plants and other medicines that have to be gathered at night. Undoubtedly, that's what she's doing." Except for the laughter and the pipes, it might even be true.

"Hmmm, you realize this presents a problem." His voice was slightly slurred. The release from pain was having the desired effect. Weariness crept over him.

"Does it?" she murmured.

"If you aren't in the tower, you have to be with me."

"The guard awaits outside to escort me back."

"No, not his responsibility, mine. You stay."

"Delacroix . . ."

"Please."

She bit her lip and stared at him. His face was more relaxed, his eyes shut, his breathing becoming deeper and more regular. He looked . . . all sorts of things, but not, she tried to tell herself, dangerous.

A long sigh escaped her. Was it really so much to ask? Sometimes the simple knowledge that one was not alone was essential to healing.

"Sleep," she said.

"You'll . . . ?"

"Stay."

He smiled faintly, his hand seeking hers.

She sighed again and cautiously settled beside him. Damnable man, finding that one word that would move her. When had he ever said "please" before?

Never, so far as Delacroix could recall, but he'd said it now and it was working. She was there, in his bed, close to his hand. Perhaps he would sleep for an hour or two, and then . . .

Was that a flute he heard? No, something else . . . pipes? A sound almost gone from the world, yet he recognized it clear enough. Odd that, he would have to find out who played the pipes so close by. But first . . . he started slightly. Surely he was mistaken to think he saw in the shadows of the room smoke swirling and in it the rising moon, bright and beckoning, drawing him gently to its silvered breast.

CHAPTER
21

A HEAVY WEIGHT ACROSS DEIRDRE'S MIDDLE prevented her from moving. She tried once, twice, before giving up and snuggling back down into the bed. Sweet, comforting warmth enveloped her. She turned her head slightly. Her mouth brushed something hard, smooth, tasting faintly of salt.

Her mind sought out of the drowsy contentment of sleep to identify what the something might be. Down deep in the same place where the little imp of jealousy lived, among other interesting things that didn't get out too often, an alarm bell began to clang.

Skin. Bare, male skin. Delacroix. Bed. *Danger.*

Instinctively, her legs moved. That was a mistake. First, they became tangled even further in the heavy silk of her gown. Second, the effort woke Delacroix.

He cracked open one eye, then another, and peered at her blearily. Slowly, with pure masculine pleasure, he smiled.

"Deirdre?"

"No," she said quickly, "it isn't me. You're having a dream, actually a nightmare. I mean think about it, would I be here? Does that seem believable to you? This is wishful thinking, wishful dreaming, whatever. Go back to sleep."

His smile deepened until he looked for all the world like that damned golden wolf again, regarding a prey he fully intended to gobble up. "Deirdre, it is you. What are you prattling about?"

"Nothing, absolutely nothing. You're better, good, I'm so relieved. I was just leaving."

"Leaving? Oh, no, not that. No more escaping for you. I'm getting too old and feeble for the chase."

"Feeble, my eye, if you don't let go, I'll be marked for a week. Stop that! What are you doing?"

"Kissing you, sweetling. I love the taste and feel of you. There's this little spot at the bottom of your throat that . . ."

"Let me go! Damn you . . . stop . . . you're . . ." She put her hands on either side of his face, straining to push him away. The night's growth of whiskers like rough velvet made her palms prickle. She moaned. "Delacroix, don't . . ."

"Don't what?" he murmured, his mouth wandering farther, seeking the scented cleft between her breasts. "You're wearing too many clothes."

But not for long, if the deft movement of his fingers was anything to judge by. The tiny buttons and intricate fastenings that had given her such trouble didn't hinder him at all.

"Just how long were you at court?" she demanded, trying to slap his hands away. "You must have spent all of it in backstairs and private chambers to gain such expertise."

He laughed. "Jealous, pet?"

"No! And don't call me that."

His smile faded, his eyes suddenly serious. Quietly, he said, "I tried to stay away from you, Deirdre, truly I did. I ran myself into the ground these last few days just so I wouldn't go bursting into your tower and take you." He sighed and shook his head. "Fate conspires against my better self. You are here now, and I cannot let you go."

With implacable tenderness, he bent her back across the bed. His massive shoulders blocked out the light. She felt the slither of silk followed by the coolness of morning air. Instinctively, she trembled.

"You were made for this," he murmured thickly as his hands moved over her, boldly savoring every exquisite curve. "Made for a man to cherish and fill. I used to think of you with Red Hugh, until I came within a hair-breadth of killing him merely to keep him from you." He cupped her breasts, kneading them gently, and watched with satisfaction as her eyelids grew heavy.

His mouth nuzzled her belly. "He was a fool to let you go, but thank God he did. No red-haired babes, sweetling, not here and not at your breast. You are mine." Fiercely, he gazed down at her, lying bared and open to his touch. "Accept me, Deirdre. I want you willing, for the thought of hurting you is a knife through me. There will be pain, but only this once, and if you will allow it, great pleasure for us both."

His entreaty left her dazed. He was so big, so powerful, so easily capable of overwhelming her. The muscles in his arms and chests clenched with the force of his restraint. She was trapped, and yet she was not. By waiting, by letting her decide, he made her free.

"Delacroix," she murmured on a thread of sound, "let there be no misunderstanding between us now. What I give, I will also take. You will be mine."

His smile was of infinite relief and breathtaking tenderness. "A better fate I cannot ask." He moved then with consummate thoroughness, hands and mouth sweeping over her, coaxing away the last lingering remnants of shyness and bringing in their place exultant passion. Not an inch of her went untouched. At last, when her head was tossing back and forth across the pillow and soft moans broke from her throat, he stroked the delicate inner skin of her thighs, his hand reaching higher to find the moist petals of her womanhood.

He closed his eyes for an instant on a wave of nearly intolerable desire. He slipped his hands beneath her, grasping her buttocks. A steely leg nudged hers farther apart.

Sweat dampened his brow as he strained for the last measure of control. The tip of his manhood pressed against her, slowly, carefully, entering only a little.

She was empty, and she hadn't even known it. The revelation stunned Deirdre. She reached out to him, her slender hand closing around his manhood, and drew him to her.

The touch of her fingers around him snapped the last shreds of Delacroix's control. A low, guttural sound erupted from him. His hips surged as he drove deep within her.

Deirdre uttered a soft cry. She felt a hot dart of pain that faded almost before it began. In its place came a great rush of pleasure so intense that tears sprang to her eyes. Her back arched, bringing her breasts close to the hungry seeking of his mouth. He sucked and teethed her nipples ravenously even as he plunged again and again within her. The pleasure built, higher and higher. She sobbed his name, straining to take all of him, gasping as wave after wave of ecstasy throbbed through her. Until at last, on the greatest wave of all, the world itself seemed to shatter and she was adrift in nothingness with only the steely strength of his arms to shelter her.

Slowly, the world re-formed. Deirdre found herself in the bed, locked against Delacroix, their limbs entwined and his manhood still within her. She stirred slowly, unwilling to end the exquisite sense of oneness.

His arms tightened around her instinctively. He drew her head down to his chest, stroking the tumult of her silken hair. "Sweet," he murmured.

She sighed and settled more comfortably against him. There was a dull throbbing deep within her womanhood, but otherwise she felt wonderful. It was as though all the tension and sorrow of recent years had been banished from her. Later, she might think otherwise, for truly the old problems still remained. But for the moment nothing mattered except being with him, safe and cherished.

Much later, after they had awakened, they were served breakfast by a saucer-eyed but silent Libbie, who fled from the room as swiftly as she could, her plump cheeks like scarlet apples.

"Amazing," Deirdre said, helping herself greedily

to warm bread and honey, "she didn't have a word to say."

Delacroix sat across from her. In deference to Libbie's modesty—and truth to be told, Deirdre's—he had a dark, swirling cloak flung around his shoulders. Deirdre herself was more scantily clad in the beribboned linen shift she had rescued from the floor.

He poured a mug of the rich, aromatic coffee he favored and laughed when Deirdre wrinkled her nose. "It's all the rage in London," he said. "The best of men spend their days in the coffeehouses declaiming on everything from the classics to the latest royal proclamation."

"They'd be better off drinking honest ale. Did you like London?"

"Some of it. You can meet the world there. Last time I went, I actually ran into a fellow I'd known briefly in Constantinople. He was in London on a trading venture. Did well for himself, too."

"Constantinople," she repeated, savoring the sound. "Truly you have seen the world."

"A part of it, but there are vast lands to the east I have only heard of, and of the new world I know almost nothing."

"Do you yearn to travel still?" Deirdre asked, thinking that his life had been so unsettled the habit of wandering might be deep within him.

But Delacroix shook his head. "Darkcroft requires my presence, as do the other estates from time to time. My gypsy days are over."

A spurt of pleasure went through her, and with it thoughts she resolutely denied. For the time, at least, she was determined to live only for the moment.

When they had finished eating, the door opened again to admit Libbie and Lizzie carrying vats of steaming water. They poured it into the large, iron tub that stood behind a screen near the fireplace. Delacroix waited until they were gone before stretching out full length on the bed. He smiled expansively. "You first."

Deirdre blushed, an absurd thing to do given the intimacies they had shared. She went behind the screen, glad of the privacy it afforded, and slipped out of the chemise. The water caressed her silken skin as she lowered herself into it.

She sighed appreciatively, still mindful of a certain tenderness. Her eyes closed, she tilted her head back and let her thoughts drift.

Her eyes shot open again when she felt a rough cloth moving over her breasts. Delacroix knelt beside the bath, shorn of the cloak, his burnished skin glowing in the sunlight. He withdrew the cloth to rub more soap onto it, then returned it to her.

"Stop," she said, trying to catch his hand. "I'll do that, there is no need . . ."

He laughed, evading her efforts, and pursued his self-appointed task. Her nipples deserved particular attention, he thought, considering the pleasure they had given him. And then there was the sweet fullness of her breasts themselves, the delicate indentation of her navel, the shadowed curls between her thighs. All these and more he attended to despite her squirming protests. Her skin was darkly flushed, her eyes wide with disbelief. That he should do such a thing, that she should enjoy it so, that she should want him to do so much more, was all astounding.

"No," Delacroix said.

Her eyes widened yet farther. She stared at him. "No, what?"

"It is too soon to take you again. This is only for play."

"Indeed?" Pointedly, she peered over the edge of the tub at him. "You forgot to tell something that."

He laughed, half shocked by her boldness but also delighted. "That part of me has a mind of its own."

"Mayhap it has no mind at all. Now, if you would kindly excuse me, I can do without this *play*, as you call it."

He winced at the biting edge of her tongue but showed no contrition. "I'm surprised at you, Deirdre. Didn't you say Libbie was a good girl, and surely her sister is the same. Why would you want to make extra work for them?"

She looked at him suspiciously. "What do you mean?"

"Only that the tub is very large, the water still warm, and I in need of a bath myself." Even as he spoke, he stood, huge and dark, and lowered himself into the water beside her. Much of it splashed over the sides, the motion upsetting Deirdre's balance and throwing her smack against him.

A wet, hair-roughened leg, steely in its strength, moved between hers. He pulled her upright so that she was half straddling him. With a grin, he ordered, "Wash me."

She picked up the cloth and tossed it in his face. "Wash yourself."

Scrambling, she tried to climb out of the tub, but he stopped her easily. The look on his face said he was being kinder and more patient than could be expected of any man. "Behave yourself, woman. 'Tis a simple task. I am confident you will be able to manage it."

"Ooohh, you—"

"Temper, Deirdre. It is most unseemly for a woman to carry on so."

"I do not carry on," she informed him tightly. "You *play* with me, as you yourself said. I resent it."

He looked at her long and deeply. "Do I understand you right? You would be in better humor if I did not stop but took you fully, even though I know it would cause you discomfort?"

"I didn't say that," she insisted hastily, even though, in all truth, he'd hit it right. "I merely—"

"You merely nothing. You are complaining because I hesitate to plow you again so soon after taking your virginity. Well, then, perhaps you are right. Let it not be said I let a woman languish when the remedy was to hand."

Before she could do more than gasp, he rose from the tub, dripping water, and lifted her with him. With no ado, without a by-your-leave, he laid her flat on the Araby carpet, spread her legs and entered her.

Deirdre was stunned, plain and simple. She hadn't believed he would do it. There was discomfort, but not as much as might have been. Like it or not, her body responded instinctively to his slightest touch. She was aroused and ready even before they left the tub.

He paused, embedded deep within her, and gazed down into her beautiful, flushed face. Softly, he murmured, "I'm sorry."

"For what?" she gasped, hardly able to speak with the pleasure coursing through her. He was so big and hard, filling her completely, and every slight motion he made set off new, exquisite sensations.

"I am hurting you."

Such a beautiful man, but sometimes just a shade foolish. Her mouth curved in a smile. "No, you aren't." As though to emphasize the words, she moved her hips slightly and was rewarded by his groan.

"I am stronger than you know," she said. Her arms lifted, reaching for him. His mouth was at her breasts in the way she loved, tugging urgently, releasing spasms of pleasure deep within her. Their bodies, still wet, slipped together as easily as silk to steel. He raised himself to drive more deeply into her, and she looked down, gazing with fascination at their joining. His manhood moved, drawing out of her only to plunge again. Her head fell back. The swollen flesh of her womanhood was achingly sensitive. Every movement he made touched off coiling waves of heat within her. She cried with the wonder of it, grasping him ever more tightly, and drove them both to wild release.

Afterward, he stirred against her. His voice muffled, he said, "I have heard of this, that a man may die satisfying a woman, but I never thought to suffer such a demise myself."

"You aren't dead," Deirdre pointed out reasonably. On the contrary, he was giving every evidence of being fully alive. Her hand wandered down him, driving the point home. "Not dead at all."

"Incredible," he said, shaking his head. "You affect me most strangely. I wonder what could be the cause." He raised his head and studied her with mock seriousness. "You are fair enough to look upon. Your hair reminds me of the night, so dark it seems to shine as though with stars. Your eyes are lovely, your mouth full and ripe, your throat tempting." He smiled as he watched the wave of color move over her cheeks. "Your nipples are a shade of plum I find particularly pleasing, and your breasts large without being too much so. As to your waist, it is small enough for my hands to meet around it."

He suited the action to the words and grasped her lightly. "Your hips are delicate and your belly infinitely soft. As for this . . ." He released her but continued to hold her in place with a leg thrown over hers. His hand moved to the juncture of her thighs. "This is exquisite," he said, "like a flower opening its petals to reveal treasures unlike any other." His thumb moved, finding the ultrasensitive nub and coaxing it forth. Deirdre cried out. She could not bear more pleasure, not so soon. Yet it seemed she could, for Delacroix demanded it. He touched and caressed her, first with his fingers and then, to her infinite shock and delight, with his mouth. Without thought for himself, he drove her to release so profound that she was lost to the world. She never knew when he lifted her, carrying her to the bed, and lay down beside her, drawing her safe within the protective curve of his body.

CHAPTER 22

"A WEDDING?" DEIRDRE ASKED. SHE LOOKED AT Delacroix uncertainly. They were sitting in a field beyond the manor. A small stream ran nearby. Earlier, several deer had come to feed near the edge of the wood that adjoined the field. The day was cool but brilliant. Darkcroft and all on it lay wrapped in golden sun. Yet now a cloud seemed to move before the light, sending a chill through her.

"A wedding here?"

The earl nodded. He was stretched out beside her, long and lean in black breeches and a white shirt open at the neck. His face was relaxed; he looked younger and more at ease with each passing day.

In the two weeks since her midnight summons to his chamber, they had been almost constantly together. He took her everywhere with him, to every part of Darkcroft, and everywhere she was received with courtesy and warmth. What his people made of it she could not say, but they seemed genuinely to like her.

She returned the sentiment. The strong Welsh folk reminded her of her own kin even as their beautiful land made her think of Eire. Slowly, without her being fully aware of it, she was coming to think of the manor as home.

That was a mistake. She was his prisoner and his mistress, nothing else. Someday it would all end and she would have to live with the consequences. But surely she did not have to think of that just now.

He plucked a fragrant stem of grass and ran it through his fingers as he said, "One of my guardsmen, Kerwin Osborn, is marrying one of the housemaids. They would be pleased if we would attend."

"You go," Deirdre said hastily. "I would be intruding."

Delacroix frowned. "Why do you say that? They would be delighted to have you there."

It was her turn to be puzzled. "I don't see why."

He stared at her for a long moment before it dawned on him that she was serious, she really didn't know. Softly, he said, "Don't you realize how delighted everyone is to have you here? Haven't you seen the smiles, the excitement, the eagerness with which you are met everywhere you go?"

"Everyone has been very kind," Deirdre acknowledged, "but a wedding is special. It should be for friends and family, and for an honored guest like yourself. Not for someone who truly has no place being there."

His frown deepened. Something was wrong. Why would she feel she had no place? What was there about a simple country wedding to make her ill at ease?

Abruptly, his brow cleared. He could be a bit dense at times, but eventually the message got through. For a moment, he was tempted to gather her into his arms and reassure her that he was no more satisfied with the present situation than she herself. He would never be satisfied until Deirdre was entirely and permanently his own. But he sensed the time was not right to confront her with that. Her emotions were still too fragile, her loyalties too divided.

"You forget," he said, suddenly stern. "Either you stay with me or you stay in the tower. I will be at the wedding, so you must be, too."

Deirdre's eyes darkened. She had almost forgotten the terms he'd set, so caught up was she in the delight of being with him. That he chose to remind her of it distressed her.

"There is nothing wrong with the tower," she insisted stubbornly. "Indeed, if the truth be known, I could use some time to myself."

She cast him a quick, sidelong glance to see the effect of that, then scowled as he laughed. "I mean it. I was always used to a measure of solitude, and I've had none for a fortnight now."

"No, you haven't," he agreed good-humoredly, "because you have spent almost every moment of it wrapped in my arms, sleeping at my side or with me deep inside you. Forgive me, sweetling, but I can't see you as deprived."

"Knave! How dare you throw that up to me? You are no gentleman."

"Of course not. I thought we got that clear some time ago. Come, don't fuss. A wedding is just what you need to set your temper right."

No, it wasn't, but she couldn't bring herself to tell him that. How could she explain what thoughts a wedding set off within her? He would only be embarrassed or perhaps saddened that she should entertain so absurd a fancy.

"I don't want to go," she said, very low.

"But you will to please me."

"You are insufferable, not to mention rude, autocratic and . . . and you snore!"

"I most certainly do not!"

"Oh, really? Then what accounts for the cracking of the wall near your side of the bed?"

He grinned. The more she talked, the more she revealed. His side of the bed? Then there must be a her side. Which was the fact, for couples invariably slipped into such patterns. When she complained of his snoring she sounded positively wifey. He liked that more even than he was ready to admit.

"Cease your quibbling, lest you set a bad example for the bride. Come, we go." He stood and held out his hand to her.

She took it with utmost reluctance. "I can't go like this. I have grass stains on my skirt and there is a rip in the bodice from when we . . ." She broke off, her eyes shadowy with the memory of their most recent lovemaking, there in the lonely field on the fragrant grass.

"You have time to change," he said gently. "The wedding isn't until this afternoon."

They returned to the tower, where he left her reluctantly, as always. There was not a moment he spent apart from her when she wasn't in his thoughts. He hardly noticed Ewan's slight smile as the steward laid out fresh clothes for his master. Nor did he pay any attention to the letter on his desk, the fine parchment embossed with Elizabeth's seal. Whatever the queen wanted of him could wait.

As soon as he decently could, he entered the tower again and climbed the stone steps to Deirdre's chamber. The guard was still on hand, the iron bar still in use, for Delacroix absolutely refused to take chances where she was concerned. Deirdre herself was pale but composed. The gown of yellow silk was more modest than some in her wardrobe. Even so, the closely fitted bodice left no doubt as to the sweet fullness of her breasts, and the narrow waist emphasized the delicacy of her figure. She looked, he thought, like an early spring flower, filled with the promise of life.

"This is for you," he said, and held out a small coffer secured by a golden latch. "Open it."

She did as he bade, and gasped. Inside the coffer, lying on a bed of velvet, was what looked at first glance to be a circlet of fresh flowers. But these were flowers that would never fade, for they were made of the finest enameled porcelain set with rare jewels.

"I cannot," she said shakily. It was a gift that proclaimed his favor and more, for only a woman who found favor with a man in the most intimate way possible would receive such a treasure.

His eyes flashed. He took the coffer from her hands, set it on a nearby table, and removed the circlet. "You can and you will. The flowers are meant to be rare white violets such as grow in very few places on earth. The sapphires at their centers remind me of your eyes." Firmly, allowing no resistance, he set the circlet on her brow. "I received this from the hand of the Rus tsar in thanks for my skill at routing his enemies. It undoubtedly possesses a long and checkered history, but I am certain no woman lovelier than yourself has ever worn it."

Her eyes misted. She turned away lest he see how deeply his words affected her. They were both silent for a moment before Deirdre said softly, "I thank you, my lord. The gift is most generous."

He shrugged, uncertain how to deal with her gratitude. There were times when he thought he liked the fighting, prickly Deirdre better than the sweet, compliant woman she could occasionally be. And then there were times when he thought exactly the opposite. One thing was certain, with her he was never bored. She filled his nights—and his days—with passion, brought pleasure to his soul, and made him think of things he had too long delayed. Definitely, he would have to do something about that, and before much more time expired.

But first to the wedding. It took place in the courtyard behind the house. The maid, Margaret, was well liked, as was Kerwin, so the servants had determined to see them right. Late autumn flowers hung in garlands strung around the courtyard. A large table covered with a fine cloth fairly groaned with food. Several vats of wine and ale had been cracked, their contents being willingly consumed.

The bride was a blushing lass of seventeen with red cheeks and a gently rounded belly. Kerwin was little older, although the seriousness of the occasion made him appear solemn and mature. He flushed slightly as his lord congratulated him.

"Thank you, sir," he murmured, "and thank you, too, for the dowry. 'Tis powerful good of you."

It was Delacroix's turn to be embarrassed, although he concealed it well. When they had walked a little distance away, Deirdre asked, "Is that usual, for you to provide the dowry?"

He shook his head. "The maid's an orphan, with no one to provide for her. Kerwin's a good lad and would have seen her right without it, but there's no harm in them having a decent start."

She squeezed his arm lightly, conscious of the eyes following them. It wasn't hard to understand why. They were the perfect match, he with his golden mane and black garb, she gowned in spring with the circlet of his flowers set in her ebony hair. Beside him, she felt small and fragile, a novelty for her but not at all displeasing. His hand covering hers, he appeared watchful, protective, and, truth be told, unmistakably possessive. Other men, gazing at her, could be pardoned for feeling a surge of lust, but even the most feckless among them repressed it hastily lest they draw the wrath of Darkcroft's master.

At the center of the courtyard, beneath a trellis of flowers, a small, wizened priest stood. He nodded respectfully to Delacroix and slipped a cautious glance past Deirdre, whom he then scrupulously ignored.

With his lordship present, the ceremony followed swiftly. The crowd parted as the young couple approached the priest. They knelt together, heads bent, for his blessing. This he gave along with an admonition to be fruitful and multiply, which they were already well on the way to fulfilling. That done, they stood, facing each other shyly. Margaret put forth a careworn hand, which Kerwin gently took. From a pocket, he fetched a narrow ring of gold that he slipped onto her finger. The giving of a ring was a custom of the gentry only recently becoming popular among lesser folk. Margaret had clearly not expected to receive one. She gazed down at it delightedly for a moment before flinging her arms around her new-hatched husband.

The crowd laughed as bride and groom exchanged a hearty kiss. When it was over, Margaret looked disheveled and triumphant, while Kerwin appeared well pleased with himself. A smiling Ewan handed cups around. When all were served, Delacroix lifted his to the young couple. His deep voice unusually gentle, he said, "Margaret, Kerwin, much joy to you on this day and throughout the years you share together. May the peace and blessing of this fair land always be yours and may your children's children always call it home."

The men looked solemn; the women dabbed at their eyes. Truly, the lord was almost cymreig like themselves, a man of the people. Blessed be the day he came among them.

As for the lady, she was all of beauty and delight. Never mind how she had come to be there, she was meant for Darkcroft as surely as the lord himself.

On such buoyant spirit, the fiddlers plunged their bows. Music filled the air, and laughter with it. Delacroix left Deirdre for a few minutes to lead the bride out with such good-humored kindness that Deirdre could not take her eyes from him. Dancing, he moved with the same lithe grace he brought to everything else. Margaret was crimson, laughing and proud when he handed her with a flourish to her delighted husband. Higher the fiddlers soared, faster the music flashed, skirts swirling, legs leaping, and in the midst of it all, Delacroix and Deirdre, she safe in his arms as the joy of the moment carried them both away.

She danced well, he thought, as he had known she would, for she did all things with artless skill. Her eyes met his, sparkling, shadows banished. Her cheeks were flushed, her lips full and curved in pleasure. The circlet gleamed against her brow, the mark of his possession.

Off on the side, seated on a rough-hewn bench, Granny Dru watched it all and nodded to herself. The priest was gone. He never lingered long at any festivity, lest he see something he would rather not. That suited her well enough, for truly they each had their place.

The music flowed on, as did the drink. Much food was consumed. Delacroix had thought to stay only a short time, but found he was enjoying himself too much to leave. So was Deirdre, who put aside all other considerations for the pleasure of the moment.

The sun was slanting west, throwing long rays of gold across the courtyard, when Granny Dru rose. Her legs were stiff and she felt the growing coolness in her bones, but that did not deter her. Leaning on her cane, she hobbled forward. Margaret and Kerwin stood, breathless with the exertion of their dance. The crowd fell silent, watching. From the sack around her waist, she drew two small dolls made of the gleanings of the wheat at harvest's end. Each of the figures was nude, one clearly female, the other male. To Margaret she handed the male, to Kerwin the female.

In the old tongue, she said, "Ye are given to one another's keeping. Cleave together as tree to earth. May the fruit of your bodies be plentiful and sweet. May you find great joy together, and at the end of your days may you return together to the beginning of all things. Blessing be."

"Blessing be," the crowd repeated as one. Deirdre, too, spoke the words. They resonated deep within her, answering an ancient need.

Delacroix was silent. He had known without having to be told that many of his people still held to the old ways. The priest's early departure had not escaped his notice. He was surprised, though, by Granny Dru's boldness. Such things were usually kept from the sight of men like himself.

The old woman turned her head and looked directly at him. For a moment, he thought she was challenging him to object, but then he realized there was something else in her eyes, a kind of gentle sympathy that warmed him even as he felt a surge of apprehension. Why would Granny Dru think him in need of such solicitude?

There was no chance to ask her, for the crowd closed ranks, the fiddlers struck up another tune, and the bent old woman vanished behind the swirling mass of dancers. When he could see clearly again, she was gone.

CHAPTER 23

WHEN DEIRDRE AWOKE THE FOLLOWING MORN-
ing, Delacroix had already left. Only his scent and the
imprint of his head on the pillow beside her remained
to remind her of the pleasure they had shared.

She lay for a time, staring up at the ceiling, until the
emptiness of the bed drove her to leave it. Libbie and
Lizzie bustled in, chattering about how splendid the
wedding had been. The morning proceeded as usual. It
wasn't until after she had breakfasted that she thought
to ask Libbie if she knew where the earl had gone.
Usually Delacroix left a message for her if he had to be
away even a short time. He would say to expect him at
dinner or in the afternoon, when they would go riding,
or something. But not this time.

The maid shook her head. "I'm sorry, my lady,
Ewan didn't say. I could ask him, if you'd like."

Deirdre hesitated. She was still reluctant to reveal
how much Darkcroft's master dominated her thoughts,

but neither could she bear not knowing where he was. "Would you, please? I would appreciate it."

Libbie bustled off about her errand, taking Lizzie with her, and a short time later Ewan himself appeared at the door. His slender face was somber.

"His Lordship has gone to London, my lady."

Deirdre stared at him. He couldn't have said what she thought he had. Delacroix would never go off to London without telling her.

But when she said as much, Ewan sighed. "He left before first light, my lady, with only a small escort. I am given to understand he will return as quickly as possible. He has left instructions that you may have the run of the manor house and the gardens immediately beyond, but no farther, and that you must be well guarded at all times."

"I see . . ." Deirdre said slowly. In fact, she did not. Delacroix had gone without a word to her. Granted, he had eased the terms of her captivity during his absence, but he had also made it clear that distrust and suspicion still lay between them.

A heavy weight pressed against her heart. "Do you know why he went?"

"He did not tell me, my lady." Ewan might have added that he, too, found the earl's behavior very odd. Hitherto His Lordship had gone out of his way to avoid London. Yet now he speeded there as though devils snapped at his heels. Still, a wise servant kept such speculation to himself.

"May I get you anything, my lady?"

Deirdre looked at him blankly. "What? Oh, no, thank you. Unless . . ." She stared at the four walls of the chamber and shivered. To be confined within them with only her thoughts to keep her occupied would be anguish indeed.

"You did say I could go out."

Ewan nodded. "His Lordship said that, my lady, provided you remain on the manor-house grounds and have an escort."

"Then I would like to visit the gardens." It was a lovely day, crisp and pleasantly cool, and she'd been meaning to view the gardens. Only Delacroix's lack of interest in them, and her absorption in him, had stopped her.

"As you wish, my lady. I will make the necessary arrangements."

He left her then, but returned a short time later to say she might proceed whenever she liked. The "arrangements" consisted of not one but two burly guards who followed her doggedly as she left the room. She spent an hour or so in the gardens, observing that they were well, if unimaginatively, cared for. The soil and drainage were excellent; there was a potential for growing many medicinal plants as well as a better selection of herbs to ease the tedium of winter fare. Perhaps she would mention that to Delacroix, provided she was still speaking to him when he returned.

As the day wore on, what little warmth there had been fled. Clouds scudded across the sky. A hint of rain dampened the air. Despite the cloak wrapped around her, Deirdre shivered. Like it or not, she would have to go back inside.

But first there was something more she needed to do. Before he left, Delacroix had been reading a work of Christopher Marlowe's, *Doctor Faustus*, which she wanted to read herself. If he had not taken it with him to

London, she might as well find it.

When last seen, the book was in his quarters. She informed the guards of where she was going and received no more than noncommittal stares in response. They followed her dutifully but waited outside while she went in. The room was as always, big, luxurious, and very masculine. But in Delacroix's absence, it seemed eerily quiet. She moved quickly, avoiding the bed, and sought the table near the window.

As she had hoped, the book was there. She had it in her hand and was turning to go when her eye fell on a scrap of parchment crumpled in a corner. Untidiness was so foreign to her nature that she instinctively bent down to retrieve it. She was about to put it in the pocket of her cloak to dispose of later when she happened to look more closely. The parchment had been folded at one time, although it was so badly crumpled as to make that hard to realize. A broken wax seal could still be seen. Her hand shook as she realized what the seal depicted—the crowned head of a lion bearing proudly the standard of Britannia.

Slowly, she smoothed out the paper. The writing on it was spidery and hard to read. She bent closer to the light from the window and picked it out word by word.

Long moments passed before she finished. By the time she did so, her face was paler even than the parchment itself.

"My dear Delacroix," Elizabeth had written. "Hold well the daughter of O'Neill. God willing, she will prove the last of her troublesome line. Mountjoy does well in Ireland. O'Neill and O'Donnell grow more isolated by the day. Those they believe are friends become enemies. Now they look to Spain for help but will be disappointed. The time has come to end this folly."

Deirdre's blood chilled. Mountjoy was Britain's most feared warrior, a killer who stopped at nothing to win and was a proven genius at devising battle strategies that overwhelmed less wily opponents. No Baganel this, but the worst possible adversary Ireland could face. The clan chiefs who should have supported her father were drifting away in the night. And now it appeared the Spanish were also set to betray him. He would be as a lamb to the slaughter.

The guards were waiting in the hall when she emerged. They followed her back to the tower and dutifully saw her secured inside. A short while later, Libbie came with her supper.

She took one look at Deirdre and put the tray down quickly. "Is something wrong, my lady?"

"I'm not feeling well," Deirdre said. That wasn't entirely a lie. Ever since finding the letter, she had been overwhelmed with dread.

"Do you want Granny Dru?"

Deirdre hesitated only a moment. "I think that would be best."

Within the hour, a small, bent figure wrapped in a heavy shawl slipped from the tower. It moved slowly across the courtyard to the stables. The donkey tethered there raised its head and whinnied. A guard watched disinterestedly. He was used to seeing Granny Dru come and go at odd hours, whenever there was need, and found nothing unusual in the scene.

The old woman released the tether and climbed onto the donkey's back. She slapped its rump to urge it forward. The animal whinnied again before it trotted swiftly out and turned onto the road leading west. The guard went on about his business.

Deirdre was well beyond the manor walls before she could breathe normally. She offered a silent prayer of thanks for Granny Dru's understanding. Indeed, the old healer hadn't even seem surprised when Deirdre begged her help. She had merely smiled slightly and said some paths had to be followed to their natural end, whatever that meant.

Surely, it didn't matter. She was free, and soon she would be in Cardiff. The coin Granny Dru had pressed upon her would buy passage to Ireland. How the old woman had happened to have so ample a sum of money on her person did give Deirdre pause, but she could not dwell on it. Ahead lay the ribbon of road, silvered by the moon. Behind, Darkcroft slumbered, and farther away still its master rode to his queen's side.

Her stomach tightened as she thought what Delacroix would make of her escape. Tears burned her eyes. How many times had she told him there could be nothing between them? He had never listened, and finally she herself had forgotten that simple truth. Now they would both pay the price.

She straightened her back and spurred the donkey on. Only a fool wept for what could never be. Which must mean that it was a fool who rode for Cardiff, tears slipping unhindered down her cheeks. They mingled with the rain that shortly began to fall.

Miles away, well along the road to London, Delacroix also felt the rain. He pulled his cloak more closely around him and urged his destrier on. His men did the same, but reluctantly. They had been riding with scant pause since before dawn. The horses were exhausted, and the men themselves in need of rest. Yet his lordship showed no inclination to stop. Indeed, he looked almost desperate to reach London.

Finally, the boldest of them rode up alongside him and dared to speak. "Sir, your pardon, but if we continue as we are, the horses will be lamed."

Delacroix barely heard him. He was lost in the tumult of his thoughts—fury at Elizabeth, worry for Deirdre, dread of where it all would lead. With O'Neill's allies drifting away and the Spanish set to disappoint him—whatever that meant—nothing would stand between Ireland and the scourge of Mountjoy. It would be kinder to let loose a plague upon an unsuspecting land than to send him with orders to subdue Eire. He would succeed, of that Delacroix had no doubt, but only at the most terrible cost.

Unless he could convince Elizabeth there was a better way.

"What's that?" he demanded, turning on the man who had dared to intrude upon him. The fellow paled but held his ground.

"The horses, my lord, they will be lamed."

Delacroix stared at him until abruptly he realized the man was right. He had lost all track of time, but clearly it was far later than he'd thought. It wasn't like him to mistreat any animal, but clearly there was an added reason not to do so now. He had no assurance of being able to find fresh mounts. With his horses lamed, his chances of reaching London quickly would vanish.

"All right," he said, reluctantly. "We camp."

The men murmured their relief. They turned off the road gratefully, and with the usual efficiency of men who have spent much time in the field, saw to what needed to be done. The horses were rubbed down, watered, and put to graze. Under the shelter of the trees, a small fire was lit. From saddlebags, food was drawn and silently consumed.

Delacroix sat a little apart, eating nothing. He stared into the flames, watching the wood hiss and steam. His body cried out for rest, but he could not so much as close his eyes. They remained, fast opened, gazing at the fire. The sound of the rain faded away. He lost all awareness of the other men and the horses moving nearby. There was only flame and the wavering smoke, rising gray against the night.

As clearly as though she stood right next to him, Granny Dru spoke. Her voice was firm but with a shade of rich good humor. "Do not hurt her."

Delacroix started. He must have fallen asleep after all, for surely he dreamt. Do not hurt her? Who? Uneasiness stirred within him. He thought suddenly of Deirdre standing on the crest of Buan-ann, the offerings to the earth lying before her. And of Granny Dru at the wedding only yesterday, holding the corn dolls in her worn hands. "You are given to one another's keeping," she had said.

How deeply did the keeping go? Did it transcend sleep and dreams to reach some secret region of the soul?

He sat up abruptly. Around him the night was still. His men snored in their tiredness. The horses nickered softly. In the high branches of a tree, an owl hooted.

The rain had stopped. Above he could see the stars,

and in the west, along the path he'd come, the pale moon. A trickle of red ran down it. He closed his eyes, opening them quickly. The vision was gone, but the memory lingered.

Reason warred with instinct. He should continue on to London, to do his utmost to convince Elizabeth the course she followed was wrong. Ireland should not be crushed. That way led only to generations more of hatred. Mountjoy was the worst man to have sent.

But Mountjoy was not in London, he was already in Eire. The fires of treachery already burned. The night wind whispered: Too late, too late, save what you may.

Deirdre. Safe in the tower, wasn't she? The wind came again, tugging at his soul. Far in the distance a wolf howled.

"To horse!" he shouted, dragging his men from sleep. They stumbled upright, fumbling for their weapons until they realized it was no attack, merely his lordship astride the night like a fury.

Down again along the London road, the pale moon showing the way. Not long after dawn, a rider galloped to meet them. Ewan drew rein beside his master. His slender face was pale with dread. Before he spoke, Delacroix knew why he had come.

"I will crush her," he said with such ferocity that all before him quailed. All, that is, but Granny Dru, who faced him squarely. They were standing in the great hall—Ewan, Granny Dru, Libbie, Lizzie, and the half-dozen guards who had been on duty the night before. The guards were gray-faced, knowing there could be no forgiveness for them. They expected their punishment to be terrible and only hoped it would be mercifully swift. Libbie and Lizzie sobbed quietly, their arms around each other. Ewan occupied himself thinking frantically of how they, at least, might be saved. That he was doomed could not be questioned. He had sent the messenger for Granny Dru. It was he who approved her entry to the tower chamber; he, too, who found her there the following morning when he went to inquire if her ladyship was feeling better.

They were all to blame, but of them all only Granny Dru had acted deliberately. And only she appeared unafraid.

Her eyes met Delacroix's unflinchingly. "You will not hurt her. She is yours as you are hers. What she has done is for good reason."

"What she has done," Delacroix snarled, "is break faith with me for the last time. I trusted her. I believed I could leave her here, protected and safe. But no, at the first chance, she betrays me yet again. Women! Truly God made nothing more treacherous."

"Indeed?" Granny Dru demanded. "You trusted her? Yet you left her under heavy guard. You went off without a word to her, leaving her to find out for herself what Elizabeth was doing. How do you think she felt to learn of that? To know that the final destruction of her people will soon be underway?"

Delacroix whirled, his face dark. "What are you saying? She could not have known."

"She found the letter." From a pocket of her homespun skirt, Granny Dru pulled out the crumpled piece of parchment. "She showed it to me last night when she begged for my help. She goes to warn her father as what daughter would not? Should she stay here while his foes weave his burial shroud? If she were capable of that, would you feel for her as you do?"

"Feel what?" Delacroix shot back. His mind reeled at the news that Deirdre had not merely seized the chance to escape him. She had gone out of the need to protect her people and her land. Yet he still could not admit his relief. "What is it you imagine I am prey to, some falsehood spun by your moon-addled magic? I am a man, and I will not be played false by any woman. She will pay."

"Only if you find her. Which you will not do standing around here prattling." She ignored the others' fearful gasps and said, "Deirdre is in Cardiff by now. How long do you think it will take her to find a fast ship to Ireland?"

Delacroix cursed. The old woman was right; he could not afford to delay a moment. He spared a hard glance at the guards before turning on Ewan. "Back to work, all of you. No trouble while I am gone, or by God I'll have your hides."

"Yes, my lord," Ewan said hastily, praising the reprieve. "Whatever you wish, my lord. Libbie, run to the stables for a fresh horse. Lizzie, to the kitchen. His Lordship will need provisions. All will be well here, my lord, have no doubt. Godspeed you."

Scant minutes later, Delacroix was mounted again, a full saddlebag beside him and his faithful servants waving him off. He went in bad humor, suspecting he'd gotten the worse of it but determined before much longer to even the reckoning.

He reached Cardiff shortly after midday and went directly to a tavern nearest the docks. The patrons were hard-bitten men washed up from every far-flung shore.

Very little impressed them. However, the big, black-garbed stranger was an exception. The sheer extent of his fury when he learned a ship had sailed barely an hour before for Ireland astounded even them. Why he should care so much that a little old woman was on board was a mystery, but the world was filled with those. As for the stranger himself, he took ship shortly thereafter, paying for his passage in gold and promising the captain the same again if they reached Eire on the swiftest wind.

CHAPTER
24

THE DOCK BESIDE DUBLIN'S LIFFEY RIVER WAS A stinking swirl of humanity from every corner of the world, brawling in a dozen languages, spitting and shrieking without a thought for the man elbowing his way among them. The ship Deirdre had taken had barely docked before Delacroix reached it, but there was no sign of her. The captain admitted he'd taken an old woman on board, but she'd kept to herself and said nothing to any of his crew. She was gone almost before the gangplank settled in place.

"A queer one that," he said, looking at Delacroix nervously. He reminded the captain of a great storm brewing out over the sea, readying itself to wreak havoc on any creature careless enough to cross its path. "I never did see her face, but she paid well and there seemed no harm in it. Why do you seek her?"

Delacroix took grim pleasure in telling him. "Because she is accursed. She steals the wits from helpless men. Seen yours lately?"

The captain gaped at him. "A witch? Saints preserve us. I thought her only a cunny woman, wise in the old ways."

"Spare me the old ways. I've had my full of them. She said nothing of where she was going?"

"Not a word, I swear. But wait . . . I thought, that is I'm not sure, but . . ."

"Spit it out, man!"

"We were still tying up and there was much for me to do, but I did think I saw an old woman talking with one of the dockside whores. It might have been her."

"Which one?" Delacroix demanded. He resisted the urge to close his hand around the captain's throat, but only because that would make it all the harder for him to talk.

"A red-headed doxy. Tess, I think her name be."

The earl nodded curtly. Now he had two women to find: an infuriating, ebony-haired Irish princess and the whore who might, just might, know where she had gone.

Tess did indeed know that and a good deal more, as she was at pains to tell him. Indeed, she fairly babbled on, struck by the incredible good luck of drawing so fine a gentleman's attention. Rich he was, that was obvious from his garb. And so big and powerful, like as not a girl would faint in his arms. Granted, there was an aura of danger about him that gave her pause. Still, she was willing to risk it just for the thrill of having such a man.

Delacroix had other ideas. He laced her palm with more gold than she'd ever seen before and said, "You're a fine lass, but the truth is I'd be no good for you. I must find the old woman you spoke with on the dock."

Tess gave him a long, level look. She raised one of the gold coins between her fingers, bit into it, and smiled thoughtfully. "She was no old woman."

"How could you tell?"

"I saw her hands, very fine they were. She's a young one, and a lady to boot." She smiled slightly. "Your wife, is she?"

"Not exactly. Let's just say she's a thorn in my side. One I intend to pluck at the earliest opportunity."

Tess laughed. "Oh, I like that, I do. A thorn in your side? Then why don't you just let her pluck herself out instead of going tearing after her?"

"That's for me to know," he said. All women were really the same when you got down to it—infuriating. Summoning all his patience—little enough effort that, for there was scant left of it—he said, "What did she say to you?"

"She asked me a question."

Mary and all the saints, he wasn't going to survive this. "And what was that?" he murmured.

Tess shrugged. She slipped the coins into a pocket of her red satin skirt. "She wanted the latest gossip on what the O'Neill was about. Whether he'd left his redoubt at Dungannon, and if so, where he'd gone."

Deirdre had asked a dockside whore for information on the movements of an army of rebels sought after by the queen of England herself. Why hadn't he thought of that?

"What did you tell her?"

"Only what I knew." She rattled the coins in her pocket and smiled again."The O'Neill was at

Dungannon until two days ago. Now he's marching south. 'Tis said the Spanish have landed at Kinsale and Mountjoy is hurrying to besiege them. O'Neill marches to their relief. He means to free all of Eire in one blow and be done."

"He'll be done, all right," Delacroix said grimly.

"I told her to head north out of Dublin. There'll be word of him in the villages for sure. Men will be rushing to join him from every hill and glen."

"If she took your advice, she can't be more than an hour or two ahead of me. Thank you, Tess."

"'Tis my pleasure, Your Lordship. If you come back this way, come see me again."

She watched him go, thinking again what a fine figure of a man he was, and felt just the tiniest twist of guilt that she hadn't been completely honest with him. Hadn't, for instance, mentioned that the old woman had also asked her where she might find a change of clothes. Tess had sent her to her own brother, thinking to keep the coin in the family, as it were. Ralph would outfit her right well. Judging from what she'd seen of the lady, she would make a fetching boy. Too bad his lordship didn't know to look for that instead of a little old woman.

Never had Delacroix pursued any quarry with greater relentlessness. Never had he experienced greater frustration as each mile passed and he came no closer to success. Deirdre stubbornly eluded him, but information on the O'Neill was more forthcoming. As Tess had said, men were rallying to his banner from throughout Ireland. Every lane and road had its share of marchers heading to him. The only trouble was, they all seemed to be going in different directions.

In the space of forty-eight hours, the O'Neill was reported to be at Monaghan in the north, to the west near Athione, or already far to the south passing through Tipperary. Truly, it was amazing how the man got about.

Of a certain cunny woman, nothing had been seen at all.

Ten days later, as the calendar settled into December and chill winds blew across the land, Delacroix began to think that Deirdre had vanished off the face of the earth. Dreadful though the possibility was, there was some faint consolation in the fact that her daft father seemed to have gone with her.

All Ireland was as one, asking the same question: Where was the O'Neill? He had left Dungannon, on that there was agreement. But what happened afterward? From Kinsale, where he besieged the Spanish, Mountjoy issued a proclamation calling on all Irishmen to give up "this dastard rebellion" upon pain of death. Had he wished to call them to arms, he could not have done better. All Eire rang with the cry "to the O'Neill!"

And then, in the season of peace and joy that precedes the coming of Christmas, word arrived. Hugh O'Neill, Red Hugh at his side, and an army of five thousand were encamped outside Kinsale, there to give battle to Mountjoy and rid Eire of the English scourge for all time. Praise be to God in his mercy that he let men live in such magnificent times.

Praise, that is, from all save Delacroix, who cursed the idiocy of fate even as he sped by the fastest horse he could find southward, racing the sun, toward the frost-dappled killing ground.

✳ ✳ ✳

Deirdre woke sweat-soaked and breathless. She lay on the narrow cot, feeling the rapid beating of her heart, and let the last of the nightmare fade into the shadows of predawn. Yet even when the images were gone, she still thought she heard the pounding of horses' hooves and saw above her head the remorseless glint of steel.

Heaven save her, she needed rest desperately, yet could find none. Since stumbling into her father's camp several days before, footsore and filthy in her boy's clothes, she had received every comfort that could be devised. The finest food, the best accommodations, the most insistent cosseting, all were hers. Even Red Hugh, who had gone out of his way to avoid her since Yellowford, bestirred himself to pleasantries. As for her father, he was all she could have wished and more. The hurt she had felt faded before his great joy at having her safe. Looking into his broad, seamed face, she saw what her captivity had cost him and cursed her own carelessness anew.

Yet for all that, the nightmares came with renewed force each time she tried to sleep. Giving up, she rose from the cot, washed her hands and face in a basin of chill water, and put on the simple gray dress provided by the good sisters of a convent near the army camp. Deirdre was grateful for the warmth of the fine-spun wool that kept the cold at bay, but she also appreciated the garment's looseness. It did well at concealing her tender breasts and the small but unmistakable expansion of her waist.

She closed her eyes for a moment and uttered a

silent prayer that God in his majesty would find a way to help the tiny babe growing even now within her. Delacroix's child, his son or daughter, and hers as well. England and Ireland united, not in any fashion either country would have desired but in the only way that truly mattered.

Had she really told him they could share nothing? Fool! They had shared the furthest limits of passion, not once but time and again. She could not claim to be surprised that new life was the result.

As she opened her eyes again, the small tent seemed to swim before her. She was dizzy most mornings and her stomach was chronically unsettled, but overall she felt surprising well. That made no sense at all under the circumstances. She could only credit it to the strange resiliency of pregnant women.

Washed and dressed, she left the tent and made her way across the small space to her father's quarters. Men nodded to her respectfully as she passed. The shock that accompanied her sudden arrival had died down, leaving in its place pleasure and a measure of relief. It was said her escape from the English was a good omen.

The O'Neill was awake and finishing his breakfast. He smiled when Deirdre entered and gestured for her to sit. "You're too pale," he said. "Have some of this mead. It will warm you and put a bit of color in your cheeks."

Deirdre took a mug obediently but contrived to only sip at it. Her stomach was still too unsettled for anything more. She gave her father a cautious look as she asked the same question she had every morning since coming to the camp.

"Have you thought any more about what I told you?"

He tore a strip off a chicken leg, chewed and swallowed before he replied. "You mean that business with the letter? It doesn't amount to anything. Elizabeth's old, she's lost her wits."

Deirdre wanted desperately to believe him, but in the days she had spent crossing Ireland, she had heard too many disturbing rumors. While ordinary men rallied to the O'Neill's cause, the clan chieftains were in scant evidence. Only O'Donnell remained at his side. The Spanish were in Kinsale, true enough, but in smaller numbers than they should have been and with a general noteworthy only for his incompetency.

"Why did you come here?" Deirdre asked softly. The question had been on her mind for days now, but there had been so little opportunity to speak with her father that she had delayed asking it. Finally, she had him all to herself, without his aides rushing about, Red Hugh coming and going, servants flitting in and out, all the hustle and bustle attendant upon a great war leader. Now he was only her father who, despite the differences between them, she loved devotedly.

O'Neill took a long swallow of his mead before he replied. So quietly that she had to strain to hear him, he said, "I came because Ireland is not strong enough to free herself. It wounds me to the heart to admit that, but 'tis true. We must have help, and that comes only from the Spaniards. But they make poor friends. I asked for five thousand men; they sent half that. I asked—nay, I expected—a general of skill and daring. They sent this bastard son of a half-wit, d'Aquila."

He shook his large head in disgust. "He squeals

like a stuck pig merely because Mountjoy besieges him. What does he expect the English to do? Give him the keys to Kinsale? I told him, sit out the winter, wait for spring and better fighting weather. He has all the provisions he could ever need. If he'd show a bit of backbone, he'd have no problem at all."

"Instead he brought you the length of Ireland," Deirdre murmured. "To do what, hold his hand?"

"I suppose." The O'Neill pushed back his chair and stood. He looked at his daughter gently. "I forget myself, this is man's business and not for a lass to worry over." She started to speak, but he hushed her with a light touch. "When this is over, we will talk. Whatever happened in Wales, you are my daughter and the joy of my heart. Never forget that."

Deirdre nodded mutely, her throat tight. She wanted to call her father back, to plead with him not to shut his burdens within himself. But he was gone already, out into the too-bright day, and she was once again alone.

The hours passed with wrenching slowness. In the afternoon, weariness overcame her and she slept awhile. The need for midday rest was becoming a habit. She awoke, for once free of nightmares, and emerged from the tent to see Red Hugh just leaving her father's.

He hesitated a moment before walking toward her. She looked pale to him and he thought she'd lost weight, although it was impossible to tell, what with the heavy cloak she had wrapped around her. Her hair was caught back from her face in a single braid that hung halfway down her back. His body stirred, as it always did when he thought of her, and he cursed the fate that had kept them apart.

"Deirdre," he said softly, "are you well?"

She nodded, thinking how odd it was that after all that had happened between them, she still felt such liking for this slender young man who held so much of Ireland's pride within him. Had she never met Delacroix, they might have dealt perfectly well with each other. She would have been spared so much—consuming passion, deep despair, love.

Ah, no, she wouldn't think that. It was lust she felt for the dark earl, not love. Love was a sweet, tender emotion, the stuff of courtly romances and troubadours' ballads. It had nothing to do with the sweat and tumble, the heat and fire of incandescent mating. Nothing at all.

"Deirdre," Red Hugh said, "is something wrong?"

She shook her head so firmly that the dizziness threatened to return. "Nothing, absolutely nothing. I was just on my way to see father. Is he busy?"

"I'm afraid so. He's had another communication from d'Aquila. The man whines like a woman." He caught the look she flashed him and flushed. "Sorry, but I can't deny he wears on the nerves. Best let the O'Neill settle down some before you go to him. There's time yet."

"Time?" Deirdre asked. "What do you mean?"

Red Hugh cast her a startled glance. "I thought you knew."

"Knew what?"

"Never mind," he said hastily. "I must have misunderstood."

"Oh, no, you're not getting away like that. You just came from talking with my father, and he told you something. Now, what is it?"

He looked into her face, no longer pale, the eyes

flashing, and sighed. Mayhap it was as well they had never wed. He would have been so much bog clay in her hands.

Softly, he said, "He's sending you back to Dungannon. It's the best place for you, surely you can see that. I was surprised he kept you here even a few days, but he was hoping he could convince d'Aquila to manage on his own until spring. Then he could have taken you home himself, but that isn't to be." He took her hands in his, pressing them gently. "You will be safe there. That is very important to your father . . . and to me."

The anger that had surged so hotly in her at his words ebbed away. She simply lacked the strength to sustain it. He was right, of course. She was a woman, carrying a child—although her father didn't know that, praise God. She had no place on what might shortly be a battlefield. But Dungannon was so far away. She would be able to do nothing there. She would be useless.

"I don't want to go," she said.

Red Hugh smiled faintly. "Of course you don't. You have great spirit and courage to match. But the O'Neill is tuath. You will obey him."

Deirdre bent her head. The weight of her sorrow pulled her down. She wanted to fight, to plead, to resist. But for what? Her father would hold firm in his decision, of that she was sure. Like it or not, she was bound for Dungannon. In that stone-walled fortress, close within the shadow of Buan-ann, the child would grow within her womb. She would be safe, and so would it. For that, she must be thankful.

"You will be in my thoughts," she said softly.

Red Hugh's gaze was tender. He slipped his fin-

gers beneath her chin. "And you in mine, fair Deirdre."
His lips brushed her brow in tender benediction.

Deep in the shadows along the edges of the camp,
a dark shape stirred. In the movement was great
strength and power barely checked. Silvered eyes narrowed to slits glinted dangerously. Delacroix strode
mightly to control himself. He stood, concealed by the
trees, as he watched the pair separate, Deirdre returning to the tent from whence she'd come, Red Hugh
going off to join his men. Only then did he relax very
slightly.

He had found her. In the face of that, nothing else
mattered. She was here, safe, and close within his
grasp, little though she knew it. A fortnight, curse it,
since he stood on the dockside at Dublin. North he'd
gone, and west, and south, everywhere but east, and
only then because water barred him. He'd seen more of
Ireland than he'd ever hoped to, but he'd found no sign
of Deirdre. Not until he reached her father's camp did
he know for certain that she had not perished.

As well she might have in a land posed on the brink
of war. Curse the woman! How dare she put him through
such anguish? When he had her to himself again, he
would make clear to her exactly what he thought of such
behavior. He would have her weeping, pleading with
him, begging for forgiveness. He would . . .

Whatever he would, it had to wait. He settled back
against the tree, concealed deep within its shadows.
Darkness would come, and with it opportunity. He
smiled grimly to himself. Let her have these last few
hours. They were a small price to pay for all the days
and nights ahead when she would be completely and
undeniably his.

CHAPTER 25

AGAIN, THE NIGHTMARE CAME. DEIRDRE CRIED out, fighting to escape the stench of blood, the gleam of steel, the overwhelming sense of terror that threatened to crush her. She twisted on the narrow cot, striking out in all directions, until abruptly she stopped.

Strong arms enveloped her. She was held hard against an unyielding wall of muscle and sinew. A hand clamped over her mouth. The voice near her ear sent shivers through her.

"Be still."

Delacroix, enemy and lover, captor and father of her child. She shut her eyes against the tide of relief that crested over her, and opened them to fury.

Delacroix here in her father's camp, daring to seize her yet again. Oh, no, not this time! She had played the fool enough where he was concerned. Her teeth clamped down, biting into his hand. She was rewarded by a grunt of pain before he suddenly twisted her around and pressed her face down into the cot. A steely leg was flung over her. He straddled her buttocks, holding her in place. Swiftly, he tied a length of cloth over her mouth. Only then did he turn her over again. She lay trapped between his thighs as he loomed over her, her hair tumbled, her nightshift slipping down to bare an alabaster shoulder, and glowered at him.

Delacroix bared his teeth in a smile. She really did look most enticing, his fey Irish witch. Once he had her away from here, he would lock her high in Darkcroft's tower and keep her there, in bed, for a week, a month, whatever it took to slake his thirst and still the raging hunger within him.

But first there was the small matter of escape. Effortlessly, he wrapped her in the cloak he found beside the cot and, ignoring her efforts to kick him, tossed her over his shoulder. She snarled through the gag. He gave her backside a sharp pat and turned to go. A movement immediately outside the tent stopped him. Cursing silently, he fell back into the darkness even as the flap was opened. A burly shape moved forward, pausing beside the cot.

Hugh O'Neill hesitated, not wishing to wake his daughter. She needed her rest, so pale was she and so unnaturally quiet. But tomorrow would be very busy, and before it was half done she would be gone. He wanted a few private minutes with her before then. When she was a child, he had gazed at her sometimes when she slept, thinking there had never been anything more beautiful or precious. Surely every child was like that, but she was his, and lately he had thought of that a great deal.

He wanted to tell her so much, that he loved her,

that she had never disappointed him, that his greatest regret was that he had not given her a more secure future. But it would be enough to simply look on her again.

He gazed down fondly, seeking the flash of ebony hair, the perfect face, the sleep-closed eyes that could glow so brightly. Seeking . . .

Nothing. The cot was empty. He glanced around the tent quickly, telling himself she was awake, she was nearby, she was all right.

A shadow moved, big, hard, unmistakable. For an instant, silver eyes hard as steel looked directly into his. Within the close confines of the tent an ancient challenge loomed. Hugh O'Neill, tuath of Ulster, champion of Ireland, and outraged father threw back his head and roared his battle cry.

"To the O'Neill!"

They came, oh, how they came. So many surged into the small tent that it was dragged from its moorings and sent tumbling across the frozen ground. In the process, a brazier was knocked over, shards of charcoal igniting a pile of hay nearby. The fire burned unnoticed, because the men were too busy trying to get a turn at the Englishman who, truth be told, gave as good as he got until a series of blows finally drove him to his knees.

That suited the O'Neill just fine. He looked down at the bruised and bloodied despoiler of his daughter and knew a surge of satisfaction so intense it robbed him of breath. But only momentarily.

It was Deirdre herself who denied him his just

deserts. She crouched beside Delacroix, holding him in her arms, her tears falling unhindered on them both. The look of anguish in her eyes was so intense it cut the O'Neill to the quick.

"Child," he murmured, bending over her, "control yourself. This man is the enemy. He came to steal you away. What was done was no more than right."

She shook her head despairingly. "You don't understand. If he dies, it will be because of me. I cannot bear that. He has been naught but kind and . . . other things to me. He didn't deserve this, truly he didn't." She bent her head again and sobbed heartbrokenly.

Hugh O'Neill sighed. If he lived fourscore years— which, all things considered, was highly unlikely—he would never understand women. Fortunately, he had given up trying.

He gestured to two of his men standing nearby, among the many taking in the scene with open-mouthed fascination. "Carry him to my tent," he ordered. Deirdre threw on her clothes and followed at their heels. She bustled about, supervising every move they made, and sent several servants rushing for supplies.

"We must remove his clothes," she said distractedly as she struggled to determine all at once everything that needed to be done. "He may have other injuries. Here, help me."

"Hold!" the O'Neill exclaimed. "'Tis not fitting for you to remain while that is done. I'll send for the camp surgeons."

Deirdre turned on him, cheeks flushed, eyes flashing, fury given flesh. Before her, even the tuath felt the pulse of primal dread.

"You will do no such thing! No stinking quack will touch him! And don't speak to me of fitting. Would you have me tell my child I let his father die?"

The O'Neill gasped. Shock roared through him, but hard upon it came the cold light of honesty. He had known, truly, when he saw her kneel beside the Englishman. There had been something in the way she touched him that spoke more clearly than any words.

"So that's the way of it," he murmured. A hard hand fell on her shoulder. He bent slightly, enough to meet her eyes. Deliberately, he cut to the core of the matter. "Tell me truly, were you raped?"

Deirdre gulped. She was embarrassed, stunned by her own audacity and fiercely, undeniably glad. No child of hers would be a dirty secret. She would proclaim it to heaven itself.

"No," she said flatly. "I was not. He is a good man. Foolish sometimes, but which of you isn't?" She paused a moment before adding, very softly, "I have fought loving him with all my strength, denied it even to myself, but I cannot any longer. For good or aught, he has my heart."

"I see. . . . And what of his? Who holds that?"

"I don't know," Deirdre admitted. "But it makes no difference. Now stand back and let me work."

Her father obeyed; he had no choice, for there was a strength and will in her that would not be denied. It hovered over Delacroix throughout the night, drawing him from pain and darkness, leading him back into the light. Until, with morning, he awoke to find himself stretched out on a simple cot, covered by a fine-woven blanket, and face-to-face with Hugh O'Neill.

"Deirdre is asleep," the tuath informed him. "I sent

her to rest when it was clear you were out of danger."

"Am I?" Delacroix murmured. His mouth felt dry, there was a dull ache in his head, and he could feel tenderness along his ribs. Little enough, considering the beating he vaguely remembered receiving.

"I thought you meant to have me killed," he added.

"The notion crossed my mind," the O'Neill admitted. "I like not what you have done."

"I didn't think you would," Delacroix murmured. Was he dreaming this conversation? Had he been the Irishman, he would have already driven a knife into his own heart. What stopped him?

"I have very little time," the O'Neill said. "Were that not so, I would go cautiously, subject you to much thought and testing. But Mountjoy grows stronger while d'Aquila weakens. I must give battle soon."

"Do not," Delacroix said quickly. "Let d'Aquila go. Return to Dungannon and wait. Elizabeth can still be convinced she gains nothing by making war against you."

The O'Neill looked at him curiously. "You, an Englishman, say that?"

"I am half Irish, but more than that, I have seen the full folly of war, and I tell you, this is madness. England and Ireland need each other. We can find a way to live in peace."

Slowly, on a piercing note of sadness, the O'Neill smiled. "My daughter is right. You are a good man, if sometimes foolish. Would that the world was as you say."

"It can be," Delacroix insisted. He sat up on the cot, spilling the blanket off his chest, and said, "All that's needed is time. I will go to London. I will . . ."

"There is no time. Do you think Mountjoy will wait on the chance of peace? That is exactly what he and others like him are determined to avoid. No, I fight now or I slink away. There is no other choice."

"And what of your daughter?" Delacroix challenged. "What happens to her? If you are defeated, what life will she have?"

He braced himself, expecting the O'Neill to say something to the effect that he would not be defeated, fate would carry him to victory, the ancient heroes of Ireland would all be avenged, and more along those lines.

Instead, it was a weary and resigned man who spoke. "My daughter will be happy. That may seem a small thing compared to the fate of a nation, but it is one thing I can accomplish. Now tell me true, why do you care what happens to her?"

Delacroix hesitated. So would any sane man when confronted by the chasm of his own self-deception. Finally, he said, "I have need of her."

The O'Neill snorted. "I know that need well; it is not enough. God's blood, man, you've faced the mightiest foes in battle. Can you not face yourself now?"

Delacroix took a deep breath. The throbbing in his skull had eased. Indeed, he felt remarkably clearheaded. Softly but with unmistakable firmness, he said, "She is life to me."

The two men looked at each other. Their eyes met in perfect understanding.

A week later, a single-masted yawl entered the river Severn near Cardiff and proceeded upriver to the holding of Darkcroft. Ewan was waiting on the dock as it drew alongside. He watched as his lord disembarked, then turned to assist Deirdre.

She smiled gently at the steward. "It is good to see you again, Ewan."

"And you, my lady." Softly, he added, "Welcome home."

He thought he spied a sheen of tears in her eyes, but they were quickly gone. The earl hovered nearby, a protective arm around her. Together, they walked up the path to the manor house.

Libbie was there and Lizzie, too, fairly bursting with excitement. But they grew more solemn when they saw how pale and fragile their mistress looked.

Delacroix allowed them to take her off to his room, filled now with dried flowers, as he had ordered, and to which her own clothes had been brought. They helped her bathe, brushed her hair until it gleamed, and slid her into a warm nightgown. Snug under the covers, she closed her eyes, thinking to rest only a moment.

Delacroix found her deeply asleep. He had expected nothing else. The past few weeks would have been exhausting for anyone, much less a woman with child. At the thought of the babe, a fierce sense of gladness took him. He slipped out of his clothes and, naked, eased himself beneath the covers close to her. With consummate tenderness, he drew her to him.

In the night, Deirdre half awoke, crying. Delacroix held her until the worst passed and she slipped away into sleep again. He remained alert, staring at the shadows beneath the high canopy. In them, he could readily imagine the shapes of men and steeds, hear the clash of battle, the cry of death, all so familiar to him.

But not this time. The battle on the plain beyond Kinsale was not his to fight. Hugh O'Neill went to his destiny, and Ireland with him. So be it. His own challenge lay ahead, here in this verdant land, in the woman held in his arms. To keep her safe, to protect the land, to build for the future, that was his promise to the O'Neill and to himself.

He turned his head slightly and in the corner of the room spied a familiar shape. A smile touched his mouth. Only Ewan would have dared to fetch his harp from the storeroom where it had rested since Dungannon. Odds were it was horribly out of tune. Tomorrow he would have to see to that.

Deirdre stirred in his arms. He stroked her hair until she quieted again. His hand drifted over the slight swell of her belly where the baby grew. His son or daughter to cherish and protect. As he would its mother, now and for all time. He would wed her with high ceremony, make her countess of Bradford and lady of all else. But she would always be to him his wild Irish lass.

His eyes grew heavy. Far off, wind blew over ancient hills, carrying the scents of fertile earth and foam-crested sea. High above, the moon threw off the misty veil of cloud and shone, bright and eternal, over all.

EPILOGUE

THE BATTLE OF KINSALE WAS THE LAST GREAT contest in the historic struggle for Gaelic independence. In a single day—Christmas Eve, 1601—the struggle of centuries was decided. The Irish fought valiantly, but ultimately could not hold. By dawn on Christmas Day, thousands lay dead, their cause in ruins. The O'Neill tried to fight on, but without success. In bitter sorrow, knowing he had no other choice, he led his surviving followers into exile. Far from Eire, they found their rest. But in the emerald hollows and on the mist-draped hills, their memory lives now and for all time.